# MAGGIE SHAYNE

## SLEEP
### with the
## LIGHTS
## ON

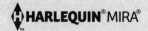

ISBN-13: 978-0-7783-1554-4

SLEEP WITH THE LIGHTS ON

Printed in U.S.A.

www.Harlequin.com

This novel would not have been the book it is without the insight and skill of my editor, Leslie Wainger. Her enthusiasm, support and sheer brilliance make me look good, and I can't imagine doing this job without her.

# Prologue

He watched the body sink in slow motion through the murky green water. Tears blurred his eyes, obstructing his view, but he wiped them away. He liked to watch. It was peaceful, the way the long tendrils of dark seaweed seemed to reach up for the bodies. Like they were waiting, eager to welcome them home. They parted, those tendrils, as the body sank deeper and then closed up again as its descent continued. Like the fingers of a loving hand, embracing them, wrapping them in the liquid softness of death. He liked to think of them resting at the bottom, sinking into the deep, soft mud. Peaceful. Easy. When the seaweed fingers returned to their former positions, reaching toward the surface, waving gently in the currents, it was as if they'd never even been there.

As if he'd never killed them.

When the last ripple faded and the water returned to green stillness, Eric backhanded the new tears from his face and snuffled hard. It was done. Again. But this was it, it was over. This would be the last time.

*You say that every time. But you know better.*

Yeah, it was true, he'd said it before. Every time, with every lanky, brown-eyed young man he bludgeoned to death with his favorite framing hammer. It wasn't that he took any pleasure in killing them. It was just that he couldn't help himself. When he saw them, he got this persistent itch in the back of his brain. And it would get worse and worse. You couldn't scratch that itch from the outside. It was *inside*. It scratched and it scratched, a rat on a wall, working until it broke clean through.

That other one inside him. *He* was the killer. And once he got his rocks off beating them to death, he crawled back into his rat hole, leaving Eric to clean up the mess, to plaster over the hole and cover up the crime, and pretend there were no rats in his house at all.

*What rats? I don't hear any rats. Look at me, I'm just a normal guy. And yeah, my eyes are red, but not because I've been sobbing over the poor fucking bastard I just dumped into the lake. It's probably allergies. There's nothing wrong with me. I'm fine. Normal.*

*Scratch, scratch, scratch.*

Nothing could make the scratching stop except killing. And it was getting so the rat demanded to be fed more and more often. It was growing, that rat. It was almost too big to stay behind the wall at all anymore.

But he told himself, as he always did, that was not the case. *He* was in charge, not the rat. He was patching that hole for the last time. He wouldn't let the rodent chew through it again. Not again. He was done with this. He was not going to kill any more pretty, lanky young men with brown hair that hung a little too long. He could beat this. He knew he could.

Nodding hard, Eric dipped his oars into the green-brown water and pushed the boat into motion. The sun was rising now over the pine-forested eastern shoreline.

It warmed the surface, drawing misty spirals and pillars upward from the water. They twisted higher, heading for the light like the spirits of Eric's beloved dead. He watched them rising, growing thinner, vanishing altogether, while he rowed in the opposite direction, west, toward the dock, the cabin.

A loon sang its heartbroken song. Tall black trees rose up out of the water without a leaf or a limb. Weak and rotting. Lily pads clustered thicker the closer he got to the shore, until it was as if he was rowing through a lake made of the waxy green leaves. There were lotus blossoms, too, mostly white, a few bright pink ones, just starting to open up as the sunbeams reached them. Bullfrogs croaked, and the birds in the forests surrounding the lake chorused louder and louder. Their morning choir. All around him, as the sun climbed higher, the Adirondack Mountains changed their character entirely. By night they were a dark world that seemed perfect for someone like him. A place where death and decay were just a normal part of the whole process, and where killing was everywhere. It was accepted. It was normal.

But when the sun took over, the mountains changed. The lake water that had been murky and green, sparkled and danced in the morning light. The forest came to life, no longer deep and foreboding, but green and lush, the ground beneath the trees, dappled in light and shadow.

He no longer fit, he with his rat-infested walls. And by the light of day it was always clear that he never really had.

He rowed the boat up to the long wooden dock. Today he hadn't even taken a life preserver or any fishing gear, the way he usually did, figuring that would make him look normal if he were noticed by some fish-and-game officer. Not that he ever had been. The lake was isolated. He'd never seen anyone when he'd been out doing his grim work. This time he hadn't even bothered to take those precautions. He'd just been eager to get it over with. To be done with it. That was how determined he was to stop killing. That was how sure he was that this would be the last time he would row out across Stillwater Lake in the predawn chill to lay a young man to rest at the bottom.

Looping the rope around a post, he climbed out of the boat, pulled himself up onto the old wooden dock, and realized that it was getting harder. He'd been putting on weight. His joints ached. Thirty-eight. He shouldn't feel this bad at thirty-eight.

He walked toward the cabin, past the tire swing that dangled from the giant maple tree at the water's edge. He and his kid brother used to swing out on that tire and try to see who could land farther out in the lake. He smiled as he remembered. They'd had a lot of fun here as kids. His own boys played the same game. Or used to. He hadn't had the heart to bring them up here in a long, long time.

He'd polluted the water with the blood of his victims. He should have found a different place to put them to rest. Hell, he should have done a lot of things differently. But he was broken, and he didn't know why. He only knew that he had to find a way to fix himself. To keep the rat sealed behind the wall, keep it there until this time it starved to death.

He walked past the cabin, not going inside. His pickup was parked in front. The hammer, already washed and dried, was hanging back in its spot in the toolshed. There was nothing more to do. And if he could just hold on to his willpower, there never would be. He got into his white F-150 and drove. He needed to be home with his family and to forget about this morning's task. Forget, if he could, about all of those pretty, pretty boys.

# *1*

If the bullshit I wrote was true, I wouldn't have been standing in the middle of a beehive where all the bees were cops—not one worker bee in the hive, either—trying to get someone interested in finding out what had happened to my brother.

Then again, if the bullshit I wrote was true, I wouldn't be holding a white-tipped cane in my hand, either. But the bullshit I wrote was just that. Bullshit.

Solid-gold bullshit, though. Which was, after all, why I kept writing it.

"Look, I'm going to need to talk to someone else," I said to the queen bee behind the tall counter. My fingertips rested on the front edge, which was up to my chest. Smooth wood, with that slightly tacky feel from being none too clean. I took my fingers away, but the sticky residue remained. *Ick.*

"And just who else would you like to talk to?" the queen bee asked.

"Are you getting sarcastic with me now?" I leaned nearer. "How about I talk to your boss, then?"

"Ma'am, that attitude of yours is not going to help.

I told you, your case is getting the same attention any other missing persons case would get from this office."

"The same attention as any other missing homeless heroin-addict case, you mean?"

"We do not discriminate here."

"Not on the basis of intelligence, anyway."

When her voice came again, it came from way closer. She was, I surmised, leaning over her tall counter. I could smell her chewing gum. Dentyne Ice. "Never thought I'd be so tempted to smack a blind woman upside her head," she muttered. It was probably supposed to be under her breath, but I had hearing like a freakin' bat. I heard *everything*. Every nuance. So I knew she meant it.

"Want to try it now?" I asked. "Because I promise you, I will—"

"Miss de Luca? Is it *really you?*"

*That* woman's voice wasn't angry. It was adoring, and coming from about seven o'clock. That was how I found things. A clock inside my head where I was always the center. You know, the pin that held the hands in place so they could spin all around me while I stood still. It was an accurate illustration in more ways than one.

I closed my eyes behind my sunglasses, shut my mouth, pasted a fake smile on my face and turned. Sometimes not being able to look in the mirror and see how far I missed the mark from the expression I *thought* I was making was a blessing, and I suspected this was one of those times.

"Rachel de Luca? The author, right?" The woman was moving toward me as she spoke. I waited until she got just two and a half steps from me before extending my hand. Any farther, you looked like an idiot. Any closer… Any closer was too damn close. I liked three feet of space around me at all times. It was one of a whole collection of quirks I held dearly.

"Last time I checked," I said, pouring sugar into the words, using my "famous author" voice. "And you are?"

"Oh, gosh, this is such a thrill!" She gripped my hand. Cool and small. She smelled like sunblock, sweat and sneakers. Tinny, nearly inaudible music wafted from somewhere near her neck, and I could hear her pulse beat behind her words. No, seriously, I could. I told you, I hear everything. My brain snapped an immediate mental photo. She was too thin, an exercise nut, five-one or so, probably blonde. Her earbuds were dangling, iPod still playing, heart still hammering from a recent run. She probably didn't even hear it. Hearing loss due to cramming *speakers* into one's ear holes and cranking the volume. Joggers were the worst offenders. Sighted people didn't appreciate how valuable their hearing was.

Also, she had a beaky little nose and bad teeth.

Don't ask. I have no freaking idea how I get my mental snapshots of people. I just do. I don't know if they're anywhere near accurate, either. Never bothered to ask anyone or feel any faces. (Give me a break, people, it's just *disgusting* to go around pawing strangers like that.)

And she'd been talking while I'd been sketching her on my brain easel. Sally something. Big fan. Read all my books. Changed her life. The usual.

"Glad to hear my methods are working for you," I said. "And it's great to meet you, but I have—"

"I'm so glad I came in to check on my missing poodle," she said. "I think she was dog-napped. But I'm staying positive. You know, I used to lose my temper all the time," she went on. "I'd fight with my husband, my teenage daughter—and don't even get me started on my mother-in-law. But then I started writing your words on index cards and taping them all over my house."

"That's really—" *fucking pathetic* "—nice to hear. But like I said, I—"

"'If you get up in the morning and stub your toe, go back to bed and start over,'" she quoted. "I *love* that one. Such a metaphor for everything in life, really. Oh, oh, and 'When you're spitting venom onto others, you're only poisoning yourself.' That's one of my favorites."

The woman behind the counter snorted derisively and muttered, "Oughtta be droppin' dead any minute now, then," just loud enough for me to hear. If I had been the metaphorical cobra in my metaphorical affirmation, I would have spun around and spat a healthy dose of venom into her eye to keep her from costing me a reader.

"Sally," I said, struggling for patience. No, that's not true at all. My patience was long gone. I was struggling to hang on to the illusion of it, though. "Like I said—" *twice now* "—it's nice to meet you, but I actually have something important I need to do here." *This is a police station after all. I mean, do you really think I'm here for shits and giggles, lady?*

"Oh! Oh, I'm so sorry." She put her hand on my shoulder. Familiar. Like we were friends now.

I *almost* cringed. People think they can touch you when you're blind. I have no idea why. I hear pregnant women complain about the same thing, but of course I've never seen it.

"I hope everything's all right. Not that I'm asking, of course."

*Yes she was.*

"I'll go." Two steps, but then the parting shot. I was ready for it, even guessing which one it would be. "Remember, Rachel," she called back, her overly happy tone making me restrain a gag. "'What you be is what you see'!"

She left as I tried to remember which of my books had contained *that* particular piece of crapola. Her sneakers squeaked as she trotted away, until the sound got lost amid the buzz of the drones.

I turned back to the woman at the counter. Her image in my mind was short, hefty, with melon-sized boobs and long shiny ringlets.

"Where were we?"

"I believe you were about to threaten to kick my ass," she said. "Or maybe you were gettin' ready to dole out one of those Susie-sunshine lines you're apparently known for." She paused, leaned back in her chair—I heard the movement—and slurped coffee that smelled stale. "So are you famous or something? 'Cause *I* never heard of you."

I placed my hands flat on the tacky countertop and leaned forward. "My brother is missing. I reported it three days ago, and I haven't heard one word from you people since."

"'You people'?"

"You *cop* people. I want action. I want my brother found. I at least want some indication that you're looking for him. Can you give me that?"

"I already *gave* you that. I *told* you, we're doing everything we can. I'll have an officer call you later in the day. I already *have* your number."

Oh, brilliant double entendre there. Apparently I was dealing with a genius.

"Thanks a million."

I turned and waved my cane back and forth, half hoping I'd whack someone in the shins on my way out. But no. Apparently the bees were parting like the Red Sea. I was not amused that my identity had been revealed in the cop shop. My agent would lop off my head for being a bitch in public at all, much less being recognized while I was at it.

What the hell did I care? I'd deny it. My legions of followers would believe me. I mean, as long as it didn't happen too often or in front of someone's cell-cam and wind up on YouTube, I was golden. And even if it did, they'd forgive me for losing it if I let them know why.

My brother was missing, for God's sake. A *saint* would be on her last nerve.

I tapped across the room and out the door, feeling the space around me widen as I moved through it. I turned left down the hall to the main entrance. Lots of doors there. I picked the quietest one and went through it and then down the broad stone steps to the sidewalk. I intended to cross the street to the coffee shop, grab a Mucho-Mocha with extra caffeine, and phone my assistant to come and pick my ass up. My mind wasn't on what I was doing, though. I was flashing back to the last time I'd seen anything.

It had been Tommy's face.

I was twelve and knew I was going blind. I had a corneal dystrophy, a rare one. At that point I could still see, but it was pretty bad. Blurry, dull. Worse and worse. I'd been having a nightmare, dreamed of being completely blind, and woke up screaming.

It was Tommy who came to my bedroom, sat on the edge of my mattress, hugged me close, told me it was all gonna be okay. That he'd be with me, no matter what. And he was, before the addictions took him away. He went from coke to crack, from the oxy-twins—contin and codone—to heroin, his standards lowering with his resources, until he was broke and homeless and taking anything he could find that was stronger than aspirin. Anyway, before all that, when he was a freshly show-ered fourteen-year-old kid with a future, he hugged me, conceded to my demand that he leave the light on and told me stories until I fell back asleep.

When I woke up, I thought he'd lied to me. I thought he'd turned the light off after swearing he wouldn't. But he hadn't. Turned out my nightmare was a premonition. I was totally blind.

I shook off the memory about the same time I heard squealing tires and a blasting horn, and realized about a second too late that I'd stepped off the curb and into the street without checking first. Sure as shit, the car hit me. I couldn't even believe it. One step, a loud horn, and *bam*. I flew fast and landed hard, hip bone, then shoul-der, then head, in that order. And then I just lay per-fectly still while pain blasted through every part of me.

Damn. I'd thought this day couldn't *get* any worse.

Detective Mason Brown had a series of rapid-fire im-pressions; *leggy brunette. Dark sunglasses. White cane. Blind? OhfuckI'mgonnahither!* He jerked the wheel and slammed on the brakes, but it was too late. The thump made his stomach heave. The car slid sideways, but only a few feet—hell, it was city traffic, he hadn't been moving very fast to begin with—and came to a stop. He opened the door and lunged out before he'd even finished processing what had happened. And then he was bending over the felled female in the middle of the street outside the station, hoping to hell she wasn't seriously hurt. Hands on her shoulders. That was autopilot. Then the brain kicked in. *Don't move her. Spinal cord and all that. Hell, her eyes are closed.*

And then they opened and looked slightly past his left shoulder. They were sky-blue eyes, and they were completely blank.

"I'm okay, I'm okay." She was trying to sit up while she talked.

"Hang on. Hold still a second, just in case."

She was lying on her side, propped up by one bent elbow on the pavement. Short skirt. A brand-new run in her stockings. Long brown hair, kind of wavy. She patted the blacktop with her free hand. "Am I in the road? Get me the hell out of the road." Her questing hand found her big sunglasses and she quickly jammed them onto her face. They were crooked, but he didn't think she knew. "Do you see my bag?"

Since she was apparently getting up with him or without him, he helped onto her feet, then kept hold of one upper arm. "It's over by the curb. Can you walk?"

"Yeah." To prove it, she started limping back the way she'd come. It was closer, though how she knew which direction to go, he couldn't figure. A couple of his colleagues had jumped into action by then, block-

ing traffic, directing it around his still sideways unmarked car. His partner, Roosevelt Jones, was standing
by the hood, shaking his shaved head and smiling so
hard his face actually had wrinkles. He was a hundred
and six—okay, fifty-seven—and still only had wrinkles
when he smiled.

"Quit your damn grinning and move the car, Rosie."

"Nossir. We're gonna need photos and whatnot." He
scooped up the handbag and cane just as Mason got her
back on the sidewalk. Rosie held her things out to her.
"Here's your stuff, miss. You sure you're all right?"

She turned her head toward him and, with a precision
that surprised Mason, reached out and took her handbag, then her cane, from Rosie's outstretched hands.
"I think so."

"Do you hurt anywhere?" Mason asked.

"All over, but—"

"Best let the medics have a look at you in the E.R.,"
Rosie said. "Just to be sure. Damn, Mason, I knew you
were desperate for a woman, but I didn't think you'd
run one down in the street." Then he laughed like a
seal barking.

The woman's head snapped toward Mason again.
"*You* were the one who hit me?"

"Damn straight he was," Rosie said and turned to
Mason. "What's wrong with you, running down celeb-
rities in the street?" Rosie smiled at her. "I'm Detective Roosevelt Jones. My partner—who talked me into
letting him drive due to my alleged aging reflexes—is
Mason Brown. And might I just add that it's a privi-
lege to meet you, ma'am? My wife quotes you to me on

a daily basis." He elbowed Mason. "Rachel de Luca. The author."

He said it, Mason thought, like that ought to mean something to him. He shrugged at Rosie, but said, "Great to meet you." Like he knew who the hell she was. He'd never even heard of her. "And I'm really sorry."

"I'm fine." As soon as she said it her knees bent a little, and he had to snap an arm around her waist to keep her upright.

"Whoa. Okay, that's it, you're going to the E.R."

"I really don't have time, I—"

"Ambulance is already here," Mason said.

"Like I said, I don't have time."

He gave the paramedics a wave. "Over here, boys." Then he turned to her again. "Just go get checked out. I won't be able to work all day if I don't know you made sure you're okay."

"Oh, well, I wouldn't want to mess up *your* day. And mine's pretty much fucked, anyway." She clapped a hand over her mouth, and he saw those blue eyes widen behind the crooked glasses.

The lady had a temper.

Just as quickly, he saw her face change. It was like she put on a Halloween mask. Only backward. In this case, the wicked witch was the one *behind* the disguise.

"So you're a detective?" she asked, as if she'd only just heard that part of his partner's spiel. Her voice was a half octave higher, softer, her attitude polite instead of pissed, as if she wasn't *really* just aching to kick him in the balls for hitting her.

"Yeah." *And I see right through you,* he thought. *You wouldn't give a damn what you said to me if you didn't know I was a cop. And that makes me wonder why it matters.* "Here come the paramedics. Hey, Reno."

"Hey, Mason." Reno, an EMT Mason had known for three years, took her other arm and led her to the back of the ambulance. She handed Reno her bag and her stick, gripped the rail, found the step without a single miss, and pulled herself up and in as Mason watched her, thinking she was really good at being blind. And then thinking what a dumb-ass thought that was.

No wonder she was on the bitchy side. He would probably be a bear if he were in her shoes.

"Look, I'll see how you're doing later, okay?" He wasn't quite able to walk away just yet. "I need to take care of things here, get that car out of the road, free up the traffic, climb the paperwork mountain. But I'll check in on you."

"No need. I'm not going to sue you."

*That's what they all say,* he thought. *Right before they call a lawyer.* That was one headache he didn't need. "I'll see you later, okay?"

She settled onto the gurney, still sitting up. "All right. Actually, there's something I'd like to talk to you about, anyway." Sweet smile, flung at him without warning. He hadn't been expecting it, so its impact was stronger than it should have been. "Maybe…maybe this little accident was *supposed* to happen."

Huh? What the hell did *that* mean?

He stood there puzzling on that after the ambulance doors closed, until Rosie came over and clapped a hand on his shoulder. "She's way better-looking in person than on her book jackets, isn't she?"

"I wouldn't know, having never seen one. Who the

hell is she, anyway?" They started back toward Mason's car. There were uniforms out in the street taking photos, another one stopping traffic to let the ambulance pull out.

"Self-help author. Big celeb. On TV a lot. Preaches nonviolence, happy happy joy joy shit. You know, like Marlayna's so into. Positive energy. Love your enemy and raise your vibe. What you get in life is always your own doing and all that. How can you not have heard of her?"

"Like *you* would have if not for your better half, pal? We're not exactly *vibing* on her level, are we now?"

Rosie grinned. "Guess not, bein' as we been up to our necks in bloodless crime scenes and MPDs lately."

Missing, presumed dead. Twelve so far. Not a single body yet, though. But back to the blind chick. "Did you hear what she said to me, just before they closed the doors, Rosie?" Rosie shook his head. "She said maybe this accident was *supposed* to happen. What do you think she meant by that?"

"Shoot, I don't know. I said I know who she is, not that I'm a true believer. I'll ask Marlayna, though. She might have an idea."

"Yeah, you do that."

Mason's phone chirped just then, and he pulled it out and looked at the screen.

His big brother Eric's face—he looked fifty but was only thirty-eight—popped up beside the text message icon. He clicked through, and the message read: Take care of Marie & the boys.

What the hell?

"I gotta go." Mason turned toward the car, moving on

autopilot, then stopping. "Shit, I need a car." He couldn't move his until he got the okay.

"What's up?" Rosie unsnapped his key ring from his belt and held it out.

"Don't know. Eric's at my place, showed up in the wee hours and wouldn't talk to me. He had a fight with Marie or something." He looked at the text again as he took the keys, a cold chill going up his spine. "Thanks, pal."

"Holler if you need me, Mace."

Mason gave a nod and headed around the corner to the parking lot behind the Binghamton P.D. Rosie's yellow Hummer stood out just like its owner, the only black detective in a mostly white police department, so he didn't have to look for it.

There was a sick feeling in his stomach as he drove the oversize toolbox out into traffic. He was worried about his brother.

Nothing new there. Worrying about Eric had become the Brown family pastime. Habit, he guessed. He told himself that there was probably nothing wrong. Maybe Eric was quoting a line from one of those damn grim poems he was always reading, scaring the hell out of Mason for nothing.

But he didn't think so.

Eric Conroy Brown had gone straight to work after dumping the body, worked the entire day and then headed home late last night just like he always did after the rat had been fed and had crawled back into its hole, leaving him to clean up the mess. It made him feel normal to lie in bed beside his wife and pretend he wasn't a monster. He knew he was, though. The rat was him. No matter how hard he tried to convince himself it was some other being, some demon possessing him, some evil other personality trying to force its way to the fore, it was him. He was the rat, which was probably why he couldn't get it to shut up and stay inside, much less kill it.

This time, however, home had provided no solace.

Marie had been angry, waiting at the door with one hand at the small of her back and the other on top of her basketball-sized belly. "Why didn't you come home last night? Honestly, Eric, I told you yesterday morning that the boys would be home from camp and I was making a welcome-home dinner."

He blinked. The boys. Baseball camp. They'd been gone all summer. Hell. "I'm sorry. I got busy at work and—"

"You left your cell phone home. Again. I called the garage three times last night."

"You know the garage phone switches over to the service at five whether we stay late or not. This guy needed his car finished, and the boss asked if I could stay late and get it done. It got so late I just slept on the cot in the storeroom. I just forgot about the boys is all."

"You *forgot?*" She'd stared at him for a second there as if she knew. Or suspected. As if she was trying to get a visual of the rat inside him.

*Don't let her see, don't let her see, don't let her see. Spackle. Plaster. Shhh. No scratching!*

"Are they already asleep?" he asked. He'd stayed late. It was hard to face the family too soon after...

"It's 2:00 a.m., Eric. What do *you* think?"

He sighed heavily. Then, unable to bear the way she was looking at him any longer, he went to the boys' shared bedroom and closed the door behind him. He heard Marie huff and stomp off into the kitchen. He imagined her waddling and stomping at the same time and smiled. She was beautiful when she was pregnant. All the time, really. A blue-eyed blonde just like Mother. But pregnant, she was at her best.

He didn't deserve her.

Joshua was sound asleep. His curly carrot mop had grown longer, and his freckles had undergone a summertime explosion. How did kids change so much over a single season? He hoped sixth grade would be a good one for Josh. He hated sending his kids to school. School had been nothing but hell for him. He'd suggested home-schooling, but Marie had insisted she had no time, and the boys had hated the idea. And really, the more they were out of the house, away from him, the better.

Besides, the boys weren't like him. They fit in. They weren't freaks.

He'd wondered, back then, if everyone would always be able to see the rat inside him as clearly as the kids in middle school seemed to. Because they saw it. He had no doubt that they saw it. Even when he could keep it mostly silent and sleeping for months at a time, and only had to feed it a neighbor's cat here and there, they saw it. Kids homed in on shit like that and tried to kill it. You know, like a litter of healthy animals, mom and all, will push the one sick one right out of the nest and leave it to die? He'd seen it on the Discovery Channel. Lions did it. Wolves did it. Birds did it. Kids were *just* like that. A weak one, a different one, a broken one, or even an especially gifted one—anything different—was to be shunned, banished, destroyed. It was probably a matter of self-preservation left over from the caveman days. You didn't want anyone evolving faster than the norm or they'd be unfair competition. And you didn't want anyone evolving slower than the norm, or they'd drag you down with them. And you sure as shit didn't want predators—the kind who would prey on their own— because they'd eat you.

Kids always knew. Adults, not so much. Adults were mostly blind. Not his mother, though. His real one. She must have taken one look at him and seen that he was broken.

Eric smoothed Josh's hair and turned toward Jeremy's bed, then stopped where he was, shocked by how much more of the bed Jeremy took up. He couldn't possibly have grown that much taller since May. Could he?

He moved closer, surprised when Jeremy rolled over and opened his eyes. They were brown and accusing. "You forgot, didn't you?"

But it wasn't his words that made Eric's blood chill in his veins. It was his *look*. He didn't look like a kid anymore. He looked like a young man. Tall, lean, lanky, with brown hair he'd let grow all summer long, and deep brown eyes with heavy brows and thick eyelashes.

*He looks just like they all look.*

And that hot scratching began deep inside Eric's brain.

"No," he whispered. "No."

*Scratch, scratch, scratch.*

"No? Well then, where were you?"

Eric backed away from his son.

Jeremy rolled his eyes and gave an exaggerated sigh. "Come on, Dad, can't you even talk to me?"

But he couldn't. The rat was coming out. He felt it scratching, clawing, gnawing. The plaster hadn't even had time to dry, and already the rat was breaking through. Its twitching nose was sniffing through the first tiny hole.

Eric backed out and closed the bedroom door. The digging intensified. That scratching rat inside his brain had caught the scent, and it was demanding to be fed. And the meal it wanted this time was Eric's own son.

He couldn't stay at the house. Not once that feeling had begun. It never went away once it started. Nothing would stop it, nothing but killing.

He heard Marie banging pans in the kitchen, warming up leftovers for him. She was always worrying about what he ate, his cholesterol, his weight, shit like that, shit that didn't even matter. His body wasn't diseased, his brain was.

He walked quietly back through the house. It wasn't a bad house. Small, only three bedrooms. The boys each had their own, but Josh had given his up to be a nursery, so they were sharing now. The living room was a mess. The boys' sneakers scattered randomly all across the rug, jackets flung over chairs, backpacks spilling out onto the floor. He looked at the clutter, at the out-of-place sofa pillows and the TV, turned on, volume muted, running an infomercial about an electronic gadget you plugged into the wall to drive away pests. Mice and ants and spiders…

*Not rats, though. Once you've got a rat, you've got a rat, that's all there is to that that that.*

He went out the front door, barely making a sound. He knew how to move in silence. He was a predator, after all. A hunter.

He got into his '03 F-150, and drove back the way he'd come, over the bridge onto 81, and twenty minutes south to Binghamton. To his brother's apartment. Mason let him in, groggy, only a little curious, but too tired to stay up long enough to grill him. Just pointed at the couch and scuffed back to his bedroom. A minute later he brought out a pillow and a blanket. "You need to talk, bro?"

"No. Maybe tomorrow."

"All right. Get some sleep, okay?" Mason handed him the bedding, and went back to his room.

Eric hadn't slept, though. He'd thought. All night long, he'd paced and he'd thought.

He guessed he'd probably been hoping to stumble onto another solution. A different answer. But he knew down deep that there wasn't one.

And now it was morning. He'd pretended to be asleep while Mason was getting ready to go to work, knowing his brother wouldn't wake him. Better that way. If he spoke to Mason first, his detective instincts would tell him something was wrong. So he faked sleep and waited until Mason left.

And now he was alone, and he was ready. Everything was done. He'd showered, and he'd gone down to his pickup to get his stuff out of the locked toolbox where he kept it. A man's toolbox was sacred. Like a woman's purse, according to Marie. People didn't snoop in a man's toolbox. Not without a damn good reason, anyway, and he'd always been careful never to provide one.

So he was ready. His duffel bag was on the floor, up against the wall on the far side of the room. He'd returned the blanket and pillow to Mason's bedroom, and unrolled a sheet of plastic on the sofa and out across the floor for several feet all around it, because this was his brother's place, after all. He didn't want to ruin it entirely. And he always had plastic in his truck. For moving them. His letter was written, and though it was short, that had taken the longest, 'cause what could you say, really? *Sorry?* Sorry didn't even begin…

Didn't matter.

The long line of driver's licenses was on the coffee table, one neat straight row. He'd texted Mason. Mason would know what to do. He would take care of everything. He always did.

So…it was time.

He picked up the gun in his right hand. It was heavy. He'd rarely used the thing, kept it just in case. He'd avoided the question, in case of what? It wasn't really his gun. It belonged to the rat. But he was going to use it now.

He was shaking hard as he pressed the barrel to his temple. It worried him how hard he was shaking. He didn't want to mess this up. He didn't want to suffer. He didn't want to feel it. Barrel in the mouth didn't always work. He'd read that somewhere, hadn't he? So, to the temple. And it wasn't like he had to be too precise, anyway. The gun was a .44. He wrapped his left hand around the barrel to keep it from bucking with the recoil and just blowing off the top of his head. And yeah, it would burn his hand—that barrel would be hot. But he didn't think he'd feel it for more than a second or two, and it was better than letting the gun buck and not getting the job done. That wouldn't be pleasant. He might survive that.

*Gotta do what must be done, burn my hand on the red-hot gun.*

*God, I'm scared.*

He had to do it. Mason would be here soon. It had to be done before Mason got here to stop him.

*Is there really a hell? God, what if there is?*

He took a deep breath. Then another.

*It's gonna hurt. I know it's gonna hurt.*

He heard footsteps outside. Hell, Mason was already here.

*Just do it. It'll only hurt for a second. Just do it already. For Jeremy.*

"Yes, for Jeremy."

The rat was scratching frantically now. Its claws had broken through. It was ripping away the plaster. If it got out, it wouldn't let him go through with it. He knew that.

*Do it do it do it!*

Mason's heavy steps came to a stop just outside the door. Then the door opened and his brother's eyes found him sitting there. They went wide with horror as Mason lurched forward, reaching out with both hands, yelling, "No, no, no!"

Eric squeezed the trigger, felt his brain explode in one all-consuming white-hot mixture of deafening noise and blinding pain. And then as blackness descended, he felt the rat squeeze through the hole in the wall and plop onto the floor. Or was that a handful of his brain?

He never did feel the hot barrel burning his hand.

# 2

A cop came to the hospital to take my statement. It wasn't Detective Brown, though.

My imagination and sixth sense had joined forces and decided to visualize Mason Brown as gorgeous, buff and sexy as hell. He probably had a wide, strong jaw and a corded neck. No long rock-star hair, though. Not on a cop.

Another cop, a short fat one, I guessed, was sitting in a chair by my bed writing down my answers to his questions. He wore glasses. I could hear him adjusting them over and over, up on his head, then down on his nose again. Up when he was addressing me, down when his pen went scritching across the notepad.

"You should just give in and get bifocals," I said.

He looked up, or that was what I guessed by the sound: movement, then stillness.

I loved this. Shocking people by showing off. It was almost like I was a magician doing parlor tricks for the crowd. Some of the blind—okay, visually impaired is the PC term, but I'm not *visually impaired,* I'm fucking blind—hated being underestimated by the sighted.

I enjoyed letting them think I was some kind of wonder kid. It was good PR and amused me to boot. And amusing myself was hard when I was in the hospital and therefore in public, and therefore forced to play my Positive Polly role to the hilt. No slips allowed. BW would have my head.

BW, by the way, was my agent. Belinda Waubach, aka Barracuda Woman.

"Those are store-bought glasses, right? You got them off a rack at a Walmart or a CVS, didn't you?"

"Price Chopper. I only need them for close-up stuff."

"It's the corneas. You need a transplant to fix it. Sadly, they save them all for people like me—not me specifically, of course. My body hates foreign corneas. Rejects them almost before the surgery's over." I smelled sweet pea and jasmine. "Are we about finished? My sister's here to see me."

"You—" He stopped, and I heard him shift positions, probably to look behind him at the doorway where Sandra stood.

"Is she messing with your head, Officer?" she asked.

"She's amazing," the cop said, thereby taking off ten pounds in my mental image-maker. Hell, he'd earned it. He still had bad acne scars and a hint of rosacea, though.

"Amazing my ass, she smelled my body wash." Sandra came close, leaned over, we hugged, yada yada. "One of these days I'll switch brands and screw you up royally, Rache," she threatened.

"It's not bad enough you pick a fragrance worn by a third of the women who shop at Bath & Body Works?"

She straightened, and I pasted a smile on my face and hoped my eyes weren't doing anything stupid. Sandra and others had assured me that they didn't, but I didn't believe them, which is why I am rarely seen without sunglasses. I mean, why tell me, right? It's not like I could check in the mirror and prove them liars.

"How are you, sis?" she asked softly.

My sister, Sandra, was my only claim to normal. She was a soccer mom in the best sense of the word. She had twin teenage daughters bearing the ridiculous names of Christy and Misty—no, I am *not* kidding—and a husband named Jim who worshipped at her feet. And why is it every great husband I know is named Jim? Anyway, this particular Jim was a pharmacist. Sandra was a real estate agent. Independent. Office in her basement and doing pretty damn well for herself. She and her family were so perfect, it was amazing I didn't have to check my blood sugar around them.

"Bruised rib and a concussion," I said. "Nothing big, but they want me overnight and they took my fu—" *Oops. Cop's still sitting there.* "They took my darn glasses."

"Did you give them hell?"

"Only a little," I lied.

"We need to get you home before you destroy your career."

"You're right. I'm not even gonna argue. I was going to go hunt the glasses down myself as soon as Officer Bob here finishes with me." I tilted my head his way. "That was your cue," I whispered.

He laughed a nervous laugh. "Okay, I have all I need. And, uh—here." He moved again, getting up, and then a plastic bag rattled. "It says personal effects, and I see some sunglasses in the bottom of the bag."

I took it from him, and felt my glasses in the bottom. "Hey, thanks. I guess I should have asked you to begin with." I fished them out fast and pushed them onto my face. My relief was so intense I felt like I melted in the bed a little.

"I hope you recover fast, Ms. de Luca." Sincere and mildly amused. He thought I was cute. I hated being thought of as cute.

"Oh, I know I will," I told him. "I'll just raise my vibe until my body has to rise up to match it." Oh, my agent would have *kissed* me for that one. Funny how no one ever responded with the obvious question: "Why the hell are you blind, then?" Maybe they did, behind my back. Who knew? I didn't care, as long as they kept buying the books. And the affirmation cards, and the annual calendar.

The cop should have left then. He really should have.

But instead he said, "If there's anything you need, don't hesitate to call."

"I need my brother found, Officer. I think I've told you that already."

"I know, I know. Look, it's not my case, but I'll see who I can nudge, all right?"

"No. It's nowhere near all right."

My sister swung her hip sideways, bumping my bed hard enough to shake it.

"But it'll do for now," I added. "Thanks, Officer."

"You're welcome, Ms. de Luca."

I waited until I knew he was gone. It's funny how you can feel a person's presence or absence. Human beings give off some kind of…I don't know, energy or force field or something. You can sense it clearly and easily if you aren't too busy looking for them with your eyes. At least, that was my explanation for it. I didn't remember noticing it until I'd gone blind. Then again, who remembered details like that prior to age twelve?

"So?" Sandra took the cop's former chair. "What happened?"

I told her what she already knew from my phone call. "Got run over by a cop. Not that one, though. A much better-looking one, according to my built-in TV. A detective, even."

"You should sue," she said. She reached out to take my glasses from my face, then put them back a second later. "Crooked," she said. "You'd get a zillion."

"I already *have* a zillion. You know, give or take. Besides, it was my fault, so—"

"You weren't in the crosswalk?"

"I speed-walked into the crosswalk without even pausing. The guy couldn't stop. I was pissed. About Tommy."

"I know."

"Besides, how is the 'make peace with the pain' guru going to look in a big messy lawsuit? It would cost me more than I'd gain."

She sighed. "I suppose you're right."

"So I'm here for the night."

"Yeah, well, you'd better stow the attitude, then. People talk." And then she was leaning over the bed, apparently forgetting the part where I'd mentioned that I had a bruised rib, and hugging me again. "God, when I think what could've happened… We don't know where Tommy is. Mom and Dad have been gone ten years now. I don't want to lose you, too."

"Mom and Dad went the way they would've wanted to. Together and on vacation." Cruise ship capsized. It was all over the news. "And we almost never know where Tommy is, so we should be used to it by now."

"I know."

"You won't lose me, too. I promise." I grunted, because she was still hugging me and the rib was still bruised. "I'm fine. And I'll stay that way if you'll quit trying to break the rest of my ribs."

Warmth on my face. Tears. Hers, not mine. I didn't believe in them. They didn't serve a hell of a lot of purpose except to rinse the eyes, and I could do that with Visine, thanks.

"So they're letting you go tomorrow, then?" she asked, sniffling, unbending, releasing me from her killer hug.

"Probably tomorrow, they said."

"Why only probably?"

"I don't know."

"I want to talk to the doctor."

"Well, you can't, big sis, because I'm of age, and that health-care proxy I gave you doesn't kick in unless I'm incapacitated. So you're going to have to take my word on this. I'm fine."

"Hell."

"I'm *fine*," I repeated. "And the last thing I want is a fan club vigil in the waiting room or, God forbid, the press showing up. So keep this to yourself and tell my right-hand Goth to do the same. Got it?"

"Of course I've got it. And I'll tell Amy. You know me, honey."

*Yeah,* I thought. *That's what I'm afraid of.*

* * *

Mason had worried all the way to his place. He'd jogged up the stairs with his heart in his throat, assuring himself that Eric was fine, but something—that same intuition that made him an uncannily successful detective, maybe—was telling him that he wasn't okay at all. The apartment was the second floor of a two-family house, and the family who owned it rarely used the ground floor but kept it vacant just in case.

More money than brains, maybe, Mason didn't know. He'd always figured if he held out long enough, they would get sick of keeping it and rent him the whole damn thing.

When he got to the top step his heart was pounding and his mouth was dry. Then he opened the door.

It was like a curtain parting on a nightmare. His brother was on the couch with a .44 Magnum jammed to the side of his head, just above the ear, awkwardly holding the piece with both hands, tears streaming from his reddened eyes. Eyes that shot to Mason's for an instant, eyes so full of pain Mason could feel it himself.

He lunged and shouted and the gun went off. Ear-splitting, that shot in the confines of the small room. The blood spray was like an explosion.

He halted midway to his brother, tripping over himself and falling to his knees in time with Eric falling over sideways on the couch. Rumpling the plastic with which he'd covered it.

"Ahh, God, what the fuck, Eric, *whatthefuck...?*" He scrambled closer on hands and knees, over more plastic on the floor. There was very little left of his brother's skull, and he just knelt there with it at eye level, shaking all over, frozen. He was also at eye level with the coffee table, so he saw the note and an odd row of driver's licenses. And then he started moving again, fumbling for the cell phone in his pocket. Somehow he punched in 911. And then he was talking, giving the address, automatic functions kicking in while his mind reeled, as scrambled as if the bullet had gone into his own brain. *Why? Mother. Marie. The boys. Why?*

Putting the phone back into his pocket, Mason blinked again at those driver's licenses.

Then he went still, and so did his reeling brain. Everything stopped. Time froze, a moment drawn out into what felt like eternity. He knew most of those faces. They were the same faces currently pinned up on the bulletin board in his office. All young men, all missing, all presumed dead. No bodies, though. Just empty wallets found in each man's last known location.

What the hell was Eric doing with these?

Frowning, he looked around the room. Everything was just the way he'd left it this morning, except for the plastic and that duffel bag on the floor, way over by the far wall. He didn't think that had been there when he'd left. Letter on the table. Eric's handwriting, always as sloppy and uneven as a third grader's. Swallowing hard, Mason looked at the note, didn't touch, just looked.

I am a monster. I kill. Over and over again, I kill. I'm the guy you're looking for, Mason, and I'm sorry. I'm so, so sorry. God, you must be so mad at me right now. But I stopped. I made myself stop. I did the right thing...finally. I know you'll take care of the boys. It had to be over. Now it is.

It's over. Thank God. Pray I don't go to hell. It wouldn't be fair. I couldn't help it. It wasn't my fault. I just…couldn't stop.

Eric looked from the note to his brother, lying in a soup of brain matter and blood on the plastic-covered sofa. He thought about Eric's sons, Josh and Jeremy. Mason loved those two boys like they were his own. Now he was supposed to tell them their dad was…

…a murderer?

…a *serial killer?*

His mind rejected the notion even though it was right there in blue ink on a white, blood-spattered sheet of printer paper.

And Marie, what about Marie? She was heavily pregnant with a little girl.

And Mother. God, this would kill Mother.

Was he really going to tell them what was in this note?

He looked at the driver's licenses again. The practical part of his brain said it had to be true. Otherwise, how would Eric have all those IDs? Trophies.

So he would have to tell them.

*For what? It's not like Eric's going to kill anyone else. The murders will stop now. No more harm will be done. And I don't have time to sit here debating this.*

A minute, maybe two, had ticked past since his 911 call. He only had a few more. Maybe five. Probably five.

He got up, picked up the licenses and the note, moved to the left, where the duffel sat on the floor. Unzipping it, he saw duct tape, coils of rope, a Taser.

*Shit.*

He fought off his heaving stomach, then stuffed the licenses and the note inside the bag and zipped it up. The blood spatter had mostly gone the other way, and the recoil spray hadn't made it that far. The duffel was clean, but the coffee table was coated with a fine mist of blood except where the note and licenses had been.

He picked up a bloody sofa pillow by one clean corner, shook it over the clean spots on the table to splatter them with blood, then replaced it where it had been on the sofa. Then he tipped the coffee table onto its side, as he could easily have done when he'd lunged toward his brother. The blood on the surface would run enough to further cover those clean spots. It wasn't perfect. But it was enough. No one was going to look too closely, anyway. He had the text message, and he'd called it in immediately. There was nothing here to suggest this was anything but exactly what it *had* been: a suicide. He'd witnessed it. He was a cop. A decorated and respected cop.

Open and shut.

Taking the duffel bag, he walked out of the apartment and down the stairs. He put the bag into the back of Rosie's Hummer, then took a quick look inside his brother's pickup, as the other detectives would do in a little while, but he didn't see anything else tying Eric to the missing men. Not on first glance, anyway, and there was no time for a more thorough examination. His colleagues would be here any second now. So he sank to the curb and tried to keep it together as he heard sirens wailing in the distance, coming closer.

He'd made a snap decision to cover up the answer to the biggest case of his career. And he would lose everything if it was ever found out. But dammit, he couldn't put his family through the truth.

He *couldn't*.

He told himself he'd done the right thing.

And then the cavalry arrived, ambulance first, cops on its bumper.

He just pointed at the stairs. "My brother shot himself."

The medics reacted, raced up the stairs. Rosie arrived and hunkered down beside him. "Lemme see your phone, partner."

Nodding, Mason handed it over.

Rosie looked for Eric's text message, found it, nodded. "You should'a taken me with you."

"I didn't think he meant *that*. Hell, maybe I did, but I didn't think he'd really *do* it."

A burst of activity on the stairs. Urgent shouts that seemed uncalled for, given that his brother was obviously dead. Mason looked up fast. Had he missed something? Did they know? *And am I going to be wondering that every day for the rest of my life? God, what the hell did I do here?*

And then a gurney came bumping down the stairs, Eric strapped to it, mask on his face, someone pumping a rubber balloon.

"He still has a pulse!"

Lightning jolted Mason to his feet. "How can he… how can that…his head…"

"Hold on, partner," Rosie said, grabbing his shoulders when he started to go to his brother.

Mason honestly didn't know in that moment, whether

he meant to go help Eric or yank the bag away and let him suffocate.

Two EMTs jostled Eric into the back of the ambulance. In seconds it went screaming away and left Mason staring after it with his guts tied up in knots.

"You'd better go," Rosie said. "Go on now. Be with your brother. Call your family. I've got this."

Nodding, Mason looked Rosie square in the eye, knowing he had to initiate the lies now, before he lost his resolve. It was the only thing to do. "I can give you the gist first, though. You need to know. He showed up last night, asking to sleep over. About 3:00 a.m., give or take. I was half-asleep, and we didn't talk. This morning I left before he got up. Then I got that text. When I opened the apartment door he was sitting on the couch with the gun to his head." He had to stop and swallow hard to get his throat to open up again.

"Damn," Rosie said softly. "You don't have to do this now, partner."

"It was a .44 Magnum. Never saw it before. Have no idea where he got it, or if it's legal. He had the barrel here." He put a finger on his skull. "His right. My left. I yelled and sort of jumped toward him. He pulled the trigger at the same time. I landed short, knocked over the coffee table. Then I called 911 on my cell, came down here and waited. I couldn't look at him like that. That's all. That's everything."

"Good enough. Good enough for now, Mason. Maybe I'd better drive you. They don't need me here."

Mason looked at his partner; he hated lying to him. "I'd feel better if you'd stay here while they process the place, see they do it right, respectfully, you know?

I mean, it's my place. I don't want it all torn up." He shook his head. "Shit, that sounds shallow."

"Sounds like someone who's seen what happens when a home becomes a crime scene. Don't you worry."

"I still need the Hummer, Rosie."

"I'll pick it up at the hospital once we finish here."

"The station. I'll leave it at the station." Mason looked down at his hands. "I need to change…before the hospital."

"Go to the station, then. You got a change of clothes in your locker?" Mason nodded. "You can park the Hummer there, then. Your wheels are already back in the lot. The blind writer didn't so much as ding it. It's all good."

But it *wasn't* all good. And Mason pretty much figured it was never going to be all good again. He wanted to crawl into a dark corner and stay there for a while. A long while. But he had to keep moving, and somehow he did.

He headed to the station. As Rosie had promised, his beloved black '74 Monte Carlo was in the lot in back. And also just as promised, the blind chick hadn't even put a dent in the bumper. They didn't make cars the way they used to. A new one would have crumpled. He tossed his brother's duffel into the trunk and made damn sure no one had seen him do it.

He locked Rosie's Hummer, took the keys inside and left them in his partner's locker, avoiding everyone he saw on the way. No one stopped him. Easy. Then he took a quick shower and changed into the spare clothes he kept on hand, a pair of jeans and a long-sleeved pullover in two-tone gray. Then he went back out to his own car and drove to the hospital, racking his brain on the way. Had he missed anything?

He undoubtedly had some of Eric's blood on his clothes. He'd crawled across that plastic, after all. That was fine. He wouldn't even wash them until he was sure his colleagues didn't want to run them through the lab. They would count on his cooperation. He had to give them exactly what they expected an innocent cop to offer. Full cooperation.

He might have left microscopic traces of blood on the steering wheel and driver's door of Rosie's Hummer. But that would be expected, too. If he cleaned that up, it would look as if he had something to hide. If anyone even bothered to check, which they had no reason to do. Looking as if he had something to hide would be the quickest way to revealing the truth, though, so he hadn't cleaned off the steering wheel or front seat.

Traces of blood in the cargo areas in the back of the Hummer, or on the cargo hatch door, however, would be *un*expected. They would be out of place. But no one was going to look for traces of blood in the back of Rosie's Hummer. No one had any reason to. Unless Eric somehow pulled through, of course. Or said something in a state of delirium. If that happened, he would deal with it. He couldn't do anything about it now.

As Mason pulled into the parking lot behind Binghamton General and looked for an empty spot, the shaking set in.

*My brother's dead. But not quite. No, dead. He's dead. No one could live like that. It's a glitch in the works, some reflex trying to hold on. But he's gone. I saw it, felt it. I know.*

*My brother was a murderer. All those guys. How many licenses? Gonna have to go through them later. And that bag. God, I don't want to go through that bag. Got to, though. And then hide it. Where it'll never ever be found.*

*I need to find the bodies. What the hell did he do with the bodies? Those families...*

*Gotta call Mom. And ohmyfuckinggod, Marie. I gotta call Marie. How do I break this to the boys? It's gonna destroy them.*

*Yeah. I did the right thing. This is bad enough without...that note. That bag. Those IDs. Those faces. It's bad enough. I did the right thing, God forgive me.*

*But what if he lives?*

"Sir? Sir, can I help you?"

He'd managed to walk into the E.R. without even realizing it, that was how far gone he was. He needed to pull it together here. He focused on the woman—a nurse wearing scrubs with big pink flowers all over them. She was behind a curved desk looking at him through an open glass partition. "Detective Mason Brown, Binghamton P.D. I'm here for my brother."

"I can help you with that. His name?" she was already tapping keys.

"Eric Conroy Brown."

"Eric." *Tap-tap-tap.* "Brown." *Taptaptaptap-big tap.* She actually backed up from the computer screen a little, and the bright smile vanished. "He's in the ICU. That's up—"

"I know where it is." He was a cop. He knew his way around Binghamton General. He was gone while she was still talking. Wishing him luck or something equally useless. Elevators, buttons to push. Autopilot.

*What if he lives?*

He still had all the evidence. If his brother lived and was anything more than a bedridden vegetable, Mason was going to have to turn it in and take the consequences for removing it from the scene. It would be the end of his job. Which was nothing compared to the possibility of his brother going on killing.

Eric. Killing. God, he couldn't even imagine it.

*Yes, you can. You know damn well you can.*

How the hell had it happened? What had driven him to this? They'd had the same childhood. Not perfect, but no trauma. No abuse. What had made his older brother become a monster?

*He's never been right and you know it. And what about all those cats, huh? Why was it we could never keep a cat? They all disappeared. And when they were gone, the neighbors' cats started vanishing. Remember how everyone thought there must be a wild animal in the area, preying on house cats? Coyotes. They blamed coyotes. And when I asked for a dog, Dad said absolutely not, and there was this look in his eyes, remember that? This look like the thought of a dog was horrifying somehow. Maybe he knew....*

The elevator stopped, the doors slid open. He stepped out into the white hallway. It smelled so clean he didn't think a germ would dare try to invade. Spotting the nurses' desk, he went over and repeated his brother's name to the guy sitting there.

"Are you family?"

Mason hated male nurses. Didn't know why, it just

chafed him. They always seemed, to him at least, to be full of themselves. People who see men in scrubs automatically assume they're doctors, and privately, he thought most male nurses got a huge ego boost out of that and almost never corrected the misassumption.

"I'm his brother."

"I'd better take you in. Your brother is—"

"I was there when he pulled the trigger. You don't need to prepare me. Just point me to the room, okay?"

The chubby Justin Bieber–haired blond came around the desk, anyway. "It's right over here. He's on a ventilator, but—"

Mason walked into the room, right up to the bed. Eric lay there. His entire head was bandaged and padded underneath, so it wasn't as obvious that a lot of it was missing. Someone had washed most of the blood away and put him in a hospital gown. His eyes were closed, sunken unnaturally back into his head.

"Have you called his—your—family?" the nurse asked.

"I was just about to."

"Good. The doctor will want to talk to them as soon as possible."

"Why?" Mason took his eyes off his brother to look at the nurse.

"I really have to let the doctor be the one—"

"Come on, kid. Do you really think it matters who tells it? Cut me some slack here. I just watched my brother blow his own head off. Just tell me what you have to say already."

The nurse lowered his head. "He's brain dead. The machine is pumping air through his lungs, and forcing his heart to keep pushing oxygenated blood through his body. But he's not coming back."

Mason nodded and exhaled long and slow. No vegetable brother wasting away slow for the next twenty years. No recovering murderer brother having to face the consequences of his crimes. No being forced to testify against his own sibling or reveal the nightmare to his mother or sister-in-law or nephews. No being driven out of the job he loved.

It was better this way. Was that selfish? Okay, yeah, a little, but not entirely. It was better for *everyone* this way.

"So the doctor wants us all here to tell him to pull the plug." It wasn't a question.

"And to ask you about organ donation, though technically his wife has to make those decisions," the nurse said with a nod in the direction of Eric's left hand. "Most families make it together."

Organ donation. That hadn't even occurred to him. He let his eyes travel up and down his brother's body, completely intact except for his head.

"The ventilator keeps the organs oxygenated until the decision is made," Nurse Bieber went on.

"I see. So he's…"

"He's already gone, Detective Brown. I'm really sorry."

Mason nodded. "Seems like it would be a shame to just waste them, doesn't it?" he asked. "The way he wasted the rest of himself."

"Yeah. It does. There's someone right now praying they'll stay alive long enough to get a heart, a liver, a kidney, a lung. Even his corneas are still good. He could make a blind person see again. Maybe for the first time."

A blind person see again.

*Maybe this accident happened for a reason.*

Mason turned and looked at the nurse, revising his opinion of him. "They should have you talk to all the families in this situation. You're good at it."

"Does that mean you're going to…?"

"Yeah, I'll convince the family. Marie…she listens to me. But don't worry, I'll let the doctor think he talked me into it. Now, about those corneas—can we pick someone to get those? A specific person? If they're the same tissue type or whatever?"

"Of course you can. Tissue typing isn't even necessary for corneas anymore. The latest studies, blah blah blah."

The nurse's words faded into the background noise inside Mason's head, where the gunshot was ringing and echoing endlessly. He was staring at his brother, remembering when they were kids, playing on the tire swing that hung from the giant maple up at the lake, seeing who could swing out farther, dropping into the icy cold water.

How do you go from a laughing ten-year-old to a cold-blooded killer?

"Detective Brown?"

He nodded to let the nurse know he hadn't lost him. "Can you, uh, give me a minute alone with him?"

"Sure. And then you'll call the family?"

Mason nodded.

The kid left and closed the door behind him, leaving Mason alone with Eric. He moved closer to the bed. "I don't know what to say to you, brother." He swallowed to loosen up the constriction in his throat. "Hell, I don't even know if you can hear me, but…what the *fuck,* Eric? What were you thinking? You—" He lowered his voice to a whisper. "You *killed* all those boys, you sonofabitch. And then dumped it all on me? What the *fuck,* man?"

He sighed, backed away. "Okay, so you win. You're badass. You make the messes, and I clean 'em up. Just like always, big bro. And now I've gotta go call Mother and Marie, and break their hearts. And they're gonna cry and mourn for a piece of shit who never deserved either of them. Much less the boys. Damn you, Eric, how could you do this to your family?"

He got up, started to leave, then turned back. "Why the fuck did you have to wait for me to get there, make me watch you do that? That's never gonna get out of my head, you know."

He left the room, closed the door, lowered his head way down because his eyes were burning with tears, and then, finally, he called his sister-in-law.

By noon my room was full of balloons, flowers and various idiotic stuffed animals. And *people,* let's not forget people. My BBF—best blind friend—Mott Killian was at my bedside, strumming his guitar and singing away, doing his usual half-a-song-then-switch thing. Mott taught American history over at Cortland State. Amy, my irritatingly twentysomething personal assistant, had confiscated my tray table for her laptop. She was clicking away, tweeting and posting hourly updates to my fifty-thousand-and-some-odd followers, and manning her ever-present iPhone to tell reporters no to every interview request. I have no idea about social media. She does it all for me. My agent, Barracuda Woman, was keeping tabs via Skype from her Manhattan office. And my sister was riding herd on the hospital staff and ordering takeout. Her twins were texting nonstop— I could hear the tapping, soft as it was—and sucking down vitamin water. I could smell it. Misty had Berry Blast, and Christy had Mango Peach. They were trying not to let me know that their social lives were positively wasting away while they were doing time at their blind aunt's bedside, but their frequent sighs were audible, and their impatience wafted from their pores like B.O.

When a nurse tried to object to all the activity in the room, Sandra laid down the law. "Do you know how many times my sister has been on TV?" she asked. "She's *important*. She needs her people around her."

My people. My entourage. And every one of them so devoted they would take a bullet for me. Well, except for Misty and Christy, who would take a slap for me, max. Maybe. As long as it wasn't in the face.

Moreover, the people in this room were the only people who knew that the real me was *not* the feel-good guru who showed up in my books and on talk shows. And they not only loved me anyway, they loved me enough to *not* sell the truth to the tabloids. That was devotion right there, because that information would've been worth a significant bundle.

There was a tap on the door before someone came in. I smelled her and heard her signature footsteps, soft and close together, and I knew her instantly. "Hold up, hold up." I tapped Mott's knee as I spoke, and he stopped strumming.

"Doc Fenway?"

"You amaze me every time, you know that?" she said with a smile in her voice.

"I do it on purpose," I confessed. "So are you here to visit, or did this little accident have some kind of impact on my eyesight? Please don't tell me I'm going blind!"

Obediently, my entourage laughed. But only a little. There was still noise all around me. Amy's clicking keys, Sandra talking on the phone—"Ham and pineapple, extra blue cheese and the hottest wings you've got"—Mott still picking a string over and over as he tuned the guitar, because apparently he thought as long as he wasn't playing an actual song he was in compliance with my "hold up" order of a moment ago.

And then Doc Fenway went on. "Actually, I came with some good news for you." And then she said it. One sentence that changed everything. "You're going to see again, Rachel."

The room went silent. I flinched as the words exploded inside my brain. "I…um…how?"

"We have a brand-new healthy set of corneas for you. Private donor. Wishes to remain anonymous, and—"

"No." I shook my head and kept on talking before the arguments could begin. "I'm not putting myself through it again, Doc. You know I reject every set I get. It's too much to—"

"Just hear me out, Rachel. Let me explain why it's different this time. Then make whatever decision you want."

I bit my lip. I didn't want to let my hopes start to climb. So far, they hadn't, but if I let her talk they might, and I didn't like the crushing disappointment of failure.

I'd had transplants before. My body rejected them. Violently. I was sick all over. I know, another one of my endearing quirks. I'm a unique individual.

"If everyone could leave us for a few minutes…?"

"They can stay," I said. "They're just going to torture it out of me later, anyway. Go ahead, Doc, give it your best shot, but you know how I feel about beating this particular dead horse."

"Okay." She cleared her throat. "It's been several years since we've tried. There's a new procedure. Descemet's Stripping Endothelial Keratoplasty."

"Oh, well in *that* case, let's go for it. Anything with such an impressive sounding name is bound to work." I loaded on enough sarcasm to clog up a black hole.

Doc Fenway sighed, then repeated herself, but in English this time. "We transplant a thin layer of the graft, not the entire cornea. The risk of rejection is minimal. Recovery time is faster. It's light-years beyond what we've been able to do before. And I think it just might be your answer."

My heart gave a ridiculously hopeful leap. I told it to lie back down and shut the fuck up.

"The donor chose you specifically, Rachel. And we can do it today."

"Oh my God." That was Sandra, and the words were damn near swimming in tears. "Oh my God, ohmyGod, *ohmyGod!*"

I wasn't quite as impressed. "Today? You want me to decide this today? Are you fucking kidding me?"

Meanwhile Sandra was still going on, "You're going to see! You're going to see, ohmyGod!"

The twins started with the teenage-girl squealing

thing that sounds like giant mice having their tails stepped on. Really, someone ought to be researching a cure for that. Screw Descemet's Stripping-whatever.

"This is a miracle!" Amy cried. And then she and Sandra were hugging and hopping around in what sounded like a circle. I don't know. *Blind,* remember? Everyone was talking and crying and laughing—and squealing, let's not forget the squealing—at the same time.

I held up my hands. "Stop. Just stop." I had to speak very loudly.

They all stopped, and I felt their eyes on me. "Okay. Okay." I took a deep breath, but I wasn't processing this. This wasn't real yet. I didn't get it. "I *do* need everybody to get out, okay? Except you, Doc. Everybody else, just…just go get a coffee or something. Give me a minute here."

I heard a keystroke and whipped my finger toward Amy. "Don't you even *think* about tweeting anything about this. Understand?"

"Yeah. No, I wasn't—"

"Close the lid, Amy."

I heard the laptop close.

"Come on, everyone, let's give her some space," Sandra instructed. She was a little hurt that I'd asked. I could tell by the texture of her voice.

"Yeah. I need space."

Mott leaned in close. "You don't have to do it if you don't want to, you know."

"Right. Like *you* wouldn't?"

"No. I wouldn't." Petulant, maybe a little combative? What the fuck?

I frowned. I mean, I knew he thought of the blind as a minority group and himself as our Malcolm X, but I didn't think he'd want to stay sightless if he had a choice. Then again, he'd been born blind. I hadn't. I'd had twelve years of vision. Eleven of them twenty-twenty. And I'd had blurry, half-assed eyesight three times, after the last three transplants, a few days each time before my body threw a full-on, no-holds-barred revolt. I *knew* what I was missing.

Mott kissed my cheek, and everyone left the room. Shuffling steps, grumbling complaints, whispers and finally the door closing behind them. I lay there in the bed, listening to Doc Fenway come over, sit in Mott's former place, clear her throat.

"What do you need to know?" she asked.

I thought for a long time, and then I said, "Is this for real?"

"Yes."

"Will it work?"

"Almost certainly. I wouldn't be here if I didn't be-lieve it, Rachel. This might be the miracle you didn't think you'd ever get."

She was telling the absolute truth, as she saw it. Lies were one of the easiest things to hear in people's voices. I felt tears brimming in my stupid sightless eyes. Damn, I did not cry. Not ever. And if I ever did, it sure as hell wouldn't be in front of anyone. Thank God I was still wearing my sunglasses. "I don't want to believe it just to have it go bad again, Doc. Not this time. It would be more than I can take."

Revealing my soft underbelly was not something I

did often. But she wasn't allowed to tell, right? She was a doctor.

"But you *have to* believe if you ever want anything to change. Isn't that what you're always writing about? How it's the belief that creates the reality, and not the other way around."

*Right. Like I was twelve and somehow believed my way into twenty years of blindness right? I would probably go to hell for the bullshit I sold to the gullible.*

"How long before I'll be able to look at my sister's face?"

She patted my hand. "Tomorrow, if all goes well. And better than the other times, right off the bat, with full recovery in two to three months."

"Tomorrow. I'll be able to see my sister's face again... tomorrow." I lowered my head, shook it slowly. Even if it didn't last, I'd have that. I just didn't know if I could handle the letdown if it was only temporary. You might think temporary vision is better than none at all, but you haven't been there. I have. It sucks.

"It'll work for you this time, Rachel. I honestly believe that."

Yes, she honestly did. I sighed, and she knew I was going to give in. "If I believed in miracles, I'd think this was one."

But of course I didn't. And as it turned out, it wasn't.

# 3

Eric thought he had blown it. He was pretty sure of it, in fact. At first he'd been in oblivion, but then a sound had brought him back. The sound of the rat, scratching, biting. It wasn't digging its way through the wall. It had escaped that prison. Eric had blown a hole through the wall. Into his own head.

So how could he be aware of anything, then? Aware but immobile, aware but in full sensory deprivation. What was this? Was this hell?

He'd intended to be dead, to kill the rat, not to let it out. But it was free. And scratching now to let him know it.

"I know it was my fault," Jeremy said.

That voice, those words, snapped his attention away from the rat's merciless, incessant claws inside him. His focus turned outside, as much as it could, anyway. He couldn't see anything. His eyes were closed, and though he tried to open them, he couldn't. He couldn't feel much either, and he supposed that was a good thing, because he'd blown half his head off earlier today. Or was it yesterday? Or a week ago? Or a year?

Steady beeping, *beep, beep, beep.* The sound of Darth Vader breathing in his ear. A rhythmic thumping. And that voice.

Jeremy's voice.

"I shouldn't have yelled at you for forgetting we were coming home. But you didn't have to do this, Dad. You didn't have to do this."

*It wasn't your fault, son.*

Damn, why couldn't he tell him?

*Scratch, scratch, scratch.*

"Are you all right, Jer?"

That was Marie. She was standing close, he could tell.

"They're gonna cut him up, Mom. How can you let them do that?"

Joshua's sobbing, which he realized had been soft background noise, took a turn for the louder. He felt like joining his younger son. What the hell were they talking about, cutting him up?

"This is no place for the boys." That was Mother. She was patting someone's hand. From the location, he thought it might be his own, but he couldn't feel it, only hear the sound. *Smack, smack, smack.* "I'm sorry I didn't do better by you, Eric. I hope you'll find peace in the afterlife."

"Josh, Jeremy, it's important that you guys understand something here." That voice belonged to his kid brother. Mason.

Mason had been yelling at him earlier. He remembered that vaguely, but had no idea when it had happened and barely recalled what he'd said. Oh, right. He was mad that Eric had waited for him to get there to shoot himself. He had it all wrong, of course. He'd been *trying* to do it before Mason got there. He'd just run out of time.

*Go on,* he thought at Mason. *Tell the boys something. Anything to make them feel better. You always know what to say.*

"Your dad's already gone."

*No! I'm not gone, I'm right here. And so is the rat. Scratching me bloody, the damned thing. Why is it so hyper? Why is it still tormenting me now that it's free? It has what it wanted.*

"He's already gone," Mason repeated. "Those machines are forcing blood through his body to keep his organs alive, but he's gone. And what we're going to do here, with the parts he left behind, is help other people. Your dad is going to save lives. He's a hero."

*Oh, that's a good one, Mason. But they must know better. Or do they? No one had mentioned the dead men. The confession. The bag of tools. Jeremy wasn't asking Marie why his father had murdered thirteen young men who looked just like* he *looked. Why hadn't he?*

*What did you do, Mason?*

Then the rest of Mason's words started to soak in, and he realized they were going to donate his organs. Well, that was good, right? He couldn't feel anything, so there would be no pain, and he certainly couldn't keep on living if they took out all his vital parts. Could he?

He would be free then.

*Scratchscratchscratchscratch!*

"Part of your father will live on in the people whose lives he saves today," Mason said softly. "You should be very proud of that."

Part of him would live on.

Part of him.

Part of him…

*No, not that part!*

A soft breath, close to his face. He heard it but didn't feel it. "Bye, Dad. I love you."

From down lower. "Bye, Daddy."

"Goodbye, son." That was Angela. Mother. Never Mom or Mommy. Mother. Cold. Like she knew.

He heard the boys' shuffling steps, Mother's clacking heels fading, the door swinging open and then closed. And then it was down to Marie and Mason.

"He kept a part of himself closed up—always. But I loved him, all of him. Even the parts he didn't want me to see. I wish he knew that," Marie whispered.

*The rat. You didn't need to see that.*

"I know. I know."

*But you saw it, Mason. You saw my rat in the end. Those driver's licenses. God, what did you do? Did you cover it up?*

A smacking sound, soft, near his ear. Had Marie leaned over to kiss him? God, he wanted to feel that.

A sob. "I can't do this." Running footsteps. The door.

It was just him and his brother now. Mason heaved a big sigh. Like he was almost too tired to stay upright. He sounded just about all in.

"I covered it all up, Eric. Your secrets are going to be buried with you. I just couldn't put them through it."

*I should have figured you would do that.*

"Maybe the lives you save now will at least start to make up for what you did. Balance the scales a little. I hope so, brother. And I hope to God you find some kind of peace now. I really do." And then he went away, too.

There were feet, followed by the sound, not the feeling, of being jostled. And then Eric faded away for a while. When he returned, he felt different. Hollow. Empty. There were still others all around him, their voices muffled. More machines beeping. He was in an operating room. Had been for some time. He wondered vaguely what was left of his body at this point.

"Scalpel."

He heard it. He heard the sound of his skin being sliced. It was like a very faint echo of butter melting in a skillet. *Sssssssss.* And then the horrifying buzz of the bone saw, and the cracking as his ribs were spread apart. No, no, no, he couldn't feel it. He couldn't feel it. He kept reminding himself of that. He was just imagining the pain.

"Transplant team, ready for the heart?"

"Ready, Doctor."

*No! No, wait until I fade away again. I know, I know, I won't feel it, but it's still too awful too awful too awful....*

*Scratchscratchscratch!*

More cutting. God! And then the squishy sounds as they pried and pulled and lifted what he thought was his heart from what he thought was his chest. Surely he couldn't keep going now!

No. No, he couldn't. He was fading, falling into a whirling vortex of darkness and turning his attention away from *here* toward *there*. A pinprick of light appeared far, far away. No more scratching. No more rat.

He felt free of it, lighter than air without it weighing him down.

*Believe me, pal, it's mutual.*

Eric spun around in his rapidly expanding consciousness, which was inflating like a balloon. He started wondering how he had ever fit into his little body to begin with. But still, that voice, *the rat,* got his attention. Where the hell was it? What was it doing?

*Hey, you made this choice, I didn't. I'm not going anywhere, buddy. Just because you shot your head, doesn't mean the rat is dead.*

And then it laughed and it laughed and it laughed, and Eric's horror enveloped him. He couldn't see that speck of light anymore. Nor could he hear the laughter. Or anything. He felt like an astronaut cut loose from his tether, floating through space, only without a space suit. Or a body. Or any senses at all. He was adrift in a vacuum that was stretching him in all directions and dimensions, and he was thinning, and thinning, and wondering when he would simply become a part of the void.

The nightmares started my first night home, barely forty-eight hours after the bandages came off my eyes. But I'm getting ahead of myself here. Because really, that was major, that day. It was fucking *huge.*

I hadn't taken the bandages off myself. Not because the doc had warned me so sternly against it—like *that* would have stopped me. I wasn't real good at doing what I was told. Or conforming. Or following rules. Or anything, really, except writing books telling people to follow their bliss. The more ways I could find to say it, the more books I sold. But the truth was, the whole premise—that you could attract good things to you by being good yourself; that a positive attitude would make life go smoothly; that belief could create fortunes and castles and bliss—was flawed. It had been drummed into me by the well-meaning adults around me ever since I'd lost my eyesight for good.

*Look for the silver lining, Rachel.*

*Everything happens for a reason, Rachel.*

*Something positive will surely come of this, Rachel.*

And I remember thinking, *My God, they actually believe *this shit!*

And when they started getting me books—audiobooks back then, though now it's ebooks with text-to-speech enabled, because let's face it, braille is kind of passé these days—that spouted the same bull, I realized they not only believed it, they *wanted* to believe it.

By the time I was sixteen I had figured out that these Pollyanna idiots would pay any amount of money for any product that supported their inane beliefs, because those beliefs were so flimsy they needed constant reinforcement. One stiff gust of logic or common sense would blow them to hell and gone. Hence, the self-help guru explosion of the first decade and a half—so far—of the new millennium. Entire companies have been born and built around the idea that one could create one's own reality. Those companies produce books and DVDs and card kits created by authors who pretend to understand quantum physics, and use their brand of pseudoscience to support their claims that *you are what you think* and all that crap.

Eventually I figured, why fight it when I could make millions off it instead?

So that's what I did. That's what I *do*. Being blind makes me even more popular among the sheep—I mean masses. Silver lining? No. Smart thinking.

But back to the subject. No, I didn't take the bandages off. I was an obedient conformist for the first time in… well, ever. I waited because I was scared shitless. I had not seen in twenty years, not really. The post-transplant unveilings of the past had been little better than the blindness that had preceded them and of course, short-lived. And before I'd lost my sight entirely, there had been a solid year of slow fading, so the final unforgettable image I'd seen—my brother, Tommy—had been dull and dark around the edges.

Point is, I was too scared to take the bandages off myself. I don't even know what I was scared of, exactly. That the transplant hadn't worked and I would still be blind, maybe, or maybe that I would be able to see again and it would be terrible.

I know, stupid, right? How can seeing be terrible? I guess it's like anything else in the human psyche. When we don't know what to expect we're all alike: terrified. And frankly, I probably would have gotten over the fear and yanked the eye patches off myself if I'd had to wait very long for the doc to do it. But I didn't. Just overnight.

So I was sitting up in the bed, listening to the clock tick and my sister yap at me in an effort to try to distract me from my impatience. My breakfast tray was still there, wafting aromas that weren't really bad but were making my stomach turn anyway. Amy was there. She was unusually quiet. Barracuda Woman was there via Skype, on a laptop beside my bed. The twins were at the mall. Sandra wisely thought maybe I'd like to see them for the first time with just us four.

Mott hadn't even shown up. Him and his idea that being blind was something to be proud of. Like we should have a freaking parade. Blind Pride. Fuck that. If I could see, I damned well wanted to.

And there it was. My hopes were high. I hadn't intended to let them climb up there, but they'd ascended to the point where they were making me dizzy. God, I was a glutton for punishment.

And then there were the footsteps and the smells that told me Doc had finally arrived.

"About time," I said.

"I said nine. It's only 8:30."

"Left my braille watch home. Feels like noon of next year to me." My voice was shaking. Why the hell was my voice was shaking?

She came closer, moved right up next to the bed. Sandra was on the other side, and she slid a hand over mine, closing it tight, and said, "I'll probably look like an old lady to you." She was shaking, nervous and hopeful, and near tears.

"Shit, *I'll* probably look like an old lady to me. At least you had all morning to do hair and makeup. I've never smelled so much hairspray in my life."

She laughed softly. "It's true, I did. Spent an hour and a half. It's not every day your sister sees you for the first time in so long. God, I was what, sixteen?"

Doc's hands were at the back of my head, and she started unwrapping the gauze, layer by layer.

"Don't worry," I told Sandra to lighten the mood. "I wasn't expecting you to still be three feet tall and wearing bunny jammies. But you'd better have kept the dimples and curls. I'm probably a hag. It's unfair."

"You're beautiful, Rachel. You've always been beautiful."

"Yeah, that's the ticket. Make me cry so I can't see shit even with my new eyes."

I wasn't even kidding. Really.

"Don't expect too much," Doc said. "It's going to be better than the last times, but still a little blurry for a couple of months. But it will improve. Every day it'll improve."

"Thanks for the warning. Will you hurry up, already? What are you, rolling the gauze back up to reuse as you go along?"

"You are such a bitch, Rachel," Amy said. But she said it with love, and her voice was thick with tears already.

The gauze was gone. I could feel it. Now there were just two thick pads over my eyes. Doc said, "Keep them closed until I tell you to open them, okay?"

"You want me to wait longer? Yeah, what the hell, it's only been twenty years."

She had her fingertips over the pads, just in case I got antsy, I guess. "Amy, can you get the lights? Sandra, the blinds? I want it dim in here for this."

They moved. The light switch snapped; blinds whispered shut.

And then the pads were being peeled away. "Not yet, Rachel. Keep them closed. Just for a few more seconds." Doc dabbed my eyes with something warm and wet. Then it moved away. "Okay."

*Okay, I can open them now.*

*No, I can't do it.*

"Go ahead, Rachel. It's all right. Open your eyes."

*Just do it already. What are you gonna do, walk around with your eyes closed for the rest of your life?*

*God, why is this so hard?*

I made myself do it. And you know, as much as you might think you can open your eyes slowly, you can't. You really can't. Try it, go ahead. There's just no way. Eyes are either closed or open. Mine were closed.

And then they were open.

And it was dim, but…I could *see*. I couldn't believe it. Had to double-check.

*Am I really seeing, or is this imagination?*

No, no, it was real. I could see people in the room. Yes, blurry, I guess, but consider what I had to compare it to. Women, three women, and I almost panicked, thinking I wouldn't know who was who and would hurt their feelings.

*Duh, you knew who was who before, didn't you?*

Right. Sandra's on the left, holding my hand. I shifted my new eyes to her, and then I clapped my hand over my mouth and the tears started up. "I can see you," I said behind my hand.

She was smiling and shaking her head, and crying, too, bending to hug me, but I pushed her away. "No, no, I want to look at you." And then I clasped her face in my hands and stared at it. Smooth porcelain skin, and blue blue eyes, and laugh lines. My big sister, all grown up. I stared at her until I saw the girl she'd been in her face, in her blue eyes. Her hair was still curly, and I thought it was still gold, but it was too dark to be sure.

I turned from her to look at Amy by the foot of the

bed. And I laughed and smeared tears off my cheeks with one hand, careful of my eyes. "You look just like I thought…only not as Goth and even cuter." She was, short, a little more rounded than she wished she was, short dark perfectly straight hair parted deep on one side. I knew it was dark red—not auburn but burgundy; I'd heard her say so. But in the dimness it looked black.

"I usually *am* more Goth, but I toned it down for this," she said, grinning, tears rolling down her cheeks.

And then I looked at Doc. And blinked. "You're *Asian?*" I burst out.

She broke into laughter, wiping tears from her cheeks.

"Well, you could have told me! What the hell kind of Asian is named Fenway?"

"A married one."

I looked at the laptop on the tray table beside the bed where BW was sobbing her eyes out from inside a little box on the screen. This must be the magical Skype I'd heard so much about. She had a predictable short, sleek silver hairstyle, but I couldn't see her face, because she had dropped it into her hands and was bawling like the rest of us.

"God, BW, look up will you?"

She did. Man, she was a classic beauty, sculpted cheekbones, big brown eyes. And sharp. Even if they were weepy at the moment.

She smiled at me. Her teeth were *so white!*

"You're gorgeous! You're *all* gorgeous." I couldn't stop looking from one woman to the other. "God, everything is…brighter. Even in the dark." Then I looked at Doc again. "Can't I have a little more light?"

Nodding, she went to the window and opened the blinds just a crack, and I could see even more. If it was blurry, I didn't know it. Since, aside from twenty-year-old memories, I had only darkness to compare it to, and the teasing glimpses offered by transplants gone by, it seemed perfectly twenty-twenty to me.

"This is amazing. Oh my God." *Please last, please last, please just fucking last this time.* "When can I have full blasting sunlight?"

"In a few days. Here." She leaned over and slid a pair of tinted glasses on my face. "You need to wear these—*these,* not your designer ones—until further notice, okay?"

I pulled them off and looked at them. "Oh, come on, these? Can't I pick out a nicer pair? You know, something trendy, with spangles or—" I stopped and looked at Sandra, grinning like a loon 'cause I could still see her. "For all I know, these *are* trendy. Are they?"

"Not in the least," Sandra said. Then she leaned over and picked up the top of the tray table, revealing a mirror.

And there I was, staring at myself. At me. Seeing me more clearly than I had in twenty years. It was so surreal my stomach twisted a little. "That's *me?*" I leaned closer, tipping my head at various angles, touching my hair. "It's like looking at a stranger."

"A beautiful stranger," Sandra said.

Amy added, "Yeah, but way more beautiful when you're not in a hospital bed, post-op, no makeup, kind of pale and tired. Trust me, you look way better on your good days, hon."

I couldn't take my eyes off myself as I searched for

the image I used to identify with, which I only now realized was a slightly older, slightly taller twelve-year-old. With boobs.

"We'll go shopping for prescription glasses in any style you want the minute you get out of here," Sandra promised. "But you really need to listen to the doctor and put those back on for now."

I nodded but didn't obey. "When do I get out of here?" I asked. Because I wanted to see everything.

"Later today," Doc said.

I shook my head in amazement. Later today I was going to walk out of this hospital without a cane, without having to count my steps or listen for traffic. "I don't see how life can get any better than this," I said, sounding like one of my own books.

Almost as soon as I said it, I wanted to snatch the words back. And not just because they made me gag. It didn't pay to tempt fate like that. I mean, maybe life couldn't get any better or maybe it could. What I knew for sure was that it could *definitely* get worse.

And it was about to.

'Cause really, miracles are just fairy tales. And reality pretty much sucks.

# 4

Being able to see was so damn good, I almost started believing my own bull. I mean, really, you've gotta give me some leeway here. After being blind for twenty years, getting your sight back is a pretty big deal, and even the bitchiest of skeptical bitches would start to waver a little.

We had agreed to keep my "miracle" quiet for a while, which was great. I just wanted to bask in *seeing* for a little while before going public with the whole thing.

I had never seen my own house, and my first day home from the hospital all I wanted to do was walk through just *looking* at it, you know?

I rode home in Sandra's minivan. Jim had to work, but the twins were in the backseat, chattering all the way about how I would now be able to watch Misty's soccer games, and Christy's cheerleading routines, and ohmygod the school play was next month. It was hard to tune them out so I could gaze out the windows at the scenery, but I managed.

We took the Whitney Point exit, left at the light and

straight through the village, and I was taking it all in. The river, really wide and shallow, and pretty, the mix of nice and junky-looking businesses, the big brick school building that had probably been there for a century or so, minus the various additions. We took a right at the Mobil-slash-McDonald's, and drove until the pavement ended and became the unpaved track that twined around the lake-sized reservoir. I lived beyond the backside of the dam, surrounded by state forest and the reservoir itself. I realized as Sandra drove just how far I had retreated from the world.

Made sense, I guess. I was in the public eye in my work. I liked to hide my private life away. I mean, I wasn't paparazzi-bait famous, but still, I *was* a total fraud. Privacy was important when you were running a scam as big as mine.

When we rolled up to the gated driveway I sat there gaping. My house was like a fairy-tale cottage on crack. Steep peaks, curved clay shingles, some sections cobblestone, others rich maple wood. The windows were tall with red-stained shutters, and the front door was a like a slice from a giant redwood tree. My curving walkway was bordered in thick beds of mums...yellow, brown, red, orange. I got out of the minivan and stood there staring at them like a jackass until Sandra put her hand on my shoulder. "You okay?"

"Of course I'm okay. Why wouldn't I be?" I looked past her at the tall, lean, pair of blonde cover models who were my twin nieces. My mental camera had totally malfunctioned on those two. I'd been picturing a pair of chubby twelve-year-olds with their mother's dimples, I guess, even though I knew they were sixteen. Everyone looked way too serious and sappy-eyed. So I grinned, going for the kind I'd heard called *shit-eating* and said, "This is *really* fuckin' cool."

They laughed. Great. Sappiness averted. We all went inside.

Family party that first night. Amy, who I considered family, Sandra, the twins—still no Mott. And, of course, no Tommy. Sandra and the kids avoided mentioning his name, and when I did, the subject was gently, firmly changed. Sandra had been in touch with the police again. Still no news. *Let's focus on celebrating tonight. Tommy would want us to.* End of subject.

Eventually everyone went home. Well, everyone but Amy, who hung back, offering to help with the dishes. But I knew that wasn't what she really wanted.

So I washed, and she dried, and while I was thinking this china pattern really didn't suit me at all and imagining how much fun I would have picking out something new, she finally got to the point.

"So there are a couple of things…"

I pulled the plug on the sink. "I could tell. What's wrong, Amy? You never keep quiet for this long. You afraid I won't need an assistant anymore now that I can see, because honestly—"

"Pshhhhh. Are you kidding? You couldn't get along without me if you had four sets of twenty-twenty eyes."

"Oh, you think so, do you?" I looked her up and down for effect. She wore short black boots with killer heels and silver buckles, a pair of black leggings under a skintight miniskirt, an off-the-shoulder top that looked like it had been caught in the gears of the washer and torn up a little, with a white cami underneath, and a silver necklace with a giant skull. "Your job is safe, kid, unless I find out you've been dressing *me* like that, in which case, you are *so* fired."

She smiled so big I got distracted by her teeth. Straight and white except for the incisors, which stuck out in front of the rest a little bit.

"You could not even hope to pull this off," she said with a look at her own getup.

"Why would I want to?"

She rolled her eyes.

"So, if you're not worried about your job, then what's up?"

Her demeanor changed. I couldn't put my finger on it until I stopped looking and started feeling again. Her body had shifted away from mine a little, and I sensed her shrinking into herself, not quite as open as before. *She's hiding something. Or wishing she could. But she knows she has to tell me, whatever it is.*

"Come on, Amy. In case you haven't noticed, I'm dying to be alone in my house for a while. Just spill it, so you can leave already."

She did look at me then, and offered a crooked smile, more on the left than on the right. "I hope you never change," she said. "You're such a bitch. I just love you so much. So yeah, there's one little thing."

"I'm listening."

"You know how we talked a while back about getting you a service dog?"

Okay, *that* was not what I'd expected. "Yeah?" I stretched out the word.

"Well, we got all the stuff, and then we never got the dog. But we never got rid of the stuff."

"The stuff," I repeated.

She nodded, and now she was hopeful, opening up a little more, I felt it, and heard it in her voice. I could see it, too, in the lift of her dark, perfectly plucked eyebrows. *Are my eyebrows that perfect? I have to go check.*

"Yeah, the dog bed, and the leashes, and the feeding bowls and dog toys, and—"

"But, Amy, I don't need a service dog now."

"I know. But I wanted a dog, anyway. I mean, I got into the idea when we were thinking about one for you. And then my friend Nikki told me about this one that really needed a home. Not a service dog, just a…just a dog."

I was starting to get a very worried feeling.

"She's kind of old, and her owner died, and none of the family wanted her and she was going to get sent to the shelter. I was gonna keep her myself, but my landlord won't let me, and—"

"But, Amy, I don't need a dog." Hadn't I said that already?

"Oh, come on, Rache. You've got all this room. The place is already fenced in. You can afford to hire someone to take care of her—hell, *I'll* take care of her. For free. And she's just such a great dog, and she's so quiet you don't even know she's here."

Not you *won't* even know she's here, but you *don't* even know…

"Just meet her, okay?"

I closed my eyes. "She's in my house, isn't she?"

"Once I saw her, I just couldn't say no. She's in the garage."

Of course she was. It's not like I had a fleet of cars

taking up space in the attached three-car garage. Hey, there was a notion. I could buy a car now. Of course I'd need a license first, which would mean learning to drive. Who the hell would have the patience to teach me? Fuck them, I'd teach myself. Practice in the driveway.

Amy took my hand. "Come on."

Right. The dog. The invader in my domain. I would nip this little scheme in the bud right now.

Amy all but dragged me across the huge kitchen, enthusiastic now that she'd broken the news. It was stainless steel and white. In fact most of the rooms on this floor were white, and *that* was going to have to change. The place needed color. Or maybe *I* needed it. Splashes of brightness everywhere. Why waste eyesight on white? We stopped at the door that led directly into the garage, Amy opened it up and said, "Myrtle?"

*Myrtle? Is she fucking serious?*

Something moved in the shadows. There was a snuffling, a snorting and then, I'm pretty sure, a fart. Amy reached around and snapped on a light switch I hadn't even known was there—*note to self, find and memorize locations of light switches*. And then *it* came shuffling and snuffling toward us, and my newborn eyes widened as this short, fat, squish-nose creature that did not really look much like any dog I'd ever seen waddled closer, not stopping until its head bumped my shin. And then it sniffed and looked up.

"Playing tricks on the formerly blind girl, are you, Amy? Thinking I don't know a dog from a potbellied pig?"

"She's an English bulldog," Amy said, hunkering

down to scratch its fat little head. "Aren't you, Myrtle? Yeah, you're just a pretty little boodog, aren't you?"

Myrtle closed her eyes, sucking up the affection like a sponge.

"Did you just say 'boodog'?" I asked.

"She needs us, Rache. She's old."

"She smells it." The dog's earlier emission was wafting to my nose now, and I waved a hand in front of my face and tried to blink back tears.

"And she's blind."

I looked down again. I didn't notice the smell anymore, and I was pretty sure that was because she'd sort of skewered my heart with that last revelation. "That's not even close to fair, Amy."

"Look, if you don't want her, fine. Just let her stay until I can find someone else to take her. Please? She won't last a day in the pound."

The dog hit me in the shin with one forepaw.

"I should fucking fire you for this," I told Amy, struggling to hold on to my bitchiness and not reveal that my insides were melting like ice cream in the sun. "Fine. Fine, one week. You find this dog a home in one week." *No way in hell is anyone else getting this dog in a week.* "Got it?"

She smiled at me, and I realized I hadn't been close to understanding what a "shit-eating grin" looked like until right then. Bitch knew me too well.

Amy left. Myrtle did not. Amy had efficiently left a royalty check's worth of dog supplies in the garage. I had no idea where they'd been before, but they were all over the place now.

I decided not to let this momentary digression distract me from doing exactly what I had planned to do. I walked through my house, taking it in visually, loving it more than I ever had before but making a mental list of things I wanted to change. To brighten up. To decorate differently, or decorate at all. My bedroom and office were all but barren.

I did all of this with the tired old dog plodding along beside me. I'd tried doing it alone, but once everyone was gone, and the house silent, and I shut the garage door on the beast, she took to howling like a Halloween sound track. So we wound up making the rounds together. She walked with her side touching my leg, so she wouldn't lose track of me.

I understood that. Being in a new place without being able to see it, you liked some kind of touch. I usually inspected new places by staying close to the walls to get the layout, so I did that with her, circling each room, letting her feel all the boundaries and locate all the doorways.

When we finished our tour of the house, which seemed to meet with the dog's approval, we went outside and walked around the wrought-iron-fenced yard. Five acres of it, with woods, a stream, lush green grass. I knew the dog must be tired, but she never slowed, never complained, just plodded along beside me, tongue lolling.

When the sun started to set over the reservoir I sat down in the grass and just watched it. Myrtle plopped down, too, and without even asking first, she lowered her big head onto my lap, her sightless brown eyes falling closed.

The sun was a giant orange-yellow ball, and as it sank, I saw a bald eagle soar right in front of it. "Wow," I whispered.

I realized I was stroking the dog's head when she released an enormous sigh. I think she was smiling. It was a perfectly serene moment. It was my *last* serene moment, now that I think back on it.

Five hours later, give or take, the first nightmare came. I was standing in a dark room, and there was something sticky all over my face, and I felt...*alive*. More alive than I had *ever* felt. My pulse was pounding, and every cell, every nerve ending, seemed to tingle with delicious sensations of arousal and pleasure. Like a full body orgasm. I was breathing fast and couldn't seem to stop smiling.

*But that stickiness...*

I wiped at my cheek with one hand, pulled it away to look. Red. *Blood.*

The pleasure tingles started to change into shivers of fear as I looked down at my body and saw more of it. I was *covered* in it.

I staggered backward, trying to wipe the stuff off and realizing there was a hammer in my other hand. And it, too, wore a sticky red coating. I dropped it, but it took its time pulling free from my palm, then landing on the floor with a clear, heavy thud.

Turning in a slow circle, I tried to figure out where I was, what was happening to me. There was just enough light in the room to let me see the dead man on the floor. His head was broken like a melon dropped from a roof, his hair so matted with blood and bone and brain that I couldn't even tell what color it was. His face was more hamburger than human.

I opened my mouth to scream, but instead of screaming I spoke, and I don't even know who I was talking to. "I don't want to see this, I don't want to. Make it go away, make it go, make it *go!* I'd rather be blind!"

And then I was awake.

I sat up in bed, blinking, but everything was dark. For one horrifying moment I thought my terrified wish had been granted and I'd gone blind again.

*No. I didn't mean it. With all my heart, I didn't mean it!*

A sob got stuck in my throat, and I pressed a hand to my chest to try to catch the panic that was trying to gallop away with me.

And then a wet nose touched my cheek. It had the same effect as when the hero slapped the hysterical heroine in one those old movies from back when that was a good enough excuse to hit a woman. I snapped out of it.

I wasn't blind.

I could sort of see Myrtle, standing beside the bed, hind legs on the floor, front ones on the mattress as she stretched to reach me. The gleam of her eyes and the shape of her head were clear in my darkened bedroom. I stroked her and leaned over to fumble for the lamp, snapped it on and went limp with relief when light filled the room and the room filled my eyes.

"Okay, good. Good. It's all good. It was just a dream."

My bedroom was just the way I'd left it. Soothing green walls—keep. Ivory curtains and woodwork—keep. Not a single picture on a single wall—big change needed. The circular dog bed lay on the plush green carpet to my left. One of Myrtle's toys, a yellow teddy bear with one arm missing and white fluff sticking out of its shoulder socket, was lying in it.

But Myrtle was still standing with her paws on my mattress.

"Yeah, okay. Why not?" I got up, moved around behind her, linked my arms around her middle and picked her up, grunting as I did. "Not a lightweight, are you, Myrt?"

*Snarf,* said Myrtle.

I got her into the bed, then climbed back in myself. She padded around until she found a spot she liked— as close to me as possible—and dropped. Myrtle didn't lay down. Myrtle collapsed.

I sighed. "So what the hell was that about, do you think?" I asked her.

She opened her sightless eyes and looked back at me as if to say, *You're asking me? I'm just a dog.*

I'd never had a nightmare like that in my life. It had been vivid. Real. And the feelings running through me in that dream had been majorly fucked up. Way out of line with anything I would ever have felt. I had never equated blood and sex. Not even in fantasy. Sadism was not my thing. I didn't have a dominatrix bone in my body. So what the *hell* was up with the sensations of sexual pleasure and all that blood?

"All right, well, I've been through a lot this week. Hit by a car, got my eyesight back and Tommy's still missing and—"

I flashed back to the man on the floor in my dream, the obvious question popping into my head. Could it have been my brother? Was I having some kind of psychic vision about what had happened to Tommy?

I sat up again, my eyes shifting rapidly side to side as I searched my brain for the memory, for any clue. What clothes was the guy wearing? What did he look like?

*Blood and hamburger.*

What the *hell* was wrong with me?

"Simple, stupid. Stress, a major physical change, every sense in my body undergoing a radical new state of being, and I'm still worried to hell and gone about Tommy. Maybe even feeling guilty that we were celebrating tonight while he was—"

*Blood and hamburger.*

"What do you say we leave the light on for the rest of the night, huh, Myrt?"

She closed her eyes and sighed.

But even then, I didn't go back to sleep.


Mason stood between his two nephews at Glenwood Cemetery. Joshua had tugged and pulled at his necktie so much it was hanging loose and crooked, and kept shifting from one foot to the other, pausing in between to tug at the seat of his pants. He'd already taken off his jacket, and Mason thought if his mother hadn't been standing there, he would have shucked the tie, the pants and the shoes, too, and gone running off in his shorts.

He intended to see to it the kid did just that once this part was over.

This part, frankly, sucked.

At least Josh seemed…normal. If there *was* a normal after a kid lost his dad. Mason had been twenty-nine when he'd lost his own, three years ago, and he still felt off his game.

That had been different, though. His dad had been sick for over a year. Pancreatic cancer was a bitch of a way to go. Had he known ahead of time, Mason would have stockpiled the morphine himself for his father. But no one had warned them how bad it would be. Those hospice nurses—they'd been so good in so many ways. Let Dad die at home where he wanted to be. But still, why don't they tell the family to stockpile the morphine? To play the pain up before it got too bad and keep asking for more? They could have gotten it at that point. No one worries about addiction when you're dying. It's not like you're going to have to get clean later on and suffer through withdrawal. All anyone wants is for you to be comfortable. Until it gets to the point where no amount of morphine can make you comfortable and instead it makes you crazy, with the nightmares and the hallucinations and the notion that the drugs are poison and everyone's trying to get rid of you, maybe because that's what they should be doing.

The thing was to stockpile the morphine before it got that bad. Then give it to them all at once when it gets too horrible to bear. It would have been merciful.

That had been, Mason realized, the first time he'd ever considered that doing something illegal might be justified. The day he'd watched his brother blow himself away had been the second—and that time he'd actually acted on the thought.

Jeremy sniffed. The sound jerked Mason out of his dark thoughts, and he looked over at his sixteen-year-old nephew. Built like a scarecrow. He'd grown a couple of inches over the summer, let his hair grow out. It was brown, curly. He attempted the comb-it-all-forward look currently the rage, but it curled at the ends in a flip that ruined the effect.

Jeremy was not doing well. He looked like a zombie.

Marie was a blond-haired blue-eyed rock, standing between her son Josh and mother-in-law, Angela. She had an arm around Josh, more to get him to stop fidgeting than to comfort him, but still. The other hand rested atop her baby bump. Her eyes were wet and a little puffy, but she'd done her hair and makeup, and she was holding it together in spades. For the boys, he figured. He and Marie had not always seen eye to eye, but he thought she was a hell of a mother. His nephews were lucky to have her.

His own mother, Angela, was standing there looking blank. She was medicated. He could tell. She had one of those doctors that only the wealthy or well-connected could afford, the kind who would pretty much prescribe whatever she asked for and look the other way when her usage seemed to be getting over the top.

As for himself, he was a wreck, too. And not just because he kept expecting the whole mess to blow up in his face at any second. Someone would find out what Eric had done—and what Mason had done to cover it up. It had to happen. That was hell to deal with on top of mourning the brother he'd thought he had, while trying to make sense out of the one he now knew had been real. The two images didn't mesh. Yes, Eric had been fucked up for most of his life, but Mason had always seen him more as the victim of some screwy personality disorder—social anxiety or whatever—than as a criminal.

Murderer, he corrected.

Serial killer, he corrected again.

No matter how often he adjusted the label in his mind, he couldn't seem to make it stick. His memory of his brother kept going straight back to "poor, mixed-up Eric, he's so awkward with people, so painfully shy, so uncomfortable in his own body."

Yeah, the family was a mess. Of them all, he figured Josh was doing the best.

The priest finished up, noting that there would be a gathering at Angela's home afterward, and that they were all welcome to stop by and pay their respects.

Mason knew it was part of the whole ritual of parting, but he honestly didn't know if he could get through it. People began to wander up to the five of them, offering hugs, handshakes, platitudes. And there would be more of the same into the evening, he knew, at his mother's brick Georgian with its perfectly manicured lawn in Binghamton's upscale suburb of Endwell. Uncomfortable people with empty words and filled casserole dishes.

Turning, he looked at the boys. "You guys wanna ride back with me instead of in the limo?"

Jeremy looked at his mother, then turned back and shook his head no, though Mason could tell he wanted to say yes. "We'd better stick with Mom."

"Good man. I'll be right behind you, then, okay?"

"I'd like to ride with you, Mason," Angela said, and she closed a hand on his upper arm, digging in with her nails, though he didn't think she meant to. "If you don't mind."

He was surprised how much his mother was leaning

on him. She weighed next to nothing, and yet her hand on his arm seemed to be holding most of that weight up. It was alarming enough that he rearranged her, sliding his arm around her shoulders, and helped her down the grassy slope to the dirt track where several cars were lined up as their owners climbed back inside.

Marie and the boys slid into their limo, Marie having to turn her back to the open door and lower herself in carefully. She was going to have that little girl in a few months. Mason thought about that, about her and the boys having something joyful to take the place of the pain and grieving. And then he thought more. His brother was a serial killer. Was it genetic? Eric being adopted, his own forebears were a mystery. But could the gene be alive, even now, in one of the boys, or in the baby on the way?

The limo pulled away. He watched it go, then finally opened the passenger door of his car for his mother. She got in, he closed it and went around, got in his own side. As he pulled away, she blinked her glassy eyes and said, "You'll need to make even more effort than before with Marie and the boys, you know."

He nodded. "They'll need me. I know, Mother."

"Eric was our link to them. We can't let Marie start pulling them away from us."

"She would never do that."

"She's angry. I know you don't see that, but I do. I'm a woman. I was his mother. She blames me."

"I don't think that's true."

She was quiet for a moment. He pulled out of the cemetery, onto the road. It was a beautiful day, too beautiful to spend it among the dead.

"You're a policeman, Mason. I never wanted that for you, never understood why *you* wanted it—but it's what you are. I expect you to do whatever it takes to get to the bottom of this."

He glanced sideways at her and didn't bother going into the old argument. He'd decided to be a cop when his best friend's kid brother had been murdered by his babysitter. "To the bottom of what, Mother?"

She shot him a *How can you ask me that?* look. *"This,"* she said. Then she shook her head hard. "He didn't just shoot himself. He couldn't have. Not my Eric."

He started to speak, then pressed his lips together to keep the words inside. His mother knew the circumstances of his brother's death. He didn't need to tell her again that he'd walked in on the suicide-in-progress. She knew. She'd insisted on reading the reports. She'd been high on prescriptions ever since.

"Mother, you know he did."

"I know, I know, I—" She fluttered a hand in the air. "I mean there had to be a *reason*. I've been asking Marie about things—their finances and so on—and she says they're fine, but I know better. Honestly, if it had become that bad, why wouldn't he just have asked...?" Her voice trailed off as she slowly shook her head. "Maybe he borrowed from the...the wrong people."

"He didn't borrow. Their finances were fine. Marie didn't lie to you."

"Drugs, then." She said it almost hopefully. "Maybe he was on some sort of drugs that—"

"He wasn't on drugs, Mother." Ironically, *she* was, but prescriptions, as she so often reminded him, were not *really* drugs. They were drugs, but not, you know, *drugs*.

Mason took a breath. She wasn't going to let go of this. "Eric had…problems. You know that."

"No." She shook her head. "Not problems. He was a quiet boy. Scared. But that's natural, of course. Six years old, coming to a new country, a whole new family, learning a new language. We don't even know what happened to his birth family in Russia." She lowered her head again. "We never asked him, you know."

"I know."

"Maybe if we'd asked him."

"*I* asked him once. He said he didn't remember anything from before he was adopted."

She seemed to mull on that for a while. "We didn't think we could have children, you know. When you came along not even a year later it was like a miracle."

"I know, Mom." He'd heard the story a thousand times.

"For him, too, though."

That part, he hadn't heard before. It got his attention.

"He lit up when we brought you home, Mason. For the first time I thought maybe he was finally coming out of his shell. He seemed happy. For a little while, anyway. Until middle school. Then he just seemed to… shut down again."

There wasn't an answer for that. Had he been older, Mason would have personally kicked the asses of the school-yard bullies who'd tormented his brother. As it was…he wondered if that had anything to do with what Eric had eventually become.

And now he was playing his mother's game, with the whys and what-ifs. It wouldn't do any good.

"I had a call from the hospital this morning," she said.

"What about?" he asked, glad of the new subject.

"The person who got the corneas is asking to meet the family of the donor."

Mason nodded slowly. He knew who that person was, but the rest of the family didn't. Mother and Marie had asked him to handle all the details, and he had. He wondered why they'd phoned his mother and not him, or even Marie, but those answers could wait. As could the reaming out he intended to give to whoever had phoned his mother about it on the day of his brother's funeral. "What did you tell them?"

She sighed, and her eyes flooded. "I said I'd ask you. I don't think I can…I don't think I can bear to see my son's eyes staring at me from some stranger's face." The tears spilled over, streaming silently down her pale, papery cheeks.

"It's okay. It's okay, you don't have to do that." He closed his hand around hers, not bothering to explain yet again that Eric's eyes were still with Eric's body, that only a thin layer of tissue had been removed. "I'll take care of this, okay? You don't need to think any more about it. Just put it out of your mind, all right?"

"Thank you, Mason. I don't know what I'd do without you." She sniffed and wiped her cheeks with two manicured fingertips. "Remind me to phone the doctor when I get home, before things get too crazy and I forget. I'm going to need a refill on my Ativan."

He withheld comment and decided in that moment

that yes, he would, eventually, agree to meet with the self-help guru who'd gotten Eric's corneas. The one who'd said maybe the accident had been supposed to happen. Maybe if he could see one good thing that had come out of this entire mess, he could shake the dark feeling of impending doom that had been clinging like a shadow ever since that day. Maybe if he could see that blind woman, looking at him, *seeing* him, because of his brother, he could start to move past all this.

But not yet. He was nowhere near ready yet.

# 5

I'd been seeing pretty much twenty-twenty for a solid six weeks. And you know, it was mostly a good month and a half. Not *all* good. And definitely not serene, with the nightmares recurring. Still no word from Tommy. Or the cops, except to say they had nothing new. Myrtle continued to make herself at home, while I continued pretending to just barely tolerate her, because God forbid my entourage should think I was going soft. I totally was, though. I was putty in that fat little dog's paws. I took her everywhere I went. I'd had a safety harness installed in my car—an '02 T-Bird convertible. A classic, she was. Inspiration Yellow, with black-and-yellow leather and every available option. Yes, I'd learned to drive, and even while my sister was teaching me, Myrtle was my constant copilot. I bought her a yellow scarf to match the car, and a pair of tinted glam-dog goggles to protect her poor useless eyes from the sun and windborne grit.

I hadn't gone back to work in any way, shape or form, though. Everyone thought I was taking time to readjust to sighted life. But it was actually because I didn't want to continue using my voice-recognition software now that I could see. I wanted to *type* my books from now on. I wanted to *see* the words unfolding on the computer screen as I puked them up. Which meant learning new software, not to mention keyboarding skills. It was bound to slow me down...for a while. Not much terrifies a writer more than the notion of changing her process. We all secretly believe that we're able to do what we do because we've stumbled onto some obscure alchemical formula that magically transforms us into the great mythical beast known as *author.* And we all secretly fear that twisting one screw or adjusting one cog, or changing the color of our ink, could mess up the entire recipe and expose us to the world as the frauds we really are.

So I wasn't writing, though I would eventually bite the bullet and dive back in and it would be fine. I knew that. But there was so much else to do, and a whole lot to learn. You think there's a learning curve when you *lose* your vision? Try getting it back sometime. Everything, everything, *everything,* has to be learned from scratch, from measuring coffee into the filter basket to remembering to turn off the lights at night. (Not all of them. *Never* all of them.) Operating the TV remote alone deserved a six-week tutorial. Personal grooming—the hair, the makeup, the matching of the clothes—well, I'd always had help before.

And yeah, I still had help for the asking, but I wanted to do it myself, dammit.

My first results with makeup had Amy giving me the kind of indulgent smile you give a four-year-old who presents you with his first piece of macaroni art. Then she marched me back to the bathroom, and made me wash it all off and start over, with her patient instructions this time. I'd improved a lot since then.

But I'd still asked for help today. I wanted to look especially nice, because this was the day when I would meet the brother of the man who had given me his corneas. And see the look on his face when he realized his brother's eyes had gone to a famous person. (Yes, Virginia, I have an ego.) And then I wanted to know if he knew anything about where these damned dreams were coming from. Because they were still coming.

I'd had several more of the horrifying nightmares. They were currently averaging about one a week. In the most recent one, I hadn't just seen the end result of the murder but had felt myself committing it. I was swinging the hammer, feeling the dull, squishy thud of it connecting, the smack of metal into meat and warm blood splattering my skin, ending once again with a sick, twisted rush of sheer, almost sexual, pleasure.

I woke up and vomited that time.

I'd been doing a little research of the woo-woo variety, as I liked to call it, and had found an alarming number of organ recipients who claim to have gotten more than just the organ from their donor. Habits. Tastes. Cravings. Even memories.

I didn't really believe any of it, but from a completely rational point of view, I had to check it out. Pretransplant, no nightmares. Post-transplant, nightmares. Simple math. And this guy I was about to meet might just be able to tell me if there was a reason for that.

I'd been rehearsing my questions in my head and writing notes in longhand, because my handwriting needed *a lot* of practice. I would phrase my questions carefully, not to give too much away. I didn't want the guy thinking his brother's eyes had gone to a psycho, right? And besides, he might talk after our meeting. To the press. And I didn't need that sort of headline. Not when BW was even now setting up future interviews in the wake of the big announcement. Her original plan to save the news for the right time went out the window when I told her I wanted my driver's license and would not wait to get it. The minute someone caught wind of that, it would be obvious I could see again. So we did a press release: *The woman who writes about how to create your own miracles has a miracle of her own.* You couldn't *buy* publicity that good, and we asked for the public's patience while I adjusted to sighted life. Fortunately *Wish Yourself Rich* was already in the can, just waiting for its holiday release date.

Our spin was that my consistently positive attitude and steadfast belief that my eyesight would one day be restored, my lack of doubt and my refusal to let my blindness become my focus, had inevitably created the miracle I had now experienced.

Because that was the spin that would sell books.

It wasn't the truth, of course. The truth was, I got lucky.

I got *unlucky* when I went blind. I got lucky when my sight was restored. Because shit happens. Good shit and bad shit. It's random, and there's nothing you can do about it. Period.

But people don't like feeling helpless and powerless against fate. So you sell them a reason to believe they're not, and you "manifest" yourself a career and a pile of money. Voila! Magic.

The meeting with the donor's brother was set for the benches near the observation tower on my end of the dam. Myrtle and I could walk that far, and I loved walking even if Myrt did not. Even after six weeks, give or take, I couldn't get enough of looking out over the reservoir. Do you have any idea how many different ways simple water can look? Choppy and dark green, or white capped and rough, or still and blue. My favorite was when the water became a mirror, and I could see the pines and vivid fall foliage reflected perfectly in it. I loved that.

Myrtle and I walked slowly along my dirt road, all the way to the paved part near the village, and then we veered onto the walking path that encircled the reservoir. It was barely October, and the leaves had turned themselves up to full power. Had the colors been this vivid in the fall when I was a kid? I grew up in New York's nether regions, the little-known places with more cows than humans, so I'd seen the trees put on their annual version of Fashion Week, but it was hard to remember. And now the colors were more vivid than anything I could recall. Like neon. Or black-light posters with the black lights turned on. *Those* I remembered.

Myrtle was resenting the shit out of the enforced walk, but I kept telling her it was good for her. Yes, she was old and blind, but she was also fat. We'd been doing a slow, easy lap around the property every evening, though she hated it. If she could have talked, she would have cussed all the way.

This was a little bit farther. And man, was she pissed.

Near the tall rectangular tower on my end of the dam, I saw my donor's brother right where we had agreed, using the hospital as intermediary, to meet. We hadn't spoken yet, even by phone. He was sitting on a wooden park bench, staring out at the reservoir most people mistook for a lake. It was huge, almost six miles long and more than a mile wide.

The guy's back was toward me, so I got to look him over without him noticing. Short dark hair, nice and thick. A broad back, really wide shoulders underneath a blue windbreaker. I closed my eyes and tried to get a mental image, but my senses were on strike, and I realized it was because I was nervous. Me. Nervous. Go figure.

I walked up behind him, and Myrtle sat down the minute I stopped walking and glanced up at me. The message in her expression was *Try to move me right now and I swear to God I'll bite your arm off. And by the way, I could use a snack.*

I dipped into my pocket for a Snausage and gave it to her, then refocused on the guy while she smacked, slurped, licked her lips and belched her gratitude. Hearing the dog, he turned, and my mouth went dry, because he was drop-dead gorgeous. I'm talking better than Hugh Jackman handsome. And that's saying something, right?

*Maybe I'd better say something before he thinks I'm in need of a voice box transplant next.*

"I saw an eagle out there one day," I said. "In fact, it was the day I got home, the first day I ever saw anything here."

He smiled a little, but it didn't reach his eyes. It was

one of those smiles that seemed like the right expression but wasn't anything close to real. Then he got to his feet, moved closer, extended a hand. "Good to see you, Rachel."

I took his hand and made my shake firm, because men respected that, and then was instantly flooded with a sense of familiarity as his big hand completely enclosed mine. Warm. Nice. I looked at the little hairs at his wrist, wondered if he was hairy all over. Then my nose twitched. His scent was familiar. Not just the aftershave but the way it smelled on him. And his voice was still echoing in my brain like a skipping record.

"Wait a minute," I said, yanking my hand free. "I've met you before, haven't I?" It wasn't really a question.

"Yeah, you have. I was—"

I help up my hand, palm flat. "Don't tell me." He shut up, and I closed my eyes, because by now I knew that my other senses pretty much refused to stay on full alert when my eyes were open. There was just too much to see, and I was entirely too enamored with seeing it. But when I closed my eyes, my other soldiers came to attention. I stopped looking at the guy and starting *feeling* him.

He was crouching down by then, petting Myrtle, his big hands moving over her as she wriggled without standing up. That dog was as lazy as I was sarcastic.

"You're just a raving beauty, aren't you? Yes, you are."

*He* wasn't being sarcastic, though Myrtle had a face only a bulldog lover could love. His voice was like velvet rubbing over gravel. His *presence*—whatever unique electromagnetic energy his body gave off—some call it an aura, but that term is just so freaking new-age-fluffy-bunny that I refuse to use it, but still, whatever you want to call it, it was just *so* familiar to me. And then it all clicked into place in one big flash.

"You're the cop who ran me over!" I opened my eyes. "Mason Brown."

He was straightening up and looking surprised, one hand still stroking Myrtle's head. "How the hell did you know?"

I shrugged. "I'm just that good. You never came to visit me in the hospital."

"Some things happened that day. I meant to come, I really did."

"I didn't really expect you to come anyway, it's fine." I looked past him, not seeing anyone else. "It's just that there was something I really wanted to talk to you about."

He shrugged. "So talk to me about it now."

I looked at my watch, then grinned, because I was actually *looking* at my watch. Little things like that still made me smile. "I would, but I'm meeting someone. It's kind of important."

"I know."

Yeah, okay, so sometimes I'm a little slow on the uptake. But it finally hit me that he hadn't so much as commented on my ability to see him standing there. And he had to have noticed, being that I was clearly blind as a bat the last time he'd seen me.

I tilted my head and frowned, and heard my inner bitch say *Duh, Rachel.*

He saw me figuring it out and filled in the blanks. "My brother died within a few hours of our—accident.

He was your donor." He smiled a little. "Do you remember what you said to me that day?"

"Get this car off of me?" I suggested. And yes, I was using sarcasm to mask my momentary shock and to give myself time to snap all the puzzle pieces into place. He hit me with his car, then his brother died, and then he gave me his brother's corneas.

He laughed just a little, lowering his head as he did. Oh, man, he was hiding something. My senses went on alert. This man was full of secrets. That energy thing you feel from other humans was all tightly coiled and staying close to him, his voice, restrained, his laugh, forced. He was keeping a lot inside. And I suddenly wanted to know what.

*Probably none of my business.*

*Not if his dead brother gave me his nightmares along with his corneas it's not. I need to know this shit.*

"Remind me," I told him. "What did I say?"

"You said, 'maybe this little accident was *supposed* to happen.'"

"Oh." I blinked twice, thinking back and guessing that I must have been trying to reposition my Pollyanna mask. As I recalled I'd been a little bitchy when he'd first peeled me off the pavement. "Well, maybe so, but I don't think even I could have suspected *this* was the reason. That I'd inherit your brother's corneas."

"Well, you *couldn't* have suspected that—unless you're psychic."

"Right. And for the record, I'm not," I said. And then I took the plunge and blurted, "Was he?"

Mason gave me a quick but very deep frown. I liked his eyebrows. They were thick and dark and screamed

*I have lots of testosterone.* It was appealing to my female parts, which tingled a little. *Bad idea, Rache. Really,* really *bad.*

"Was he what?" Mason asked.

"Psychic." I watched his face. He didn't give away a thing.

"No, he wasn't psychic. That's a strange question. Why do you ask?"

I shrugged and looked past him at the water, glittering in the sun. It was blue today, and the little ripples were gold flashes sending Morse code greetings back to the sun. Mason Brown was telling the truth. I felt it. He was hiding something, but not that his brother had been his secret weapon in solving crimes. It would have been a cool scenario. His brother sees crimes through ESP, then Mason solves them without letting on where he got his insider info. I inherit the "gift" along with the corneas, and we team up to fight crime. Hell, maybe I should write fiction.

Wait, I already did.

Mason was waiting, looking at me. I guess it was my turn to talk. "I've been feeling like I want to know more about him. Your brother. Who he was. What he was about, who his family are, that sort of thing."

Myrtle tugged her leash, and I looked down to see her straining close enough to hit his shin with her paw. *Pet me, stupid. What do you think those hands are for?*

He bent to obey her, and she smiled. I'd learned to recognize her smile—when her bottom fangs stuck out, up and over her upper lip, that was a bulldog smile. And she was smiling to beat the band just now.

"I don't know how much of that can happen, really,"

he said. He wasn't looking up at me. I was standing, he was crouching, his eyes on the dog, his face hidden. Like he didn't want me to read too much in it.

I did better reading what I couldn't see, though, so he was doing me a favor.

"My mother's…she's still in too fragile a state, and the others—" He bit his words off there, apparently to keep himself from telling me anything about the rest of his family. Or maybe to keep himself from telling my anything. Everything about him was closed. He couldn't have been more obvious if he'd been wearing a sandwich board that said KEEP OUT on one side and Trespassers Will Be Shot on the other.

"I don't need to *meet* them. Maybe you can just… tell me about him."

"Not much to tell. Eric was…" He stopped there, and I almost heard the "oops."

"So his name was Eric." I smiled, and not only because he'd let the name slip out unintentionally, but also because knowing the name of the guy who gave me back my eyesight meant something to me, I guess. I know, saccharine, right? *Gag.*

"He was just an ordinary guy. Quiet. Kept to himself." Still crouching, head down, pretending to keep his attention on the dog but actually focusing on not saying too much.

"Sounds like what the neighbors always say about the guy who goes postal and murders a bunch of co-workers."

He snapped his head up so fast he probably pulled something in his neck. His eyes were wide, probing mine. I felt the tension in his body coil so tight it must have hurt. I'd said something wrong. He was alarmed, defensive, maybe even hostile.

I looked away because he was skewering me with his eyes as if he was digging inside my brain. I stared at the water. He wasn't going to tell me anything, was already covering up the reaction, and I didn't want him all defensive. So I would pretend I hadn't noticed the telltale response. "The dog's name is Myrtle, by the way."

A beat passed. Then he said, "That's the perfect name for her."

"She's blind and needed a home. My assistant figured she could guilt-trip me into taking her."

"Looks like it worked."

"She's still on probation," I said.

I felt him relax, heard him exhale deeply and fully, felt him uncoil a little, and I faced him again as he straightened.

"What *did* you mean?" he asked me. "When you said the accident might have happened for a reason?"

I frowned as I realized we'd circled back around to an earlier spot in the conversation. And that he was basically changing the subject entirely, even though I hadn't learned a single thing about my organ donor, other than his name and that his brother wanted to keep him buried.

I moved to the park bench and sat down. Myrtle took the opportunity to plop flat out on the ground. She lay on her belly, short legs straight out behind her like a big furry frog, chin between her forepaws. She started snoring before she even closed her eyes.

"I'm really sorry about your brother," I said, leaning back on the bench, opening the flap of my handbag and digging inside. "I should have said that first. I know how it feels. I was at the police station that day because of my own."

He didn't come and sit beside me. Just stood there waiting—impatient, I thought, to have this meeting come to an end. "Your own?" he asked.

"Brother," I said. "And since I didn't get much help from your colleagues at the Binghamton P.D., I thought maybe a detective racked with guilt for running me down like a dog in the street—sorry, Myrtle—would be a good asset to have."

"Your brother is...?"

"Missing." I found my brand-new iPhone, and flipped through my recently added photo collection—thank you, Amy—until I found a recent shot of Tommy, and then I got stuck on it. I hadn't *seen* him since he was fourteen. The photo Amy had gotten from Sandra looked nothing like the Tommy I'd known back then. I'd never seen it, but I'd sensed it. You could feel a person fading away—well, I could, anyway. But the sight of him was still a shocker. Skinny, with a gray cast to his skin, teeth stained and crooked, one missing right in front. That stupid tattoo on his neck that I'd heard about but never seen—a climbing tiger. Even drug-ravaged, he looked younger than his age. Closer to twenty-four than thirty-four. He'd always kept his teenage looks, Sandra said. His soft brown eyes, his long brown hair. I wished I could see him again and nag him to get it cut.

Sighing, I turned the phone toward Mason Brown. "Of course, you had to go and assuage your guilt by giving me back my vision. So I don't suppose I have any leverage left to get your help on this."

He was staring at my phone. Staring *hard.* "How long…has he been missing?"

Wow. Something had changed in him. I lowered my head so I could close my eyes without being obvious.

*He knows something.* I turned my senses up to full alert.

"He disappeared a week before our accident," I said. "As near as anyone can figure, anyway. That was the last time anyone who knew him saw him. But it's impossible to say for sure how long he's been gone."

"Why's that?"

His voice was softer, his energy all broken up and uneven. Like the water when you do a cannonball off the tire swing.

*Now that was an odd thought. I've never done a cannonball off a tire swing in my life.*

"You can probably tell by the photo, can't you?" I asked, looking up again.

"He's an addict." He turned the phone toward me and handed it back.

"And a transient." Polite-speak for bum. Street person. Homeless. "I imagine that's why the police didn't take me very seriously, which was why I went stomping into the street that day without paying attention, which is why you hit me with your car, which is why, I would hazard to guess, I got your brother's corneas."

He nodded as if that all made sense.

"It's almost as if the stuff in my books really *does* have some merit," I muttered, only because the thought had just then occurred to me and it was a little bit mind-blowing.

"I'm sorry?" He was inside himself, barely listening to me.

I looked up fast. "Nah. Nothing. Nothing worth repeating, anyway." But I filed it away under "synchronistic coincidence," knowing it would get an entire chapter in my next bullshit book. It made just enough sense to be believable and fit perfectly with my "everything happens for a reason" line, which was starting to get stale.

"Listen, I know you've done more than enough for me already, *way* more. I shouldn't ask for anything else from you, but I still think we met for a reason. Not so I could get your brother's eyes, but so you could help me find Tommy. So what do you say? Will you do it? Will you help me find my brother?"

I watched the way his Adam's apple bulged and then sank again, like a whale breaking the surface and then receding into the depths. "I'll do everything I can."

Shit. That's what they all said. And with that exact same inflection and attitude that revealed the rest of the sentence, the part they didn't say. *I'll do everything I can, which is absolutely nothing.* I sighed, then nodded and tried to hide my disappointment. "Great. That's just great. I filed a missing persons report, so they'll have all the info you need."

He nodded. "Height, weight, hair and eye color...?"

"Tall, skinny, brown and brown. Thomas Anthony de Luca. Like I said, it's all in the report."

"Okay. I'll look into it."

Maybe he would. Barely. He had something else on his mind, though. Something heavy. I could hear it weighing down his voice like a lead weight. I was quiet for a few ticks, not knowing what else to say. And then it occurred to me what I hadn't yet said, so I said it. "Thank you. Your brother's gift changed my entire life. Mainly that's what I wanted to come here and say. I hope you'll pass my gratitude on to your family for me."

"I will."

"But I'd still like to know more about him."

He stared into my eyes for a long moment. Not in a sexual way, and not in an adoring fan way, either. This was like he was looking for something in them. And I knew what. His brother. His brother, Eric, whose eyes were inside my head. You know, sort of.

Damn, the guy must have really loved his brother.

"I actually have somewhere I have to be," he said, looking away. "I meant to reschedule it and completely forgot. I'm sorry I don't have more time."

"Oh." It was bullshit. He was feeling uncomfortable as hell for some reason, so he wanted to end this. Nothing I could do about that. "All right, then."

"I'll call you, though, if I find anything on your brother."

"Yeah, sure," I said, and gave him my number, which he entered into his own phone.

"I'd still like to know more about Eric," I told him. Again. "Maybe…some other time?"

"Sure," he said. "Some other time." Then he gave me a stiff smile, a stiffer nod and walked away, taking the path in the opposite direction from the way I had to go. I watched—so did Myrtle, whining twice—until he was out of sight, around the bend in the path, moving fast, as if he couldn't get away from me fast enough.

I scratched Myrtle right in front of her ear where she loved it best. "You ready to head back, old lady?"

She lifted her "eyebrows" as if to say, *Are you fucking kidding me?*

And yet she got up, heaving a long-suffering sigh.

Something about this meeting had gone wrong, I thought, but I was damned if I knew what. We turned and headed back along the walking path, onto the road and toward home. We went slowly, for Myrtle's sake, and I replayed my every word, trying to figure out where the hell I'd messed up. Something I said had shaken that big detective right to his toes. And I didn't think he was the type who would shake all that easily.

Mason pulled into the driveway of his apartment, the place where his brother had died, and sat behind the wheel working up the resolve to go inside. He'd only been back once since Eric's suicide. Just once. Long enough to clean up and pack some of his things. He'd hauled the sofa to the curb, along with all the plastic that had been over it, the end tables, the coffee table, a couple of lamps and the area rug.

His considerate big bro had covered that in plastic, too, but he knew how blood was. It always got through. He'd had a compulsive need to get every trace of his brother *out*.

But even with that, he couldn't stay there. He'd been using a guest room at his mother's house while looking for a new home. That had worked pretty well at first, because his mother needed the company. But after a couple of weeks he'd started using a local motel instead.

Eric's duffel was still in the trunk of Mason's car. It made no sense to leave it there. It was ridiculously *risky* to leave it there. Hell, maybe he'd been hoping someone would find it and force him to spill. He'd been intend-ing to go through it, burn everything burnable, bury the rest, but he just hadn't been able to work up the will to do it yet. And yes, he knew it had been six weeks. The truth was, he didn't know if he would *ever* be able to face what was in that bag.

Well, hell. Now he didn't have a choice, did he?

He opened the trunk, took the bag out and glanced around for spectators, but he wasn't too worried. Tak-ing a bag from one's trunk into one's apartment didn't really scream suspicious activity.

Slam trunk. Up the stairs, keys in the lock.

When he turned the knob and opened the door, there was one brief flash of Eric with that gun at his own head, one echo of that deafening explosion and the forced mist of blood spray. He jerked reflexively. It was that real. Then he blinked the flashback away. He saw a bare wood floor, an all-but-empty living room. The TV and stand were the only pieces of furniture left.

He moved quickly through into the kitchen, where a sour smell reminded him that he needed to clean out the fridge and cupboards, and soon. Maybe he would hire someone to get it done. The less time he spent here, the better.

He slung the duffel onto the square Formica-topped table and grabbed the zipper, and then he froze, shak-ing all over. He couldn't move for a second. Couldn't unzip it. Was paralyzed.

"Get on with it. You're a cop. It is what it is, that's all. Open it up and get it over with."

He had no choice. Rachel de Luca knew something.

Or at least suspected something. Why would she be so interested in Eric?

*Who wouldn't be interested in their organ donor?*

No, this was more. It was in her eyes. He was a good cop, had been a cop for a long time, and he knew better than to doubt his gut. His gut had put him on high alert from the second she opened her pretty plump lips and asked if his brother was a psychic or something.

What the hell did that mean, anyway? What was she getting at?

One quick tug and the bag was gaping open. He looked inside. The letter was on top, his brother's suicide note, speckled with blood spatter. Mason pushed it aside. The driver's licenses had all worked their way to the bottom, of course, being small and having been bounced around in the trunk of his car for the past six weeks. So he was going to have to either paw around feeling for them, or take everything out.

Face it all, item by item. It had to be done.

He reached in, closing his hand around the first thing he felt. A framing hammer. A heavy one, like Dad used to build their tree forts when they were kids. He'd always given the boys little hammers, the kind meant for trim nails and tiny hands. But he'd preferred the big heavy ones for himself. Used to say why hit the nail ten times when you can hit it twice and be done with it?

Mason shuddered a little, wondering if his brother had applied the same logic to his victims. Was this how he'd done it? With a hammer?

He turned it in his hands. No visible blood. He probably ought to make sure there was no *invisible* blood, either, before he got rid of the thing.

Next in the bag, duct tape. Ten rolls. Fuck.

Beneath that was a pile of shiny new chain that turned out to be two pieces, each about six feet long, each with manacles on one end. Where the hell did a person buy manacles?

A roll of plastic sheeting, thick and two feet wide, the kind some people bought to staple over their drafty windows in the wintertime. Several coils of brand-new rope, not the cheap plastic stuff but the real deal, in different sizes from slightly-bigger-than-a-clothesline to tow-a-car. Finally the bag was empty and he took out the driver's licenses, lining them up on the table one by one.

There were thirteen of them, he realized. But he stopped dead at number nine, as he stared down at the face he'd burned into his memory at the Whitney Point Reservoir this afternoon. Thomas Anthony de Luca.

He looked healthier in the license photo. Not as skinny. His teeth were better. So was his color. The license had expired long before he had.

Mason pressed a hand to his forehead and closed his eyes. "What the hell did I do to you, Rachel de Luca?"

*My brother killed her brother,* he thought. But it was worse than that. It was way worse. He'd only been trying to help, trying to make amends for Eric's crimes by doing good with his leftover parts. But he had inadvertently given a woman the eyes of her own brother's murderer.

If she ever found out, he imagined she would want to claw those eyes out of her own head.

"Then she can't find out," he said softly. But didn't he owe it to her—to all of them—to try to figure out where Eric's dumping ground was and get those thirteen young men a decent burial? Give those thirteen families a chance to say goodbye, to have closure, to put their nightmares and beloved sons, brothers and husbands to rest?

Yeah. He owed them that. He owed them all that.

Which would mean an investigation, an investigation that, if successful, would lead the police right to Eric. And once that happened, Rachel would find out. They all would.

And while he might not have known he was giving Rachel the eyes of her brother's killer, he *had* known he was giving her a killer's eyes.

All the organ recipients had gotten pieces of a killer. Every last one of them.

He'd never stopped to wonder if they would have wanted those organs, had they been asked. He'd never stopped to think about that.

Would they?

*Would you?* a voice inside him asked.

He closed his eyes, shook his head. "I don't even want the apartment he died in. What the hell have I done?"

# 6

As she was on her way out the door at the end of the day, Amy had slapped a slick, full-color tri-fold brochure into my hand and said, "I think this might help you figure things out."

Bitch was gone before I could even decipher what it was she thought might help. But I knew exactly what it was she thought I needed to figure out. This transplant thing. I'd filled the damn house with books about transplant recipients who believed they'd received a little something extra from their donors, and whenever I wasn't researching Eric Conroy Brown on the internet, I was reading those books. Amy had noticed, and also remarked on, how my tastes had changed. In music—reggae? Really? In food. What was with the hot sauce? I wasn't sleeping well, because I was scared shitless of those nightmares, and though I hadn't told her about them, I was cranky enough that she knew something was up.

Hell, I'd even yelled at Myrtle today.

I looked at the folder in my hand. O.R.G., for "Organ Recipient Group," a support group for transplant patients. Great. Amy knew perfectly well that I'm not exactly known to get good grades in "works and plays well with others." I thought about tossing the brochure aside, but for some reason I didn't. I took it with me when I headed out the back door with Myrtle on her completely unwarranted leash—like she was gonna what? Sprint away from me? We took our evening walk around the perimeter of my piece of paradise, and I let myself bask in it for a while, then reined myself in when I started sliding too far into the mind-set I preached to the masses, and instead opened the leaflet and started reading.

*We're a group of people who've been given something precious and welcome the chance to talk about what that means to us. Non-recipients can't come close to understanding all the things that come with such a generous gift. What does it mean for us long term? How do we feel about our donors? Are we obligated to donate our own organs when we pass? Should we feel guilty if that's not what we want to do? There are no right or wrong answers to any of these questions, nor to the thousands of others that can sometimes haunt us. But here we can discuss them openly. Nothing said in this safe space is judged, and nothing is repeated. We meet Wednesday nights at 7:00 p.m. at the Legion Hall, out back under the oak tree when weather permits, inside the meeting room in back otherwise. Service animals welcome.*

Wednesday. Tonight. "Huh."

I realized I'd stopped walking, and glanced down at Myrt. She was lying down, her head on her front paws, eyes closed, snoring softly. Hell, I'd only been standing still for like forty seconds. "What are you, Myrt? Narcoleptic?"

She snarfed at me without even opening her eyes.

"Aw, come on, Myrtle, you need to walk. Let's get going." I bent over her, put my hands underneath her "armpits" and lifted.

She behaved like a sopping wet blanket. Okay, make that ten sopping wet blankets.

Sighing, I straightened, looked at the brochure, looked at the dog again. "Want to go for a walk into town?"

Her head rose, and she opened her eyes and looked up at me, though I knew she couldn't see me.

"Walk into town?" I repeated, and she tipped her head way to the side, one floppy ear perking up a little. "Come on, let's go for a walk into town!"

Myrtle sprang upright. Well, okay, "sprang" is probably a bit of an overstatement, but she got the hell up, and we headed back to the house for my purse. Myrt knew that "walk into town" meant a treat. It had become my way of bribing her into exercise. If we made it as far as the McDonald's on the corner, she would get a Chicken McNugget or two. Myrtle loved her some Chicken McNuggets, and the Legion Hall was a stone's throw from their golden arches.

An hour later we were there.

The meeting was inside, probably because it was pretty dark already by seven at this time of the year. There were chairs around a long, banquet-style table, about half of them occupied by men and woman of various ages, shapes and sizes, a big coffee urn with towers of cups, and packets of powdered creamer, sugar and every sugar substitute known to man all in the same oversize salad bowl, and plastic spoons scattered loose on a white plastic tablecloth.

I walked in with Myrtle. A man saw us and came right over. Probably forty, blond hair with a few gray strands, good-looking in a *GQ* sort of way, with a sexy smile, my eyes said. He extended a hand and I took it, looking down as I did so I could read him without my eyes mucking things up.

*Younger than he looks, thirty-five, maybe less. Grip not as strong as it should be. Looking for love.* "Welcome," he said. "David Gray. Heart."

"Wow, that's the big time, David. I just got a layer of corneal tissue myself."

"There are no small transplants, Ms.…?"

"Rachel," I said. "And this is Myrt."

He looked down at Myrtle and smiled, because it's impossible to look at Myrtle and *not* smile. She's just got that kind of face. So ugly she's cute, you know?

"She's a service dog?"

"Well, she was." It was a bald-faced lie, but how would he know? He didn't have my skills for detecting a lie in a word or gesture, did he? Of course not. "She's retired now that I got my eyesight back. Not a moment too soon, either, since she lost her own recently."

"Awww." He crouched and scratched her head. Myrtle turned around and presented her butt instead. She loved to be scratched right above her stub of a tail. He obliged but only for a few seconds, then he straightened again.

"Come on in, Rachel. Sit down. Coffee?"

"Sure."

He waved me to a chair, then, on his way to the coffeepot, said, "This is Rachel. Corneas."

"Hi, Rachel," the others said en masse. Like cult members. Or an AA meeting. *Ugh.*

I lifted a hand and wiggled my fingers in reply. Yeah, *awkward.* I was already regretting my decision to attend and plotting a suitable retaliation for Amy when "David, Heart" returned with my coffee. He took the chair right next to mine. Myrtle collapsed on my feet and began to snore. A woman giggled, drawing my eye. Pretty, blonde, too thin.

"Emily," she said. "Liver."

I was getting the format here. Name, organ. It was like a secret code for a secret club.

"Terry," said an oversize guy with leather chaps to match the jacket on the back of his chair, and tattoos that made sleeves unnecessary. Or totally necessary, depending on your taste. "Bone."

"Bone? How the hell does *that* work?" I glanced fast at David Heart. "I'm sorry, am I allowed to ask?"

"Terry?" David said.

Terry grinned. He had gold caps on both incisors, and that really creeped me out. Then he patted the top of his crew cut. "Ditched my bike. They had to patch my skull back together with bone grafts."

"Holy shit."

He grinned at David. "I like her." He said it in a way that made me expect "Can we keep her?" to follow. But it didn't.

I then met Carolyn Skin Graft, Ken and Matthew Kidney (not really a couple), and Blake Lung, who didn't look as if he was going to be coming back for too many more meetings. Everyone had coffee, and Emily walked around with a plastic tray of bakery cookies that looked to die for.

As she did, the door opened to admit a newcomer. Tall, very slender, and the only one in the group wearing a suit.

"Hey, Dr. V. We have a newbie," Emily said as the man hung up his coat. He had thinning, but longish blond-and-silver hair, which he wore straight down, combed behind his ears, with a girlie little flip at the ends. Kind of like Custer, sans the pointy beard.

He met my eyes while I was inspecting him and held out a hand. "Welcome. I'm Dr. Vosberg."

"Rachel…um…" I didn't want to give the whole thing away, just in case. Though I had glimpsed recognition in the eyes of a couple of them already. Then I realized I didn't have to. "Corneas."

"Ahh. And how are you enjoying sighted life?"

"Great so far."

He frowned. As if he knew it was a half-truth. Huh.

Finally Dr. V sat down and said, "Who wants to start?"

"How about our new girl?" Terry Skullbones asked, grinning at me.

I shook my head. "Yeah, no. Can I just sort of hang out and listen? It's my first time."

"I'll start," said Ken Kidney. "I met my donor family last weekend."

Everyone smiled, like this was a great achievement among this crowd.

"How did it go?" Carolyn asked.

"It…it was weird. It was like they expected something from me. And they were watching me so close, like…too close. You know?"

Dr. Vosberg nodded. "They were looking for your donor in you. They always do. They want to see some sign that their son is still alive inside you."

"Yeah." Ken nodded real slow. "Yeah, that's exactly what it felt like."

Yeah, it was, I thought, remembering the way Mason Brown had looked into my eyes during our meeting.

"They hugged me like they knew me, you know? Invited me to freaking Thanksgiving."

I closed my eyes. That poor guy.

"What did you say?" Emily asked.

"I said I'd let 'em know, but I don't want to go. And now I feel obligated."

"You don't need to feel that way," said Dr. Custer. Okay, Vosberg, but really. Custer. "You're *not* obligated."

"God, why do the families always act like we're supposed to channel their dead relative for them?" That was Matthew, the other Kidney in the room.

Emily was eating a cookie, but she raised her hand, even though no one else had, and tried to rush it down with a swig of coffee so she could talk. "It's because… wait." Another swig. Rinse, swoop the tongue around. *There you go, girl, get those crumbs.* "It's because a part of their loved one lives on in us."

"It's a piece of meat," Terry Skullbones said. "It's like taking the battery out of a Harley and putting it into a Yamaha. How much sense would it make to start expecting the Yamaha to look or sound or ride like the Harley? It's the same thing."

"People aren't machines, Terry." Emily shifted in her chair, bit her lip and sent a slightly sheepish look at Dr. Custer.

*She has a crush on him.*

"I mean, I can totally see your point," she went on, correcting her transplant group etiquette, I guessed. "I see it differently, though. I think we do get a little bit of the personality—the soul, if you want to call it that—with the organ."

"That," I said, leaning forward in my chair, "is fascinating. Did you feel that after you got your liver, Emily?"

"Yeah." She made the word swing upward at the end, like a question, all uncertain, and looked around the room, expecting to be judged, and her eyes lingered longest on the shrink, who nodded encouragement at her. "Did any of the rest of you?" she asked.

Everyone looked at each other, waiting for someone else to go first. I said, "Not me. Not yet, anyway." And that set off the murmur of denials. Em was on her own in roomful of liars. Oh, yeah. I felt it. They were all afraid to admit it. This was a revelation.

"Tell me more, Em," Terry Skullbones said. "What kind of stuff are you talking about?"

"I don't know." Head down, shoulders slumping. "I probably just imagined it."

I felt bad for her, and for lying, because what good would it do? So I said, "There is this thing with the hot sauce, now that I think about it."

I could feel the ears perking, even though human ears can't perk.

"Yeah, I never liked the stuff before, and since the

graft, I put it on everything. Gotta admit, I wondered if maybe my donor was a hot-sauce nut."

The minute I said it, I knew I was right. Mason Brown's brother, my donor, had been a hot-sauce nut. I didn't even need to confirm it. I *knew*. And that gave me the creeps as I wondered if he'd also been prone to having visions of murder victims or nightmares about bashing brains in with heavy hammers.

"With me it's The Beach Boys," Em said. "I only listened to country music before, but a few weeks ago I heard this Beach Boys song, and started singing along before I even knew what I was doing. I knew the words. That knocked me for a loop, because I *know* I don't know that song."

"Which song?" Terry asked.

Terry, I decided, was kinda dumb.

"What difference does *that* make?" Em asked.

Terry shrugged. "I make up rhymes."

Silence. All eyes on Terry now. He shrugged. "It's stupid, I know. Little two-line rhymes inside my head for damn near every occasion. It's freaking weird."

"You can say that again," I blurted. "Shit. Sorry. I just…I can see why that would freak you out a little."

"I think Em was right," David said. "This might be our imaginations. When you're looking for evidence of something, you tend to find it."

That could have come right out of one of my books.

"How's everyone doing with the antirejection meds?" he went on.

Smooth. Nice change of subject. He was very uncomfy with the woo-woo talk, I decided. His heart donor must've been a skeptic. I almost wished I'd said that out loud, then decided this wasn't the place for my warped brand of humor.

There was a drawn-out pause, during which my gracious bulldog let out a fart that sounded like a Bronx raspberry. Emily clapped a hand over her mouth, her eyebrows arching high. Terry slapped his leather-clad tree-trunk thigh and laughed out loud. And then the smell spread and the people nearest me started waving their hands in front of their faces.

"Damn. I am *so* sorry." I got up, and shoved Myrt until *she* got up, heaving a giant sigh at the inconvenience. "Look, I won't bring her next time. I'm really sorry."

I had her almost to the door when David Heart hurried over and reached past me to open it. I sent him a grateful look, and he sent me back a cow-eyed one. "I'm glad to hear you'll be coming back."

Shit, he'd almost just made me decide against it.

Then again, he wasn't bad-looking. Why was I automatically assuming a date would be a bad thing?

Based on past experience.

*Yeah, but I was blind then. I can see now.*

*And that's gonna help, how?*

"I'll see you next Wednesday, Rachel."

I smiled sweetly while my inner bitch called me ten kinds of idiot. "See you then…David."

Then I retreated, taking my stinky dog with me.

I didn't dream that night. Slept like a log, in fact. Maybe knowing that other people were having odd experiences like mine had validated my own enough to make me believe I wasn't slowly losing my sanity.

* * *

Two days later I hit a mailbox and wound up in the ditch. I was driving my T-Bird with the top down, despite it being only sixty-five degrees. It was sunny, and I liked having the top down. I had a mission, and I was on my way to complete it. I'd been calling Mason Brown at his desk every day for the week since we'd met by the dam, looking for my brother, and he'd alternated between dodging my calls altogether, and taking them and giving me bullshit answers. I could tell by a slight hitch in the back of his breath in between his words that he was holding something back. And that pissed me off. I'd called this morning, too, only to be told he was coming in later in the day, so I asked for his partner, Rosie, who was all too happy to spill the beans that Mason was moving out of his apartment today. I pulled out my smartphone and did a little online research—I was getting good at it and had learned a few useless tidbits about his dead brother already—and I scored an address on Washington Avenue. Figured that was the place he was moving *from,* and that I'd best get there, because it might be a lot harder to track him down at a new place.

I got lost three times before I found the street, then creepy-crawled along it reading house numbers from a distance.

I didn't spot it, though. I hit it instead.

I don't know what the hell happened. It was like my eyes stopped seeing what was in front of me and decided to play a movie clip instead. I was blind, but not *blind* blind. I was seeing, just not seeing what was really there, you know? Instead I was seeing an ordinary scene taking place on a different street. A scarecrow shaped guy in skinny jeans—God, I hate skinny jeans on men. Of all the sights I've seen since getting my vision back, that one's in my bottom ten. Anyway, it was just that. Tall, skinny guy, brown ponytail, teal T-shirt with Legalize Love emblazoned across the front in white, jeans so tight I didn't know how he pulled them over his big feet, walking down a sidewalk, past a shop window with a neon coffee cup complete with three wiggly strips that were supposed to be steam coming off the top.

And then I felt the bump and the slow tilt as my passenger side front wheel dropped into a ditch.

The flickering film reel was gone. I was back. Footsteps were jogging toward me across the blacktopped drive, and I blinked myself back into focus. Mason Brown had stopped and was standing at the edge of his driveway, looking from my gorgeous ride to his mailbox's new angle, and shaking his head.

I shook my head clear, still not sure what the hell had just happened. I'd taken a mini-vacation to la-la land. But why? And oh, shit, what about my car? My gorgeous yellow car!

"Rachel?"

"Hi," I said. "Guess I found your place."

"Found it? You assaulted it."

I shrugged. "How bad is the car?"

"Better than the mailbox, I'd guess."

"Don't be a drama queen, it's still standing." And it was, though leaning severely to the left. "How do I get my car out of your ditch?"

"Do you even have a license?"

"Brand-spanking-new one. Got it a few weeks ago." Hands on his hips, he heaved a big sigh. His chest expanded with it, and my libido followed suit, but I told it to settle down. I was on a mission here, remember?

"I can pull you out. Hang tight a minute." He started to turn away, then stopped. "Are you okay?"

"Nice of you to ask." *Eventually.* "Yeah, I'm fine. Except these damn corneas you gave me seem to be malfunctioning. Was there a warranty or anything?"

He furrowed his brows, a flash of genuine worry. About me, for once, not his deep dark secrets. "They're failing? Are you rejecting them?"

"No. Just thinking of sending them back. Get me outta here before a cop comes along, will you?"

"I *am* a cop."

"Well, yeah, but *you're* not gonna bust me and take my new license away for this. This was your fault."

He shrugged his big shoulders and walked up his driveway, where his boat-sized black car sat with a U-Haul trailer attached to its rear bumper. "I'll let you explain how it's my fault after you're out of the ditch," he said. He opened a shed near the back of his driveway, and when he came out again he had a heavy, rust-colored chain over his shoulder, messing up the flannel shirt he was wearing with smears of rust and dirt. He spent a few minutes under the back end of the T-Bird, then headed up his driveway again for his car—that big black beast that I knew intimately. Quick as a minute he had the trailer unhooked. He pulled his car into the road, then quickly backed it up close to the rear of mine, blocking traffic, should any come along, though none did. He got out and hooked the chain underneath his, then told me to shift into Neutral. And then he just pulled me out, easy as pie. When he finished and unchained me—shut up!—I drove up into his driveway. He backed in neat as a pin beside me.

I parked, then hurried to the front end to inspect the damage to my precious. There was some sod and mud wedged under her bumper, but not a scuff or a scratch to the paint that I could see.

"Doesn't look like you did any damage," he said, coming to join me in my inspection. "Sweet ride, by the way."

"Thanks. I like bright colors." I was finding out I liked a lot of things I hadn't known about before. Lots of them because I could see now, but some that seemed completely unrelated. Like the aforementioned hot sauce. And reggae. When the hell did I ever like reggae?

I was still crouched and pulling weeds from my grille. He was still standing behind me. And finally he said, "What are you doing here, Rachel?"

I stood up straight and brushed off my hands, but I kept my gaze on them, not on him. I was feeling him. His voice had the slightest tremble underneath it. He kept shifting position; I could hear him moving. And he smelled good enough to eat. I made him nervous. And he made me horny. But I wasn't getting a thing beyond that.

"Look, I want to know what you've found out about my brother."

"It's only been a week since you told me about him."

"And you've given me nothing. So I figured I'd take the initiative. I've been doing a little digging myself, and I thought we could compare notes." I went around to the passenger side and reached in for the paisley print binder on the gorgeous black-and-yellow leather seat, then faced him again, holding it to my chest. "So? You gonna invite me in?"

"I don't exactly live here anymore. I'm in the middle of moving."

"You're not in the middle. You're just starting."

"How do you know that?"

"You moved that trailer too easily for it to be full. Your tow chain was still in the shed." I pointed. "Your trash can is still out back. Your mountain bike is still on the porch. There are curtains in the windows."

"You don't miss much."

"No, I don't. Where are you moving to?"

"If I tell you, are you going to come and run over my new mailbox?"

"No, but if you don't tell me, I'll find out, anyway."

He sighed, lowered his head. "An old farmhouse in Castle Creek."

"Sounds like quite a change from an apartment in the city." Why, I wondered?

"Yeah, well, I need some peace and quiet."

"I'm with you there. I'm all about the peace and quiet. My place is practically on a desert island. So is it the upstairs apartment, then?"

I knew by his look of defeat that it was, so I headed up the exterior covered stairway and waited at his door. He sighed heavily, and his steps were slow and deliberate as he came up behind me. He was not eager. Reaching past me, he turned the knob, swung the door open, waved a hand.

I went inside, took two steps and felt a fucking wrecking ball slam into the right side of my head. It came with a flash of blinding white light, and I was on my knees holding my head in my hands just that fast.

"Jesus, Rachel, what the hell?" Mason crouched in front of me, bending over me, hands on my shoulders.

I was like jelly. Just quivering as I lifted my head, lowered my arms, peered up at him and blinked like a mole in daylight. "Damn. What the hell *was* that?"

"That's what I'm asking you."

"Bomb went off inside my head. Hurt so much I should be dead." An ironic smile pulled at my lips on one side. "Hell, that rhymes."

He rose and took a single backward step. When I looked up he was staring down at me as if I'd just sprouted antlers or something. "What are you trying to pull, Rachel?" His voice was softly furious and oozing with accusation.

"I don't particularly like your tone, Mason." I got myself upright, though I had to call a nearby wall into service, because my knees were still watery. He reached out to help me, but I dodged his hand. "Just one more bizarre side effect from your brother's fucking crazy-ass eyes, I guess. I'll call Doc Fenway tomorrow. Meanwhile…" I looked around the room. No sofa. No carpet. Nothing on the walls. The living room was barren. "You weren't lying about moving out, I see." Oddly though, the kitchen still had a table and chairs, and there were a coffeemaker and toaster on the counter. Also, I could see an unmade bed through an open door. Those rooms still looked lived in, more or less.

I looked at him and frowned.

"This is where my brother died."

My attitude disintegrated as fast as my hand moved to the side of my head again.

"Yeah. Shot himself in the head. Right side."

"No fucking way."

"Like you didn't already know? Then what was that little performance all about just now?"

I held his eyes for about two heartbeats. The son of a bitch thought I was putting on a show. Acting. Faking him out. "Fuck this." Then I just walked. Out the door, down the stairs, straight to my car. I was backing out of the driveway within ten seconds of his parting shot, and I laid rubber when I left.

I didn't know I knew how to do that.

# 7

She'd left her binder.

He would have it sent to her. Sure as hell couldn't risk going there himself. She was sharp, that was for sure. Hot, too. If she'd been anyone other than who she was, he might have thought about— Nah.

Freaking famous people. You just never knew what the hell they were up to. Some kind of PR thing, probably. Pretending she could feel his brother's final moment. Maybe she claimed to have some kind of ESP in those books of hers, or planned to start claiming it to capitalize on the transplant. He would have to ask Rosie if that was part of her gig. He knew for sure she must have come here already knowing how Eric had died. There was no other explanation. The rest had been a very dramatic act.

She'd been pretty pissed off that he hadn't bought into it. Well, it served her right.

He carried the binder into the kitchen, sat down at the table and opened it up. And then he frowned at what he saw.

*Sister Mary Catherine at the St. Bart's Shelter says*

*Tommy was staying there for 4 days. He left on the morning of August 15th and didn't come back. Wouldn't be odd except he left his stuff there. Sister says she gave his belongings to the police when they came asking about him a week ago. (Ask Mason Brown about that.)*

*Malcolm Rainbow (probably not his real name). Smells like a schizophrenic. Usually in the Catholic shelter. Saw Tommy on 8/15. Doesn't know what time. Says it was dark outside. Sunset that night was at 8:04 so had to be later. Couldn't remember what he was wearing, but was sure he had a light jacket on. Said he seemed okay to him. Wasn't lying but was afraid of something. Probably something in his own mind, though.*

*Kelly Summers—waitress at the Bullpen, sports bar, same block. Said he was there that same night from 9:30 until almost midnight, drinking beer with another guy who seemed to be doing all the buying. Didn't know who the other guy was, didn't think he'd been in before, but says he left an hour before Tommy did. Then Tommy left alone and pretty drunk. She thought he was wearing black jeans, a plain white T-shirt and a windbreaker. Jacket might have been maroon or red. Companion was an older guy, middle-aged, balding, dark hair. Had a uniform shirt with a logo patch over the pocket.*

"Shit," Mason muttered. "That sounds like Eric." He'd gone to every bar in the area, including the Bullpen, flashing her brother's photo, but none of them had panned out. How she'd gotten anywhere when he hadn't was beyond him.

No, it wasn't. He'd lost his touch. He'd been off his

game ever since he'd watched his brother blow a hole in his skull.

*Kelly didn't remember what the patch said. Bar manager says security cameras have been busted for 6 months. Kelly is a hottie, looks 10 years younger than she is, married and miserable, and had something going on with Tommy. Can't tell how far it went. Need to dig deeper.*

Frowning, Mason flipped pages. She had conducted interviews with a dozen people who'd seen her brother on August 15. Every one of them was detailed and filled with little insights she hadn't gotten from the individuals themselves but from her own intuition. She was an observant thing.

*Or maybe her ESP act wasn't fake.*

*Bullshit. No such thing.*

His cell phone chirped. He reached for it, still skimming entries. "Brown."

"You seen the *Binghamton Press* today, partner?"

It was Rosie, and he sounded grim. Mason got up and went to the counter where the newspaper lay, still rolled, just as it had been when he'd picked it up in the driveway earlier. He unfolded it and looked at the headline.

Binghamton's First Serial Killer?

"Oh, shit."

"Press has even given him a name. The Wraith."

"You're kidding, right?"

"No. It's because of the way he doesn't leave a trace."

"Well, it's a stupid name."

"Maybe all the good ones have been taken. Better postpone your plans for the day, pal. Chief wants you to come in."

"On my way."

He took the binder with him, having no doubt he hadn't seen the last of Rachel de Luca today. When she caught wind of what all the victims had in common, all hell was gonna break loose.

Chief Subrinsky's office was stark, as if he didn't expect to be there long. Then again, he'd only been in it for a month. Maybe he was taking his time about settling in. Nothing on the walls. Bookshelves collecting dust. The opposite of the paperwork swamp on his desk.

He was a middle-aged man with a middle-aged look to him. Close-cropped hair, brown that had probably once been shot with gold and now was shot with gray. Small eyes a nondescript shade between blue and green that wound up looking like neither, square face. And right now wearing an angry scowl.

"So who talked to the press?"

He stood behind his desk instead of sitting, while Mason sat in front of it, beside his partner, who'd had to squeeze into the wooden chair. The seats were not designed for comfort, much less for guys the size of Rosie Jones.

"It didn't come from us," Rosie said. "This is only gonna make our job harder. Why would we talk?"

"*Someone* talked." Subrinsky sighed.

"Look, with this many missing men who all match the same descriptions, the press was bound to pick up on it sooner or later, Chief," Mason said.

"Well, thanks to the press putting the heat on, the mayor wants to ask the FBI for help."

That got Mason's attention. He tried not to look star-

tled or panicked, but if the Feds came in, he was probably toast. "That's a leap, isn't it? Aren't we skipping
a few steps?"

"Such as?"

Mason shrugged, shaking his head. "I don't know.
Special task force, maybe? That would buy us some
time without the Feds charging in here and taking over."

"Yeah, that's what I told the mayor."

"And?"

Subrinsky nodded. "She agreed. You're heading it
up. But I need you on the ball, Brown. I need the Mason
Brown you used to be, the guy whose gut instinct was
damn near uncanny, *not* the guy you've been for the
past few weeks. I don't want to be a hard-ass, Mason,
but you're a cop, a good one, until lately...."

"I know."

"It's hard losing a brother, Chief," Rosie said. "He's
coming back from it, but it takes time."

"Time is one thing we don't have."

"I still don't get why the press has jumped on this
now," Mason said. "There hasn't been another missing
person in almost two months. Maybe it's over."

"It's not over until we catch the guy," Subrinsky said.
Then he leaned over to press his fingertips to a manila
folder and slide it across to them. "And as for why now,
he's *not* done. We've got another one."

That was the last thing Mason expected to hear. He
shot his eyes to the chief's, but Chief Sub didn't look
like he was kidding. So he leaned forward to take the
folder, opened it, and started looking for what he knew
he would find. Differences—marked differences—between his brother's crimes and this new one.

As he scanned the pages, the chief narrated as if reading over his shoulder. "Jack Patterson, twenty-seven, one-sixty, brown eyes, brown hair on the long side. Last seen at a coffee shop downtown, left alone around noon. Responding officers found a wallet on the sidewalk between the coffee shop and Patterson's car. Nothing missing but the driver's license."

The same. Exactly the same. And the bit about the licenses had never been released to the press. How could a copycat know that?

"This isn't possible." Shit, he hadn't meant to blurt that out loud.

"Why the hell not? The last thirteen were." The chief finally sank into his chair. "I'll give you three men to start. If you need more, say so. Pick your team and meet me in the briefing room in an hour. And, Mason, I was serious before. I need you on your game here. You gotta get over this thing and get back to being the cop I know you are."

Mason nodded. "I hear you, Chief." Then he looked at Rosie. "You with me on this?"

"Always, pal."

Mason got up and went back out to the bull-pen, but he wasn't really there. He was in his head, trying to figure out how he was going to prove that this was a copycat. He knew it wasn't the same killer, because Eric was that killer…and Eric was dead.

Dammit, he should have known covering up his brother's crimes would come back to bite him in the ass. And now he had to ride the wave he'd created, follow it through to the end. And try his best to do it without compounding his guilt by telling more lies to cover up the ones he'd already told.

TV was freaking amazing. I had it on all the time whether I was watching it or not, because it just blew me away. I'd known, of course, of its evolution, and I'd listened to it over the years. But looking at it in high definition on a fifty-inch screen was beyond anything I'd imagined on my inner-eye-cam, lo these past couple of decades.

Everything else in my living room was covered in drop cloths. I needed a project to distract me from the knowledge that my cornea donor had shot himself in the head in his hot detective brother's living room. I hadn't been able to get that little image out of my head since I'd found out. I'd already scanned the internet for photos and any other tidbits about Eric Conroy Brown. I'd found very little. His obit had given me a little bit, but no details about his death. Obits never mentioned things like suicide or murder. It's always either "died unexpectedly" or "died after a long illness." Useless as far as causes. But great for vital stats. Eric had been married to Marie Rivette Brown. They had two sons, Jeremy, sixteen, and Joshua, eleven. His kids were online, but not him. Still, there were a couple of family photos on his older son's social sites, and the guy had looked positively ordinary. Potbelly, receding hairline, no resemblance whatsoever to his brother. Nothing about what he did for a living.

There was a lot more about Mason Brown. Yes, I'd looked. He was apparently some kind of super-cop with instincts bordering on eerie. Single, too, but I'd deduced that on my own.

"Running over the mailbox wasn't the worst of it," I told Amy. She was standing on a ladder rolling saffron-colored paint, just this side of cinnamon, onto my walls, and I was trying to explain why I'd been in such a bitchy mood before she'd left last night. You know, as a part of my apology. Because she was a good assistant and I wanted to keep her.

"Oh, come on. How can it get worse?" she teased.

I was rolling paint, too, and loving the way the room was slowly being transformed from its former bland shade of off-white into a color so rich I could almost taste it. "Turns out my cornea donor was a suicide."

She didn't answer, but I felt the ripple of her reaction from the other side of the room and turned to verify it with my eyes. Yep, she was freaked out, holding her roller in midair while it dripped slowly onto the plastic-covered floor. Her thick eyeliner made her worried stare even more penetrating.

"Creepy, right?" I asked.

"*Way* beyond creepy."

"You're dripping."

She looked down, gave her head a shake, resumed her painting. "How did you find out?"

Should I tell her? Hell, did it matter? I trusted her. She wouldn't be working for me if I didn't. "All right, this is where it gets really weird. And listen, Amy, this is between us. Don't mention it to Sandra. She'd freak, probably have me in a mental ward before I knew what hit me."

She glanced my way with a grin, like she was sharing the joke, but the smile died when she got a look at me. "Shit, Rache, you're serious."

"Yes, I *am* serious. You promise?"

"You want a blood oath?"

"Paint'll do."

Sighing, she made three more passes with her roller and her task was complete. Then she came down the ladder, and dropped the roller cover into the contractor-sized trash bag and the handle into the bucket of paint-tinted water. "Tell me," she said, finding a spare rag and wiping her hands.

I kept painting, as I still had a two-by-three-foot rectangle of bland eggshell to obliterate. "I walked into Mason's apartment and could have sworn someone pasted me upside the head with a friggin' mallet." Oh, hell. Bad metaphor there. Too much like those nightmares. I shook it off and continued. "There was an explosion inside my head, a blinding white flash, excruciating pain and then nothing. I was on my knees holding my head, and Mr. Hunky Cop was staring at me like he thought I might need an exorcist." Hell, maybe I did.

Amy's eyes went wider, but she tried to hide her shock by turning and sauntering over to the paint can, where she picked up a narrow brush to use for detailing. "And?"

"He told me his brother had shot himself in the head right there in that apartment."

She barely missed a beat before she nodded slowly. "And this is the brother who gave you his corneas?"

"Yeah. Nice of him to let me know, right?"

Then I shook my head and finished up the wall. "Then again it's stupid to think it matters. I mean, it's a layer of tissue. It's not like it has consciousness. Memories. You know, that kind of thing."

"Unless you believe what's in those books you've been reading." She climbed the ladder again and began carefully dragging the edge of her brush along the place where ceiling met wall, filling in the remaining white bits without getting a single spot on the ceiling. If I tried that the ceiling would end up looking bloodstained.

*Nice. Can you get blood out of your head at all these days, do you think?*

*No, probably not.*

"You've been reading them, too?" I asked her.

"Yeah. Look, I wasn't snooping. I've been worried about you." She paused and looked my way, her mouth tightening as if she'd just bitten into a lemon. "Actually…" Then she trailed off, went back to painting.

"Actually *what?* Just spit it out."

"I got another book for you. But now I'm not sure whether it'll help or make things worse."

"Where is it? Did you bring it?" I'd finished my wall, climbed down and was washing my hands in a sudsy bucket. We were nothing if not neat about this project.

She nodded and used her paintbrush to point to the coatrack near the front door, where her drawstring burlap excuse for a purse was hanging. "Help yourself. Just be prepared. It's a little…intense."

I headed over to her bag and dipped inside for the book. There was an image on the cover of a skinless body, with all the muscles and veins showing—you know, like in a high school health class textbook. *Cellular Consciousness* by Dr. Raymond Vosberg. "Hey! This is the shrink who runs that support group!"

"I know. That's why I bought it. But like I said, it's a little intense."

"Intense how?" I flipped open the back cover, and sure enough, the author photo was of Dr. V.

She shrugged. "He claims transplant recipients get a lot of extra stuff from their donors. Cravings for the dead guy's favorite foods. Feelings of déjà vu when they go to places their donor used to go. They start using certain turns of phrase, and sometimes even have memories that aren't their own and turn out to belong to their organ's previous owner. His theory is that part of the soul comes with the organs."

"You think it's for real?" I asked her.

"You tell me. You just felt a guy shoot himself in the head. How else do you explain that?"

"I don't. It could have been just a fluke."

She sighed. "Maybe you ought to read that book. You know, just in case."

I could feel my forehead pucker in thought. "I will," I said. And I definitely would, probably tonight in one red-hot session. Because too many weird things had been happening to me since I'd gotten my eyesight back. That dream of murdering some poor SOB with a hammer. That flash of seeing some stranger in a Legalize Love T-shirt that resulted in my nailing Mason Brown's ex-mailbox. And that bullet through the head. That more than anything. There was no freaking way I could have known that. None.

"Hey."

I was still standing there staring at Dr. V's head shot. He really did look like Custer, I thought.

"Yeah, yeah, I know, the edges still need—"

"No, not that," she said, then nodded at the TV. "*That*. Something's up."

I followed her gaze to see Binghamton's slick, AARP cover girl of a mayor standing on the steps in front of city hall in a designer suit, not a pale coifed hair out of place, with two men slightly behind and flanking her. I knew one was Police Chief Subrinsky, because I'd seen his face in the newspaper every now and then. I knew the other guy because I'd run over his mailbox and he'd run over my body.

"That's Mason Brown," I told her. "The one on the left."

"You're right, he *is* hot."

I snagged the remote and cranked up the volume.

"The recent piece in the *Press* and *Sun Bulletin* was, at best, speculation. At worst, it was dangerous and irresponsible reporting," Mayor Katherine Spencer said in tones as smooth as butter. "While it's true that a number of men have been reported missing, there is absolutely no reason to jump to the conclusion that there is a serial killer on the loose in Binghamton."

Cameras flashed, and reporters shouted questions, but the mayor held up her perfectly manicured hands. "I'm going to let Chief Subrinsky take it from here, but rest assured, we have this well in hand, and there is no reason for anyone to be afraid. Binghamton remains one of the safest cities in these United States. On that you have my word."

"Word of a politician," Amy said. "That's good enough for me."

"Shhhh!"

I felt the look she shot me, but I didn't return it. My

eyes were glued to the screen as the police chief stepped up to the mike.

"I don't have a lot to add to what the mayor has said. While we do have several missing persons cases, we haven't found any bodies. That's key. Not one single body has been discovered. It's a huge leap of the imagination to jump to a serial killer based on what we know to date. Even so, we take the safety of our citizens very seriously. That's why I've created a task force to focus specifically on these cases. That task force will be headed up by Detective Mason Brown." He held out an arm, and Mason, apparently with some reluctance, stepped forward and let the chief clap his shoulder. "Detective Brown is highly decorated, with a stack of commendations higher than my head. I have every confidence that he will have answers for us soon."

Cameras flashed and, again, more questions were shouted.

"Is it true all the missing men match the same description?"

"Why a task force, unless the cases are connected?"

"How many men have gone missing, Detective Brown?"

"Is the FBI being called in?"

The chief smiled at Mason, patted him hard and stepped back from the mike, turning it over to him. I read his body language, that smile, plain as day. It said, *I am now officially passing the buck, Detective. Knock yourself out.*

Mason looked at the microphone as if it might bite him, cleared his throat, lifted his chin. I was furious with him and sorry for him at the same time. Furious because I was already putting the pieces together in my head and guessing that my brother was one of these missing persons cases the press were attributing to a serial killer. Sorry because the responsibility for Tommy and all the other missing men had just been dropped on those wide shoulders of his, and I'd sensed they were already in danger of buckling under the weight of his brother's recent suicide.

But he stood straight and tall, and spoke with so much confidence that even I believed him. "The first mission of the task force is to determine whether these cases are connected."

"How many cases?" someone yelled.

"Fourteen."

The chief looked surprised that he'd admitted it. The reporters all started talking at once again.

"Why wait 'til now to form the task force?"

"Do you have any suspects?"

"How far back do these missing persons reports go?"

Mason looked left at the mayor, then right at the chief. They both looked impassive. Clearly there was no help coming from either quarter. Then he faced the crowd again, leaned close to the mike and said, "That's all I can say at this time. This is an open investigation. You're just going to have to be patient. Thanks." Then he turned and walked up the steps and through the glass doors of city hall.

I watched him go and knew by the way he carried himself that he was pissed at being thrown to the wolves like that by his superiors. Well, *I* was pissed at being kept in the dark. And if he thought the crowd of voracious reporters was bad, he'd better hang on to his knickers when I got my hands on him.

"I gotta go," I said to Amy.

She looked at the TV, then at me. "You think Tommy was one of these missing men they're talking about?"

"That's what I'm about to find out." I looked at the walls, at the paint cans.

"Don't worry," she promised. "I'll have this finished in an hour, and I'll clean up the mess when I'm done. You go."

"Don't hang anything on the walls. I want trim or stencils or a great big mural…or something."

"'Kay."

I started for the front door.

"Rache?"

"What?"

"Don't you want to change first? You have paint on your…everything."

I looked down at myself, and for a moment the dark red spatters on my oldest jeans, on my hands and forearms, seemed like blood. My heart started pounding; my head started swimming. I swayed, then grabbed the ladder, almost knocking it over.

Amy lunged, latched onto me, eased me down onto my sheet-covered sofa. "What the hell? Are you okay?"

I blinked until my head cleared a little, then nodded, but I didn't meet her eyes. "Yeah. I'm okay."

Only I wasn't. I wasn't okay, and I think it was right then that I realized way down deep in my gut that my brother wasn't okay, either. My brother was dead.

And that sonofabitch Mason Brown knew it. He knew it, and he hadn't told me.

# 8

"Why the *fuck* didn't you tell me?"

Mason looked up from his desk the minute he heard the by-now-familiar voice. Rachel de Luca was stomping toward him wearing purple skinny jeans tucked into tall black boots and a long green cowl-necked sweater that hung off one shoulder to reveal a hot pink tank underneath. Her color choices made his teeth ache.

And everyone in the office was turning to gape at him.

He got up. He'd been expecting this visit, rehearsing his explanation. "There was nothing to tell. This is pure specula—"

"*That* is pure bullshit." She was at his desk now, hands flat on it as she leaned into his face. Well, flat on top of several piles of paper. She was so close that he could look directly down the sweater at her cleavage, and he felt his brows go up. *Nice* cleavage. Who knew?

"Up here, Detective. Crap. How many of you Y-Chromers got away with that before I got my eyes back?"

"All of us." He stood up and dragged his gaze with

him. "Can we talk about this in private?" he asked as his eyes finally met hers.

But hers were looking past him, and widening, and he turned to look, as well. Rosie had just come out of the conference room that Mason was about to take over for his task force. As the door swung slowly closed behind him, the corkboard on the far wall, where the photos of all the missing men were hanging, was in plain sight. That was what she'd seen.

Rachel had rounded his desk, brushing past Rosie like he wasn't even there, and barged into the room before he could catch up to her. She stopped right in the center and just stood there, staring at the photos.

Mason came in behind her, closing the door to give them some privacy. Her brash manners and loud mouth made him want to hate her guts, but he couldn't. Not just then. Not when she sniffled unashamedly and took two steps closer, lifting her hand, pressing her fingers to the 8 x 10 glossy of her brother.

He knew how it felt to lose a brother, after all.

"I'm sorry. I'd have had my ass handed to me if I'd been the one to let this information out."

She didn't turn, didn't move her hand. "Then it's true? There *is* a serial killer?"

"There's no proof of that." God, he felt like an ass for lying to her. "We haven't found blood or bodies. Nothing. It's like they just…vanished."

"He takes them somewhere before he kills them."

"Excuse me?"

She finally turned to face him, a tear still damp on her cheek. His gut churned with guilt. "If you don't find anything, then he must take them somewhere else, right? It's common sense."

She was covering. His cop sense was tingling. This woman *knew* something. Just like she'd known how his brother had died.

"Where do you think he takes them?"

"Isn't that sort of your job to figure out?"

"Why don't we sit down and have a long talk?" he suggested. "You're right. I should have told you that your brother was one of thirteen missing men. I'm sorry about that."

"Fourteen." She dropped the word as if it was nothing.

"As of this morning, yes. Fourteen. We don't have a photo of the most recent victim yet." She was still keeping something from him. Something important. He was sure of it. "Listen, Rachel, why we don't we get some coffee somewhere? Maybe lunch? Talk about this at length?"

"Not yet," she said. "I want to know about the new guy first." She slid into a chair in front of his new desk, and her steady gaze went right back to the photos.

"Why would you want to know about him?"

She shrugged. "Maybe there's a connection between him and my brother. Something you've missed that would be obvious to me."

And if that wasn't a good enough reason, Mason thought, she would make up another. Because he was sure she wasn't telling him everything. Yet.

"I'm not supposed to discuss—"

"Come on, Mason. You owe me that much. I can guess a little. They're all on the scrawny pale side. They all have longish hair in varying shades of brown." She leaned forward, squinting a little. "And brown eyes, too?"

"Yeah."

"All around the same age?"

"Range is from twenty-three to twenty-seven, except for your brother."

"Tommy looked young for his age. But they're not all addicts, are they?"

"No." He was being interviewed here, and he needed it to be the other way around.

"Tell me about the new guy," she said again.

He was about to say no, but she shifted her focus and her eyes locked onto his. And he knew, he knew damn well, they were not his brother's eyes, but it felt for just an instant like they were.

He looked away first. "Let's get some lunch, and I'll tell you what I can."

She nodded. "Okay."


Lunch was at a Mexican *cucina* near the P.D., where I sat in front of a chicken quesadilla that covered the entire plate, and handed the little containers of sour cream and salsa back to the waitress. "I don't need these."

"Oh, okay. You want something else?" Her smile was a real one. Went all the way to her eyes.

"No, I'm good."

She nodded and bounced away. I took a sip from my mug and nodded. "The coffee's good, and the staff are happy. You get better food in places with a happy waitstaff."

"And how do you know they're happy?"

I was still angry. I was grieving for my brother. I was scared shitless about my visions, and pretty sure I knew who the fourteenth victim had been. Not his name or anything, but what he looked like. I didn't want to be right, but I felt in my gut that I was.

And yet I understood on some level why Mason couldn't tell me. It helped that I could feel the guilt weighing down on him for it. So I could cut him a little slack. Not much, but a little.

"Close your eyes for a second, Mason," I said.

He frowned, but he did it.

"Now listen."

I knew what he was hearing. I'd been hearing it since we came in. One waitress was humming, sometimes singing a little, as she moved back and forth between tables. A waiter and another waitress were chatting by the cash register, friendly tones, easy conversation. Somewhere in the kitchen, someone laughed.

"That's the sound of happy people."

He opened his eyes. "You really do have keen perception."

"You think?"

He nodded. "Yeah. You left your binder at my apartment. I went through it. It shows up there, too."

"I need it back."

"It's in the office. Remind me when we get back." He dug into his burrito.

I reached for the hot sauce and started shaking it all over my quesadilla. "I spent more than twenty years blind. Had to depend on my other senses, so I guess they got stronger."

I looked up. He was watching me as I continued to

shake the hot sauce. I shrugged and set the bottle down. "It's a recently acquired taste. Weird, I admit, but…" I cut a big bite and slid it into my mouth. "Damn, that's good."

He took a gulp from his water glass, then put it down with care, setting it precisely in the ring it had already formed on the Formica. He was nervous. Why?

I could guess. "Your brother loved hot sauce, too, didn't he?"

"Yeah."

I sighed, nodding. "I thought so."

"What does that mean?"

He wasn't ready to hear it, so I shrugged and changed the subject. "I have a sort of inner camera. When I was blind I would imagine what people looked like by their voices, their mannerisms, and…I don't know, I guess you'd say their energy. It's not ESP woo-woo bullshit. It's just that some people give off…I don't know. A vibe, I guess."

"So you really believe the things you write about?"

I clamped my jaw to prevent an honest answer from leaking out and reached for my own water glass.

When I set it down I changed the subject again. "What about the latest missing guy? You gonna tell me?"

"I don't see the harm. He's twenty-seven, a perpetual student and apparent science geek. No known enemies."

"Known enemies aren't the ones to worry about, though, are they?"

He smiled a little. "I guess not."

I kept eating, because my quesadilla was to die for. Why had I never eaten here before? The place was fantastic, everything vivid and bright. Green, yellow and red, each trying to be louder than the other, like competing mariachis. And there was music, a little too soft but creating the perfect ambiance, trumpets and castanets. I took another long drink of water. "So, where was he last seen?"

"Getting into a car in front of a coffee shop on Front Street."

I stopped with my fork halfway to my mouth and looked over it at him. "Shit."

"What's wrong?"

Blinking fast, I shook my head, ate my food. But I was scared. I did not want to believe I'd seen the murder victim just before he'd been killed. It wasn't possibly, was it?

*Why not? Tall, scrawny, brown hair, brown eyes, coffee shop? Test it. Go on, ask what he was wearing. No, tell him what he was wearing, because if I'm right, he's going to have to believe me sooner or later.*

I wanted to prove the voice in my head wrong so badly that I went for broke, even though I would probably come off looking like an idiot when he refuted my vision. "I don't suppose he was wearing skinny jeans and a bright blue Legalize Love T-shirt?"

He didn't answer me. I was feeling a little queasy. Too much hot sauce, that was all. I eyed the last of my quesadilla for a minute, debating whether to stuff it down or ask for a take-out box, and feeling the silence lengthening and growing tense. I looked up.

He was looking at me as if *I'd* killed the guy. And then it hit me that was probably close to what he was thinking. I hadn't considered that possibility.

"How do you know what he was wearing, Rachel?"

I set my fork down. A box, definitely a take-out box. "I don't know."

"I asked you before, do you claim to be some kind of a psychic?"

"No. I don't even believe in that shit."

"Then how do you…?"

"I saw it."

"You saw it? You saw this guy getting into a car with someone? Can you describe—"

"No. No, just hold up. I didn't *see* it see it. I saw it… in here." I tapped my head. "I was driving down your street, looking for your house number, and it flashed into my head like a pop-up ad. I saw this tallish, skinny guy, long brown hair in a ponytail, skinny jeans, bright blue T-shirt with white lettering, walking down a side-walk past a window with a neon coffee cup in it. Then I hit your mailbox and it…blinked out."

He just kept looking at me. I looked right back, holding his gaze, keeping my own eyes steady, so he could see that I wasn't making shit up or losing my mind.

He swallowed hard. "We're going to have to talk about this."

I sighed. "Are you leaning toward 'she's batshit crazy' or 'she's a fucking serial killer'?"

"Are you?" He stared hard into my eyes. I'd never seen eyes like his were just then. Sharp. Penetrating. Hell, he was as good at reading people as I was.

"Am I what? A killer? No. Absolutely not. Batshit crazy, on the other hand…I'm beginning to wonder."

He nodded very slowly, still holding my eyes. "You ever have…visions like that before?"

He didn't think it was a vision. He thought I was a suspect. I shouldn't have said what I had, but damn, I'd been so sure there was no way in hell what I'd seen would match the latest missing man. "No."

"Interesting."

"What is?"

"That I can tell when you're lying. Maybe I'm not losing my edge after all."

"You thought you were? You, with the commendations and awards the chief was singing about on TV this morning?"

He didn't answer. "You've had visions before. What were they?"

"Is this an interrogation?"

"I've got thirteen missing men on my hands, Rachel. I have to follow up every lead, and you just gave me the biggest one I've had so far."

"Fourteen." Why the hell did he keep getting that wrong? "So now I'm a suspect. I should've kept my mouth shut."

He sighed, shaking his head, and then clearly deciding to go ahead and tell me more. "You have an alibi," he said.

I frowned at him and wondered how he could know that when I didn't. Oh, right, he knew the date and time the guy went missing. "I do?"

"The guy was seen getting into that car about the same time you were running down my mailbox."

"So I saw him as it was happening?" I lowered my head and tried to quiet the questions that were swirling through it, but they wouldn't go silent. Those nightmares of murder by hammer, they'd felt like something in the past. I'd seen the same one again and again. That couldn't have been happening as I'd dreamed it, could it? That had been some kind of flashback.

Over and over I tried to replay that damn unwanted video clip of the latest victim in his blue T-shirt in my mind, to grab onto a detail or two that I'd missed. But there was nothing. "What kind of car did he get into?" If he told me, it might jog something loose.

Mason shrugged. "The witness said it was a dark blue or dark green or maybe black sedan. Not old but not new, either."

"Not a motor head, was she?"

"How do you know it was a she?"

"Not old but not new? That's not a car person."

"Not all guys are car people."

I sent him a look, and he shook his head as if he was almost, but not quite, confirming my guess. The waitress came back and asked if we needed anything else, and I asked to have my leftovers boxed up, never taking my focus away from Mason. The guy was going through some shit, that was for sure. And he had been, even before his boss dumped this case on him. And now here I was, telling him details I had no way of knowing. I hoped he was as strong on the inside as he looked on the outside.

He was puzzled right now, uncertain about me, about the case, about how to proceed, and still keeping something inside. I realized that I had a momentary advantage with him and, sensing that was going to be a rare thing, decided to press it. "Is my brother dead, Mason?"

To his credit, he didn't look away. "I'm pretty sure he is, yeah. I think they probably all are."

I lowered my head. The waitress came back with my food in a box and a white paper bag. "Chocolate chip cookies, free with every meal this week."

"Thanks," I said, but I didn't look up, because there were hot tears burning my damn eyes.

She walked away, and Mason said, "I'm sorry, Rachel. I know how it feels."

"I know you do." I swallowed hard.

"We'll talk again."

I nodded, blinking until it felt safe to lift my head. "You're not gonna keep dodging my calls?"

"Not now. I've gotta figure out how you know what you know. And I *will* figure it out. Count on that."

I pulled a cookie from my bag and handed it to him. "When you do, let me know, okay? Because it's freaking me out."

I don't know if he believed me or not. But he took the cookie and the check, then got up. Lunch was over. My brother was dead. And I was having visions. Accurate ones, apparently. And now I was, if not a suspect—albeit one with a cop for an alibi—at least a person of interest.

I got up, too, and followed him to the door. He held it open, then walked with me to my car, which was parked at the curb in front of the police station, with ten minutes left on the meter. I stopped beside it, fished for my key and unlocked the door while he studied me as if any move I made might be the slip that revealed my guilt. Of what, I didn't know. He couldn't think I'd done it. He'd already admitted being with me at the time.

I finally met his eyes. "While you're investigating me, Detective, take a few minutes to look into your brother's deep dark secrets."

His shock was impossible to hide. There was something in his eyes. Just for an instant. Fear, quickly masked. "What does my brother have to do with any of this?" he asked. But there was…something behind his words, and a slight change in his breathing.

"I don't know. I only know that I didn't start having these visions until his eyes were in my head. And I promise you, Mason Brown, I'm going to figure out why. So whatever secrets you're keeping about him won't be secret for very long."

He blinked twice, shook his head. "My brother's life is an open book, Rachel. I don't have anything to hide, and neither did he."

I leaned in closer, my face right up near his, and whispered, "There's a subtle change in your breathing when you're lying. Did you know that, Mason?"

I didn't wait for an answer, just got into my car and took off. But I no longer had any doubt. Mason's brother had known something about the serial killer. Either he was psychic, or he knew the guy, or one of the victims, or…*something*. And whatever it was, Mason knew it, too.

The rat had emerged into a den with tunnels veering off into many directions. He'd crawled around, exploring them one by one. Most were completely inhospitable to him. Most rejected him with the first of his urges. And one of them—one was out to destroy him. Could see him. Could feel him. The one who had Eric's eyes. *She* was going to have to go, because she could stop him. She was the only one who could.

But first he'd had to find the right host.

And this, he thought, seemed to be the one. It had already proved itself compatible with his…needs, at least to a degree, and now he would see whether he could continue to control it.

It was a big body, strong, with a brain that wasn't overly bright and a soul that was a little bit mean. A little bit hungry. Like his own. Mean and hungry enough? That remained to be seen.

He'd taken the victim, offered him a ride and a cup of roofie-laced coffee that had him passed out in the passenger seat within five minutes. And now he was chained up in his host's basement. But would he be able to follow through? Killing a man was harder than drugging him, chaining him up, even than torturing him.

Already his host was resisting, feeling guilt and pity for the begging, crying, soon-to-be-dying prisoner in the basement. His will was stronger than Eric's had been.

Oh, but to kill again… To feel the hammer cracking through the skull and sinking deep into the softness of brain matter, to see the delicious fear in those brown eyes just before landing the first blow, and then the pain and tears and horror. And then the light just…blinking out. It was going to be so good. It had been too long. Much too long.

Tonight. He couldn't wait any longer. His new host lived with a mother, who would be returning home from vacation in the morning. It had to be tonight.

"Here. These are all I have." Rosie brought a stack of hardcover books with paper dust jackets into the living room, and set them on the coffee table in front of Mason. Mason had filled him in on his bizarre lunch conversation with Rachel and, knowing Marlayna was a fan, asked to borrow any copies of her books she might have lying around.

Marlayna came in from the kitchen with a brimming cup of coffee and a plate of her "special apple crisp," and placed them nearby. "Now you make sure I get my books back, Mason. Rachel de Luca is one of my all-time favorite authors."

"I promise they'll be safe with me." He reached for the plate and took a big bite, making sure to "mmm" appreciatively.

"It's good to see you taking an interest in spiritual things, Mason," she said, patting his hand. "Sometimes it takes a loss like you've had to call us to it."

"Spiritual? Is that what you'd call what she writes?"

"Yes. But not religious. Just…spiritual. You read it, you'll see."

"Thanks, Marlayna. And thanks for this, too." He took another bite.

"You come around more often and I'll plump you up. A woman likes a man with some meat on his bones." She slid her arm around her husband's ever-widening middle and hugged.

"Damn, woman, not in front of company." Rosie was grinning, though, and when she turned to leave the two of them to talk shop, he swatted her backside and made her jump and giggle like a teenager.

Mason lowered his head, almost jealous of what they had.

When she was gone, he picked up the book from the top of the stack. "*Being Human: An Owner's Manual.* Cute."

"I don't know why you're so interested all of a sudden. You said yourself, she couldn't have done it. She was at your place when the guy got into the car."

Mason set the book back down and ticked off reasons on his fingers one at a time. "We don't know for sure that the guy he got into the car with is the guy who killed him. That could have happened later. He might've just been catching a ride with a friend."

"Wallet on the sidewalk, pal. Driver's license missing. Just like all the others."

"Could be coincidence."

"Uh, I don't think so." Rosie plucked a book from the middle of the stack, and held it up. The title of the book was *Why There's No Such Thing as Coincidence.* "Besides, you told me what she's driving. A yellow T-Bird does not resemble a dark-colored sedan."

"She knew what the guy was wearing. She knew what time he was taken. She knew the freaking words on his T-shirt. She knew—well, guessed—the witness was female."

"She said she had a vision," Rosie countered.

"She could have lied." Mason finished the dessert, and started on the coffee while Rosie searched his face and shook his head.

"You honestly think a little thing like—" Rosie dropped his voice to a whisper "—a little thing like Rachel de Luca killed all those men? Most of them while she was blind?"

"No. I think this was a copycat crime. And I think she's looking like the closest thing to a lead."

"Now where the *hell* did you get that idea, partner? Copycat? Since when?"

Mason shrugged. "Gut feeling."

Heaving a sigh so big it probably qualified as a gust, Rosie shook his head slowly, sadly. "I'm glad your gut's talking to you again, my friend. I just wish it was makin' a little more sense."

"It will. Give it time. I'd bet my bottom dollar this woman is hiding something. A whole *lot* of something. And I'm gonna find out what." He drained his cup and set it down, then gathered up the books and headed for the door. He paused with his hand on the knob and turned back. "Marlayna's into all kinds of new-age, supernatural shit, isn't she?"

"She calls it woo-woo."

"She have anything on…" Mason licked his lips, hoping he wasn't going to give anything away. Then again, Rosie didn't know de Luca had Eric's corneas. "On organ transplants?"

"What's woo-woo about organ transplants?" Rosie looked worried. "Or is this a whole different topic? You thinking about Eric now? About those people he helped with his leftover parts?"

*Easy,* Mason told himself. *Just take it easy and go with it.*

Marlayna had come back into the living room with a plastic dish of apple crisp for him to take home. If the soft and sympathetic look in her eyes was anything to go by, she'd heard the whole thing. And then she said, "As a matter of fact, I have exactly the book for you." She handed the apple crisp to Rosie and dashed out of the room, returning seconds later with yet another book. *Cellular Consciousness* by Dr. Raymond Vosberg. She put it on top of the stack in his arms, and Rosie topped it off with the dessert.

"The man's ahead of the curve in the psychological implications of organ transplantation. And he's local. Maybe it will give you some comfort," she said, and blinked back a tear or two.

"I think your theory is dead wrong, partner," Rosie said. "But you know I got your back either way."

"I know you do." Mason looked at his watch. "I gotta go. Dinner with the family tonight, then reading if there's time." He looked at the books, knowing he would dig into them tonight, and half dreading what they might tell him about the sexiest, mouthiest, most compelling female he'd met in years. Or ever.

# 9

It was Wednesday night, so like a freaking lemming, I went to my O.R.G. meeting. I swear, if I was in charge, I'd have called it the Organ Recipient Group and Support Meet-up, because it would have made a much cuter acronym. Well, at least a more memorable one. I mean what the hell was their website? Org.org?

I had a couple of reasons for going. Now that I knew Dr. Custer was an expert on the topic, I was hoping to hear more about the phenomenon of organ recipients inheriting memories and tendencies from their donors, and a group setting seemed like a safe place to try angling for that. I also wanted to see David Heart again. Not that I was dying to jump his bones or anything. But the very fact that I didn't was fascinating to me. Because I should be, right? He was a great-looking guy, we had a major shared experience, and he'd fallen over himself showing his interest in me. Why the hell was I not falling back? It was stupid. I needed a distraction, and a little flirtation was just the ticket.

Far better than being frenemies with the far too perceptive detective.

I smiled at the rhyme. "Perceptive Detective is hot on my trail. I stupidly wish he was after my tail." I laughed at my own ridiculous fantasies, then spent ten minutes on the floor hugging my dog and feeling guilty for leaving her alone for what would amount to an hour and a half, tops.

I arrived early in hopes of catching the good doctor for a conversation before the crowd arrived. It was chilly tonight, windy and glum. Gray skies of autumn, thick as oatmeal. The lights were on inside, though, and a couple of cars were already there: a beige sedan and a black Audi TT with M.D. plates.

Good. Custer was already here. And who else?

I went inside, pleased that Dr. Vosberg had apparently arrived early tonight.

"…seems more intense to me now, Doc. More important. Like I'm suddenly aware of how limited our time on this planet is and every single second has taken on this urgency and—"

I cleared my throat, because David Heart and Dr. Vosberg were clearly in deep and important conversation and I didn't want to appear to be eavesdropping. They both looked my way. Doc looked irritated, but David smiled so warmly I couldn't help but notice. Nice face. Nice eyes. Blue. So what if he drove a beige sedan?

"You came back." He said it the same way a kid says, "It's Christmas!" and came to grab my hands. I figured that was an impulse move. I knew it was an honest one. "I'm really glad."

"Me, too." Could I have poured any more saccharine into two words?

"Dr. V and I were just—"

"Hey, no," I said, holding up both hands. "You don't need to explain to me."

"But I want to." He smiled again. "Maybe…after group we could go out for coffee and dessert?"

"I'd like that."

Would I really? Probably not. I *should* like that, that was the thing. So I was going to try. It wasn't as if I was going to be able to capture Custer for a "casual" conversation about his theories. I'd seen how everyone crowded around him after the meeting last week, so I'd just have to hope for a chance next time.

The meeting went by all too fast. David had parked himself in the chair right next to mine, and was hanging on my every word. It was clear to me that everyone in the group knew who I was. I'd been sure last week that Emily, at least, had recognized me. This week they all had that look about them, but true to the group's policy of anonymity, no one mentioned it.

When it was my turn to speak, I brought up having bad dreams since the transplant, though without giving details of course. I didn't mention that I apparently did ride-alongs with a phantom who was bashing in heads during those dreams. Or that I thought he might be a real killer. Who'd also murdered my brother. Because the other group members wouldn't have believed me, and the good doctor would probably have ordered me up a straitjacket if I had. Sure, he theorized you could pick up tastes and tendencies and habits from your donor. But I was pretty sure having a serial killer inside my head would have seemed crazy even to him.

Terry Skullbones talked a lot about feeling like someone else was rattling around inside his head sometimes.

Emily did, too. She was showboating. She wanted it to be true, because she was clearly one of those types who watched *Celebrity Ghost Stories* and *The Haunted*. She craved a real live paranormal experience so much that she was willing to convince herself she was having one. Terry wasn't being honest, either, but I got the feeling he was erring the other way. Downplaying something he wasn't ready to share fully—sort of like I was doing. David didn't talk at all at this meeting.

*Saving it all for me over coffee? God, I hope not.*

*Knock it off. You want to go out with him, remember?*

*No. I want to want to. But I don't really want to. Clear as mud.*

I'd read Dr. Vosberg's book until three in the morning, and I wanted to ask him some questions about it, but I'd come to the conclusion that group wasn't the place. Some of these folks seemed a little wobbly on the old mental balance beam, and I didn't want to shake it. I mean, if he wanted to push his book to the group, he would have copies on a table at the meetings. No, I got the feeling this group of his was more about researching his own theories. Brilliant, really.

So the meeting broke up, and I hadn't really gotten any further intel that I considered reliable. I followed David's beige sedan to Aiello's, the best restaurant in town. Granted, there were only five others to compare it to, including a McDonald's, a Subway, and the very recently—and much to my delight—opened Dunkin' Donuts, but still, it really was good. We ordered coffee and a great big homemade brownie with two forks. His idea. I would have gladly eaten the entire brownie myself.

"I'm really sorry about walking in on you and Dr. V,"

I said, after three consecutive bites, just to get a jump on the lion's share. "I didn't know whether to back out quietly or let you know I was there."

"It was fine, we were finished. He gives private sessions before the weekly meeting at no charge. First come, first served, and it's only a half hour. But he does one a week."

"I didn't know that."

He nodded. "I got there before Terry for a change. Lucky break."

I nodded, took another bite. He was eating slowly, and I thought it was because he was being generous. Another point in his favor, right? "So you're having trouble since your transplant?"

He shrugged. "I just seem to be more…emotional, I guess."

"In a good way or a bad one?"

"Both. Everything feels bigger. Deeper."

I nodded. "Well, it *was* a heart transplant, after all."

"Yeah." He sipped his coffee, nodding at my fork to tell me to go for broke on the remaining brownie.

"Do you know anything about your donor?"

"No. I don't think I want to."

"Really? I was dying to know about mine." I shook my head. "Gosh, as much trouble as I've had since a simple tissue graft, I can't even imagine what you must be feeling after something as big as a heart transplant."

He shrugged. "You've been having trouble? I mean, I know you said you'd had some odd dreams. Is it more than that?"

I drew a deep breath, looked around the restaurant and lowered my voice. "Can I trust you, David? Because the truth is, I'm dying to talk to someone about this, someone who would understand. Someone who's been through it."

He nodded and set his cup down, then focused on my eyes like nobody's business. "I promise."

I really did want to get his thoughts on this whole thing. "I think my donor might have been a psychic. I think he might even have helped the police solve crimes or something. But they won't admit it, of course."

He frowned at me, not in disbelief but in rapt interest. "What makes you think so?"

Okay, deep breath, spill it. Not too much, but a little. See if he freaks. "I've seen some crimes in my dreams. And at least one of them really happened, either during my vision or right after. I've verified it. And it scares the hell out of me."

"Well, damn. Who was your donor?"

"Brother of a cop," I blurted. It felt good to get it off my chest. "And the thing is, I think the cop knows his brother had this thing going on, but he won't admit it."

"Of course not."

"Look, keep this between us, okay?"

"I promise, hon. I won't breathe a word."

"Thanks." Wait a minute, did he just call me *hon?*

He reached across the table, covered my hand with his. "For the record, I don't think you're crazy."

That, at least, was good to know. "It helps to hear that." I ate the last bite of brownie, followed by the last of my coffee.

"You should get away from it all. That's what I do when I'm stressed out. Go camping in the mountains up north. I could take you."

"I….think it might be a little too soon for that."

He shrugged. "Well, maybe you should schedule a session with Dr. V. He's a really great listener."

I shrugged. "I intend to. But I kind of think it might be even more valuable to talk to people like you. You know, other people who've had transplants."

He leaned across the table. "Rumor has it, he has."

"I didn't know that."

"Well, he won't talk about it. It's one of the topics that's off-limits. His personal life isn't supposed to enter into our group meetings. I figure he'll open up after a while. We've only been having the group sessions for a couple of months now. Still, everybody speculates. Someone thought it was a kidney, someone else said skin grafts after a fire."

"And someone else probably thinks it's a convenient rumor he started to help him sell books."

He smiled ear to ear when I said that. "Most of the group don't even know he has a book out. But I think that's a really smart theory. I never even thought of that. What made you come up with it?"

I shrugged. *Because it's what I'd do.* But I wasn't going to tell him I was that mercenary. I looked at the empty plate, resisted poking around for crumbs and said, "I guess we should probably get going, huh? Myrtle's been home alone a lot longer than I'd planned to leave her."

"And where is home, Rachel?"

I looked up, and my expression apparently revealed my reluctance to tell him that, because he smiled and patted my hand.

"How about just a phone number? For now, I mean."

I nodded.

He got out his cell phone and started typing while saying "Ra-chel-cor-neas. Okay, shoot."

I gave him the number. He keyed it in, nodded once and pocketed his phone. "Great." The waitress brought the check, and he handed her his card before she could scoot away. Then he said, "I hope we can do this again. Maybe a whole dinner next time?"

There was absolutely no reason not to say yes. So I said, "Sure, I'd like that."

And even before the words were out of my mouth, I wanted to take them back. Who was I kidding? This wasn't going anywhere. Nice guys were apparently not the sighted Rachel de Luca's cup of tea. She preferred dark moody cops with secrets behind their eyes and dead psychic brothers. It was a pain in the freaking ass.

Angela Brown lived in a large and lush home in comparison to the others in her neighborhood. It was, she'd often told Mason, a classic Georgian. He'd never cared enough to find out what that meant. But it was big and square and brick, three stories, not counting the basement, the topmost of which had been his father's personal space and hadn't been touched since he'd passed.

His own childhood bedroom was similarly enshrined, and so was Eric's. Nothing had been touched since Eric had left home to marry Marie Rivette right out of high school. Wednesday nights were their traditional family dinners. Once a week, no matter what. So far, Marie was still honoring that tradition.

Pork loin with pineapple glaze, baby red potatoes cooked with carrots and bathed in butter, homemade applesauce, undercooked just enough so that tiny chunks of apple remained, just the way Eric had always liked it best.

They sat around the formal dining room table, the boys on one side and their mother on the other, beside the empty chair that had belonged to their dad. It was painful to see that every week, but Mason didn't know what to do about it. His mother seated everyone the same way, week in and week out, until forced to make room for a new family member. He used to sit right where Josh was sitting now. When his father died, Mason was promoted to the head of the table and Jeremy sat alone across from his parents until Josh came along. Now Mason mused on whether Angela would put the new baby beside Marie, sticking a high chair in Eric's former place, or whether she would move Jeremy to that spot and put the baby beside Josh. Probably the latter.

Josh hadn't shut up since they'd sat down, and it was a good thing, because everyone else was as silent as a thick fog. He'd talked about his new sixth-grade teacher, his tae kwon do lessons, his Halloween costume—Captain America—and the about-to-be released must-have video game he was hoping to wheedle his mom into buying for him.

Jeremy was brooding. Rolling his eyes at a lot of his kid brother's antics, sighing heavily whenever his mother tried to pull him into the conversation. Marie eventually gave up and shifted her focus to Mason, passing him dishes he hadn't asked for, offering to get him a refill on his raspberry iced tea, asking him how things were going at work. Fussing over him like she used to fuss over Eric.

"Well," Angela said when Josh paused for a breath, "it's time we discuss the plans for when you go in to have the baby, don't you think, Marie?"

Marie shot her a surprised look. "Plans?"

"For the boys. You'll be in the hospital for at least a day or two."

"Oh. Right." Marie sent Mason a look, one of those unspoken-message looks. *Here she goes, micromanaging again.*

He smiled a little, enough to sympathize.

"They're more than welcome to stay here with me until you're home and ready for them again, Marie. We'd have a great time together," Angela said.

Joshua's eyes widened a little, and he sent Mason a pleading look. Jeremy just heaved another dramatic sigh and kept on eating.

"I was thinking they might want to spend a couple of days with their uncle Mason," Marie said, sliding her eyes from Angela's to his. "You could come and stay at the house with them, Mason. I know you've been avoiding your apartment since…for the past few weeks."

He saw the boys' hopeful gazes pinned on him. Even Jeremy had cut out the sixteen-year-old "everything sucks" routine for a moment.

"I have to work during the day," he began.

"We have school during the day," Josh chirped. "It's perfect!"

"Besides, Mason will be busy looking for his new place, I imagine," Angela said.

"Actually, I already bought one."

"You bought a house?" Marie asked. "You didn't tell us."

"I was saving it for dessert. It's an old farmhouse in Castle Creek." He watched everyone's reactions. Angela's was disappointed, no doubt because his new place was a few miles farther from her. Marie looked delighted, because it was a few miles closer to her and the boys. "And it needs a lot of fixing up," he said. "I think you guys coming to spend a couple of days might be just the ticket."

"Well, this is very sudden," Angela said. She set down her fork and picked up her napkin.

"You knew I was looking for something outside the city, Mother."

"Yes, I did." She blinked fast and dabbed her mouth, covering her hurt.

And he could tell that he *had* hurt her. It was easy to do, but even so, he wasn't happy about it.

"When are you moving, son?"

"I've already started, but I'll finish this weekend." He looked at his unfinished meal, feeling stuffed to the gills from his visit with Rosie's food-pushing wife but not wanting to offend his mother even further. "Actually, I could use your help. All of you. Boys, I'm gonna need some muscle to unload the U-Haul. And, Mother, the place is a real fixer-upper. No one I know decorates a house like you do. You could have made a living at it."

It worked. She smiled, lowering her head as her cheeks went pink. His mother was still a class-A beauty.

Marie was looking at him, waiting. She needed the distraction as badly as his mother did.

"You, too, Marie. Living in a house is a whole different ball game than living in an apartment. I need help getting organized, figuring out what I need that I don't already have." He swept his gaze back from the two easily offended and always needy females to his chief concern, the boys. "Are you guys free? No games, practices or parties to attend?"

"Soccer's over, and basketball hasn't started up yet, Uncle Mason," Jeremy said. It was, to Mason's recollection, his first complete sentence of the evening. "It sounds like fun. I'm glad you're moving closer."

"It's a deal, then. I'll text you the address, and you can meet me out there first thing Saturday morning."

"I'm looking forward to it," Marie said.

He got through the meal, turned down dessert and saw Marie and the boys to the door. Then, as was his tradition, he hung out just a little bit longer with his mother. He'd spent a few weeks here in his old bedroom right after Eric's death. Since then, he'd been mostly holing up in a hotel. He'd tried to stay in the apartment three times and ended up leaving in the middle of the night every time.

"I'm worried about Jeremy," Angela said. "Marie says the last words he exchanged with Eric were angry ones. He's blaming himself."

He nodded. "I know. I'll talk to him again. Actually, this move gives me a good opportunity for that."

She nodded. "Thank goodness we have you to lean on, Mason. I honestly don't know what this family would do without you."

"You'd be fine."

"I'm serious." She handed him the post-dinner coffee she'd made, and then took her own cup to a chair near the bay windows that overlooked her spacious back lawn and garden. There was still a wealth of flowers in autumnal colors, gold and russet and burnt orange. A few decorative scarecrows and Indian corn on drying stalks had been placed strategically. Angela really did have a touch.

"I asked you this once before, Mason, when your father died, and you made me promise never to bring it up again, but..."

He'd known this was coming, had expected it. "I'm not leaving my job, Mother."

"Eric has left us. You're the man of this family now, and we need you, Mason. If you should be cut down in the line of duty, we—"

"You would be fine."

She stared into her cup and shook her head. "We would *dissolve*." Then she took a sip and let the topic die. "We need one last trip to the lake house. To close it up for the winter."

"Halloween weekend?" he asked. "Like always?"

She nodded, sighed. He had a subject he wanted to bring up, but he hated upsetting her. It took so little, and he was sure his request would be more than enough, but he didn't have a choice. "Mother, I'd like to spend some time in Eric's room."

Her head came up fast, and she blinked in horror. "For God's sake, *why?*"

Since he couldn't tell her why, he just said, "He was my brother. I miss him. I want to know why he...did what he did."

"Well, you won't find any answers to that question in there. He was a happy little boy when he lived at home. If anyone's to blame for his depression, it's that Marie. She never understood him the way I did."

He lowered his head so she wouldn't read his complete disagreement in his eyes. His mother had understood less about his brother than any of them. Even Marie had known something was off about her husband. She'd told him as much at Eric's bedside, when they'd all gathered there to say their goodbyes.

"I need an hour. Alone. If you can't handle it, I can come back another time, when you're out, or—"

She set her cup on its saucer and got to her feet. "It's fine. Take as much time as you need." Then she left the room, moving through the big dining room and into the kitchen. She always handled dinner on her own. Sent the maid home by four to get out of her hair, as she put it, and then took care of the meal and the ensuing cleanup solo. She would never let anyone help, himself included, and certainly not Marie, who she'd always seemed to think of as competition in some weird, twisted way.

He looked at the clock. It was already nine, and he had more to do tonight. But for now, this was his top priority.

By a quarter to ten I was falling asleep with visions of my mini-date with David Heart replaying in my mind. He was interested, and I knew I should be, too. It was about time I entertained impure thoughts about someone besides the stubborn cop with the secrets behind his eyes. You just didn't get involved with a guy who had secrets. It was a bad idea. Maybe almost as bad an idea as dating your cornea donor's brother, which was just as bad an idea as dating the cop who was investigating your missing brother and refusing to tell you what *his* brother—*your* cornea donor—knew about the case or how he knew it.

Mason Brown was a secretive, cagey character. I didn't want to pursue anything with him. And the fact that he didn't seem to like me very much had nothing to do with it.

Okay, yes it did. What the hell was wrong with him? I was a perfectly acceptable-looking female specimen, mostly sane, with a steady job and a luscious income. What was his problem, anyway?

*"You were thinking about David, remember?"*

Yeah, David. Blond, blue-eyed David. Interested David.

*I shouldn't have told David as much as I did. What the hell was I thinking?*

I fell asleep thinking about that, and petting my dog and letting her soft snores be my lullaby. Myrtle was on the passenger side of my bed, her head on my pillow like she was trying out for human. Her weight on the blankets made it impossible for me to pull them at all, so I'd learned to tug them mostly to my side before letting her plop down. She was like a sack of lead. Solid.

So I sank into oblivion, and then I was there again. In that same fucking horror movie. There was a dark room with concrete walls and floor. It smelled like a basement. There was a man lying on the floor, with duct tape wrapped around his head, covering his mouth, and heavy chains leading from his wrists to rings driven into the wall.

I was looking at him. I couldn't see myself, only him, and the absolute terror in his eyes. I felt excited by that fear. Turned on, horny, call it what you will, but I was feeling it. All wound up, like I was about to get it on with Mason—or maybe David. No, definitely Mason. Like we'd already worked our way through a solid half hour of steamy foreplay and I was squirming to go.

But dream-me wasn't hot for sex, I was wound up for what I was about to do. It was time. I felt it, knew it, like knowing when it was time to eat. A hunger gnawing at a part of me that wasn't my stomach and wasn't my libido. It was a dark hunger.

The man on the floor looked up at me. I saw his eyes, his pupils growing bigger in the dim room as I moved closer to him. His chains rattled as he skittered backward into the corner and cowered. He would have crawled into the wall if he could. He was muttering behind the tape. *Please, please, please,* I thought, but it could have been anything.

I felt the hammer in my hand, its rubberized grip giving beneath my fingers as my grip tightened around it. I moved closer, and my feet briefly caught my attention. I was wearing boots, black boots with silver buckles. A man's boots.

And then the hunger that wasn't quite hunger pulled me back to the cowering, whimpering man, and I drew my arm back and brought the hammer down. He screamed and cringed, and I only struck a glancing blow, the hammer sliding down one side of his head. It made a groove in his skin from above his left ear down to the ear itself, tearing the top part of it almost off. His cries were like an animal's now, not even human. I brought the hammer down again. Oh, yeah, this was what I needed. Right on target. Dead center, top of the head, a direct hit. The hammer cracked through his skull and sank deliciously into the meat of his brain.

I had to yank it hard to get it free, but it came loose with a splat of goo that hit me in the face. I smiled.

He was jerking now, still pressed against the wall, arms still up, trying to protect himself, but the sounds he made had risen an octave, and there was a lot of gurgling behind them. I kicked him with my black leather boot so he fell face-first to the floor, then stepped on the middle of his back to keep him there. His arms and legs were slapping up and down on the concrete, like fish out of water. Enough of this. I brought the hammer down for the killing blow, right to the back of his head.

Another satisfying crunch, more splattering brains, and then he didn't move anymore. Turning the hammer in my hand, I noticed my black leather glove for the first time, and I saw the hair on my wrist between the edge of the glove and the cuff of my shirtsleeve. There was a tattoo on the inner part of my wrist. A crude blue peace sign. A peace sign. That was funny as hell.

I rolled him over with the toe of my boot, so I could see his face. His eyes were closed. *It's so much better when they stay open.* His face was streaked and spattered with his own blood and brain matter, and his bright blue Legalize Love T-shirt was soaked in it.

He was a mess. And this was not the fun part. I never enjoyed the cleanup as much as I enjoyed the kill. That was why I usually left someone else to take care of it.

*What the fuck does that mean?*

I sat down on the floor, close to him, and smoked a cigarette, enjoying the afterglow, because I had enjoyed the *hell* out of this kill. And as I sat there, the I that was not me seemed to be staring straight at the I that I was. And very softly, the I that was not me spoke, and he said, "I see you watching. Pretty soon I'll get to you, too." And then he laughed and laughed and laughed.

# *10*

I opened my eyes slowly, and every part of me went cold as the sick, twisted dream returned full throttle and I realized the deliciousness I'd felt in the dream wasn't my own. And more. He'd seen me.

He knew!

Everything in my stomach tried to escape all at once.

I flung myself out of the bed, stumbling into the bathroom, and made it to the toilet before I lost it all, and then I knelt there, shaking, pushing my hair off my forehead, reaching up to flush.

"What the fuck is happening to me?"

A cold nose nudged me in the rib cage, and I lowered a hand automatically to Myrtle's head.

*Call Mason.*

Right, and give him more evidence that I was crazy.

*Come on, Rache. You need help on this. Who the hell else are you gonna tell? Something's happening to you. You need to tell somebody.*

I got myself up onto my feet. No easy task, with my knees still roughly the consistency of grape jelly. I ran water, rinsed my mouth, washed my face and decided fuck it, I needed a full-blown shower. I cranked on the taps, then headed back to my bedroom for something clean to put on.

I looked at the clock and saw that it was only 10:38 p.m. Had that dream really only lasted half an hour?

*If you call him right now, he'll probably still be up.*

Sinking onto the edge of my bed, I picked up the telephone. I'd called Mason enough times in the past couple of weeks, both on his cell and at the police station, to know both numbers by heart. I dialed his cell and waited while it rang.

Mason was on a mission. He began to systematically dismantle his brother's childhood bedroom in search of…something. He didn't know what he was looking for—some explanation about why Eric had become the monster he had, when he'd started to change. Or if he'd changed at all. Maybe he had always been a predator and had just been very good at hiding it.

But he didn't hide it. Not really. Everyone knew something was wrong with Eric. He'd never had friends, never fit in at school, always seemed cut off, walled up, unemotional. He'd seen it, Mason realized. He just hadn't known what it was.

No one had.

So he started with the bed, stripped off the covers, the sheets, the pillowcases. He turned the pillows over, squeezing and feeling for any odd lumps inside. Then he removed the mattress and ran his hands over every inch of it, followed by the box springs.

He put everything back together, of course—had to.

He couldn't let his mother know what he was doing in there. After he finished with the bed he started on the dresser, removing every item from every drawer, and then the drawers themselves, looking underneath and inside them, then under and behind the dresser itself. Nothing.

He was just getting started on the closet when his cell phone chirped, and he grabbed it automatically. "Brown."

"Mason? It's Rachel."

His frown was automatic, but reason followed only a heartbeat later. She sounded wrong. She sounded scared. She did not sound like sarcastic, cocky Rachel de Luca.

"What's wrong?"

"I'm that obvious?"

"Your voice is shaking."

"Shit." There was a pause, a deep breath. "I don't know if I can do this on the phone. I don't suppose you could come to my place—no, never mind, that's stupid. It's after ten-thirty."

"I'm up. Whitney Point, right?"

"Yeah. Keep going past the dam where we met. It's two and a half miles out that road, on the left. I'm the only house out here."

"Half hour, maybe a few minutes longer."

"I'll make coffee."

I felt like an idiot, like a stereotypical helpless female calling on a man for help over a nightmare. But I knew—way down deep, where you know the things you don't really *know* you know—I *knew* this was not just a nightmare. I knew, somehow, that what I'd seen had been real.

So I got off the phone, turned on every light in the house and damn near had a heart attack when I saw headlights moving slowly away along the road. Like someone had been sitting out there just outside my gate, watching the house, until the inside lights came on and scared them off.

*Right. Or maybe like someone was out doing some end-of-season night fishing and driving past my place on their way home. Get a grip already.*

I took my damn shower and washed the vomit out of my hair, and I brushed my teeth to the brink of obsession. I put on plush pajama bottoms, gray ones, big cushy socks, and the softest T-shirt I owned, and then I grabbed a little brown felt blanket and wrapped it around my shoulders like an old-lady shawl. Comfort. Every bit of it was for comfort.

Myrtle was content to snooze on the bedroom floor as long as she could feel me tromping around, in and out of the bathroom, but as soon as I stepped into the hallway to go downstairs, she was up and plodding after me.

Stairs were not her friend. Being a bulldog, she carried most of her weight up front, head and shoulders big and broad, tapering to a little bitty butt. Her front legs were shorter than her hind ones, making her very prone to going ass over elbows down a flight of stairs. I reminded myself about that and waited for her at the top, then walked down slowly so she could descend in her preferred manner: with her head bumping up against the backs of my calves on every step.

We reached the bottom, and she sighed in relief and

headed for her favorite downstairs spot, the round, plush doggy bed close to the fireplace. It didn't occur to her that the gas flames wouldn't be turned on at that hour, so I went over and hit the switch for her. She deserved comfort, too.

*Yeah, you might just be spoiling her a little bit here.*

*Fuck you, voice in my head. She's* blind, *for God's sake.*

*Yeah, I suppose you're right.*

I left Myrtle there to soak up the heat and headed into the kitchen to put on a pot of coffee. Mason was ringing the doorbell before it finished brewing.

Nervous as hell for some reason I couldn't name, I went and opened the door, met his eyes and wished I hadn't. He was too damn good-looking. I hadn't even come close in my pretransplant mental picture of him. I'd envisioned him hot, but not *gorgeous*. The guy was good-looking like Clooney was good-looking. Like Jackman was good-looking. It was above and beyond just garden-variety hotness, and it knocked me off my game a little bit every time I saw him.

So I looked away as I stepped back and waved him inside, and I let myself feel him instead.

He was curious. I got that from the silent way he entered and the touch of his gaze as it took me in, head to toe, then swept the room, my living room. I heard him sniff the air.

"You just paint this place?"

"Yeah. You like the color?"

"It's…vivid."

"I like vivid. After twenty years of black, vivid is a good thing."

"I imagine it is." He still hadn't said he liked it, though.

*What the hell do I care whether he likes it or not?*

I led and he followed, and I waved a hand toward the crackling fireplace, where Myrtle was snoring like a hibernating bear. "I'll get the coffee."

"Cream and two sugars," he called.

He didn't have to tell me that. I remembered from our lunch, because I was apparently paying way too much attention to the guy. I could not for the life of me recall what David had put in his coffee a few hours ago.

I went and fixed us two cups, and by the time I returned he was all comfy in a big plush chair and bending over to stroke Myrtle's head. I brought his coffee to him. He took the cup from me with one hand, and lifted up a white bag with pink-and-orange lettering that wafted the luscious scent of donuts at me.

"How did I not smell those before?" I reached into the bag and pulled one out without looking. Score. Boston Cream with chocolate frosting.

"You were upset. You ready to tell me why yet?"

I heaved a sigh, paced to the chair that matched his except for being a darker shade of brown. His was caramel. Mine was chocolate. I sat down and bit into the donut to give myself time to construct a sentence that wouldn't sound like the disjointed ravings of a lunatic off her meds. Washed it down with a long drink of just-right coffee and nodded just once.

"I'm pretty sure the guy in the Legalize Love T-shirt is dead."

I kept my eyes on him when I said it. He was good at hiding his reactions, though. His hand twitched a little.

I saw the ripples in his coffee, but aside from that, he was still and his expression didn't change. There were about three beats before he said, "And you know this because…?"

"I saw it. In my sleep."

This time his reaction was obvious. He relaxed a little. "So it was a dream."

"I don't think so."

"What do you think it was, then?"

He was watching my face intently, and I reminded myself how alike we were. We both read people not by what they said or how they looked, but by everything they didn't say and everything they hid.

I met his eyes because I wanted him to know I was being straight up here, and if we were anything alike, he would know that's what steady, solid eye contact meant. *Look at me all you want,* I was saying. *Read me and know I'm telling the truth.*

His eyes narrowed a little, refocused. He got the message.

"I was asleep, and I saw the blue T-shirt guy. He had shackles on his wrists, and he was lying on a floor, chained to a wall, with duct tape over his mouth. I think he was in a basement. Scared shitless, too."

Mason kept his eyes right on mine. I wanted to blink and look away, but I forced myself not to.

"I was seeing him through someone else's eyes. Like I was riding along inside a body that wasn't my own, looking out through his eyes, feeling everything he felt as he walked into that room."

"Who?"

"The killer. In the dream, I was him. And I felt… I felt…"

He set his cup down, got out of his seat and came closer to me, then knelt down in front of my chair, still holding my eyes. "Go on. You've gone this far. You felt…?"

"It's sick. I felt turned on. Excited by what I was about to do. Only they weren't my feelings, Mason, they were his."

"The killer's."

"Yeah. He just walked up to that poor guy and bashed his brains in with a hammer and—"

"Okay, okay, slow it down for me. I need to know it all, step-by-step. How do you know the killer was a he and not a she?"

I blinked. Did he believe me, then? Or was he just humoring me? Or maybe he was taking a wait-and-see approach to my claims? I couldn't tell, couldn't read him. He was expressionless, giving nothing away.

"I saw my—I mean *his* boots. Black leather biker boots with silver buckles. Big feet, man feet."

"And what else?" he prodded.

"His hand, when he swung the hammer. I saw the skin between the glove he was wearing and the edge of his shirt. Caucasian, and hairy. Dark hair. On his wrists, anyway." I blinked. "And there was a tattoo. Amateur, blue ink, a peace sign. A fucking peace sign."

He exhaled, and his breath warmed my face. "How about the glove?"

"Black leather, like the boots. And the shirt wasn't a dress shirt. More like a long-sleeved T, dark blue or black."

He nodded, still gazing into my eyes. "What about the hammer?"

I saw it again, felt myself swinging it, felt the impact when it broke through skull and mushy brain. I felt the wet splash of brain matter on my face and flinched as if it had hit me just then, turning my head to one side and closing my eyes tight. Damn, hot tears were burning in them.

Fingertips on my cheek, warm, firm, turning me to face him again. "It's okay. Tell me about the hammer."

I went back in my mind, slowing the images down as they replayed, noticing details I'd seen but hadn't acknowledged before. "It's big. Blue, like gunmetal, with a rubber grip. The end of it, you know, the business end, has a grid, like a checkerboard grid, cut into it, it's not smooth like a hammer snout should be. It has to hurt like hell when it connects." I closed my eyes. "Three blows. First one glanced off, taking off a strip of scalp and part of his left ear. Second one landed here." I lifted my hand, saw it was shaking, and pressed two fingers to the top of Mason's head, where a baby's soft spot would be. "It was awful. Sank in deep. The guy was crying, moaning, gurgling, spazzing out. Then the killer kicked him over and stood on his back and nailed him again." I moved my hand over his head, down the back of it to the spot that seemed right. "Once the guy was dead, the killer sat there next to the body, smoked a cigarette and looked right at me. He said he was watching me and he'd get to me pretty soon. Those were his exact words. 'Pretty soon.'" I shook off the chill that memory evoked. "That was the end of it. I woke up and puked, called you, took a shower, and here we are." I looked at my donut, no longer the least bit interested in it.

He was still watching my face. I took a deep breath and let it out, nodding. "I had to tell you. Now I have."

"Why do you think you're having dreams like this?"

I shook my head slowly. "I don't know."

"After all that, Rachel, why are you lying to me now?"

I blinked, caught red-handed. "You're good."

"Not as good as you are. But good enough. So tell me, why do you think you're seeing this kind of thing in your sleep?"

"I think you know the answer to that better than I do."

He held my gaze and didn't flinch, not even a little. I couldn't see any falsehood in his eyes as he waited for me to answer his question.

"All right, fine. I think it's because I'm connected somehow to this killer. And I think *that's* because your brother must have been connected to him, too."

He stood up fast. "Come on, Rachel, we're back to that again? It's ridiculous."

And then I could see it. Now *he* was the one lying.

"Think about it, Mason. I had the first nightmare right after I got my sight back. It was a murder just like this one, and I kept having nightmares just like it. And then I had that…vision right outside your place, when I saw the guy in the T-shirt getting into that car—*right as it was really happening.* Then I heard the gunshot and felt what your brother must've felt when he blew his brains out the minute I set foot in your apartment. And now this. Nothing like this ever happened to me before I got your brother's corneas. So what the hell else could it be?"

He shook his head, pacing away. "You're reaching. A million things could explain it. Hell, sensory overload, first and foremost. Your brain must be dealing with a million times more input than it's used to. Every sight, every color—every photon of light, for God's sake. Your mind's overwhelmed. This is stress, nothing else."

I stood up slowly. He'd walked over to the fireplace and was standing there with his back to me, staring at the flames. Myrtle was still snoring away by his feet. "Why is it you can't look me in the eye when you're spouting this bullshit, Mason?"

His head came up and he turned. "Come on, Rachel, you've gotta admit, this is all pretty far-fetched."

"You know something you're not telling me," I said, reading him like an open book. "I know you do, I smell it on you. What is it, Mason? Was your brother some kind of psychic after all? Was he the reason you solved so many crimes, earned so many commendations, before his death and have been floundering ever since? Was he your secret weapon?"

Everything in him relaxed. His shoulders eased, his chin lowered a notch, and his jaw unclenched. Oh, he was trying to hide it, and his reactions were subtle, but the ones I couldn't see were more powerful than the ones I could. His soft exhale, the prickly defenses I'd felt as clearly as an electric charge, now blinking out one by one.

He was relieved, hugely relieved, that I'd said *psychic* and not some other word. The question was, what other word?

"No," he said, and the hard, tight undertone was gone from his voice. It was soft, almost comforting. "No, to my knowledge, Eric was never in possession of any sixth sense or ESP or anything like that. I don't think he even believed in it."

I lowered my eyes, no longer willing to let him see into my soul. "So what, then? Why am I having visions of murder that feel just as if I'm seeing them through the eyes of the killer? And that he can see me back? What else could possibly explain—"

"Stress. That's all. Come on, sit down, let *me* talk for a minute, all right?"

He came closer, hands on my shoulders, gentle, his face near mine. "Sit. Try eating something again."

I nodded, the movement jerky, and sat so he would take his hands off me and back up out of my space. He was a liar, and I had to find out why, see through his masks, figure out what he was hiding, all the while without revealing my own thoughts to him. Especially not the one where I was sure he was lying to me.

I ate a bite of the donut, drank some more of my now cooling coffee, and nodded at him to go on.

"Look, you just got your eyesight back after twenty years. You just learned that your missing brother is probably dead, mostly likely the victim of either a serial killer or a copycat. You—"

"Copycat? You think there's a copycat?"

He shrugged. "It's one possibility we're looking at. But you have to let me finish."

"Why? Why a copycat?" I studied him, watched his face. "Was there a difference in the most recent abduction that you haven't told anyone about?"

He shook his head, then was interrupted when his phone buzzed. He pulled it out, glancing down. Then he looked at me again. "There is now."

"What's that supposed to mean?" I got up and leaned closer, looking down at the phone in his hand and reading the text message that had just changed his mind.

Body found. The W screwed up. 210 Orange.

"What's the W?" I whispered, a beat late on the up-take. "The Wraith?"

He looked sideways at me. "Yeah." He texted On my way and pocketed the phone. "I've gotta go."

"I'm going with you." I walked to the door on shaking legs, and grabbed my jacket and keys.

He came behind me, laying a heavy hand on my shoulder. "I can't take you with me."

"I didn't ask you to. I'm driving myself. I already have the address."

"Rachel, you could cost me my job."

"I'm an author. A self-help author. Researching for my next book on….oh, hell, let's say the nature of evil. I heard the address on my scanner."

He looked around my living room. "You have a scanner?"

"No, but my sister does. Her husband's a volunteer fireman. But I can have it here by the time anyone comes to check, should it be necessary. So let's get going already."

He sighed heavily, and I ran back to my sleeping bulldog, crouched low and rubbed her ears. "I'll be back soon, Myrt. Hold down the fort, 'kay?"

# FREE Merchandise is 'in the Cards' for you!

Dear Reader,

## We're giving away FREE MERCHANDISE!

Seriously, we'd like to reward you for reading this novel by giving you **FREE MERCHANDISE** worth over $25. And no purchase is necessary!

You see the Jack of Hearts sticker above? Paste that sticker in the box on the Free Merchandise Voucher inside. Return the Voucher promptly...and we'll send you valuable Free Merchandise!

Thanks again for reading one of our novels—and enjoy your Free Merchandise with our compliments!

*Pam Powers*

Pam Powers

P.S. Look inside to see what Free Merchandise is **"in the cards"** for you!

# W e'd like to send you two free books

to introduce you to the Suspense Collection. These books are worth over $15, but they are yours to keep absolutely FREE! We'll even send you 2 wonderful surprise gifts. You can't lose!

**REMEMBER:** Your Free Merchandise, consisting of **2 Free Books** and **2 Free Gifts**, is worth over $25.00! No purchase is necessary, so please send for your Free Merchandise today.

## FREE MERCHANDISE VOUCHER

Please send my Free Merchandise, consisting of
**2 Free Books** and **2 Free Mystery Gifts**.
I understand that I am under no obligation to buy
anything, as explained on the back of this card.

**191/391 MDL F44Z**

*Please Print*

FIRST NAME

LAST NAME

ADDRESS

APT.#          CITY

STATE/PROV.          ZIP/POSTAL CODE

### NO PURCHASE NECESSARY!

▲ Detach card and mail today. No stamp needed. ▲

© 2013 HARLEQUIN ENTERPRISES LIMITED ® and ™ are trademarks owned and used by the trademark owner and/or its licensee. Printed in the U.S.A.

FM-SUS-13

She sighed, opened one eye and went back to snoring. I interpreted her commentary as *Bring me back a treat or you're on my shit list.*

When Mason arrived on the scene, he saw the flashing lights of two police cruisers bathing everything in red and blue strobes. Uniforms were already there, talking to a weeping, bathrobe-clad woman on a sidewalk lined with orange carnations. Neat little saltbox house, more flowers along the front. The front door was open, but one of the uniforms was standing nearby with the yellow tape ready.

He watched Rachel de Luca pull in behind him as he parked a block up, because he wanted her bright yellow convertible out of sight. The thing was like a neon sign announcing the fact that he'd brought a civilian to a crime scene. Since she knew the address, trying to shake her would have been a waste of time, but no way was he bringing her in his car as if he'd invited her.

This had to be a copycat. Had to be. It was a relief that there was such a marked difference in this murder. Leaving the body to be found had definitely not been Eric's M.O.

Rachel hurried to join him on the sidewalk. She'd thrown on a jacket and a baseball cap, but her hair was still wet and sticking out the back, ponytail-style. No makeup. She didn't look like a celebrity tonight.

She looked scared.

They speed-walked past the side-by-side houses. Not real nice ones. Sagging porches loaded down with crap, like something out of *Hoarders,* shingle siding with missing patches, dogs on chains with about four square feet of worn-bare dirt to stand on.

Rosie was already there, standing in front of one of the nicest places on the block. Small, but neat. Well kept. He spotted them coming and came to meet them halfway.

"Mason, hey." He sent him a questioning look as he nodded at Rachel.

"I was with her when I got the call. She wouldn't take no for an answer," Mason explained.

"I do have a vested interest," she snapped. Then she directed a phony but potent smile at Rosie. "Besides, I'm researching the nature of evil for my next book. It's my way of dealing with what happened to my brother. I have to be here."

Rosie went soft, like he was chocolate and her sunny beam was melting him. "I understand, Miss de Luca."

She reached out and touched his arm. "Rachel. You can call me Rachel."

Hell, Mason thought. If she was this good with the chief, they would be clearing out office space for her at the station in no time. How was it no one saw through her but him?

Fuck it, it wasn't important. "What have we got, Rosie?"

"Uniforms responded to a suicide. Found the SOB hanging in his bedroom. Bloody footprints in the hall-way outside his room led 'em to check out the basement, where they found the body of our latest missing person. Come on, this way." He stopped on the front porch to pull on paper shoe covers and a pair of latex gloves, then handed a set to Rachel.

Mason snatched them just as she reached for them and put them on as he said, "No. Look, you can't go in there, I'd get my ass handed to me. Just wait outside, and for God's sake, don't talk to anybody." He looked at the uniform standing at the door with the tape. "No one else comes inside unless it's the chief or forensics. Got it?"

He sent Rachel a final warning glance.

She was pissed, but he could tell she was a little bit relieved, too. That fear in her eyes had noticeably eased. It wouldn't have, he thought a minute later, if she had followed him inside.

The house was small and simple. You entered straight into the living room, furniture there all draped in flowery throws and way too many pillows. Eat-in kitchen on the right. No dining room. Then a hallway, with a bedroom on either side. One was smaller and had a bathroom beside it. The other was bigger, and farther down the hall. He noticed the bloody boot prints that led from a doorway at the far end of the hall—basement?—to the bigger bedroom. When he got close enough to see past Rosie, into the bedroom, he saw a man dangling from a rope tied to a ceiling light fixture.

"Couldn't somebody have cut the poor bastard dow—"

Suddenly the fixture tore free of the ceiling and the dead man hit the floor, the light bashing onto his head with an explosion of dust and plaster, and a spark or two as the wires came apart. Rosie jumped backward so fast he flattened Mason to the wall.

"Easy, partner. He's already dead."

"Jesus, Joseph and Mary." Rosie crossed himself as

Mason squeezed out from behind him, then moved past him into the room.

"His wife know what he was depressed about?"

"It's his mother," Rosie said. "But we didn't ask. It's pretty clear. Follow me. We'll come back to this."

Nodding, Mason moved back into the hallway, stepping over the bloody prints rather than on them, and followed Rosie to the last door. It was already open, revealing a set of stairs going down into a basement with the lights on. Blood on those, too.

At the bottom there was a pile of bloody clothing in the corner. Wait…no, there wasn't. It was a body. He realized that as soon as he spotted an arm and a small patch of the bright blue T-shirt that wasn't soaked in red. The victim's head had been smashed in.

"There's a pretty likely murder weapon right there," Rosie said, pointing.

Mason turned in that direction and saw the hammer. Blue metal with a black rubber grip. He moved closer, crouched low and tried to get a look at the head. Even though it was packed full of hair and blood and bone, he could see the checkerboard pattern.

Just like Rachel had said.

He closed his eyes, lowered his head, stood up again. The forensics guys were there. He could hear them chattering upstairs.

"Looks like all those murders finally caught up with him," Rosie said. "At least it's over now."

"Looks like," he lied. Because this guy was not the Wraith. The Wraith—*his own brother,* he thought—had always made his victims disappear. Until he'd made *himself* disappear, that was. Eric was dead. This was a copycat, and not a very good one.

If he was smart, Mason thought, he would plant all those driver's licenses somewhere in this house before the team finished up. But no, he was too honest for that. Why put that poor woman outside through any more grief?

How the hell had Rachel known about this?

Voices floated down from upstairs, one of them female and all-too-familiar, clearly coming from inside the house. "I don't care, I need to talk to Mason *now*." And then, "Oh, my God."

He met Rosie's eyes briefly, then turned to jog up the stairs. In the hall he saw Rachel standing outside the dead guy's bedroom door, her hands to her mouth and her eyes wide as she stared in at the tangle of dead man and light fixture.

"That's why I told you to stay outside, Rache," he said. He took her by the shoulders, turning her so she was looking at him instead of the body. "It's hard, this kind of thing. You're not used to it. It's—"

"I know this guy." She pulled away from his hands and refocused. "I know this guy."

Every head turned turned their way, and Mason grabbed her shoulders again. "Not another word." He turned her around, marching her straight out the front door and all the way to the street. The cop at the door knew who she was, Mason had seen the recognition in his eyes. It wouldn't be long before word got around, dammit. To his amazement, she didn't speak again until he got her out of earshot of everyone else.

"What the hell, Rachel? Do you *want* to be a suspect in this mess?"

"It was a suicide."

"Yeah, *he* was a suicide. The guy in the basement wasn't. His head was bashed in with a hammer, one with a grid pattern on its snout. And yeah, I'm dying to know how you knew this guy, and how you knew what you did about this crime scene, but for right now, you're putting yourself in a helluva situation just by being here."

"I have a right to be here." She backed up three steps, hands deep in the pockets of her long leather jacket, shoulders hunching up a little. Maybe against the chill wind, or maybe something else. More cops were arriving all the time. He had to get her the hell out of here. "This guy killed my brother."

"I told you before. I don't think so."

Her head came up fast, her eyes searching his. "Your copycat theory? You never told me why you believe that."

Dammit, he had to be careful with her. She was as good a detective as he was.

"How did you know him, Rachel?" He glanced around while awaiting her answer, knowing this was starting to look fishy. Rosie would cover his ass, but still…

"Support group. For transplant recipients."

His eyes shot back to her. "You're shitting me. He got a transplant?"

"Bone. Said he ditched his Harley, smashed his skull in, had to have bone grafts." She lowered her head. "I met him last Wednesday and saw him again last night.

His first name is Terry." She lowered her head again. "Did you see those fucking boots he was wearing?"

"I saw."

"Just like in the dream. Did he have the tattoo?"

"I don't know yet."

"I never saw it at group. Never noticed it, anyway. This is lunacy, right?"

"Seems like."

"What's going on, Mason? How can any of this be happening?"

The chief's Mercedes pulled up to the curb. "Go home now," Mason said firmly. "I can't help you if I lose my job, and I sure as hell can't help you if you get arrested and charged with multiple murders."

"Oh, like that's gonna happen."

"You know too much, Rachel."

She stopped talking, blinked twice, her gaze briefly turning inward, and then she met his eyes again, her expression worried. "You're right. I do, don't I?"

Not the response he'd been expecting. She turned toward where they'd parked, then turned back again. "Will you come back? After? Tell me what the hell's going on?"

"I'll come back," he said, not promising anything more.

She nodded. "Okay. Okay." Her eyes shifted past him, toward the house, then back to him again, quick, jerky. "Yeah, okay. I'll see you."

He watched her all the way to her car, then jumped guiltily when a hand fell onto his shoulder. "You okay, Mace?"

He nodded at his partner. "Fine."

"Something goin' on with you two?"

Mason frowned, then barked "No" a little too emphatically.

"I see."

"She's a little freaked, is all. This guy was a transplant recipient, too. She met him at a support group she attends. I guess there's some kind of common bond there."

"A bond, huh?"

"I know. It's bull, right?"

Rosie shrugged. "I don't know." He paused, seemed to be thinking. "I guess if someone got parts from the same donor, maybe that might create some sort of sentimental attachment, but…"

Rosie's voice was drowned out by the sudden buzzing sensation inside Mason's brain. *The same donor.* Eric?

Could it be that his brother had been this guy's donor, too? No. It was too much of a coincidence, and that way lay madness. He wasn't even going to bother following that ridiculous thread any further.

Yes he was.

He was going to read the book by that local shrink and maybe even give the guy a call come morning.

# 11

The host the rat had chosen hadn't been the right one. Oh, he'd allowed the rat to kill through him, but afterward, he'd self-destructed. Shame. It was a body he could have enjoyed inhabiting for a while.

No matter, he'd found another. One who would allow him free rein for far different reasons. Curiosity. A need to know.

The rat liked this one even better. A clever mind, but a willing one. It was perfect. With this sharp brain at his disposal, he knew just the way to take care of his unwilling observer.

I couldn't stop pacing, and I was shaking, too. I felt like puking but there was nothing left to puke. No matter what Mason had said about a copycat, as far as I was concerned the man who had murdered my brother was dead, a man I'd sat in the same room with—twice now—and I hadn't even realized who and what he was. Terry Skullbones had been the serial killer the press had dubbed "the Wraith," and his final victim was in his basement. *Unless Mason was right and he was just a copycat. Which means the true Wraith is still out there. My brother's murderer, still running free.*

*I saw him do it, though. This time, at least, I watched it just as clearly as if I was there for the whole thing. And he saw me. He saw me!*

I couldn't keep denying it now, even if I wanted to. Not when I'd seen every detail before ever setting foot at that crime scene.

*Zero chance now that there could be any other explanation. This killer got inside my head somehow.*

I paced and muttered to myself so damned much that I disturbed Myrt's comalike sleep. She opened her sightless eyes and shifted her ears to follow my progress back and forth across the living room but didn't bother picking up her head.

I poured a drink—vodka, stiff—and turned on the TV to try to distract myself with an episode of whatever the hell mindless reality show was currently airing. I found one, tried to focus on it. Every contestant sucked. The judges might not hear that slightly off-key warble, but imperfect pitch rang in my ears like a dog whistle in Myrtle's. Real talent was rare.

My drink was empty. I poured another. I was contemplating a third when I must have drifted off in my comfy chair, lulled by the heat of the fireplace, because the door chimes startled me awake again.

Two hours had gone by. I got up and picked up my regrettably empty glass. The doorbell rang again.

"Rachel, you up?"

It was Mason's voice. I dragged my feet to the door and turned the lock. "Come on in, it's open." Then I headed back to the bar for a refill and poured one for him while I was at it. I made mine weaker this time, though, and added soda. Yeah, image. I didn't want him seeing me drinking straight vodka like water. People tended to form certain opinions of women who did that.

Turning, I offered him a glass, ice cubes clinking, and as he took it from me, his fingers brushed over mine. Ice-cold, and not all that steady. He looked like hell, and it wasn't just exhaustion.

"So?" I asked, watching his face.

"Yeah, I can't tell you all that much."

"You don't *have to* tell me all that much. I saw it. Remember?"

"You know that's not possible." I could tell by the lack of conviction behind those words that even he didn't believe them.

"Then how do you explain what's been happening to me?"

He shrugged and averted his eyes. Aha. He had a theory.

"I need to know if the details I saw were accurate, Mason. I *have* to know, okay? You can understand that, can't you?"

"Yeah." He drew a breath, let it out again. "Yeah, I can't even imagine what this must be like for you. I really didn't believe it, to tell you the truth. Until tonight."

I wanted to ask if he believed me even now, but I was afraid of the answer. There was still no proof, I knew that. He'd been with me when the call came in, yeah, but before that I'd had all night. I could have slipped out, bludgeoned one guy, hanged another…yeah, right. He had to know as well as I did how impossible that was.

Terry Skullbones must have had eighty pounds on me. Maybe a hundred. Probably a hundred.

"So? Were my details accurate?"

"Several of them were, yes."

*Yes?* Not yeah, not uh-huh, not yup, but yes. Formal now. He was keeping a physical distance, too, now that he had his drink. Like I was carrying some virulent bug he didn't want to catch. He was probably spooked. Hell, he oughtta try being me for an hour and see how fucking spooked he was.

"Which details?" I demanded.

"I can't—"

"You can't tell me that. You're like a broken record, you know that?" I moved to the fireplace and cranked it up a notch, took a big gulp from my glass and decided to make the next one a little stronger. "What *can* you tell me, Mason?"

He shrugged. "There'll be an autopsy, but it's pretty clear he died from the hammer blows."

"Three of them. The one that glanced off the side and tore half his ear off, the one dead center, topside, and the one in the back." I touched my own head as I spoke. "Right?"

His body tightened. I felt it, knew it, even though I didn't see it. He tensed up, sure as shit, and there was a hitch in his breath, just a small one.

"I'll take that as a yes," I said.

Shooting me a look, he said, "How do you do that?"

"Do what? Read you?" I shrugged, downed the rest of my drink, paced to the bar and made another. "You?" I asked with a lift of my tumbler.

"I'm sipping."

"God forbid you get drunk and tell me what the hell is going on, right?" I didn't sip. I gulped.

"If I knew—"

"I know you don't *know*. *I* don't know, either, but I've got some theories. And the one I keep coming back to is your brother."

I didn't have to look at him to feel him react. The ice cubes in his glass tinked the sides more loudly than before the second I said "brother."

"My brother is dead."

"I know. But his organs live on. What if Terry back there got his bone grafts from your brother just like I got my corneas?"

I turned to look at him. He was taking a long, slow pull from his glass. When he lowered it, he moved closer to the fire and stood staring at the flames, his back to me, and I knew what he was doing then, too. Trying to focus on something so intently that I wouldn't be able to keep reading him the way I was. "What if he did? How would that explain any of this?" he asked.

He was picking every word so carefully, speaking so slowly, making sure nothing he didn't want to reveal would leak out, and that made me even more certain that he was holding something back.

"Don't you see it, Mason? It would connect us. I've got the corneas, Terry got some skull bone, both from the same donor. Somehow that linked me to the killer. I was seeing the stuff Terry was doing." I lowered my head. "Maybe your brother *was* a psychic and you just didn't know it. Maybe he was seeing the killings, too, and that's what he couldn't live with."

His breath rushed out of him. Relief? And for the

second time he was feeling it when I talked about his brother being a psychic. *Why?*

I walked up beside him, ostensibly to stare into the fire but really so I could see more than just the back of his light blue shirt. "I know you think Terry was a copycat, but I don't. The thing is, why would he suddenly off himself like that? I mean, after killing thirteen other men, why kill himself after number fourteen? And without even bothering to hide the body, as if there was no point in trying to keep you from knowing it was him. Were you getting close to catching him?"

Mason shook his head slow. "He was never a suspect. But they'll search his place, anyway."

"For his trophies. The missing driver's licenses."

He nodded, then stopped himself. "You're not supposed to know about those, either." He turned to search my face. "How do you?"

"I don't know. I must have seen it. It's just there with a pile of other useless crap I didn't have before the transplant."

"What kind of crap?"

I shrugged. "A love of hot sauce and reggae music. A fondness for very lame rhymes." I blinked. "Wait a minute, wait a minute. Terry said something about that at group."

"Something about what?"

"Rhyming." I gulped, then shook my head. "Look at me now. I'm one of those woo-woo freaks, seeing signs and omens in every little thing. This is ridiculous. Terry's dead. I guess the guilt must've gotten to him. Maybe that's why he didn't hide the last body. So the families would have closure and the police could stop wasting time looking for a killer who was already dead. His way of atoning for his sins or something. At least it's over now. No one else will have to die. And maybe...maybe we can find where he dumped the bodies, right? Find my brother. Give him a decent burial."

"I hope so."

"Then why do you sound like you don't believe it?"

He lifted his head but didn't look at me. He looked at his drink instead, then quickly downed it. "I should go."

"Really?"

*Then* he looked at me.

I shrugged, rolled my eyes. "Look, I'm not hitting on you, okay? But it's a big house, and I've had a rough night."

"You're scared."

"Shitless, to put it delicately. And I know it's stupid to be. He's dead. The Wraith is dead. This is over now. Right?"

He almost relaxed, nodded. "All right, Rachel. I'll sack out on your couch." With one blow, he broke the tension that had been squatting on my shoulders. Knocked it right off me.

"No need. There's a perfectly good guest room upstairs."

"Okay. Is there a perfectly good shower to go with it?"

"Oh, *hell* yes. But breakfast is gonna consist of instant oatmeal and coffee. I'm no cook."

"Neither am I."

"No worries. We'll muddle through." I slugged back the rest of my drink and set the glass down. "This way, Detective." And I headed up the stairs.

Myrtle jumped up—or what passed for jumping with her—and came scrambling up behind me, scrambling also being a relative term. I mean, she was an overweight bulldog, after all.

"Aren't you going to lock the door?"

"Oh." I paused on the stairs. "Yeah, I guess so. I don't usually. It's… I mean, you know, quiet out here. I'm in the middle of fucking nowhere. And there's a gate."

"Which you left open. How do you think I drove right up to the door? Humor me."

I waved an arm. "Be my guest."

He went to the front door, and turned the lock and dead bolt. "Are the other entrances…?"

"Already locked. I keep them that way, since we hardly ever use them. Will you come to bed already?"

He sent me a look, a quick, unguarded, surprised one.

I winked at him. "Just wanted to see your face. You're a little bit scared of me, aren't you, Mason Brown?"

"A little bit, yeah."

I was surprised he'd admitted it. "Good," I said. "You should be. This way." And I headed up the stairs again.

He didn't sleep. Hell, he wasn't about to sleep. He had to keep an eye on the mouthy, spooky chick, because he was half-afraid she really was the serial killer. Okay, not really.

Or maybe.

He didn't know what to think. But he was sure this wasn't about his brother, couldn't possibly be about his brother. There were no ghosts, and there were no such things as unseen connections made through body parts, no matter what some psychiatrist thought. Tissue and bone did not have intentions or minds or evil in them. And the thought that kept on coming to him, that somehow his brother was still killing...no. Just no.

But he had the shrink's book stuffed inside his jacket, anyway. *Cellular Consciousness.* So he lay awake reading it. At first he was just skimming, and then it sucked him in. This Dr. Vosberg had a lot of documentation. Page after page of cases—the names turned into aliases, of course—where transplant recipients not only developed cravings for their donors' favorite foods but felt inexplicable familiarity with their favorite places, started using turns of phrase their donors had used, even recognized the donors' family members, though not by name.

Eric had loved reggae music and hot sauce. And his most irritating habit had been those weird rhymes he came out with. Used to drive Mason crazy when they were kids.

Mainly because it never seemed like Eric who said them but like someone else. Someone mean.

Was there any way Rachel could be making up her newfound love of hot sauce and reggae? Had she faked the vision that knocked her to her knees when she stepped into his apartment, or lied about having seen the latest murder go down? Maybe, but where the hell would she have gotten the information? And why would she want to? What would she have to gain?

PR? She was a writer, after all.

*But not a psychic. She's making a killing off her books as it is. She has no reason to add to the positive thinking thing she hypes, not when it's working so well for her as it is.*

Maybe sales were down and she needed to heat things up.

He fished his phone out of his discarded jeans to go online and did a little scoping out of her latest few titles. But they'd apparently been her bestsellers to date. The most recent one had spent seven weeks on the *New York Times* bestsellers list. She didn't seem to be hurting for money or fame.

So he was forced to consider other options. Options like the one where maybe she was telling the truth. Maybe she really was seeing the things she claimed to be seeing, and maybe it was because a part of his brother really was alive inside her head.

He hoped to God it wasn't true, then went back to his reading.

I didn't sleep well, what with Mason Brown in the room right next to mine, though probably better than I would have if I'd been there alone, given all the horrors of the night before. God, Terry Skullbones, a serial killer. Who the hell would have thought?

Eventually I must have slept, because it was the sound of Mason's banging around that woke me. I got up, pulled a robe on over my typical nighttime attire— big T-shirt and undies—and wandered toward his room.

He was freshly showered, hair still wet, and dressed in the clothes he'd worn the day before. He looked over at me, then sort of kept looking at me. Suddenly self-conscious, I pushed a hand through my hair and wondered why I hadn't bothered to look in the mirror before coming to his room.

"You're up early," I said, while bitching myself out for being such a girl.

"Yeah, have to get to work. Important meeting this morning."

"Yeah? With who?"

"Can't say."

Well, that felt like a slap. "Oh. Sorry for asking. I guess I thought we were sort of…teaming up on this."

He lowered his head, like he felt a little guilty or mean or something. "I can't really do that, Rachel. I mean, I admit you're getting some valid stuff, but I'm still a cop and you're still—"

"Oh, come on, I can't be a suspect. The Wraith is dead."

"Did I say suspect?"

I shook my head. I was being petulant, and that wasn't like me.

"Civilian. I was going to say civilian."

I sighed heavily. "It doesn't matter. It's over now." *God, please let it be over now.* "Besides, I have an important meeting this morning, too."

"Good. I'll get out of here and let you get to it."

"Good."

He was shoving his wallet and phone into his jeans, then turning to look around the room to be sure he hadn't forgotten anything. He'd even made the bed. *Neat freak.*

I rolled my eyes, swallowed my pride. "Thanks for staying with me last night."

"You're welcome." He came to the doorway. "If you want me to come back and do it again, I will."

"You will?"

"Sure. You've been through a lot. Besides, we still have to figure out where your brother is. I'm not going to give up on that."

Wow. He was actually being...nice to me.

*Yeah, what the hell is up with that?*

Before I could ask, he was cupping a hand around my nape and leaning in. His lips brushed over mine, and I damn near had a heart attack. Then he just backed off and moved on past me, trotting down the stairs and out the front door almost before I'd opened my eyes.

What the fuck?

I had a breakfast date with my BBF, Mott, that morning. I'd phoned him last night—before the murder, the vision, the visit to the crime scene and Mason's mind-warping goodbye kiss.

*That was no kiss—barely a peck, in fact—but it sure left me thinking about one.*

I needed my friend right now, and I had pretty much guilted him into getting together, but I'd be damned if I was going to let him ruin our friendship just because I could see and he couldn't.

He'd agreed to the meal, but got all huffy when we discussed a place. The conversation went something like this.

Me: "So I'll meet you at the Hollywood, then? Eight sound good?"

Mott: "Oh, sure, because it's easier for you to come to Cortland than for me to go Whitney Point, you being sighted at all."

Me: "Yeah, Mott. Everything's easier for me now that I'm sighted. Deal with it."

Mott: "So you think you're more capable than I am now. You see why this isn't going to work anymore?"

Me: "Fine. You come here. The Country Kitchen. MapQuest it, fuckface."

I used to avoid the small, crowded diner. I loved it now. It had everything a small-town diner ought to have, right down to the mouthy waitress. I'd bantered with her a few times over coffee. She was almost as good at Sarcasm Ping Pong as I was.

I waited outside for Mott, because the place wasn't exactly blind-guy friendly. Before he arrived, I got the eeriest feeling I was being watched, and I hunched deeper into my coat while looking all around.

Then his taxi pulled up, and he got out. I couldn't help it. I ran over and hugged him. Damn, I'd missed him. "You're an idiot to pay cab fare when I offered to come to Cortland."

He hugged me back, not as enthusiastically as I would have liked, but he wasn't ice-cold, either. "You bought a car and *I'm* wasting money?"

"I don't care, I love her. She's a classic. Come on, let's eat. I'm starved." I looked Mott up and down, loving seeing him clearly for the first time. I'd known he was a Brillo head, but the sheer depth of his brown curls amazed me. And his face was nicer than I'd pictured it, too. Close to my imaginary picture of him, but better. Small features, an elfin nose and narrow mouth. "I've missed the hell out of you, Mott."

He lowered his head. "I've missed *you,* too. But here I am, feeling self-conscious about how I look. I never felt like that with you before."

"You look great, and I don't care about that anyway, and you know it." I hooked my arm through his.

He pulled it away. "Don't do that to me."

"Do what? There are three steps, here, I was just—"

"Then tell me there are three steps. Don't guide me like I'm helpless."

"Wow, bite my head off, why don't you?" I walked ahead of him. "Follow me and hope for the best, then. You're at the steps now." I walked up and let him follow behind, trying not to touch him or help in any way. "Door is on your right, I'm opening it and going through now. Stop when you're two steps in."

He did fine, and continued to do fine, until we were sitting at a table, had placed our orders and were waiting for them to arrive. He'd chosen one of the specials the waitress—not my favorite sassy one, who must be off today—had rattled off. I knew that was to avoid asking me to read him the menu but didn't point it out and ordered the same thing.

So we ate. Western omelets, with toast on the side, three cups apiece of luscious coffee, and we each got a homemade cinnamon bun to take home.

"I got a dog," I told him while we ate. "You've got to meet her. She's a fat little blind bulldog named Myrtle. You're gonna love her."

He smiled, and it was genuine. He was starting to relax a little. "I can't wait to meet her. Never figured you for a dog owner."

"Me, neither. This was all Amy's doing. She wanted to adopt her, but her landlord put the kibosh on it, so…"

"So you went soft."

"The minute I set eyes on her." I bit my lip. *Dammit, watch the eye references, you dumb ass.*

He stiffened a little. Not too much. And then I said, "Mott, I'm pretty sure Tommy's dead."

He dropped his fork, and sat there real still and quiet behind his sunglasses. Then, "Only pretty sure? Does that mean there's still hope?"

"No, it just means we haven't found his body. Looks like he was murdered."

"Murdered?" He'd been feeling the table for his fork again, and once he found it, he held on to it while gaping in shock.

"It was that serial killer who's been all over the news."

"The Wraith?"

I rolled my eyes at the ridiculous name the press had given him. "Yeah. All the victims matched Tommy's description." I wanted to tell him more, about my nightmares, the vision, all of it, but not just then. *Let's mend the friendship first,* I thought. "I need my best friend back, Mott. I don't want to go through this without you."

He sighed, nodded. "I've been too hard on you, I guess."

"You've been a bastard to me. You can't stop being friends with me just because I can see. I mean, who does that? What would you think of me if I ditched my blind friends just because I can see now?"

He was quiet for a moment, and then he said, "That's kind of what I expected you to do, actually. And being that I'm your only blind friend…"

"You decided to beat me to the punch."

He nodded.

"You're an idiot, Mott. But I love you, anyway."

"You're a bitch, Rachel, and I love you, too."

Mason had read Dr. Vosberg's book from cover to cover while lying awake in Rachel's guest room and trying not to think about her just a few steps away down the hall. Now he was sitting in the man's office, wondering if he ought to ask the shrink's opinion on why he'd done something as stupid as kissing Rachel this morning.

It was a dull office, walls on the brown side of tan, dark plush chairs, floor-to-ceiling bookshelves on one wall and an aquarium on the other with colorful tropical fish swimming lazily back and forth. The man himself was a handsome fortysomething with a fake tan and blond hair with streaks of silver that looked a shade too perfect. Might have been a rug.

"I appreciate you shuffling your schedule around for me this morning, Doctor."

Vosberg nodded, and his smile was genuine. "You said it was urgent."

"It is. And it's confidential, as well. I'm here off the record."

Vosberg's brows rose, and Mason noticed that they had a red tint to them and wondered if the guy was a naturally pale-skinned carrot top. "Now I'm even more curious."

Mason got that. He was taking a risk coming here, but he had to know. "Okay, here it is. I'm working a serial killer case, but the killer is dead."

"You're talking about the Wraith," Vosberg said, getting up from his chair and crossing the room to the large coffeepot in the corner. "I read that he killed him-

self after his latest murder." He paused and looked in-
quiringly at Mason. "I'm having tea," he said, pouring
steaming water from the steel carafe into an earthen-
ware mug. "Would you like some?"

"No, thanks."

Vosberg took his time choosing a tea bag from an
assortment in a fancy wooden box. "Please, go on."

"The man who killed himself the other night? He's
not the man I was chasing. That man died weeks ago."

"So you were wrong, then. The man you thought was
the Wraith *wasn't*." Vosberg had finally unwrapped a
tea bag, and was dipping it slowly and rhythmically in
a way that was almost hypnotic.

"No. There was no question that I had the right man
and that he was dead. But he was an organ donor. And
if I didn't know better, I would have sworn he went on
killing. Somehow. Maybe. I just want to believe he's
done now."

"This Wraith…you believe he went on hunting from
beyond the grave?" The doc turned slowly and looked
at him.

"The man who committed the last murder was a recent transplant recipient. And another recipient seemed
to see the crime as it happened. Having dreams, visions."

Vosberg stopped dipping his tea bag, and his eyes
flashed excitedly. "Did they have the same donor? And
was that donor your dead suspect?"

"I don't know."

"Detective, you need to find out. If they did, this
could be groundbreaking."

Mason blinked, not quite sure the doctor was saying

what he thought he was saying. "So if their common donor was the original serial killer, then you think—"

"That one person who got his organs continued his crimes, then killed himself, and another was able to see those crimes. What sorts of transplants were these? Corneas on the second one, I'd bet."

Mason lowered his eyes, because the doc was doing that same thing Rachel did, watching him and reading him like a neon sign. He could feel it. "I can't divulge that."

The doctor was silent for a moment, pacing to his desk, retaking his seat. "Well, if I were you, I'd try to find out if there was a common donor. Somewhere there has to be a master list of, at the very least, the hospitals where each of the original donor's organs were sent. You combine that with the date and you could compare with suspects' health records."

"Medical records are confidential. And I don't exactly know how to use this theory to justify a warrant," Mason said, thinking out loud.

Dr. Vosberg gave a short bark of laughter. "I guess you're right. This would sound insane to a judge."

"Yeah." Mason sighed. "Sounded insane to *me,* too, which is why I came to see you."

"So that I could tell you it's not insane at all? That I believe it's entirely possible, and, in this case, even probable?"

Mason looked at him, waiting.

The doctor nodded. "In my opinion, it is both possible and probable, Detective Brown, that a patient who received body parts from a killer became a killer himself. And I think that if it happened once, it could happen again to other recipients of organs from this same donor."

Mason was stunned. And scared. "A nurse told me one donor could be used to help over a hundred patients."

Vosberg nodded. "I understand your alarm, but no, I don't believe every one of them would turn to killing. Your visionary hasn't, after all." He shrugged, then he looked down at his tea as if reading answers there. "No, I would expect most people would not be compatible with such urges. Most would drown them out with their own moral compass, bury them, reject them. This killer would have to find a host that was compatible." He nodded as the thoughts seemed to gel in his mind. "The man who committed suicide, he must have been receptive to the notion of committing murder but afterward couldn't live with what he'd done, so he took his own life and the killer inside him moved on."

"You say that like the killer's a separate being."

"He's the evil part of the original donor. The part that lived on beyond him. The part that didn't die. Or, should I say, parts. In times past, he might have been seen as a demon."

Mason lowered his head, shaking it. "I don't believe in demons, Doctor."

"Neither do I. No, my research is leaning toward the notion that our habits, tastes and tendencies are largely due to unique mutations in our DNA. Mutations that make each of us different from every other human being. But don't you see, Detective Brown? The DNA lives in every single cell. It goes with the organs into their new bodies. This is why so many organ recipients experience cravings for the donor's favorite foods, have flashes of the donor's memories and so much more. It's all in my boo—"

"I know, I read it. Tell me, are any of your…colleagues on board with this theory of yours? About cellular consciousness?"

"No. No, but I'm gathering more data all the time."

"I see." So he was really nothing but a quack with a wild and unproven theory. Mason liked evidence, facts, *proof.* Until he had it, he would stick with the old adage that the simplest solution was usually the right one.

The doctor sighed. "This must be quite upsetting to the person having the visions. I imagine it would help her immensely if you would let her know that you don't think she's crazy."

Mason nodded, started to get up, then stopped and turned. "How do you know it's a she?"

"I believe I met her last Wednesday."

What had Rachel said about last Wednesday? Right, that support group where she'd met Terry Cobb, or Terry Skullbones as she called him.

"You run the support group?"

Vosberg nodded. "Corneal grafts aren't so common that there would likely be two in the same relatively small geographic area within such a narrow timeframe."

Mason had no doubt that Rachel had sought out the support group and Dr. Vosberg for the same reason he had. To ask questions. To try to figure out what was going on. She was a wannabe sleuth if he'd ever met one. And she was a natural at it, too. He wondered if she'd managed to get any further than he had.

He got up from his chair, and the doc did likewise,

extending his hand across the desk. Mason shook it. "Thank you very much for your time, Doctor. And again, this has to remain confidential."

"Of course," Vosberg said. "It's not as if anyone would believe it, anyway."

## _12_

The Wraith lives on
Though Cobb is gone.
He's entered Number Three.
To find out more
Best watch the whore.
Was blind, but now she sees.

The note was in Mason's email when he arrived at the station later that morning, and it gave him chills right up his spine. There was no point in trying to delete or hide it. First, because Rosie came to his desk just as he opened the email and read it right over his shoulder, and secondly, because he was done covering things up or hiding the truth, however crazy it might sound. He was straight-up honest from here on.

"Sounds like he's talking about Rachel de Luca, doesn't it?" Rosie asked.

"It does." Mason saw the chief's office door open and waved him over to read the note.

"Gotta mean the de Luca woman," Subrinsky said. "So she's connected to all this somehow?"

Mason nodded. "Which we already knew. Her brother was one of the victims. She knew Terrence Cobb, though she'd only met him twice."

"I want her under surveillance tonight," the chief said. "We have no way of knowing what this means, and I'm not having the Queen of Nice murdered on my watch. Not with a warning flashing like a neon sign."

"Queen of Nice?" Mason blinked in shock as the chief headed back into his office and slammed the door.

Rosie shrugged. "All that positive living stuff she spouts."

"Trust me, she is not the Queen of Nice. She's not even the Queen of Civil."

Rosie grinned. "Not with you, anyway, huh? Then again, you didn't make the best first impression."

Mason took a deep breath and decided to withhold any further comment. "Let's get the net guys to give us some help on this, see if it can be traced."

"I imagine he's too smart for that, but yeah, I'll get them on it."

Unmarked units had been following Rachel de Luca without her knowledge all day, because Mason had thought it would look fishy if he'd insisted he be the only one keeping tabs on her.

When he arrived to take his shift that evening, though, her house was dark and quiet, and apparently empty.

He drove on past, then pulled in beside the other vehicle, which was parked in a pull-off alongside the dirt road where it made a slight bend just past her house. The spot was one fishermen used to put their boats into the reservoir. He could tell by the way the tall grass and reeds on the downward sloping bank were flattened all the way to the water, with telltale tire paths on either side. Parked where he was, he had a good view of the house.

He rolled his window down.

Mark Richards, a twenty-year vet marking time until retirement, did the same.

"Anything going on?" Mason asked.

"She's having dinner at Aiello's."

Mason blinked. "Then why are you here?"

"Dennison's there. He wanted to get a pizza to take home for the family tonight, so he's keeping an eye on her, said he'd text you when she left and follow her to the end of her driveway, then take off. Seemed okay to me."

Mason nodded. "She alone?"

"No, looks like a date. Denny's gonna see if he can get a look at the guy's plastic when he pays up so we can run him."

A date? Rachel was on a date? Why did that surprise him? Better question, why did it piss him off?

Mason nodded. "Anyone else in and out today?"

"Just her assistant, one Amy Montrose. She left a little after five."

"Anything else?"

"Yeah, she walked her fucking dog before she left to meet her date. You want the full report before I go home, or do you think you can wait till it's typed up?"

"Sorry. Go on, get out of here."

Mason rolled up his window, cranked up his heat against the autumn chill and watched Richards's tail-lights disappear. He was thinking that if she'd met this date at the restaurant, it couldn't be very serious, and then thinking he was an idiot for thinking about it at all. She was tied up in a string of murders. She was, at the very least, the sister of a victim in an ongoing case. She had his brother's eyes in her head, and she was perilously close to figuring out things that could cost him his career. Besides, he was a confirmed bachelor. There was no way this thing was going anywhere.

He got the text within ten minutes. They're leaving. Separate cars.

U get his name? he texted back.

David R. Gray. CC # too. Shd I run it?

I will. He paused with his finger over the keypad. Kiss goodnight? he finally texted. He had to know, and Dennison could think what he wanted.

There was a long pause before the reply came. Yep, w tongue. :)

Not fucking funny, Mason thought. Not funny at all. Probably served him right for asking. He pocketed the phone, picked up his binoculars, turned off the engine and got out of his car, then walked along the dirt road so he could have a better view of her front door. He crouched in the bushes and waited.

She came home, alone, ten minutes later, and went inside. Another hour and the lights went out, all but one on the second floor.

Three hours crawled by with nothing more to show, and he was thinking about heading back to the car to sit with the heat on for a while when his thoughts were broken by the mechanical hum of the garage door ris-

ing, followed by the sound of her T-Bird's engine starting up. Then the headlights flashed on and the car came
rolling out.

He ran back to his own car, started it up and left the
headlights off. She pulled out through her gate, which
she'd left open as she usually did, and he followed, keeping his headlights off until they hit the main road and
staying a good distance behind her even then. She didn't
take the highway but drove north using side roads that
ran parallel to it, all the way to the small city of Cortland, where she turned onto Main Street, which was
one-way. A minute later she pulled the T-Bird into one
of the diagonal parking spots that lined both sides of
Main, got out and started walking down the sidewalk
just as bold as you please. She wasn't wearing anything
but a T-shirt and a pair of satiny blue panties.

What the *hell?* Was she *drunk* or something? She
hadn't been driving as if she was, and she was walking
a fairly straight line.

As she moved beneath a streetlight he noticed that
the shirt had two hands on it, one with its middle finger straight up and the other pointing at whoever happened to be looking. The message was clear and not
even close to in keeping with her public image. Probably
not a shirt she would normally wear in public. *Queen
of Nice, my ass.*

He tried to notice the crude logo instead of the long,
lean legs and the dark blue satin that showed at the tops
of them. But he noticed them, anyway.

He parked and got out, too, still giving her a little
space but keeping her in sight. Then she stopped and just
stood there, looking down at something on the sidewalk.

He walked a little closer, waiting for her to do something else. To go wherever it was she'd been heading or…hell, he didn't know.

But she just stood there.

Frowning, he moved still closer and then decided to reveal himself, because a car or two had passed and somebody was gonna call a cop to report a suspicious beauty in her underwear on the streets in the wee hours. "Rachel?"

Nothing.

He got an odd inkling, a little shiver up his nape, and moved around to stand in front of her. He almost tripped over something on the sidewalk but ignored that and crouched a little to get a look at her face. "Rachel?"

Her eyes were wide-open and completely unseeing. He waved a hand back and forth close to them, but she didn't blink or flinch. She was asleep.

Come on, *really?* Was that even possible?

But he knew it was. There had been cases of people doing all sorts of things in their sleep, including driving vehicles, cooking meals, committing murders.

Shit, could that be it? Was she dreaming of the crimes because she was committing them in her sleep? No, she'd been with him when one victim was abducted. But since then?

Had his brother's parts taken control of her, the way they had—maybe—taken over Terrence Cobb?

Her arm came up and she pointed at his feet. He looked down, remembering the thing he'd nearly tripped over. And then everything in him turned icy cold, because a thin, black leather wallet was lying there, open.

And the clear plastic slot where a man would keep his
license was empty.

She hadn't put it there. He hadn't taken his eyes
off her.

So how had she known?

And how was a killer who'd already died twice still
taking victims?

He moved closer and put his hands on her shoulders,
shook her just a little. She sucked in a sharp breath before her eyes came back online, blinking a few times,
and then looking at him like *he* was the one losing it.

"What the fuck, Mason?" It was an accusation. She
looked around, then down at her T-shirt, and finally
seemed to get it. "Shit, where are we? How did we—
I'm not even dressed!"

"We're in Cortland, because you drove here in your
sleep. And I'm here because I had you under surveillance tonight."

She opened her mouth, no doubt to bitch about that,
but he held up a hand. "It's a good thing I followed you,
Rachel, because you apparently drove here to find that."
He pointed. She saw the wallet and staggered backward,
then spun around and grabbed hold of a nearby lamp-
post to hold herself upright. "Tell me it's not missing
the driver's license."

"Looks like it is." He grabbed her shoulder. "Hold
on, if you can. I've gotta call this in to the local P.D. as
well as my own, since this isn't my jurisdiction." And
then he had to figure out how to explain what the two
of them were doing there.

Hands braced on the post, she leaned there for a
second, then finally straightened and turned. She was

calm, no longer on the verge of panic as she'd been a second ago.

"Did you have another dream?"

"No." She wasn't looking at him. Her huge blue eyes were glued to that wallet.

"Then how did you know?"

"I have no fucking idea. Aren't you gonna pick it up or something?"

He crouched over the wallet, which lay open on the sidewalk, facedown. Using his car key, he managed to flip it over without the risk of contaminating evidence. A credit card had fallen out and had been lying beneath it. The open wallet had an empty spot where a license would normally go. "No license. Just like the others."

"But who—"

"Hang on, hang on." He turned his head to view the credit card at the right angle. "Dermott Allan Killian."

"Mott," she whispered. "Oh, my God, it's Mott."

It felt like a tornado inside my head when he said Mott's name. I don't remember falling, but I wound up ass-to-sidewalk, hands covering my face.

Mason was right there, though, scooping me up. And I thought he must be strong, because I wasn't one of those pixie-stick chicks. At that moment I felt like one, though, and gave in for just about a nanosecond to the whole damsel-in-distress, head-on-a-strong-shoulder, damn-he-smells-so-good bullshit I would hate myself for later. He was carrying me. His arms were solid and his chest warm against me. I could have relished the sensations a lot longer than I allowed myself to.

But then I twisted free and landed on my bare feet

on the sidewalk again. The concrete was cold, and so was the night air. I rubbed my arms to get the goose bumps to go down. "We have to find Mott. We can't let this maniac kill him." Then I shook my head. "How can there even still *be* a maniac? It was Terry Skullbones, and he's damn well dead."

He stood there blinking at me for an elongated second before his brain clicked on. I wondered if he'd been feeling all knight-in-shining-armorish, then corrected myself. Men didn't feel mushy, men felt horny. Totally different thing.

And then I wondered if he'd been feeling *that*.

"So, you…know this one, too?" he asked once his system rebooted.

I nodded. "He was my best friend until I got my sight back. He was being a real dick about that. Because he thinks he's the fucking Malcolm X of the blind. Oh, God. Mott."

"Maybe this isn't what it looks like, then," he said, obviously thinking more clearly than I was. "Maybe he just lost his wallet. He's blind, so he wouldn't have a driver's license, anyway."

"Yeah, and I came straight to his lost wallet in my sleep just because he dropped it," I said sarcastically. "Besides, he had a state-issued photo ID. You need one when you're blind."

"I didn't think about that. So his ID is missing?"

I nodded. "It would have been in the driver's license pocket."

"You want to try calling him before I bring in the cavalry?"

"Yeah. Can I borrow your cell? 'Cause I don't think I have mine stuffed in my underwear."

He nodded. "Get in your car, you've got goose bumps from your toes to your—" He stopped there, eyes on my thighs, which were exposed all the way to the crotch of my panties.

Yep, horny. Typical male. I rolled my eyes and didn't bother to think about whether I was irritated by his attention or my girlie-girl reaction to it. I just headed for my car. I got in, started it up and cranked on the heat.

Mason got into the passenger side and handed me the phone, then waited while I punched in Mott's number. It rang four times, then his voice mail picked up. And when I heard his voice, my stupid eyes burned. "He'd better fucking be okay."

"What would he be doing here?" Mason asked, looking up and down the street.

I looked, too. "He has an apartment a few blocks from here. He teaches American history at SUNY here in Cortland."

He didn't say anything, just held out his hand for the phone. I handed it to him, and he scrolled through numbers until he found what he wanted, but he didn't hit the call button. He said, "I really do need to call this in. I want you to go home. You were never here, okay?"

"So I'm not a suspect?"

"Depends on when he was taken. *If* he was taken. You've been under surveillance for most of the night, so—"

"What if I'm working with a partner? Did you ever think of that?"

"Yes, I have."

The answer surprised me, not to mention it felt like a smack upside the head. "Shit, Mason, you really *do* think I've got something to do with this, don't you?"

He pressed his lips together and looked at my dashboard instead of my face. "We both know you're connected in some way. Beyond that? I don't know what to think."

"Well, thanks for that vote of confidence. Hell, Mason, what about your gut feeling? Aren't you detective types supposed to have gut feelings about shit like this?"

He looked at me for a long moment, then just shook his head. "Go home, okay? If I really thought you were a killer you'd be heading to the station with me for a lengthy interrogation. Just get the hell out of here, all right?"

"And what about you?"

He scowled at me so hard I thought he was going to bite, but I didn't let that stop me.

"How the hell are you gonna explain how you just happened to find the wallet?"

"I haven't decided yet. Anonymous phone call or text or email or something."

"Won't they check your phone?"

"Not right away."

I looked straight into his eyes. "You keep this up, *you'll* be a suspect."

"That's a distinct possibility." He got out of the car but stood there with the door open. "This stays between us, okay? If I'm keeping quiet about it, you've got to do the same."

"I know." I got a lump in my throat. "I thought the killer was dead."

"So did I," he said, and then he shut the car door and brought the cell phone to his ear.

I drove home, my mind racing about a zillion miles an hour. Terry Skullbones had kept Blue T-shirt alive for a day or two before bashing his brains in with that hammer. A day or two. That was how long we had to find Mott.

Why couldn't my fucking dreams tell me something useful, like where to begin looking?

## 13

By daybreak Friday he and Rosie were together at the station. Rosie was at his desk, and Mason was sitting on the edge of it, so he wouldn't have to talk too loudly.

"This is bending my brain," Rosie said. "The Wraith's dead. We found him hanging, with his latest victim still warm in his cellar. How can he still be hunting like this?"

"I don't know, pal. What if Terrence Cobb didn't kill the guy in his basement? What if he was set up?"

"What do you mean? His prints were on the hammer. The victim's blood was all over his clothes."

"Okay, I'll rephrase. What if he was *brilliantly* set up?"

Rosie frowned, leaning closer. "It would have to be beyond brilliant. Forensics didn't find any hint of anyone in that house besides Cobb, his mother—who'd just come back from Atlantic City—and the victim. Not a fingerprint, not a blood drop. And no sign he had any help hanging himself, either."

"I know all that. But the fact remains, we've got another victim. If Cobb was the killer, we wouldn't have, would we?"

*Why not?* he thought in answer to his own question. The killings had continued after Eric's death. Why not after his successor's?

"Yeah, another victim," Rosie mused. "Dermott Killian. Who the hell lets a blind guy leave a bar all alone after midnight, anyway?"

"Anyone who drank with him, that's who." Killian had last been seen by several of his colleagues around midnight, leaving Hairy Tony's, one of his favorite bars, to walk to his apartment several blocks away, just as he did a couple of times a week. The witnesses all said much the same thing. Killian was zealous about being treated the same way a sighted person would be. If they'd offered him a ride, he would have been furious for at least a month.

Mott Killian fit the profile, with the exception of his hair. It was the right color, but curly, not long and straight like all the others.

"So...Rachel," Rosie said, dropping his voice. "She knew *this* guy, too?"

"Yeah. And that stays between us for now."

"Shoot, no reason to spread it around, anyway. It's not like *she's* the killer."

"Exactly." Even though his cop sense had been out of whack since his brother's suicide, Mason was leaning toward trusting it where Rachel de Luca was concerned. She'd been blind during most of the crimes and with him during another. She wasn't big enough or strong enough to move the dead bodies of grown men, lanky

or otherwise, and the only vehicle she owned was beyond memorable.

Of course he already knew beyond a shadow of a
doubt that she hadn't killed the first thirteen. Those victims had all been Eric's. But someone was damn well
continuing Eric's crimes without him, and though he'd
thought it was Terrence Cobb, the biker was dead now,
too, and someone was still at it.

Someone who'd received another one of Eric's organs? Could that crazy fucking shrink be right about
that?

"Maybe you were right about Cobb being a copycat," Rosie said. "Maybe the guy in the basement was
his only victim and he couldn't take it, and now we're
back to the original killer."

"Maybe." But no, Eric had been the original killer,
and Eric was dead. So what, then? Two copycats? A
team of copycats? Or his current pet theory, a setup,
which made a lot more sense. One copycat, setting up
others to throw the cops off his scent. But the organs…
And Rachel's visions… How the hell did those fit in?

His desk phone rang, and he went over to pick it up.

A vaguely familiar female voice said, "Hey, Mason.
It's Patty. Patty Emerson. You left a message asking me
to call you back."

It took him a minute, because it had been a couple
of days ago he'd placed the call. Then his brain put everything together. Patty was a nurse from the Transplant Unit. He'd gotten to know her while handling all
the details of Eric's organ donation. She'd made it clear
that she was interested in him, but he'd been in no shape
emotionally to take her up on what she was so clearly

offering. But since Terrence Cobb was a local and his bone grafts had, Mason had learned, been done in the same hospital, he'd figured Patty would be the person who could tell him what he needed to know.

"Hey, Patty. Hang on." He covered the phone with one hand, looked over at Rosie and said, "Personal."

Rosie nodded and headed for the coffeepot.

Mason returned to the call. "Okay, I'm here. I have a question, Patty. It's vital, and I swear to you now, your answer will go no further."

She sighed, and he wondered if she was disappointed at the reason for his call. "I'll tell you if I can."

"You know about the recent suicide of Terrence Cobb, the man we think was the serial killer, the Wraith?"

She hesitated. Then, "Yeah?"

"He'd had a bone graft of donor material. I need to know if my brother was his donor."

"Mason, you know I can't tell you something like—"

"But you could save lives by telling me, Patty. And that's what you do, right? Save lives?"

There was a long pause. Finally she said, "I could lose my job if I told you that Eric was his donor. So I can't tell you that. I can't tell you that he was."

"He was." Mason repeated it.

"I can't tell you that."

"Thank you."

Part of him had known all along that it had to be true. The gears in his mind started turning, trying fit the cogs together into a machine that actually worked. One of Eric's recipients committed a murder just like Eric's murders. Another got his corneas and started having visions of the victims. Maybe it was time to start believing in that shrink's crazy theory after all.

"Thank you, Patty. I hate to ask, but do you think you might be able to find out something else for me?"

"Depends what it is," she said, her wariness evident. "I'm not losing my job for you."

"I need to know where all my brother's organs went."

"I couldn't get that information for you if I tried."

"But you know who could."

"And I'm not telling you."

He sighed, but he wasn't about to give up. "You're right, and I don't want you risking your career. You've put yourself on the line for me already, and I appreciate that." *Okay,* he thought. *Here goes.* "I really appreciate you getting back to me. How about if I take you out sometime to say thanks?"

Her reply was immediate. "How about tomorrow? It's Saturday, and I'm off."

"I'm moving tomorrow." He'd put it off long enough. The motel was eating into his savings, and he had a perfectly good fixer-upper ready and waiting. "And I'm going to have my nephews that night, but I'll tell you what, how about breakfast Sunday morning?"

"All right. Sunday breakfast, then." She sounded disappointed. "Where do you want to meet?"

He needed her alone, so he could talk his way into finding out where to get those medical records. "How about you drive out to my new place and I'll cook for you? I'll give you the address."

He rattled it off, but he wasn't thinking about Patty anymore.

He was thinking about whether one of those organ

recipients had known about Eric's secret life as a serial killer and had decided to carry on in his memory. Some warped sense of gratitude or some delusion of being possessed or some other fucking mental contortion. The why didn't matter. The fact that Recipient One had framed Recipient Two for the most recent killing—brilliantly framed him, and probably hanged him, too—meant that he might be doing the same with Rachel. Trying to set her up.

*By planting dreams in her head? That's a little farfetched, isn't it? What about Dr. Vosberg's theory? That the killing gene is being transplanted with the organs? Can you* really *explain all of this in any other way?*

He shook his head until his inner voice went silent, because the good doctor's explanation, the one the UFO freaks and ghost hunters of the world would jump on, was even more ludicrous than his own theory.

And no matter who was right, Rachel might be at risk.

So he needed to figure out who else had received organs and rule them out as suspects one by one. And he had to keep Rachel safe in the meantime.

He had to keep her in the dark, as well. He couldn't tell her what he thought. Not until he knew for sure. She was already scared shitless, and *she* probably *would* jump straight to some freaking paranormal explanation. Besides, he couldn't tell her without also telling her that his brother had been the original Wraith. That she had the eyes of a killer in her head. Her own brother's killer.

God, she was going to hate him if that ever came out. So he couldn't tell her. But he couldn't let her far from his sight either, just in case. If nothing more, she would have an alibi. That was the best he could do for her right now.

The twins had a soccer game Friday afternoon, and it was cold as hell. Wind blowing, sky gray, air damp so that it chilled straight through to the bone. I had every right to be miserable.

And I was, at the beginning. Muttering about the cold while my sister handed me a mug of hot cocoa from her Thermos. But once the game started I forgot to be miserable. I was on my feet so much my ass barely touched the frigid bleacher seats, no doubt deliberately designed to be as uncomfortable as possible. I was sitting on the bottom row, because I'd brought Myrtle, along with a blanket for her to lie on. She was wearing a pink fleecy sweater. I'd had to buy an XL. Whoever invented dog sizes oughtta maybe try owning one first, I swear. She's a foot tall. Yes, two feet in diameter, but still, if that's an XL dog, then what the hell is a St. Bernard?

She was lying on the blanket snoring, not the least bit into the game she couldn't see. But every time I jumped up and yelled for the girls, she would lift her head and look my way. It was cruel, what she was missing.

It had been cruel that I'd been missing it for so long, too.

"I wonder if they do cornea transplants for dogs?"

Sandra reached down to pet her head. "I never thought I'd see you go soft for an animal, Rache. Myrtle has you wrapped around her forepaw."

"She does not."

"No? She owns more outfits than you do."

I shrugged. "I don't do the frou-frou shit, you know that. I'm getting my inner girlie-girl off vicariously."

"Oh, so *that's* all it is."

"Yeah, that's all it—holy shit, Christy's gonna score. Go! *Go, Christy!*"

She had a shot but passed the ball instead. The red-headed Amazon she'd passed to flubbed the kick, and the goalie was on it like white on rice. I sat down, deflated. "Damn."

"Easy, Rachel. It's just a game."

"Bullshit. It's self-esteem, is what it is. I need to have a serious talk with that girl."

Misty and Christy were nearly identical on the field, but Misty played fullback and Christy was front line. They both wore black spandex leggings under their black-and-gold uniform shorts, and long-sleeved spandex turtlenecks under their jerseys to keep warm. On top of the leggings, white soccer socks and shin-guards. Hot-pink cleats. High blond ponytails, and smudges of black under their eyes.

*Mercenary-Barbie, your favorite doll goes rogue.*

The thought amused me so much I laughed a little bit.

"It's good to see you smile."

I shot Sandra a look. "What do you mean? I always smile."

"Not lately. Actually, I've been wanting to talk to you about that."

"About what?" The other team was speeding toward our goal, and I jumped up again. "Boot it, Misty! Get it out of there!"

Misty complied. The black-and-white ball sailed a hell of a lot farther than I ever could have sent it and was promptly claimed by one of her teammates. I sat down again.

"You've been looking rough, honey," my sister said. "You have dark circles under your eyes."

"They're just tired from all this seeing. They're not used to it, you know."

"Amy says you're short-tempered."

"More than usual?" I asked with an innocent blink.

Coach called a time-out. The girls came jogging to the sidelines, gathering around their bench for a thirty-second conference.

Sandra was still going on. "She said you fell asleep at the computer yesterday. Is something—"

"Be right back." I handed her Myrt's leash—you know, just in case my comatose dog decided to get up and go for a romp—and marched to the huddled mass of sophomores, yearning to breathe free. I put a hand on Christy's shoulder and, leaning in close enough to speak for her ears only, said, "Next time you have a shot, you damn well take it, sweetheart. Fifty bucks in it for you, hit or miss."

The coach sent me a scowl, but I didn't care. I was back at the bleachers seconds later, looking at the scoreboard and wondering how long five more minutes was in soccer time.

"Amy says you've been seeing quite a bit of that cop."

"Amy's got a whole lot to say about my personal life, doesn't she?"

"She loves you, and you know it."

"She's gonna love herself right out of a job if she's not careful. Did she mention I've been on three dates with David Heart from the support group?"

"No. She must not think you're serious. I agree with her, considering you're still not using his actual last name."

"I keep forgetting his actual last name."

"So you're not serious."

"He tried to stick his tongue down my throat after dinner the other night. How's that for serious?"

"You sound more grossed out than turned on."

I sighed. "Yeah, I was. I don't think it's going anywhere."

"And what about Detective Brown?"

I rolled my eyes. "Yes, big sister, I've seen Detective Brown a few times—because I want him to find our brother so we can bury him."

She lowered her head. "We don't know for sure that he's—"

"Yes, we do, Sandy. I'm really sorry, but we do. His wallet was left behind, just like all the others. I told you that." I also told her that Mason believed Terry Skullbones had been a copycat. A one-time killer. That scared the hell out of her, too.

She blinked as the whistle blew and the girls ran back out onto the field. "Is your detective getting any closer to finding the…to finding who did it?"

"No. Not yet." I ignored the fact that she'd called him my detective, bit my lip and decided I was going to have to tell her about Mott. She'd hear about it sooner or later anyway. "Sis, last night Mott went missing."

Her head came up fast, eyes round as platters. "*What? Oh my God,* was it the same…?"

"Yeah, it looks like the same guy."

She muttered something under her breath. I heard

cuss words in there, and my sister *never* cussed. The girls were playing again, but Sandra was staring at me. "Rachel, that's two victims who are close to you. It's beginning to look personal. Have you thought about that?"

How could I not think about that? It *was* personal. But I couldn't tell Sandra that or she would have me on the first flight to Timbuktu. Thank God the action on the field picked up just then, giving me an out.

"Hey, look at your daughter, sis."

Christy was dribbling for the goal, when she hesitated and faked a shot, swinging her foot past the ball so the goalkeeper dived in the wrong direction. Instantly my brilliant niece turned and took a real shot. The ruse worked, and the ball sailed straight into the net.

I rose to my feet and pumped my fist. *"Yes!"*

The buzzer sounded, and the girls formed a screaming, squealing happy huddle in the middle of the field. I knew they would be busy for ten more minutes with the obligatory "good game, good game, good game" high fives with the other team, then picking up their equipment, and after that Sandra would still have to wait to sign the coach's clipboard so she could reclaim the girls and drive them home. This wasn't my first soccer game. Just the first one I'd been able to see. And I was damn near giddy about that.

I got up and coaxed Myrt to her feet, as well. "I'm gonna put Myrtle in the car and turn on the heat. She's about frozen."

"She's warmer than any of us."

"I'll meet you by the van to say bye to the girls."

She sighed. "Are you sure you're all right?"

"Yes, I'm sure I'm all right." *I am so far from all*

*right it's not even funny, but I need to go home so I can sleep and dream of Mott and maybe find out where he is, because it's the only thing I can think of to do.* "Meet you at the minivan."

"What are you doing this weekend, sis?"

"Helping a friend move," I said. I'd been shocked as hell when Mason invited me along to meet his nephews and see his new place, and I hadn't actually given him an answer, only said I'd call him and get the address if I could make it. And I'd only just now decided I would go. I assumed he had motives that had nothing to do with anything personal and everything to do with the case. He wanted to keep me close. I just wasn't sure if it was because he thought I might be in danger or because he thought I might lead him to the serial killer. I was at least pretty sure he didn't think I *was* the serial killer. Either way, it was cool with me. I wanted to keep *him* close, too, so I could learn everything he knew, one way or another.

When I arrived home, I put the car into the garage. I didn't always, especially if I was in a big fat hairy hurry, as I was then. It was just starting to get dark. The soccer game had run into the dinner hour, so I'd joined Sandra and the twins for a celebratory fast-food fest at the combination McDonald's, Mobil station and convenience store, making sure to display suitable excitement over Christy's goal. Okay, so that hadn't really been a challenge. I'd handed over the fifty I'd promised her, and given another one to Misty to keep things fair. By then it was pushing seven. Another few minutes home, but only because I drove really slowly over my rutted dirt road, then through the gate—which I closed for once—and into my driveway. After I put the car in the garage, I closed the door and locked it, too. Myrt and I went in through the door that led from the garage into the kitchen, and I locked that for good measure. And I set my alarm system for once, so that it would start chirping if the door was opened without the code being entered first. I did not want to be driving around in my sleep again. That was freaky. I could have killed someone. I wished there was a lock on my driveway gate. I'd never thought it necessary, but now it was on the top of my to-do list.

At least with the alarm on the door, the chirping would wake me if I tried that little trick again. I hoped. God knew I didn't use the security system often enough to be able to enter the pass code in my sleep.

Myrt danced around my feet once we were inside. That was as active as she ever got, to be honest. She'd been quite content to snooze on the passenger seat until after my McMeal with the fam, but when I came back out to the car, she was done with that. Her interest became focused on sniffing the red-and-white bag I'd brought with me, knowing it contained a cheeseburger just for her. I know, she was already chubby, bordering on fat, but we hardly ever had junk food, and everybody needs to indulge now and then, right?

I opened the bag as soon as we were inside the kitchen, broke the burger into pieces and fed one to her. She ate it with the same relish I eat chocolate.

I couldn't wait to get to sleep, thinking maybe I'd dream about Mott and figure out where he was or who had him. Part of me was scared, too, because I didn't want to see him die. I couldn't stand that.

As it turned out, it didn't matter. I couldn't sleep. I didn't think I would ever sleep again. My fear apparently outweighed my worry about my friend. I thought about taking a pill, but I needed to be able to wake up fast if I got a clue where Mott was. I turned off all the lights except for the bathroom one and lay there staring at the ceiling for several hours. Eventually I turned on the TV and propped myself up on pillows to try to manually put myself into a coma by watching one of the twenty-four-hour news channels. The same six or so stories, over and over and over, word for freakin' word. By the third cycle, my eyeballs were drooping.

A car door slammed, and they popped open. Was it a real sound, or had I dreamed it?

Seconds passed, then there was some kind of a thud from downstairs. Myrtle sprang up onto all fours—no shit, she *sprang*—and let out a low growl, while I sat up in bed, frowning. The TV was still on. I found the remote and hit the mute button. Tires spun as whoever had been down there sped away.

I had this weird moment of wondering if I was in a dream or actually awake, and then decided the only way to find out was to head downstairs and check for myself. The night-light was on. I turned on the big lamp beside the bed, got up and pulled on the bathrobe hanging from the bedpost. It was the ugly green one. It was fluffy and plush, mint-colored, and made me look about twice my actual size. But it was also my fave because it was so snuggly cozy warm.

Shoving my feet into slippers, I went into the hall.

Myrtle hustled down the little portable steps I'd put by
the foot of the bed for her so she could get up and down.
It was the first time she'd used them without me putting
a hand on her back to guide her. She reached the bottom
and hurried ahead of me, cutting me off so short that I
damn near tripped over her.

"Easy, girl. It was just a car." Though it had sounded
like it was on *this* side of my gate.

She gave another low growl, still blocking me.

I'd never seen her like this. The fur along her spine
was standing up. I had cold chills up my own spine, but
something made me keep going. I don't know what. I
made it to the bottom of the stairs with Myrt practically
walking between my feet, but I did, and then I went into
the kitchen to grab my cell phone off the counter where
I'd dropped it when I'd come in last night. I gave the
battery a quick check. Low, but on.

Okay, I was being a big chicken, but Myrt was acting weird, and *I* was feeling something, too. Her senses
were sharper than mine, and mine were sharper than
most humans'. Something was wrong.

I walked to the front door thinking about the peignoir-
clad waifs in all the horror novels I'd listened to on au-
diobook over the years, walking *toward* the scary noise
in the dead of night instead of running away from it. I
usually call them every kind of idiot. I sure as hell never
thought I'd ever be one of them. But I had to keep going
toward my front door, even though it loomed ahead of
me like maybe there was a hungry lion waiting on the
other side. My hand was shaking as I reached out, turned
the lock—*yes, still locked, that's good. Alarm light still*

*green. Also good. No one has been inside.* I punched in the code, gripped the knob and pulled the door open.

There was a pile of rags at my feet just outside the door, blocking the threshold. Wait, no, what was at the end of that stained… Was it a shirtsleeve? Was that a *hand?*

I hit the light switch beside the door. The outdoor light came on. The pile of rags was being worn by a person. A dead person, lying facedown. My eyes jerked from the pale, bloody hands to the jeans-clad legs to the head, all bashed to hamburger, with a few tufts of curly hair still sticking up here and there.

"Mott, oh, Jesus, it's Mott." Everything in me wanted to back away, slam the door, scream my brains out, but there was one little piece of reason left, and it told me to check for a pulse, just in case he might still be alive.

I crouched down and reached out. My hand touched his shoulder, and the entire lump of what had once been my friend flopped over in cinematic slow-mo. Myrtle started barking her brains out. Mott was staring up at me through wide-open eyes that had never seen, set in a face painted in his own blood.

That was when I started screaming and leaped to my feet, spasmodically smacking every button on the security panel just inside the door until I hit the one that called the cops.

# 14

"Drink this." Mason shoved a glass under my nose. It looked like Coke, but I could smell the vodka. Hey, don't tell me it has no odor. It totally does, and it's an aroma I know well. I took the drink, chugged it and smacked the empty glass down onto the end table next to my chair.

Cops were outside, flashing cameras just beyond the closed door, and their cars were all over the driveway flashing their bubblegum lights. My living room looked like a damn disco from the police flashers outside, and I realized I still hadn't turned on the lights. I didn't remember calling Mason. I remembered hitting the alarm system's panic button for the first time since it was installed, and not much more. I don't know how the hell I got from the front door to the overstuffed chair.

I decided it was time to pull my head out of its hidey-hole and face reality.

*Never face a reality you don't like. Create a better one instead.*

Had I really written that? God, I was an asshole.

"Rachel?"

I blinked a couple of times, and managed to lift my

head, look him in the eye. "Yeah, I'm here. And yes, it's Mott."

"Are you sure?"

I nodded. "His face was intact. Bloody, but intact. It's him. That bastard killed my friend." My jaw went so tight my teeth hurt. I picked up the empty glass and handed it to him.

He held it up and someone else took it from him. Rosie, his partner. I'd met him twice now, once when Mason hit me with his car about a hundred years ago, and again at Terry Skullbones's house. I liked him. Rosie vanished from my line of sight, but I heard him pouring, heard the splash of ice going into the glass. "Turn on some freakin' lights while you're over there, will you, Rosie?" I called.

"Sure, Ms. de Luca. You got it."

I narrowed my eyes against the sudden glare, but it was better than being in the dark with all those strobing cop lights.

"Can you tell me what happened, Rache?"

Mason was hunkered down in front of my chair, watching my face like he thought it was going to put on a show.

"What the fuck do you think happened? Someone killed Mott and dumped his body on my doorstep."

He held my gaze and didn't flinch. He didn't deserve my anger. The bastard who'd killed Mott did, and I think that moment right there was when I decided I was going to have to find him and kill him myself, because this shit had to end.

I didn't know if I could really do it, though. I'd never even entertained the notion of killing anyone before. But

this guy had taken my brother and how many more?
Fifteen that we knew of. And Mott. Blind, arrogant,
activism-prone Mott with his stupid guitar and his constant performances of half of a song. He never finished
one. Always forgot the rest and petered off, then thought
a minute before starting a new one and not finishing that
one, either. Drove everyone fucking crazy.

My breath hitched in my throat, and I lowered my
head and choked on tears. Rosie's big hand held the
drink under my nose, and I took it and drank deep.

Mason said, "Tell me what you heard, what you saw,
what you did tonight, everything leading up to finding
the body."

I nodded, and then I told him. I told him about the
soccer game, and that no, I didn't know the names of
anyone else who'd been there besides my sister, Misty,
Christy, a referee named Sanchez who was more blind
than I'd ever been, if her calls were anything to go by,
and Coach McElroy. I told him about going to McDonald's, then coming home and trying to fall asleep early,
and watching CNN to help with that. About starting to
drift off, and then hearing the thud from downstairs,
the slam of the car door and the squealing tires, and
that I needed to get a fucking lock on my fucking gate.

Rosie was standing close by, listening, making notes.

"Where the hell was her surveillance?" Mason asked.

He sounded as angry as I felt. That made me feel better somehow. That he was furious on my behalf.

"Alarm went off at the bank. They were closest, and
their relief was due in twenty, so dispatch sent them to
check it out."

"And?"

"Brick through the bank's window," Rosie said. "Probably a distraction to get them out of the way so he could dump the body here without being seen."

Mason nodded. Their killer was clever, he'd give him that. "Let me see your hands, Rachel."

She held them out. "I touched him. I was going to check for a pulse, but his body rolled, and I knew he was gone."

Mason looked her hands over. "Barely any blood on them."

"Do I need a lawyer, Mason?" I asked. "Does anyone really think I bashed my best friend's brains in, then dumped him on my own doorstep and called the cops?"

"No. No one thinks that. It's standard procedure to check everyone at the scene of a murder. I want my ducks in a row on this. You do, too. Trust me on that. Should any evidence turn up later, you need your ass covered now." He turned to Rosie. "Have Dennison get in here with the camera. Photograph her hands so we have it on record they were virtually blood-free and clearly hadn't been washed."

He was trying to help me. I got it now.

Someone came in and shot my hands. Someone else scraped under my nails and put the scrapings into a plastic evidence bag, sealed it with red tape and walked away writing on it with a Sharpie. I didn't argue, because I didn't have a thing to hide.

Rosie said, "The tire tracks in the driveway support everything you said, Ms. de Luca. Someone spun out of here, and there's a blood trail from where the car stopped to your front door. Forensics wants permission to take a look at your car's tires for a tread comparison."

I nodded. "It's in the garage. Knock yourselves out."

"Absolutely not!" The voice came from the kitchen side of the house as my sister, who had her own set of keys to my place, came charging into the living room. "If you want my sister to answer any questions, she's getting a lawyer first."

"Hell, her and her damn scanner," I said to Mason. Then I met Sandra's eyes, shook my head. "Don't, sis. Just…don't."

"I'm going to call Victor Kent, Rache. He's the best criminal attorney I know of. Meanwhile, don't you dare answer any further questions until you and he speak." She pulled out her cell phone and walked away to make her call.

"You know I have nothing to hide. She's just over-protective." I met and held Mason's eyes.

He stared back into mine for a long time, long enough that I knew he was looking for the truth there. So I let him look. He had to know I was telling the truth. And I knew that he was the one keeping secrets from me, not the other way around.

Meanwhile, it was clear to both of us that I was into this mess up to my neck. The killer was fucking with me, with the people I loved. I might not be able to do anything about that, but I was damn well going to find out Mason Brown's secrets.

"Your home is a crime scene at the moment, Rachel. We're going to need to check it thoroughly, and we're legally allowed to keep you out until we do, even if your lawyer insists on us waiting for a warrant."

I reached for my vodka, then thought better of it. I needed to stay sharp. I didn't even know who to trust right now. "So it's safe to say you guys are going to be here awhile?"

"Yeah. Like I said, it's a crime scene."

"What about me? Am I allowed to leave?"

"To go where?"

I blinked and looked at Sandra.

"To my house," she said. "She just lost a friend, Detective Brown. That *is* who you are, isn't it?"

"Yeah."

"I thought so." She nodded, softened just slightly. "I'm taking my sister home with me." She pulled a business card from her purse and handed it to him. "My office is in my home, so that's the address. Phone, too. Let us know if you need anything."

Mason looked at me, then at her, then at Rosie, who shrugged. Sighing he said, "All right. Go home with your sister."

"Can I get dressed first? Pack a bag?"

"Nothing leaves the house until we've finished. Including your car, Rache. Sorry."

I got up from my chair. "I love that car. Don't you dare let them rip her to shreds."

"There's no reason to do that."

He lowered his voice a little. "I'm trying to protect you here, not convict you. The killer was here, on your property. We need to check everything he could have touched."

I nodded. "Car keys are on the hook in the kitchen." I got up, felt the weight of my cell phone in my bathrobe pocket and decided it was coming with me whether the cops liked it or not. "Come on, Myrtle. Let's go ride in Sandra's car."

Sandra, Myrt and I went out through the garage. I certainly wasn't going out the front, where Mott's body was still lying. Even Myrtle was less excited by a ride in the car than usual. It was as if she knew our lives had been turned upside down.

Sandra only lived two miles away so it wasn't a long drive. I was putting off telling her my plans because I dreaded the inevitable fight. I needed her help to execute them, and she would need her computer to give it to me, but she was going to do her damnedest to talk me out of them, and it wasn't going to be pretty.

I looked back at Myrtle, already snoozing on the backseat by the time Sandra pulled into the driveway, cut the engine and headlights. I realized it was now or never. Better to argue out here than in the house, where we would wake the twins and Jim.

No such luck. The porch light came on, and I saw my sister's perfect husband silhouetted behind the glass pane of the front door. Shit. This would be harder with him awake. Two against one wouldn't be fair.

I got out, resolved to take them both on and scooped my too-heavy bulldog out of the back. I carried her, because she was tired and this wasn't her usual domain (and I tended to over-coddle her) as I walked to the house beside my sister. Jim opened the door before we got to it, came out in his pajamas, complete with striped robe and loafer-style slippers, and hugged me, dog and all. "Come on, kiddo. I made you some chamomile tea." He patted Myrt's head. "And I have a leftover piece of beef for you, chub."

I let them lead me into the haven of their home. The

entrance was just a landing, with a short flight of stairs that went up to the main part of the house and another set that went down to their finished basement, game room, laundry room and guest room. I carried Myrtle up so she wouldn't have to negotiate the stairs. Shoes off first, though, like any normal visit. It always smelled good here. A combination of fabric softener sheets and Lemon Pledge. My dog would probably take care of that in short order if we were here long enough. I resolved that we wouldn't be.

The living room had a railing around the stairway. We walked through into the combination kitchen/dining area. Everything else was down a hallway to the left, where I presumed the twins were asleep in their beds.

No, I didn't. They were eavesdropping for sure.

I sat at the table and let Jim pour me a cup of tea, while Myrt accepted her treat and sank onto the floor near my feet to chow down. They left me alone for a few minutes, but the minute they returned I opened my mouth to launch into my case. Then I closed it again when Jim held up a hand and started to speak.

"Sandy tells me she's hired Victor Kent," Jim said. "I'm sure you don't think you need a lawyer because you're innocent, but a lot of people who thought that are in prison right now."

Sandra turned to me, taking my hands in hers. "Look, you have to protect yourself. Just do what the lawyer says."

"And what does he say?" I asked. "Not to cooperate? To make myself look as guilty as possible? It's obvious to anyone with a brain that I had nothing to do with these murders. I was blind through most of them, for God's sake."

"The police are desperate to solve these crimes, Rachel," Jim said calmly, reasonably. He was the calmest, most reasonable man I knew. "You're walking through a minefield here. Victor has already been in touch with Police Chief Subrinsky. He's told them they can't search the inside of your home without a warrant, and that will take time."

"But what do I care if they search the house? I have nothing to hide."

Jim heaved a sigh. "If someone is trying to make you look guilty, how do you know they didn't plant evidence earlier so the police could find it after they dumped the body?"

"Okay, fine." There was no point in asking for Sandra's help, I realized. With her logical, clear-thinking husband around, she would never go along with my plan. I was on my own.

"I'm going down to the guest room," I said. "I'm exhausted, and I need to get some sleep and think more about this in the morning." I took a long drink of the foul-tasting tea to soak up any residual alcohol, gave them each a perfunctory hug, then picked up my bulldog and went down to the basement—and straight into my sister's home office, the place where she made real estate deals left and right, even in a down market. She was good at what she did. The office was beside the garage, with its own ground level entrance for clients.

After setting Myrt on the floor, I closed the office door softly and turned on Sandra's computer. Its start-up chime made me want to punch it in the monitor, but since no one came running, I guessed they hadn't heard it upstairs. Quickly, I went to her business page, entered her user name and password—which were the same everywhere on the internet. Her user name was SandralovesJim, and her password was Misty-Christy. Then I ran a search for recent sales in Castle Creek, New York.

Mason Brown's new home was the first one that popped up. Small town, and not exactly a booming real estate market. There were photos of the place, date of sale, name of the Realtor he'd used and the one who'd sold it, and, of course, the *pièce de résistance,* the address.

Now all I needed was a set of wheels. I got up and looked down at my attire. And a set of clothes, I thought. Luckily the laundry room was also in the basement. A pair of mom-jeans and a T-shirt were just the ticket. The twins' shared first vehicle was sitting at the end of the driveway, which had just enough of a slope that I would be able to coast away a little before starting the engine. The keys were on the rack in the garage, and Myrt and I were on our way to investigate the investigator.

Mason Brown sat in the driveway of Rachel de Luca's impressive home, watching the place long after everyone else had gone.

They needed a judge to sign a warrant before they could search the house, or the car, thanks to her high-end lawyer's intervention, and the delay was frustrating.

Rachel herself had been cooperative until her sister had come charging in like the cavalry. He supposed that could have been an act, but he didn't think so.

At least he was here, watching the place. No one was going to tamper with any evidence tonight. And by morning, noon at the latest, he'd have that warrant.

In the meantime, he pulled out the book the shrink had written. The guy's theory was ridiculous, of course.

But he'd seen Rachel's penchant for hot sauce first-hand. And she'd said that she'd never liked it before she got her eyesight back, and that she found it odd she loved it so much now.

His brother had loved hot sauce. Eric had sprinkled the stuff on everything.

*Coincidence.*

He'd figured he would toss the book, but instead, sitting here for the next several hours with nothing but time on his hands, he decided to skim through it again. And as he did, he started to question his own certainty. Dr. Vosberg had cited some pretty extreme cases. The vegan health nut who woke from her surgery with a craving for a Big Mac and fries—and later learned it had been her donor's final meal.

Then there was the man who'd never played a note of music in his life but sat down at a piano and started playing after receiving a heart from a concert pianist.

Was it possible that Eric's organs had carried his warped need to kill on to a new host? More than one, even?

And if so, was it someone else? He already knew it couldn't possibly be Rachel herself. She was the most logical candidate, given that she was connected to each of the murders since Eric's death, and he was very afraid the current killer was targeting her now, either to frame her for his crimes or to make her one of his victims.

But while he didn't think she was a murderer, he *was* convinced there was *something* going on.

He knew the house wasn't locked. Why lock it when there was a cop sitting in the driveway watching the place? He could easily go in and take a look around. But no. He was doing this by the book. He'd broken the law he was sworn to uphold once already, in covering up Eric's crimes, and that was enough for one lifetime, thanks very much. Not to mention it was biting him in the ass every time he turned around.

No, he'd just wait for the warrant. If there was evidence inside, it wasn't going anywhere.

Mason's new house was cute, a neat little turn-of-the-century farmhouse with a small barn off to the side. The house was white with red trim, the barn red with white trim, and both looked to be in decent shape, given their obvious age. The U-Haul trailer I'd seen in his apartment driveway the other day was parked in front, closed but not locked. That would be my first stop. I was half hoping all his belongings would still be in it, and I wouldn't have to break and enter a cop's home. I left Myrt in the car and went to see what I could find. But when I opened the trailer, jumping as the door squeaked on its hinges, I found it empty.

I closed the door again, then stayed quiet for a minute, just listening, watching the place. It was dark as hell, dead silent. I heard crickets somewhere, a night bird or two. But nothing else, except the wind and the cars passing on distant Route 81.

Okay, I had to do this. I had to.

I headed up the porch steps but then stopped halfway, because I'd caught sight of something in the barn, and for some reason it brought me up short. Through the slightly open door I could see the nose of a white pickup truck.

*Isn't this a stroke of luck? Little brother kept the truck.*

The voice in my head was so clear and so unexpected that I jumped as if I'd heard it out loud. And yet, despite how freaked out I felt, I found myself walking toward the barn, toward the truck. A few spindly weeds hidden in the tall grass grabbed at the legs of my borrowed jeans. They were Sandra's and a size too big, but the twins' would have been a foot too long and too tight to let me breathe. I'd opted for comfort. There was a night breeze, soft but chilly, sending shivers down my spine. Or at least I thought they were caused by the wind.

I stopped at the barn door, gripped it and slid it open. It had casters in a track up top that squealed in protest. I cringed at the noise, and something inside flapped its wings and moved deeper into the barn, scaring the hell out of me. Then all was quiet again.

I looked at the truck and just for the hell of it tried the driver's door.

It opened. Cool. There wasn't much inside. A pair of leather work gloves. A broken ratchet on the floor. A travel mug that hadn't seen a dishwasher in way too long.

I reached for the glove compartment and opened it, flipping through the stuff inside and finding an expired insurance card.

Eric Conroy Brown. It was my donor's truck, all

right. Maybe this was where I could find out more about him and get some answers to my questions.

I dug around the rest of the truck but found nothing of interest except for a pair of sunglasses I just loved for some reason and was tempted to steal. I put them back instead, got out and walked around to the back. The bed was lined with chrome toolboxes, all of which were locked.

I had to get into them. *I had to.* Impulsively, I ran my hands underneath the wheel wells, and lo and behold, I found a magnetic box affixed to the inside of one with a key inside. I climbed up on the tailgate and slipped the key into the lock of the first toolbox. It turned, and I lifted the lid.

The only thing inside—well, besides lots and lots of tools—was a satchel, like a duffel bag. Frowning, I pulled it out and sat down on the barn floor to unzip it.

Mason was reading about a perfectly wonderful husband who began beating his wife after receiving the kidney of a man who'd done time for domestic violence, when his cell phone rang. He closed the book and picked up the phone. "Brown."

"Hey, pal, it's Rosie. We got the okay to take the imprint from the tire of her car, but the judge said no more than that until he's had time to review the case. Chief Sub says just get the imprint and then surveil the place from outside until morning. Someone will relieve you then."

"All right."

He got out of the car, taking his kit with him. The garage had two overhead doors and a side door, which was the one he used to go inside. He found the light switch, flipped it on and headed over to take a rubbing from the tread of the car's rear tire. It was an easy task. Lay the paper on the tire, rub the charcoal back and forth to get the impression, take the whole thing in to the station and have an expert compare it with the cast taken from the tire tracks in the driveway. He also noted the size of the tires. To the naked eye, they were narrower than the tracks he'd seen earlier in the driveway, but a comparison would say so for sure.

Then he straightened and, in spite of the rule book, took a look at the inside of the garage, walking slowly around the car but carefully touching nothing on the way. There was a utility sink in the back. Something on the front of it caught his eye, and then his heart sank a little. It looked like blood, smeared along the top lip of the deep sink.

"Probable cause, right? I got permission to get the tire imprint. I saw blood. I had to follow up." He moved closer, half holding his breath.

Inside the sink was a hammer, and it was covered in blood, bone and what looked to him like brain matter.

"Shit, Rachel, what the fuck did you do?"

He turned, still without touching anything, and walked out of the garage. He was going to have to call this in and get the team back out here to photograph the hammer *in situ* before bagging it and taking it in.

A white sedan pulled to a stop in the driveway, bathing him in its headlights, as he headed toward his own car. Rachel got out of the driver's side, slammed the door and came striding toward him. "What the fuck are you doing in my garage, you fucking lunatic?"

"Getting a tire impression for evidence."

"Yeah, evidence. I don't think I trust you to be getting any evidence, Detective." She had a sheet of paper in her hand.

"What the hell is that supposed to mean?" And why was she so furious at him? He thought he'd convinced her that he was on her side.

"What the hell is *this* supposed to mean?" She waved the paper at him, storming closer.

"What is it?"

"I'm pretty sure it's your brother's suicide note. You know, the one confessing to thirteen murders?" She closed the distance between them and backhanded him hard across the face. "You gave me your brother's eyes knowing he was a fucking lunatic serial killer! What's wrong with you?" She drew back a fist to punch him in the chest. He just stood there and let her, so she pounded on him over and over, until, sobbing, still clutching the note, crumpled now in her fist, she sank to the ground.

He sank down beside her.

She pressed her fingers to her eyes. "I want them out. I want them out of my head!"

"I know, I know. I'm sorry."

"Sorry? You're *sorry?* What the fuck were you thinking, hiding this, Mason?"

He gripped her shoulders, stared hard into her eyes, willing her to look at him and see that he was being honest. "I was thinking about his pregnant wife. His two boys. Hell, Josh is only eleven. How was I supposed to tell them what their father was? It was enough that he was dead, that he couldn't hurt anyone else."

"But he is. Somehow, Mason, he still is. You realize that, don't you?"

"No. It has to be something else."

She lifted her head, her eyes red-rimmed and wet. "I want these eyes out of my head."

"I didn't know about your brother," he whispered. "I swear to God I didn't know."

"You knew about *yours,* though. I don't want to see what I'm seeing anymore. I can't handle it."

"You *have to* handle it, Rachel."

"Why? Just give me one good reason why!"

He looked toward the garage, looked at her again. "Because there's a bloody hammer in your garage. And I'm betting it's the one that killed your friend."

## 15

I stood up fast, then felt this whoosh, like everything in my body just sort of rushed down to my feet, and my head was left without anything to hold it up. It couldn't be true, what he was saying. It couldn't be.

He was grabbing my shoulders then, and I jerked away as if his touch was dirty. "Get off me."

"You were swaying like a punch-drunk boxer." But he let go.

I reached through the hurricane in my mind and grabbed hold of myself, yanked my brain into focus, looked him in the eye. "I want to see it. This hammer."

"You can't. I have to call it in, and the garage needs to be sealed off until then."

"Bullshit."

"I'm sorry, Rachel, this is procedure."

"And was it procedure to cover up the fact that your brother was the fucking Wraith?"

He flinched, looked away. I had him and he knew it, so I pushed my advantage. "Look, Detective, *I* know for a fact that I didn't kill Mott. So if the murder weapon is in my garage, it means someone put it there. Someone who's trying to set me up. Was it you, Mason?"

His head came up fast. "I wouldn't try to frame someone else for my brother's crimes."

"Yeah, and *I* wouldn't bash someone's brains in with a hammer. But I can't expect you to take my word for that."

He looked down. "You've been connected to every murder since Eric's death."

"Maybe because I have your twisted fuck of a brother's corneas."

He shook his head. "That's not even a real theory."

"You want to know what's real, Detective Brown? Let me just fill you in on what's real. You call in that bloody hammer, and I'm going to call in this suicide note." I held it up, realizing belatedly that I'd crumpled it up pretty badly in my fit of temper. I knew, too, that he could take it from me. He had a gun, and I didn't. "I made a copy in my sister's office before I came over, so don't even think about taking it from me. I'm not an idiot."

I had made no such copy, of course. I was, in fact, an idiot.

He surrendered. His stance softened; I felt it as well as saw it. It was in the breath he released, the slight bending of his spine, the movement as his shoulders relaxed a little. I thanked my stars he was too fucked up right now see through my bluff. I had no doubt that normally nothing so transparent would have worked on him. But he was off his game, because I knew his secret.

"That hammer is evidence," he said, and it had all

the earmarks of a last-ditch effort to convince me. "We cover it up, we lose whatever it might have told us."

"Then take it out of my garage and toss it in the weeds, over there where the guy's car was parked while he carried what was left of Mott up onto my front porch."

He looked where I pointed, toward the curve in my driveway. "They could still find your fingerprints, your DNA…."

"I promise you, they won't. I don't think I've picked up a hammer in a year—if ever. It's not a common tool among the blind. I didn't kill anyone, Mason."

He was watching my face like a cat watching a rat hole, waiting for me to give something away, or to reveal my true murderous nature. Then he said, "You drove all the way to Cortland in your sleep. How can you be sure you didn't kill someone?"

"And bring the body home in a car I don't own, and carry it—not drag it but carry it—to my own front door? Mott was a beanpole, but a heavy one. He weighed a solid one-ninety. There were no drag marks in the driveway, were there?"

"No. Blood trail, but no drag marks."

"No. And even in my sleep, I think I'd have brains enough to toss the hammer into the reservoir. I mean, it's right there, Mason." I gestured at the dark water just a few dozen yards from my home, out across the narrow dirt road. "And then somehow I drove away and left myself sleeping in the house, and then I got up and called you guys?"

"You were painting," he said. "You sure you didn't use a hammer?"

"I didn't use a hammer."

"To pull nails or hang pictures?"

"Haven't gotten that far yet."

"Do you own a hammer?"

My brows went up. "Yeah. There's a little girlie tool-box kit my sister got me when I first bought the place. Said everyone should have one. The hammer in it has a pink rubber grip and is about big enough to sink a thumbtack. And that's the only hammer I own."

He seemed to be thinking hard. Then he said, "Okay, we'll move the hammer."

*We?*

"And we have to be smart here. Make sure someone on the force finds it. Whoever he is, he knows he put the hammer there. He'll know we're onto him if it doesn't turn up in the evidence room."

"How will he know if it did or not?"

Mason shrugged. "Maybe he won't, but we can't take that chance. Like I said, we have to be smart. Stay one step ahead. Figure out why he's doing this."

My lips trembled. He'd believed I was innocent, earlier. I'd been sure of it. But now I wasn't, and I couldn't ask, because I was afraid of what his answer would be. And since when did it matter to me what this lying cop thought about me, anyway?

"You should get back to your sister's. I'll take care of the hammer."

The guilt he felt over that was in his voice, as thick as butter. "I'll do it. I don't want you risking your career for me."

"My career is already over," he said. Sad as hell, that tone. "It'll come out, what I did. It has to."

"Yeah, well, on that we're gonna have to agree to

disagree. I don't think it has to come out. I just think we have to find this killer. I don't suppose you know a private lab that would run a bloody hammer without asking questions, do you?"

He made a face.

"Right, I didn't think so." I heaved a sigh and walked into the garage, folding his brother's suicide note and tucking it into my pocket on the way. "Where is it?" I asked. My pretty car was sitting there like a silent, gorgeous witness.

"In the utility sink in back." I flipped on the light switch with my sleeve pulled over my hand. I don't know why. That switch was probably covered in my fingerprints already, but I did it anyway, then I walked back to the sink. I was such an idiot. I'd locked up the whole place last night but forgotten the garage's side door, probably because I hardly ever used the thing. Dammit.

"How did you find the note," he asked. "You ransack my whole place?"

"I didn't even go inside. It was pretty fucking strange, actually." I walked closer, then stopped, looking down at the disgusting tool in the deep stainless-steel sink.

"Strange how?" He came up behind me, looking at it over my shoulder.

I shrugged. "I glanced around the place, saw the truck in the barn, just showing where the door wasn't shut quite all the way, and I heard this stupid rhyme in my head."

"Rhyme?"

I nodded. *"Isn't this a stroke of luck? Little brother kept the truck."*

I felt him react. Shock bounced from him like a static

charge. He'd gone still, stopped breathing until he had to in order to say, "Where the hell did that come from?"

I turned to see that same sense of shock reflected in his eyes. "It's what I heard in my head. I told you, it's fucked up."

He said nothing.

"Why? Why are you looking at me like that?"

The man literally gave his head a shake. Like a wet dog shaking off the water. "Get the damned hammer. But don't touch it barehanded."

Frowning, knowing there was more—this guy was a bundle of secrets, but hell, how many could there be?—I looked around the garage and spotted my collection of grocery bags hanging from the wall in their cutesy paisley print holder. Amy's Christmas gift to me a year ago. I snagged a plastic bag from it. Using it as a glove, I picked up the hammer.

"Make sure it doesn't drip," he instructed.

"It's pretty…congealed. God, this is gross." I tried not to think about there being Mott's blood and God knew what else all over the hammer. I tried not to think about how scared he must have been, or how much it must have hurt to die like that, and I followed Mason out of the garage, holding the bloody hammer as far from my body as I could. Blood had a smell to it. It was a cross between fresh meat and sulphur. I'd never smelled it quite this strongly before and had to actively suppress the urge to gag.

Mason walked across the driveway, but I don't know how he didn't fall, because he was watching me the whole time. He finally stopped and pointed into the woods off to the right. "Toss it out that way."

I tossed it, feeling like it was the most important throw of my life. It landed with a rustling of underbrush. "What do I do with the bag?"

"Burn it."

"And the sink?"

"Bleach. But for crying out loud, rinse it really, really well afterward. Crime scene guys smell bleach, they get suspicious. Wear rubber gloves to clean it, and then burn the gloves, too."

I swallowed hard, thinking the guy knew a little too much about covering up crimes. But no, he was a cop, that was all.

I got another plastic bag and put the bloody one I'd used for a glove inside it. I'd add whatever rag I used to clean the sink, and the gloves I used.

He was staring at me. Looking me up and down.

"I'm not a murderer," I told him, and I held his eyes when I said it, knowing he had the same ability to sense a lie as I did. He could see the truth in my eyes.

"I believe you."

Good. God, the relief that rushed through me at those words was beyond any kind of reason, especially now that I knew the huge secret he'd been keeping from me. Now to push my luck. "Mason, I think part of your brother is still alive. I think it's inside me somehow. And I think it was inside Terry Skullbones when he killed that guy, and I think it's in whoever killed Mott and planted that hammer here."

He pressed his lips together. "I think that's probably the least likely of the half-dozen scenarios that could explain all this." Then he tipped his head and shrugged. "But let's play with it a little. Where's the bleach?"

I blinked, because the change of subject threw me, but I caught up quickly and walked to the far side of the garage where the washer and dryer were tucked out of the way in a corner. I grabbed the bleach and a pair of rubber gloves from the shelf, and headed back.

He took everything from me, turned on the water, pulled on the gloves and began cleaning the sink. I'd expected him to let me do that, but I wasn't going to argue.

"So you think Mott's killer is also an organ recipient?" he asked.

"That would make sense."

He nodded. "I agree with you that my brother's organs seem to be the connection between these crimes. I don't believe it's because he's somehow still killing from beyond the grave, but I do think he's the connection. Either way, the next step is the same."

"And what is the next step, Mason?"

"We find the recipients."

"All of them?"

"The ones local enough to be involved."

"How do we do that? The list is confidential. Can you get a court order or something?"

"I don't have anything solid to base one on. But I do have other resources. I hope to have the list before the weekend is out, and then I can start ruling them out one by one."

"I can help you do that." He started to say no, but I held up a hand. "This guy took my brother and my best friend. And my life is on the line here. You know I can read people just as well as you can, maybe better."

He didn't even argue with me as he rinsed and rinsed and rinsed the sink. I took the bleach back to its shelf, and returned to see him dropping the used gloves into the plastic bag. "Make sure it burns. Every trace of it."

The idea of burning plastic in my fireplace didn't appeal, but then I remembered the barbecue pit out back and thought that might be a better option. "I will."

"It'll be daylight soon."

"And my poor dog is still in the car. Do you have to sit here until morning?"

"I'm not supposed to leave the house until my relief gets here in the morning—to keep you from removing evidence until we have a search warrant." He said it with an ironic look at the bag in my hand.

"When will you have that?"

"After they compare the tire tread I took from your car with the one taken from your driveway last night, and the judge has time to review the rest of the case. And that'll happen in the morning, when I can get back to the station."

I heaved a sigh. "Well, if you're staying, then I'm staying. You want to come in?"

"We're not supposed to be in the house."

"So we'll get out before anyone knows the difference."

He shook his head.

"I'm tired. My dog is tired. We've already broken every freaking rule in your cop-shop handbook. *And* I've got a serial fucking killer after me. I'm going inside. You wanna come, then come. Because my feeling is that this sicko is watching my every move, and I would like to be out of his sight. Or do you disagree that he's after me?"

"He's after you. I just don't know if he wants to kill you or frame you for his crimes."

"Well, I'd just as soon not be alone when I find out." I went to the car and let Myrt jump out. As we headed to my front door, I picked up the bag full of evidence. "Besides, you can help me burn this stuff."

He made me burn it in the fireplace. Said the bastard might be watching and would catch on if we burned it outside. No shit, and he might have seen us plant that hammer just now too, I thought, but didn't say it. He was the cop. I was just the killer's latest victim.

So I sat staring into the flames of my gas fireplace as he wrapped the plastic up in newspaper and tossed it on top of the fake logs to burn. Some of the plastic residue dripped, but soon enough it burned, too.

"I hate this," I said, after a long time.

"Feeling watched, set up, all that?"

"Having your brother's corneas. I keep thinking, they saw my brother die. These eyes in my head saw my brother die."

He sighed, lowered his head. "It's just tissue. It hasn't got a mind or a soul."

"I had the first nightmare the first night after I got home. I saw him—*me,* only I knew it wasn't really me— standing over the body of a man who'd been bludgeoned to death with a hammer."

He handed me a glass of wine, and sank onto the sofa beside me. "Good wine," he said after a sip.

"I only buy good wine."

"So do you remember details? Of the dream?"

I took a sip, too, and tried to think back. "It was like

I was a passenger in his head, looking out through his eyes. I could see his arms, his hands, a little bit of the front of him if he looked down. He wore overalls, you know, like a uniform, with a patch on the left side, his left, the kind that usually has a name on it, but I wasn't looking at it dead on, so I couldn't read the name."

"What about his hands?"

"Gloves."

"And the hammer?"

"Red handle with a black rubber grip. Smooth nose, not grilled like the second one."

He nodded.

"I could feel how much he'd gotten off on the killing. But then, right after, there was this awful sense of grief. Heartbreak. It was like two different people. And I remember him thinking how much he hated cleaning up afterward."

"Who?"

"I don't know." I blinked at him. "Could your brother have had multiple personalities or something?"

"No."

"You sure?"

He sighed and leaned back on the sofa.

"Do you think he'll try to kill me, Mason?"

He looked at me like he was going to give me some bullshit reassurance that he didn't believe, but when he met my eyes, he gave up on that and offered me honesty instead. "I don't know, Rachel. I'm gonna try to find him before he has the chance."

I nodded. "Can't ask for more than that." I got some clean clothes, even though I'd been told earlier that I couldn't take anything from the house. I knew he figured that bridge had been burned by now. Still, I didn't want to cause him more trouble, so I was careful to leave everything exactly the way it had been the night before. Even rinsed the wineglasses and put them away.

When I joined him on the couch again, he reached for the remote, flicked on the television set and slid a little closer to me. I don't know when he put his arm around me and I leaned my head over on his shoulder, but that was the way we were when I woke up to the sun streaming in through the windows and my sister yelling at me through the front door. I was stunned when I went outside to find David Heart standing there beside her.

"Where did you go, Rachel? I was worried sick when I woke up and found you gone!" That was Sandra.

David was talking at the same time. "Why are there police here? And who the hell is that guy?"

I looked past him. Sure enough, a cop car was pulling into the drive. Thankfully Mason's partner, Rosie, was the one behind the wheel, and he was alone.

"Don't act all proprietary with me, David. We've had three dates." I called Myrt, and she jumped into action for once, joining me outside the door but carefully skirting the spot where Mott had been lying. Just like Mason and I did.

Mason pulled the door closed behind us, and we all moved down the steps and onto the lawn.

"Was he here *all night?*" David was yelling now.

Sandra blinked and turned to him. "Did you not get the part about the three dates? And shouldn't you be more concerned about what happened last night that warranted an overnight with a cop?"

"What's going on, Rachel?" David said, after a dismissive look at my sister that effectively ended our relationship. Not that there had ever been one.

I took his arm, moved him aside and said, "David, what the fuck are you doing at my front door at this hour of the morning? No, wait never mind. It doesn't matter. I have a lot going on here. It was fun going out with you, but I think it's safe to say we're not compatible. I'll see you at group, okay?"

He blinked as if I was speaking in tongues or something. "You're breaking up with me?"

"We're not going steady, David. We had three dates. I'm just saying there won't be a fourth."

"Is it because of *him?*"

I gaped, then clamped my jaw. "Go home, David. I've got my hands full here."

He stared at me, first hurt, then angry. Angry enough to send a chill down my spine. But he finally turned and stomped to his car, then spun the tires and left. I shook my head and wondered if the cops should maybe get a cast of *those* tire tracks, then I glanced toward Mason.

He met my eyes and nodded just once. Flawless communication. It would be done. I smiled my thanks and went to deal with my sister.

Mason's relief showed up right behind Rosie, while Rachel was arguing with her sister and just after the jerk she'd been dating had left in an angry hurry. Fortunately they were both outside by then, trying to look like they'd never been otherwise.

He said his goodbyes and headed in to drop off the tire tread rubbing.

Dammit, he liked the woman. He liked her spunk,

her sarcasm, her wit, and he found her sexy as the devil. There had been some serious chemistry going on last night on that sofa. Hell, there'd been serious chemistry going on since they'd met, but he knew following up on it was a bad idea. More than bad. Idiotic. Suicidal. She was a suspect, though she was going to be cleared, if only because he'd helped her cover up the evidence. Oddly he felt less guilty about that than he did about hiding his brother's ugly truth. Maybe because he knew Rachel was innocent. Didn't doubt it. Hadn't in a while now.

And now he had the weekend off, and he had the boys coming over to help him unpack, and spend the night. He'd invited Rachel and she was going to come over, too, unless all this chaos had changed her plans. The search warrant for her house would either come through in his absence or it wouldn't. He needed this downtime. He needed it badly.

And the boys needed *him*.

Before he left, he managed to pull Rachel aside long enough to tell her not to let herself be alone for a while. Not until they got to the bottom of this whole thing. She made a face, and he knew she wasn't loving the idea. "Fiercely independent" was a term people threw around a lot, but in her case it fit. Especially the fierce part.

He went to the station to clock out twenty hours after his shift had begun, mentally counted up the overtime pay and drove back to his new home in Castle Creek.

He drove his aging big black beast along the rutted dirt driveway, past the weed patch of a lawn and right up to the lonely little farmhouse, fantasizing about adding a four-wheel drive vehicle to the "family" and turning that big barn out back into Taj Ma Garage. The hills that surrounded the place were lined in deep green pines with patches of hardwoods here and there, mostly bare now, but they'd been vivid only a few days ago. Beyond the trees, the sun was climbing into a blue sky. But the peace that usually settled over him when he arrived here was lacking this morning. He was worried. His secret wasn't a secret anymore. Rachel knew the truth about his brother, about the evidence he'd hidden. And while he didn't think she would tell, he didn't really know her well enough to be sure of that, did he?

So why was he more worried about her than about the damage she could do to his life?

Didn't make sense, but there it was. He was worried about her.

This being his case, he probably should have taken her in already for questioning, whether as a suspect or simply because a body had landed literally on her doorstep. It was probably going to look fishy if he didn't do it soon.

He knew she didn't have anything to do with the murders, but he had yet to come up with an explanation for what she knew and how she knew it.

He glanced down at the book on the seat. He'd read the entire thing nearly twice through, and no matter how hard he tried, he couldn't dismiss the possibility that there might some truth to it. Maybe it was time to give Dr. Vosberg another call.

He shut off the engine and headed into the barn to move his brother's truck. The boys would be over later, and there was no point having it in plain sight and reminding them of their loss. He drove it into the garage-slash-shed attached to the house, red and white like the barn, all of it peeling, and closed the double doors. Then he headed into the house and tried to distract himself by starting to do some unpacking. Within an hour Marie showed up to drop the boys off. If he hadn't heard her car, the sound of cattle stampeding over the front porch would have been a dead giveaway.

Joshua barreled through the front door first and plowed into him for a hug, almost taking him down in the process. "This is such a cool place, Uncle Mason! The barn is awesome. Can we explore in there?"

"Sure you can," Marie said without asking him first. She was standing in the doorway, leaning against the frame, one hand on her baby bump. Jeremy was a few steps ahead of her, dwarfing the kitchen with his height. He had to be six-two already. He'd really grown over the summer. "Jeremy, take your brother out to the barn."

Jeremy rolled his eyes. "I came to help Uncle Mason move in, not babysit."

"I don't need a babysitter! I'm almost twelve, for cripe's sake."

"Easy, boys. I'll go with you. I haven't explored the whole thing myself, so I don't know for sure how safe it is yet."

Marie lifted her brows. "I should have asked first. Sorry, Mason."

"It's fine. You boys can check out the rest of the house if you want," Mason said, and Joshua was gone like a shot. Jeremy shrugged and went after his kid brother, long lazy strides on great big feet that didn't try to step lightly.

"Thanks for bringing them," Mason said.

"Thanks for having them." She looked around the kitchen as she straightened and stepped farther inside, eyeing the red-and-white floor tiles. "It's nice. Needs some new appliances and a woman's touch, though."

"That's what I've got you and Mother for. Any ideas?"

She shrugged, walking through the little kitchen. It was old-fashioned, with white painted cupboards and tan Formica countertops, a double stainless-steel sink with a window behind it, and a giant of a refrigerator from the 1960s that looked and ran like new, according to the Realtor. The range was newer, and he hated it and hoped to find a vintage model to fit in its spot. No dishwasher, no island, nothing fancy. And he liked it that way.

"You going to modernize or go retro? Looks like you could swing either way."

"Retro, I think. Really old-fashioned."

"Classic, like your car." She nodded. "That's one thing you and your brother had in common, that love of old cars."

"That we did."

The sadness came back into her eyes. It rarely went away these days. "I know I said I'd help, but…"

"You go enjoy your weekend," he said. "I can handle the boys from here. You need some downtime. A little mental health break."

"Actually, I was thinking about a day at the salon. I just don't want to saddle you with—"

"There's no saddling happening here. I've been looking forward to spending time with the boys," he said. "We'll have a guys' day, you know?"

"They need it," she said softly. "And you're a good man to realize it."

"I love them, Marie."

"They love you, too." She sighed. "Okay, I'm going. Might even get a massage while I'm at it. Walk me out? The lazy bums left their backpacks in the car."

He nodded and then followed her out the door and over to the minivan, opened the sliding side door and pulled out the two backpacks he found there. "Is that it?"

"Yeah, that's all." She got in, sending him a wave and looking at least a little bit relieved, he thought.

"I'll see you tomorrow when I bring them home. Bye, Marie. Try to have a good day today, all right?"

"I will. Thanks again, Mason." And then she was pulling away, and he was heading through the front door and kicking it shut behind him.

The boys were in the kitchen waiting for him, so he slung their backpacks at them. "So, whattaya think of the place?"

"I think I want to see that barn," Josh said.

Jeremy elbowed him. "It's awesome, Uncle Mason. You've got a ton of room. You planning to get married and have kids or something?"

"Not in this lifetime, Jer."

"That's a relief."

"You should get a dog or something, then," Josh put in. "A dog would love it here."

A dog. Hell, that wasn't a bad idea. He'd never been able to have one as a kid, because his parents would never let him. The suggestion brought Rachel's chubby little bulldog to mind, and he caught himself smiling a little.

His cell phone chirped, and he pulled it out, immediately feeling dread pooling in his chest. Had something happened to Rachel?

Rosie's smiling mug was on his screen and he tapped to answer and brought the phone to his ear. "What's up, partner?"

"Got that search warrant for Ms. de Luca's place. Inside and out. Thought you'd want to be the one to tell her. Team's on the way over there now."

"They need me to lead it?"

"Chief's taking the lead himself."

That didn't feel right. Felt like maybe the chief was already wondering about him and Rachel. Or maybe he was just being paranoid. "Can you go along, Rosie? Make sure it goes down as easy as possible, don't let her stuff get trashed."

"All over that, my friend. You gonna call her?"

"Yeah, I'll do it now. Thanks for the heads-up." He sighed, eyeing the boys and then the phone. Rachel was going to have a shit fit about the cops pawing through her stuff, even though she knew they needed to find that hammer if they hoped to use whatever evidence might be on it. He couldn't risk her blurting out something she shouldn't in a moment of frustration.

"You guys ever meet a famous writer before?"

"No," they chimed in unison.

Jeremy had literary aspirations himself, so this ought to be an easy sell. "You want to?" he asked.

# 16

My attorney had earned his pay by telling me the cops had no right to keep me out of my own home, and that he'd convinced the chief I couldn't very well eliminate evidence with a cop watching the place. He told me not to start a fire in the fireplace, so as not to set off any suspicions, though.

I didn't bother telling him that I'd already burned all the evidence necessary, so I wouldn't have to.

By eleven the police were at the door with their promised search warrant, and my nemesis wasn't even among them. Even though I knew this was coming, that it was the way it had to go, I still wanted to bite nails in half as I stood there holding the door open but blocking it with my body.

My phone rang. I already had it in my hand. Glancing down at the screen and seeing Mason Brown's name, I held up a finger at the waiting jackbooted thugs, closed the door and took the call.

"Rachel, it's Mason. How are things?"

"Fine, if you don't count the army of Nazis demanding entrance into my house."

"Yeah, I was calling to warn you. Your lawyer couldn't hold them off any longer."

I sighed. "Mason, am I a suspect or not?"

"No. No, you're not. At least not as far as I'm concerned. You have nothing to hide, right?"

"Not that I know of, but if you recall—" I lowered my voice to a whisper "—I didn't know about what we found in the garage last night, either. How do we know this lunatic didn't plant something in my house?"

"Your alarm system was still activated. That's probably why he left it in the garage and not the house. The garage door isn't wired. Just the one from the garage to the house. Something you should remedy, by the way."

"Yeah. I'm adding it to the list." I sighed. "Mason, what if he knew the code? What if he switched the system off and back on again? What if he put something else here to make me look even more guilty?"

"He didn't. The alarm hadn't been switched off all night."

My brows bent until they touched. "How do you know that?"

"We checked with the company."

"And they just told you?"

"We didn't ask for anything sensitive enough to worry them. And for what it's worth, Rachel, that bit of information has you cast in the role of potential target more than suspect. That's a good thing."

"None of this is a good thing, Mason."

He sighed into the phone. I imagined I felt the warm breath of it on my ear, then batted the thought away. "What should I do?" God, did I sound enough like a helpless female yet?

"Tell them to search the place with your blessings, that you've been terrified by all this, that you think you might be in danger, and then—"

"Don't be ridiculous. I'm not going to lie to make them feel sorry for me."

He drew a breath. "Are you saying you're not terrified and don't think you might be in danger? Because if that's true, you're a fool, Rachel. And I know you're no fool."

I took a deep breath, and for the first time considered that he might be right. I mean, I didn't like admitting it, I didn't like even thinking about it, but if there was any chance this guy might come after me, then I really ought to be scared. And he kind of was doing that already, right?

A chill went up my spine, and I resented the hell out of Mason for putting it there. "So I tell them to go ahead and search, tell them I'm afraid I might be in danger, and then…?"

He paused for a beat too long, then said, "Then come over here."

"Over…where?"

"My place. I invited you to help me unpack and move in, remember? And I already know you have the address." That last bit was delivered with just a hint of teasing sarcasm.

It was my turn to pause for a beat too long. "Um, Mason, I don't know what's…you know, I'm not looking for…um…"

"My nephews are here. We're unpacking and getting the place into some kind of livable state. We're ordering pizza and wings for lunch. You'll be safe here, and not sitting there stewing and feeling violated every time an officer opens a drawer."

I lowered my head. He wasn't up to anything. I wondered why I felt disappointed instead of relieved. "What are you getting on the pizza?"

"Hold on." Then I heard a muffled yell. "Guys, what do you want on your pizza?" followed by a jumbled multipart reply that included ham and pineapple and pepperoni and sausage.

"No mushrooms?" I asked.

"Why? You want mushrooms?"

"I hate mushrooms."

"So do we."

I smiled a little bit. "Then you're on. I'll see you in a little while."

"Rachel?"

"Yes?"

"Apply some of the positive Pollyanna crap from your books to the cops outside. It'll go a long way. Crank that smile up to high beam, okay?"

I sighed, but said, "See you later," and ended the call. Then I opened my front door. "All right, sorry about that." I extended a hand to the guy in the suit who seemed to be in charge and put on the same persona I used for all my talk show appearances. "Come on in."

The cop's face registered surprise, but then he composed himself to all business again and shook my hand. "Chief Subrinsky, ma'am. I know this is uncomfortable for you, but—"

"Actually, I don't mind at all, and I apologize for my reluctance earlier. To be honest, Chief, I'm scared to death. I don't know how I've attracted the attention of a serial killer—maybe because of my persistence in trying to find out what happened to my brother. But now that I have, I'm terrified I might be next on his list."

He frowned a little, but nodded. "We're going to do our best to make sure that doesn't happen."

I stepped back. "Please come in. Search all you want. I hope you don't mind but I would rather not be here while you do. Would you lock up when you leave?"

"Of course."

"What about my car? Am I allowed to take it now?"

"Not yet, I'm afraid."

That pissed me off. I bit back my knee-jerk reply and offered a calmer one. "It's a collector's car, as you can tell. Please don't damage it."

"We will treat your possessions as carefully as we would our own, ma'am," the chief said.

Then a more familiar voice said, "I promise, Ms. de Luca, everything will be handled with care." I smiled when I saw that Mason's partner was among the cops filing into my domain, and nodded my thanks to Rosie, then turned. "Myrtle? Where are you girl?"

I heard movement from beyond the sofa, and then Myrt dragged her butt into sight, shuffling and hanging her head, eyes only half open.

"You want to go for a ride in the car?"

Her head came up and tilted all the way to one side, ears perking.

"Well, go get your stuff then."

Turning, she trotted away, and came back with her tinted goggles and pretty yellow scarf in her mouth. The cops all laughed, and several of them bent to pat her as she moved past them, stopping at my feet.

"Come on, dog." I squatted and gathered her up into my arms, then carried her past the half-dozen men and out to my nieces' car, which was mine for the day, according to Sandra, though I wasn't sure Misty or Christy had approved that arrangement.

Nor was I sure they would appreciate the bulldog ass sitting on the plush front seat, but that was the least of my worries just then.

I showed up at Mason's with pizza and wings in the backseat, wafting their deliciousness through the car like some kind of ingenious torture device. Halfway there, I'd had another call from Mason to say the local pizza place didn't deliver, so he wondered if I would mind picking up their order on the way. He'd even reassured me that he'd paid for it over the phone.

And the truth is, I wouldn't have minded if manners hadn't dictated that I *not* pull off onto the shoulder and wolf down a slice or two without them.

As it was, the ten minutes from the little bar-slash-pizza place to Mason's house were brutal. Myrtle thought so, too. The measure of her discomfort and yearning for a taste was in direct proportion to the length of the drool strand extending from her left lip and about to drop off onto the seat of the twins' car. I willed it to hang steady as we bounced over the driveway and up to the house. Then the three Y-Chromers were spilling onto the porch and I was too distracted to pay attention.

The older boy was taller than his uncle by a couple of inches, with long arms and wide shoulders, but otherwise skinny. He had a neck like Ichabod Crane with an

Adam's apple I swear was the size of an *actual* apple. I wouldn't have known if he was sixteen or twenty-three, to be honest. He had brown hair that was apparently being grown out. It was at that awkward stage where it flipped a little at the ends.

The younger boy was cute as hell. His hair was reddish-brown, shorter, swept all forward into uneven bangs, and he had freckles.

Both boys were smiling, and I was glad to see it, reminding myself that they'd lost their father not long ago.

Their father. A serial killer. God, it was hard to reconcile that with the two ordinary-looking kids in front of me. Going by their smiles, Mason must be doing a good job of keeping their minds off their recent tragedy.

I got out and went around to open the passenger door for Myrtle. She jumped down immediately, the way she always did.

"Oh, man! Is that your dog?" said the younger boy, and he came running, and dropped right down onto the ground in front of Myrt, rubbing her head and ears. Her bottom teeth emerged and she started to wiggle her butt, a sure sign of delight.

"What a cool dog."

"Her name's Myrtle." I bent down to take off her goggles and scarf. She always wore them in the car, even if it was dark. Habit.

"Myrtle!" The boy laughed, and I snapped a leash on her collar, then handed him the other end. "You're Josh, right?" I asked.

He nodded and took the leash from me.

"Well, Josh, I'm Rachel. Myrtle is old and she's blind, so you have to lead her wherever she goes."

"She's blind? Awww, poor doggy." He petted her some more, looking sadly at her eyes.

"No, she's a very happy, very lucky dog. She barely notices that she can't see. All her other senses make up for it by being much sharper. At home she finds her way around fine. But this is a new place, so she'll need a guide."

"I'll show you around, Myrtle." Josh stood up, proudly holding the leash. "Come on, come with me."

Myrt turned her head in my direction. "Go ahead," I said. "I'll be right behind you with that pizza you've been drooling over." Oh, yeah, right, drool. I glanced through the still open door and saw the splotch of it on the seat, then yanked a napkin from the stack I'd stuffed in my pocket and wiped it up.

Then I opened the back door to get the pizzas, but by that point Mason and the tall skinny boy were there, and Mason reached past me to pick up the food.

"I've got it. Rachel, this is Jeremy. And you've already met Josh."

"Yeah, I think I might have trouble prying my dog away from him, to be honest. Look at that."

The two followed my gaze. Joshua was picking Myrt's front paws up one at a time and setting them on the first step, talking to her as he went. I grinned, and my heart went a little soft. Kids and dogs, right? They'll do it every time. I turned my grin on Jeremy. "It's nice to meet you."

"Same here." He looked at Mason. "So are you two, like…dating or something?"

"No!"

We both said it at the same time, with the same horrified inflection and extra volume. I shook my head, then looked at Mason, wondering just what he had told the boys about who I was. I was pretty sure it wasn't that I was the person who'd wound up wearing their father's eyes.

Mason started for the house, and Jeremy and I fell into step on either side of him. We caught up to Josh on the front porch as he was easing Myrtle through the door. She didn't need anywhere near the amount of help he was providing, but she didn't seem to be minding all the attention.

"Rachel's had some weird stuff happening out at her place. The police are looking into it," Mason said. "That's how we met."

"That's *not* how we met," I countered. We went inside, and Mason set the pizzas on the table. Jeremy was already dealing paper plates like a round of poker, and Mason headed to the fridge to pull out a two-liter bottle of root beer as Josh escorted Myrtle into the room. So I sat down, as eager as they apparently were. "We met for the first time when your uncle hit me with his car."

The boys both stopped what they were doing to stare at me. "No way!" Josh said.

"Yeah, but it was my fault. I walked out in front of him. He probably didn't tell you, but I used to be blind."

"Just like Myrtle?" Joshua asked.

"Uh-huh. But I had an operation, and now I'm not."

"Wow."

"That's an understatement."

Jeremy sat down and opened one of the pizza boxes.

Then Josh grabbed the first slice, put it on a paper plate and laid it on the floor in front of Myrtle. I opened my mouth to object, then closed it again. Who was I to argue with a gift like that?

Mason, bringing glasses filled with ice to the table, sent me an *Is that okay?* look, and I shrugged back an *Of course it is* reply.

Myrtle sniffed for about a half second, then went to town, and even Jeremy was smiling and shaking his head.

It was a good time, scarfing down pizza and wings and root beer with Mason and his nephews. But I kept thinking, *So these are the sons of Mason's brother the serial killer.* Hard to believe. They were normal. They were great kids, actually. I mean, animals know these things, right? Myrtle was practically claiming Joshua as her own puppy before the meal had ended, and I didn't think it was *entirely* because he'd plied her with pizza.

After lunch she stuck to him like glue while the three of them showed me around the place, and then we argued good-naturedly about the placement of the living room furniture, all of it brand-new. Some pieces still had bits of plastic clinging to them. And that reminded me that Mason's brother—the boys' father—had shot himself on Mason's old couch.

Okay, all right, I got it. I got why he couldn't tell them the truth. I got why he hid the suicide note. I met his eyes, and saw him wondering, and I gave just the slightest nod to tell him that yeah, I understood now.

You couldn't tell a kid like Joshua that his dad had been a murderer. Who could do something like that?

And Jeremy's head would melt if he ever knew. Being a teenager was hard enough.

Yeah, Mason had done the right thing. He'd done the only thing he could have. I really believed that. The only thing he could possibly have done. I couldn't be angry at him for that.

We unpacked for hours. I mean *hours,* and I put myself in charge of the list of must-haves as we went along. Top thing on it was curtains. He had maybe three sets from his apartment, and they were not only ugly but too small for any of the windows. Besides which, he had a lot more windows to cover now.

We worked until almost ten, and I was shocked when I saw the time on my cell phone, then added "Clocks" to the list.

"I'm starved," Jeremy said.

"You're always starved," Mason replied.

"I'm starved, too. We totally worked through dinner." I sank onto the new sofa, green and colonial-style, which made it look both out of date and a perfect fit for the house. "How about we finish off the leftovers?"

"And watch a movie?" Mason asked. He and Jeremy had managed to anchor a flat-screen TV to the wall, making it the most modern-looking thing in the entire house, though there was no cable hooked up yet—if it was even available this far out of town, which I doubted.

"How are we going to watch a movie?" I didn't see a DVD player, just a game system I assumed was for the boys' entertainment.

"We'll stream one through the Xbox," Mason said.

I lifted my brows, impressed. "I had no idea those things could do anything more than play games."

"You've got so much to learn," Mason said, then he crooked a brow at me. "Have you ever even *played* a video game?"

I pointed at my eyes. "Blind for twenty years, remember?"

He smiled slowly, as if he was up to something. "Screw the movie, then. Did you guys see which box had the games?"

Jeremy crossed the living room, picked up a backpack, brought it to the coffee table and dumped it. "No, but Josh brought every game we own. I kept telling him we were only staying overnight."

"I wanted us to have a wide selection," Joshua said, sounding important.

"Pick an easy one, okay? I don't want to look like too much of an idiot."

They grinned at me, probably knowing that wasn't possible. But Joshua fished out an innocuous-looking copy of Super Mario Bros., and it was on.

I don't think I ever laughed so hard in my entire life.

And then everything stopped. Everything.

I dropped my controller, because I couldn't see the TV screen anymore. Everything went dark, and for a horrifying instant, I thought my eyesight had blinked out. Turned off. Like a light. But then I realized the volume of the noise around me had turned itself down, too. It was there, but muffled, dull. Maybe Mason was saying my name. I'm not sure. But I was seeing…something. Bushes. Branches. Trees. Brush. All blocking my vision. And then my hand—*no, not my hand. That's not my hand at all*—came up. Black glove. Big hand, male hand. And it moved some of the branches aside. And there was a house.

*My house.*

*The killer is in the brush watching my house.*

# 17

"Rachel, hey, come on." Mason took her by the shoulders, shook her a little. She'd gone weird all of a sudden, dropping her controller and just sitting there staring straight ahead, seeing God only knew what. Not the here and now, that was for sure.

Another vision?

"Rachel?" he said again.

Suddenly Joshua threw a glass of water into her face—just grabbed his glass and splashed it on her. Just like that.

She blinked and scrunched up her face, turning away in reaction. Then she wiped her cheeks with one hand.

"Joshua, what the hell?" Jeremy asked.

Joshua shrugged. "It's what they always do on TV."

"TV isn't real life, dork."

"Well, it worked, didn't it?" Josh yanked a couple of paper towels from the roll they'd been using in lieu of napkins and handed them to her. "You okay now, Rachel?" he asked, all innocence.

She blinked a few times and wiped her face with the towels. "Yeah, I'm okay. Thanks, Josh."

"Anytime," he said. "What happened?"

"I don't know." But she sent Mason a look that said she *did*.

Mason said, "Why don't you guys play a round without us? We need to clean up this mess, and then we all need to hit the hay. It's after midnight."

"Okay, Uncle Mason." Josh picked up the controller that Rachel had dropped, her lapse forgotten. Jeremy wasn't so easy to brush aside. He was looking at her oddly and, Mason figured, trying to guess what had just happened. He wasn't going to guess right.

"It's all right, Jer. Go ahead, finish up the level and don't forget to save our game so we can pick up where we left off next time."

"You sure I can't help?"

"I'm good, Jeremy," Rachel said. "But you're a great guy to offer. Thanks."

Jeremy shrugged and returned to his game. But Mason knew that wasn't the end of it. There was never an end to anything where Jeremy was concerned. He observed everything, remembered everything and was curious about everything.

Rachel got to her feet, seemed to take a second to make sure she was steady, then picked up the empty pizza box and wing container, all but overflowing with saucy bones. She headed for the kitchen. Mason grabbed the paper plates, empty glasses and wadded-up napkins, and followed.

When they were out of earshot, he looked at her expectantly, waiting for her to speak. She shoved the refuse into the wastebasket, folding the pizza box in half to make it fit. Then she turned to face him, leaned back against the counter, crossed her arms over her chest and said, "He's at my house."

It hit him like a mallet between the eyes. *"What?"*

"The killer is at my house. He's standing in the bushes, right near where we threw…what we threw. He's watching the place."

Mason didn't know if he believed her or not, but he didn't see the need to waste any time. He pulled his cell phone out and started to text Rosie.

Rachel moved closer and put a hand over his. "You can't do that."

He lifted his head, met her eyes.

"What will they think if you call them and tell them to go out there and look in the brushy woods near the edge of my driveway, and then, when they do, they find…the hammer?" She barely whispered the final two words. "That's gonna look suspicious as hell, Mason."

"If he's there, they can catch him."

"And how are you going to say you knew?"

"Rosie's on surveillance tonight. I trust my partner," Mason said. "He won't sell me out without asking me how I knew first, and he'll come up with an explanation. I promise." He finished the text. Make excuse to check woods near edge of drive, opposite garage. He clicked Send.

Seconds ticked past before the reply came. One letter. K.

Then nothing. Minutes ticked past, and still only silence.

Finally his phone rang. He looked at Rosie's face on the screen, then grabbed Rachel's arm and moved them out to the front porch before putting the call on speaker. "I'm here, Rosie. What did you find?"

Rachel was pale, as nervous as he'd ever seen her. As nervous as she had ever let him see her, he amended. He was pretty sure she, like any sane person, was terrified over everything that had been going on, but unlike most people, she didn't like showing vulnerability. Weakness. She had a tough shell, but inside she was afraid. Shaken to the core.

"How did you know, buddy?" Rosie asked.

"What did you find?"

"Someone was out there. Not long ago, either. Footprints were fresh. And I repeat, how did you know?"

"Anonymous tip. I can't tell you more than that. Can you cover for me?"

Rosie hesitated, then, "Yeah. I'll say I thought I saw something out of the corner of my eye. I called for backup, and they're close. If he was on foot, we'll get him."

"They won't get him," Rachel whispered. "He's long gone."

"Let me know what you find, okay, pal?"

"Will do."

Mason disconnected, and looked at Rachel. She shook her head at him. "Don't."

"Don't what?"

"Don't look at me like I'm some broken fragile flower in need of saving. I'm not that."

"No, not a fragile flower. More a milk thistle. Pretty purple flower that stings like hell." He drew a breath. "Look, I don't think you need saving. I do think you'd be an idiot to go home tonight. I'm a cop, and I'm armed, and *I* wouldn't want to spend the night there with this maniac on the loose."

Her forehead puckered in thought. "Yeah, that *would* be stupid, wouldn't it? I wonder if he plans to kill me."

"That's what he does."

"Not women, though."

"But he knows that you're...inside his head somehow." He rolled his eyes. "Listen to me. What the hell am I saying? Inside his head?"

"I *am* inside his head. You fucking know I am, and you fucking know why. Don't you think we're beyond denying it any longer, Mason? I'm in his head because I have a piece of your warped brother in me, and he has a piece in him, and that connects us somehow. Just like it connected me with Terry Skullbones."

He drew a breath, then let it out slowly. "Okay, okay, I admit it looks like it might be true."

"Might be?" It was her turn to roll her eyes, and then she turned away.

"I don't know how, but...but, Rachel, doesn't that make it even more important for you to stay alive? You might be the only person who can help me catch this guy."

As he said the words, he realized they were true and turned her to look at him. "If he's figured that out, then you really aren't safe."

Not a single sarcastic reply emerged. She just lowered her head, so her hair fell down over one eye. "Thanks for believing me. Finally."

"You're welcome. Please don't go home tonight."

She looked him in the eyes then and pushed her hair behind her ear. "I'll go back to my sister's."

"It's almost one. Just stay here. It'll be morning before we know it, anyway." When she didn't seem to
jump on the idea, he said, "We've got chaperones, Rachel. You'll be perfectly safe. I promise not to try to
seduce you."

"You think I'm worried?"

"Come on, soothe my pride, act worried."

She smiled. It was an unwilling smile, but in a second
it was full-blown and he had to return it. "You know you
could charm the socks off a centipede, right?" she asked.

"I've been told as much, though never in quite those
words." And he'd never expected to hear it from her.
"Spend the night with me, Rachel."

She met his eyes for a moment, then turned and
walked back inside. "Okay."

So Myrtle and I spent the night in Mason's bed. He
slept on the new sofa, and his nephews were in one of
the other bedrooms on the bunk beds we'd put together
earlier.

I didn't sleep well, partly because I was in a strange
bed, but mostly because a serial killer was stalking me.
Okay, and maybe a little bit because I was spending
the night so close to Mason, a guy I wanted to bang in
the worst way, even though my gut said it would be a
bad idea.

I hadn't contemplated why overly much. But since
I had time on my hands, I let my thoughts go there. I'd
been blind through my teens and my entire adult life. I
hadn't dated. I hadn't flirted. I hadn't had any steady re-
lationships, nothing beyond a couple of poorly-thought-
out one-night stands that meant nothing. Now I was a

sighted adult for the first time in my life. I needed to figure out what that meant, who the sighted Rachel was, before I brought another person into my life. And there was part of me that knew sleeping with Mason would mean just that—bringing him into my life. It wouldn't be a meaningless roll in the hay. Not with him.

So there couldn't be any roll in the hay at all. Period.

I tossed and turned, dozed and started awake a dozen times over, and by six-thirty was up and taking a shower in the adjoining bathroom, where the only supplies were strictly male. Mason was apparently a man's man. He had one single product in his shower, a combination body wash, shampoo, conditioner that I hadn't even known existed. It smelled rough and woodsy. Familiar, too. It smelled like him, I realized, as I sudsed up and rinsed off again. The stuff wasn't bad, though I imagined my hair would look like hell all day.

*Look at me, being all girlie-girl and worrying about my hair. Since when, Rache?*

I shrugged off the voice of my inner bitch, then wrapped myself up in a towel and walked back into the bedroom just as the door opened and Mason walked in.

He stopped dead and stood there looking me up and down. I stopped, too, holding on to my towel and starting to shiver. He didn't retreat and I wasn't about to, so I said, "My eyes are up here, Mason," while pointing at them for him.

His gaze rose and I said, "That's better. Did you want something?"

"Yeah."

I tipped my head to one side. He looked completely flustered and I felt a little flattered by it. "Well?"

"Um…"

And then someone walked in behind him, a tiny curvy big-haired blonde with cleavage up to her chin. She spotted me in my towel and her jaw literally dropped.

"Who is this, Mason?" she asked in a squeaky voice that made me want to pull out her tonsils, preferably through her nose.

*That was completely unjustified.*

*Not it wasn't. Look at her, she's everything I hate in a woman.*

*Yeah. She is. You're right.*

My inner self agreed with me for a change. Imagine that.

"Mason, who *is* this?" she demanded again.

*"This,"* I replied, "is someone who wishes you would get the fuck out of her bedroom and let her get dressed." I held up an arm, forefinger extended, though the middle one was itching to take its place. "Out. Now."

"Come on, Patty, I'll explain in the hallway." Mason took the bimbo's arm and turned her around, and I told myself I was being unfair. I had nothing to base the term on except her low-cut blouse, overdone eyeliner and big hair. Okay, yeah, that was plenty. Bimbo.

"Sorry, Rache," he said as he hustled her out and closed the door.

I turned to look at Myrtle. She was lying on her back under the covers, head on the pillow, "arms" sticking out, jowls flopped backward to reveal enough teeth and gums to make her resemble a horror movie monster, and snoring.

"A lot of help you are."

By the time I got dressed, combed my hair and went downstairs, the bimbo was nowhere to be found. The boys were apparently still sleeping, and Mason was pouring coffee that smelled like heaven.

"Where's your, um…friend?"

"Honest to God, Rachel, I completely forgot I'd invited her. She left in a huff after finding a half-naked author in my bedroom."

"Somehow I don't think it was the author part that bothered her." I slid into a chair at the kitchen table. "I'm sorry if I messed things up for you. She your girlfriend?"

"No. And don't be sorry. I really was hoping I could get what I wanted from her without having to date her."

"And by *date* you mean *bang*."

"Yeah, to be crude about it."

"To be honest about it, you mean."

He set a cup of coffee in front of me and my mouth watered. I added cream and sugar a little too eagerly, stirred and sipped. Ahhh. Like a the prick of a needle to a heroin addict. Nice.

"So do you regularly lure women here hoping to get something from them without having to bang them? I'd think it would usually be the other way around."

"You have a mean streak, you know that?"

"You should be flattered. I don't reveal it to just anyone."

He smiled. "I kinda figured that out all by myself. You're nothing like your books."

I shrugged. "I'll take that as a compliment. So, what's the story on the blonde?"

"I met Patty while I was arranging for Eric's—I met

her because of Eric. I needed a favor from her, so she came by to help out."

I shrugged. "She was certainly...buxom."

"That she was. And helpful." He laid a sheet of paper in front of me—no, it was three sheets, stapled together. With a long list of hospitals, complete with their addresses. "What is this?"

"It's a list of the hospitals where Eric's organs and tissues were sent for transplant."

My eyes widened and I lifted my head. "The bimbo got you this?"

"She's not a bimbo. She's a nurse. And yes, she got me this."

"Just in hopes you'd screw her?" I blinked and shook my head. "Are you *that* good?"

He leaned closer. "You'll never know."

"Hell, Mason, I could bang you right now if I wanted to."

"What makes you think so?"

"You're a guy. I'm female and breathing. Any further questions?"

"Okay, I concede the point." He snatched the sheets of paper back. "We need to start checking out the hospitals on this list, see if we can find surgical admissions around the date of Eric's death, try to generate a list of suspects."

"There must a hundred hospitals here, and for all we know, maybe more than one donation went to some of them."

"Yeah. Hard to believe one organ donor can impact that many lives."

"Hell, this *particular* donor impacted a lot more lives than that."

He looked wounded. I bit my lip. "That was cruel. I'm sorry. So we rule them out as suspects one by one."

"A lot of them probably live in other states, way beyond driving distance. I think we should start with the locals."

I liked how he kept saying *we*. Like we were a team. He really thought I could help solve this thing. It was about freaking time he took what was happening to me seriously.

"I think we should work from somewhere else, though," he went on. "Somewhere safe, somewhere the killer doesn't even know about. He could find out about this place too easily, since it's a matter of public record that I'm on the case."

I lifted my eyebrows. "Do you think he knows about my sister's place?"

"If he's been watching you, yeah. He might."

I think all the blood rushed from my brain to my feet at that point. He was still talking, something about his family having a lake house in the Adirondacks, but I wasn't hearing him anymore. I was looking for my purse. Still up in the bedroom. I sprinted there and back again in about three and a half seconds, fumbling for the car keys as I ran into the kitchen, passing him on the way. I was kind of surprised that my backdraft didn't spin him in a full circle as I ran by.

"Hey, hey, hold on a sec." He grabbed my shoulder, and I turned and looked at him but my mind wasn't on him at all. It was on Sandra, and the twins, and Jim. Shit, what would father of the year Jim do in the face of a serial killer? Probably try to reason with the guy, talk him down. You couldn't talk down a psychopath.

"I've got to go. I've get to make my sister get the hell out of town until this is over."

"Can't you just call?"

"I'll call on the way. You can write me a ticket after."

"I really don't think he'll go after her so long as you're not there."

"Don't even pretend you know that, Mason. My family is in danger." I glanced back toward the stairway I'd just descended. "And maybe so is yours, since you're the lead detective and it wouldn't be hard to find out your address."

In seconds I was out the door and diving behind the wheel of the twins' car. Five miles later I realized that I'd forgotten Myrt.

I clapped a hand to my forehead. *How could I?*

My phone rang, and I grabbed it fast without even looking at the caller ID. "What?"

"It's me," Mason said.

*It's me. So our nonrelationship has reached the "It's me" stage, has it?* "I forgot my dog. I'm a horrible human being."

"That's why I'm calling, to let you know she's fine."

"Fine my ass." I hit the speaker button and dropped the phone on my lap to avoid a ticket. "She's blind, she's in a strange place, and she's on the second floor."

"She got up and apparently followed her nose into the boys' room, where she whined until Josh woke up and brought her downstairs. He took her outside for a walk, and right now he's sharing his pancakes with her."

I exhaled, and some of the tension eased from my

spine, which had been so tight I'd thought it was about to snap. "I'll deal with my sister and the kids, and then I'll be back for her."

"Deal with your sister and the kids," he said. "Then go home and pack a bag for you and one for Myrtle. Your house has been cleared, and given the footprints in the woods from that guy lurking there last night, so have you."

"Did they find the hammer?"

He paused a beat before replying. "No. I think he took it with him."

"God, Mason. Why?"

"I don't know. Just do what you need to do and pack, okay?"

I blinked, harkening back to our earlier conversation. "Is this about your lake house in the mountains?"

"Yes. We'll head up there this afternoon. We can work the case from there. Okay?"

I wanted to say no. But how the hell was I supposed to say no when I was also wondering if it would be safe for me to return to my own home—my fucking haven—for long enough to pack?

So instead of arguing with him, I said, "Okay."

"Okay? Why was that so easy?"

"Because I'm wondering if this bastard is going to be lurking in my bushes with that fucking hammer when I get home."

"I'll be there waiting when you get there. I've just gotta run the boys home first and pack some stuff."

"Do you think they're safe, Mason?" The killer was their father, after all.

He paused for a long moment. "If this is what you think it is, someone continuing Eric's crimes because they inherited his illness through his organs, I don't see how they could be targets. My brother would never have harmed his sons. But I'm going to try to find a way to get Marie to let them take a few days off school and come with us, just in case. Why don't we meet at your place at noon?"

I nodded at the phone and felt my throat going tight, and there was a burning behind my eyes.

"Okay?" he asked when I didn't answer.

I cleared my throat, but my voice still came out tight. "You're really a decent guy, aren't you, Mason?"

"I try to be."

"It's weird. I mean, that your brother turned out... the way he did."

"Keeps me awake nights. We were both raised in the same home, by the same parents. He was adopted, but still..."

"I didn't know that." I was starting to like this guy. You know, as a person, not just as a sex object.

"Noon at my place, then," I said. "Take good care of my dog, okay?"

"You're not really the tough, thick-skinned chick you pretend to be, are you?"

"If I wasn't, I'd never have made it this far in life. Trust me on that." I hit the end call button and headed straight to Sandra's, but I was on the phone the entire twenty-minute drive with my favorite travel agent.

*"The Bahamas?"* Sandra blinked at me as if I'd lost my mind.

"Yep. One weeks, all-inclusive, at a really high-end resort. It'll be amazing. The chance of a lifetime."

"And you say you *won* this?"

"Yep. Sweepstakes I forgot even entering. I guess my luck is changing, right? But it's a trip for four, and I don't want to leave Myrtle, and I'm way behind on the current book, so I thought of you. Misty and Christy will go insane."

"Yeah, I imagine they will."

Sandra pushed herself back from her desk. She'd been hard at work when I'd burst in to interrupt her and offered her a dream vacation wrapped up in a package of lies.

"This is too much. We can't accept it."

"Call it an early Christmas present."

"It's only October."

"Then call it an early Halloween present. Call it birthday presents for all of you for the next three years. Call it whatever you want. But you'll lose it if you can't leave tomorrow."

"Tomorrow?" She shook her head. "The girls have school, soccer, I have deals pending, Jim has—"

"None of that is as important as the trip of a lifetime, Sandra. You can make this work. Come on, start delegating your important stuff and delaying the rest. Wrap up what you can, have Jim talk to his boss. You can do this. I guarantee you the girls would rather spend a week at Flip-Flops All-Inclusive Beach Resort than play soccer. And they both get straight A's, so a few days off school won't kill them."

Sandra lowered her eyes. "This week's a bye. They'd only miss one game."

"So?"

"So what's really going on here, Rachel?"

I hated when she got that look. The one that said she could see right through me. It was way worse than our mom's had been, that penetrating gaze of hers.

I licked my lips, lowered my head. "Okay, you want the truth, I'm gonna give it to you. I don't have time to dick around here. The guy who killed our brother is still out there. He's obviously trying to get to me, and since I'm going out of town to a safe haven with Mason for a few days myself, I'm afraid you and Jim and the girls might be in danger. He might try to get to me by harming you or the girls."

She went completely white and dropped back into her desk chair as if her knees had turned into oatmeal. I wished I hadn't said it, but it was done and I couldn't take it back.

"The girls!" Her head came up, eyes wide. "The girls are at school."

"There. That fear right there, that's how I'm feeling. That's why I want you out of here, out of his reach, until Mason and I can find him."

She already had the phone in her hand, dialing I don't know who. The school office or, more likely, one of the girls' ever-present cell phones. She paused while it was ringing—I could hear it. "*Mason* and you?"

I got up, not ready to pick up on that topic of conversation. "Be ready. Your flight leaves at 2:00 p.m. tomorrow. Your itinerary and links to check in for the flights are in your email. I have to go."

"Rachel—" She stopped there as one of the girls finally answered.

"I've got to go," I repeated. "Get your family out of here, sis. I'll talk to you later."

She nodded at me, and I was outta there.

\* \* \*

She hadn't been arrested. The rat's plan hadn't worked. But that was only because he hadn't known about her relationship with the cop who'd now cast himself in the role of her protector. And now he was taking her with him on a road trip. He was watching, through high-powered binoculars from a little boat out on the reservoir when the detective met her at her house, put her suitcases into his car and took her away. It didn't take him long to figure out where. He knew everything Eric Conroy Brown had known, after all. Ironic, that this would come to a head there, of all places. It was perfect, really. Lucky. He started scratching at the brain of his host, urging him toward what needed to be done.

The host didn't put up much of a fight.

*To stop the itch and cure the ache, put one more body in the lake.*

# *18*

Even without my eyesight, I would have known the place was beautiful. First off, there was the smell, pine and wood and earth, with hints of musty scented fungus wafting in and out again like ghosts underneath the rest. The air was clean, not that it wasn't clean where I lived, but it was somehow even cleaner here. All those pine needles, bazillions of them, filtering every single breath, I figured.

We were in the sturdy Jeep Mason had rented for the trip. He'd left his beloved boat of a Monte Carlo behind. Thank you, rutted back roads. And my T-Bird was not meant for this kind of travel. She was unharmed after her recent violation at the hands of the BPD forensics team. Nothing incriminating had been found, and she was safe and sound in my locked garage. I hoped.

"Are you sure Marie and the boys will be okay?" I asked, still bugged that the kids hadn't come with us.

"I put Rosie on them. He'll keep 'em safe until they can join us tomorrow. Marie wants to come along, but she insisted she needed a day to work out the logistics. My mother heard about it and insisted on coming up with them, and claimed she needed a day to pack. I asked Dennison—I don't think you've met him—to keep an eye on her."

"I guess we can't ask for more than that."

"He has no reason to go after them," he reminded me.

"I know."

I missed my car. I missed being the one behind the wheel. I'd been relegated to the passenger seat on every trip for twenty years, and I really disliked being back there again.

Myrtle didn't mind at all. She wore her tinted goggles, smiled with her bottom teeth and relished every second of the trip, even though she was in the backseat for the first time in her life. Well, her life with me, anyhow.

"I've got to ask," Mason said as we meandered along narrow, twisting dirt roads with nothing but trees on either side and majestic, snowy mountains in the distance. "What's up with Myrt's goggles?"

"Probably me projecting my issues on the poor dog." He frowned at me, so I elaborated. "When I was blind, I never believed that my eyes weren't doing acrobatics without my consent, even though everyone told me they were fine. I just couldn't be around anyone without my shades on. Just in case."

He tilted his rearview mirror to look at Myrtle. "So you think she's worried about her looks?"

"Not really. But I do think her eyes are sensitive to the sun. Mine were. She squints really badly when the light hits them."

"Ahhh. And the scarf?"

"Well, it matches the goggles. Which match the T-Bird. A girl's gotta have a little style, you know."

He smiled, drove for a minute, then said, "You didn't need to worry about it. Your eyes, I mean."

"That's right, you saw me without my sunglasses, since you personally knocked them off of me. With a car."

"Am I ever going to live that down?"

"Not in this lifetime. So my eyes weren't doing anything weird that day?"

"Nope. They were perfectly gorgeous eyes."

"Were?"

He shrugged. "Still are. Though a little more haunted now."

"Yeah, that part's your brother's fault."

He nodded, sighed, then said, "I'm honestly sorry about that, Rachel. Giving you his corneas, giving anyone his organs now that I...know."

"Why did you?" I asked.

He took his time about answering, really seemed to be searching for the right words. "I think I did it to assuage my own guilt. For covering up his crimes. I suppose I thought helping other people would...not make up for it, but maybe balance the scales a little bit."

I nodded slowly. "I guess I can see that. I appreciate the honesty."

"Thanks." Then he turned his attention to something up ahead. "We're almost there. Right around this next big bend in the road, you'll be able to see it."

And I did. It was a gorgeous chalet-style house, with a steep roof and scalloped shingles, all oak brown with darker wood trim. It looked like a gingerbread house, only bigger.

"It's stunning. This is yours?"

"My parents own it. Just my mother now. She always said she'd leave it to Eric and me in her will."

"Just you now?"

"Unless Marie wants Eric's half. If she does, I won't argue against it."

He steered the Jeep over the rutted, curving driveway right up to the front of the house. There was a garage dead ahead, below ground on two sides, and beside it a steep incline up to the main level of the house, with beautiful stone steps curving right up to the front door.

He stopped the car, and I got out eagerly and quickly let Myrt out so she could check the place over, as well. I took off her goggles and scarf, then stood close so she wouldn't be nervous as she sniffed the air and then the ground. Then she peed.

"It's a nice place, huh, Myrt? Frankly, I don't know if we're ever going to want to leave." There were birds singing, way more than I was used to hearing. Just a raucous pile of them. It was like the inner city of nature up here. Myrt sniffed and moved carefully forward, and I stayed close, talking to her as we made our way to the steps and up to the door.

Mason was already unloading our bags. I'd brought three. One for my laptop and the work in progress, a follow-up to my holiday title, which had been so sadly neglected lately that I might have to ask for an extension on my deadline. One for my clothing and toiletries, and one for Myrtle's things. Her bed, leash, dog food, treats, toys, dishes and baby wipes. Don't ask.

He'd brought just one backpack, and somehow he managed to carry all our gear at once up the stone stairway to the front door, which was made from several wide knotty pine planks with a full-length oval glass mosaic of a heavily antlered buck posing in front of a sunset. Stunning.

He paused. "Um, yeah, keys."

"I'll get them. Where are they?"

"In my jeans pocket."

"Right. Sure they are."

"I'm not kidding. Front, right."

I shrugged. "Well, hell, I'm not shy." I dipped into his front pocket and got the keys, tickling his thigh with my fingers on the way out.

He jumped.

"Serves you right," I told him, and then I unlocked the door and pushed it open while he stood aside to let Myrt and me pass.

"Wow." The place was huge, with an open floor plan, cathedral ceilings, windows everywhere, although I couldn't see much through them at this point, because darkness was falling fast as the sun fell behind the mountains. We'd packed my stuff, stopped for a late lunch and driven the four hours up here, with one extended bathroom, snack and gasoline break, so the sun had been well on its way down when we arrived. Some of the tall trees stood in silhouette against the deep purple sky, and I could see a vast and slightly darker expanse with no trees or hills at all. The lake, I presumed.

A huge fireplace, giant multitiered chandelier made of fake—I hoped—antlers, big brown teddy bear furniture that would hug you when you sat in it. What more could a person want in a lakeside mountain retreat?

Once the door closed behind us, Myrt's confidence rose a little and she wandered a few feet farther from my side to explore a bit on her own.

"There are four bedrooms, two upstairs in the loft and two down below, right underneath our feet. One bathroom on each floor. Mom keeps the place pretty well stocked. Perishables are in the freezer."

"This place is fantastic." I crossed to the rear of the giant living room and saw there was a huge deck off the back of the house. Because the house had been built into the mountainside, the living room was ground level in the front and second story in the rear. There were French doors, and in spite of myself, I opened them and stepped out onto the deck. I still had my coat on. No hat though. The breeze was chilly on my ears, but I could hear the water lapping softly against the dock down there below, and I could taste it in the air, too.

I turned, my back to the railing, when I heard Mason's footsteps as he came out to join me.

"This is my favorite place in the world," he said. "There's nowhere else this peaceful."

"I'd be hard-pressed to think of anywhere."

He looked at me for a longish minute. I looked back. It went awkward pretty fast, so we both looked away.

"So…" he said.

"So. I suppose we should unpack, get some dinner and get to work."

"And start a fire," he said. "Since I don't have much to unpack, I'll handle the fire and the dinner, while you and Myrt pick a room and get settled in. Upstairs or down?"

"Which stairs are going to be easier on Myrtle's joints?"

"Up," he said. "They're wide, carpeted and less steep." He pointed at them as he spoke.

"Perfect." I moved past him back inside. Myrtle was standing in the open doorway but hadn't come out yet. "It's okay, Myrt. Come on, I'll get your bed and put it by the fire for you. That's your favorite thing, right?"

I crossed to where Mason had dropped the bags and unzipped hers. I heard him come in, too. He closed the French doors and started messing around with the fireplace, while I unpacked Myrt's things. I took her dog dishes to the kitchen, and she followed. I poured her favorite food into one, then filled her water dish, set both down on the floor and watched her dig in.

By the time she'd finished and we returned to the living room, Mason had lit the kindling and paper in the hearth, and laid Myrt's bed right in front of it. She found it fast, and within a minute she was snoring softly and soaking up the heat.

"She'll have to go outside again before bed, but she'll hold it until she can't anymore. And meanwhile, nice kitchen."

"Yeah, it is, isn't it?" He set a larger log on the already blazing small stuff and, crouching, watched the fire.

"So I should just go up and put my stuff in one of the bedrooms?"

"Yeah. Um, you can use mine. It's on the right."

I had picked up my bags and was starting for the

stairs, but I paused at the bottom. "And whose is on the left?"

I turned toward him and knew the answer before he said it. "That was Eric's. Mom and Dad always preferred the big suite down below."

I blinked and looked up the stairs.

"Seriously, take my room. I'll take Eric's."

I took a breath, thought it over, lifted my chin. "No, you know what? I'll take his room. I told you a long time ago that I wanted to know more about him, and I meant it."

"He hasn't used it since he was a kid. Marie and the kids would come up on their own sometimes, but the boys liked the basement room so they could walk straight outside and down to the lake, and Marie would usually use Mom's. Eric hasn't been here in years."

"I wonder why?" I asked.

He shrugged. "Don't know."

"Well, all the same, I'll take the room on the left." I started up the stairs, reached the top and looked at the hallway that stretched in both directions. One wood-stained door to the left, one to the right, and one dead center, straight head of me. That one was open, and I could see the fixtures of a gorgeous bathroom that I was dying to check out. But later. I glanced back downstairs briefly, thinking about changing my mind. Mason was on the floor, rubbing Myrtle's head and watching the flames dance in the fireplace.

No. I wasn't going to chicken out.

I mustered my nerve and marched straight to the bedroom on the left, told myself it was completely idiotic that my hand was shaking and opened the door. I found the light switch and flipped it on.

I don't what the hell I'd expected. Some big hairy monster to duck quickly back into the closet as light flooded the room? Wall-to-wall B-movie posters of slasher flicks? A clichéd collection of newspaper clippings about missing young men, even?

I almost laughed at myself when the terror behind Door Number One turned out to be a neatly made full-size bed with a wagon wheel headboard, a tall dresser with six drawers, a few wildlife prints on the walls, and a set of blue-and-brown plaid curtains that matched the bedspread. That was it. There was a shelf on one wall, with books and some board games, and a clock radio on the nightstand. The floor was covered in the same brown shag carpeting as the hallway and the staircase, outdated but immaculate. One door was on the same side as the bathroom and presumably led straight into it, and the other was no doubt the closet.

I stepped farther inside and dropped my bag on the bed. "You're an idiot, Rachel," I said.

*There's still that closet, though. Don't even pretend you didn't notice that.*

"Yeah, I know."

*Might as well open it now, right? It's only gonna be worse if you try to sleep tonight without knowing what's in there.*

"Shut the fuck up, voice of reason." I moved closer, reached out, stiffened my spine and made myself just yank the door open. Just like jumping into a pool when the water was a little too cold for comfort. Just like pulling off a Band-Aid. You did it fast, you got it done, and it was never as bad as you thought it would be.

The closet was dark, but there was a dangling pull-chain. I pulled it, and the light came on. There were clothes hanging there, a few shirts, but mostly hoodies and jackets, a big parka, and a pair of snow pants, all big enough for me, I imagined, but sized for a kid about Joshua's age, maybe a little older.

"See? All good. No boogie man." I looked up at the shelf above the clothing rod. Snowmobile helmet with a thick layer of dust on it, some cassette tapes piled up in their cases. Duran Duran's *Hungry Like the Wolf.* That made me shiver. I backed out, pulled the cord and closed the closet door.

And in spite of myself I got down on all fours and looked under the bed. But it was clean, as clean and spotless as the rest of the house. Which made me wonder why the stuff in the closet was all dusty. Why hadn't Mason's mom cleaned in there?

I was still down there when the door creaked, and I twisted my head around, dropping the ugly plaid bedspread as I did. Mason towered over me from this angle.

"Everything okay?"

I nodded and got up onto my feet. "Yeah. Just checking for monsters under the bed."

"What about in the closet?"

"Already done. It's all clear, by the way."

"Good to know." I hadn't noticed, but he was holding a sturdy little tumbler in his free hand. "Vodka and Coke. I didn't make it very strong, but I figured—"

"You figured right." I took it, drank and said, "Thank you."

"You're welcome." He looked at my face for a long second, then said, "Have you seen the bathroom yet?"

I shook my head, sipped my drink. "Only in passing. It was next on my itinerary."

"Well, be my guest." He crossed the room and opened the third door, which, as I'd guessed, led into the bathroom, then stood there, waiting for me to enter first.

I walked in, and my jaw dropped. All thoughts of boogie men or closet monsters fled my mind when I got a load of it. "This is fucking awesome." Fully as large as the bedroom, which was very roomy, the bathroom was straight out of a high-end spa. Cedar boards lined the walls. I could tell by their delicious scent. An elevated Jacuzzi occupied one corner, and a double shower stall with frosted glass doors stood in another. Double sinks set in a long countertop took up one entire wall. Everything, including the ceramic tiles, was done in ivory shot through with amber and gold. A stand-up ornamental fountain took up a third corner. It was turned off now, but ready with a crooked tower of smooth round stones and a shallow basin at the bottom to catch and recirculate the water. A little marble stand held a dish of sand and had a porcupine's back worth of incense sticks stuck in it, with a lighter standing nearby.

"Wow, this is something. Is that a *heated* towel rack?"

"It is when it's turned on."

"I am seriously lusting after your bathroom, Mason."

"I think that's the first time a woman has ever said that to me."

"Any woman who saw it would say it, and if she didn't say it, believe me, she was thinking it."

"Well, the only women who've been up here with me are Angela and Marie."

"Who the hell is Angela?" I closed my eyes. "That was not, by the way, jealousy in my voice just now."

"Jealousy over the bathroom, maybe," he said. "Angela's my mother."

I shrugged and decided not to wonder why he hadn't brought any of the women he dated up here with him. He undoubtedly got around enough. And this place would charm the panties off most of the women I knew. But it was none of my business, and I wasn't going to ask. "So will anyone care if I make very thorough use of this room after dinner?"

"Why don't you make thorough use of it right now? How much time do you need?"

I shrugged. "Two hours?"

He smiled, as if that was a surprisingly long time.

"I can make it one."

"I have plenty to keep me busy for two hours. You're not here to entertain me, you know. Enjoy it. It's probably just what the doctor ordered, given all the stress you've been under lately."

"Yeah, well, if that's your rationale, you should probably book yourself a couple of hours, too. After I'm done."

"Maybe I will." He reached out to flip a button on the towel rack, then turned on the Jacuzzi and adjusted the temperature.

"I'll show you the rest of the place while your water runs."

I took the tour, saw the finished half of the basement—two bedrooms, the big one his mother preferred and a normal-sized one, with a game room in between and a utilitarian bathroom—and even the unfinished half, which combined the garage and a small woodworking area full of tools. It made me want to ask about Mason's father. He'd talked about his mother but never his dad. I presumed he'd died, but I wanted to know when and how, and how Mason felt about it.

*How he* felt *about it? What am I, freaking Oprah now? Getting all touchy-feely? Yuck.*

So yeah, tour completed, drink refilled, I sat in the delicious Jacuzzi with the jets running full throttle, leaned my head back on one of the tub pillows I'd found on a shelf nearby and thought, *This is the life* and *Why do I not have this bathroom in my house?*

It didn't matter why. I would have one before another year was out, period. In fact, *mine* was going to be even bigger and include a hot-stone sauna room.

The candles were glowing—mine would be electric, with a flickering effect and less danger of fire—and the incense was burning. I would do an electric simmer pot with essential oils, because smoke, even tiny tendrils of incense smoke, would dirty up my planned white ceiling in a hurry. I'd found the little sound dock on the shelf above the one that held the pillows and stuck my smartphone into it, then hit my "mellow" playlist, which hardly ever saw any use. Amy had put it on there for me. The first song was James Taylor, so I decided her taste was better than I'd feared. Above the two shelves, behind a set of cabinet doors, there were bottles and jars galore, body washes, shampoos, lotions, hair products, enough to get my inner girlie-girl all revved up.

*What the hell? I'll indulge her for a bit. Maybe I de-*

*serve it, after all this. Or maybe that's the vodka talking. Either way...*

By the time I got out of the Jacuzzi, I had a very slight buzz, and was feeling all relaxed and loose. I wrapped myself up in my prettiest robe and didn't even bother drying my hair. Just combed it and left it hanging, drippy and, so long as it was wet, dead straight. That was how I went back downstairs, wet and mellow, makeup free. My stomach had been growling sporadically, so it jumped for joy when I smelled food wafting up from below. I'd been a little less than the two hours I'd predicted, but only because I was too lazy to refill the tub with hotter water for the third time.

*Mmm, that smells like Italian. I love Italian.*

"There you are. Not only on time but actually early." Mason was right where I'd left him, on the floor in front of the fireplace, loving on my bulldog. But he hadn't been there the entire time. There was a fresh stack of logs in the round iron firewood rack, and the dining room table, in the open space between living room and kitchen, was set for two. No candles, thank God. I would have run screaming if he'd lit candles, because that would mean he was thinking romance, and I had no interest in romance.

Sex maybe, but definitely not romance.

*What the fuck was* that? *Didn't I already decide that would be* Bad?

I watched him get up off the floor and stretch his arms above his head to work the kinks out. His shirt rose, and my stupid lecherous eyes latched on to the expanse of flesh that was left exposed. His jeans rode low, so I could see the slight indent below his hip bones, and the fine dark hairs making an arrow pointing to his button fly and beyond.

*It's the vodka. I'm fine. I just need to lay off the vodka.*

Arms down. Skin covered. He nodded at the empty glass I'd brought down with me. "You need another drink?"

*Say no.*

"Definitely."

He took my glass, then sauntered across the room to the kitchen. I looked at his ass, then looked away, then jumped out of my skin when he was suddenly a foot from me, handing me the fresh drink.

"Hungry?" he asked.

*Okay, come on, that was sexy. Deliberately sexy. That gruff edge in his voice, just then? That had to be on purpose.*

"Ravenous."

*Okay, sound slutty much? Shut the front door, Rachel.*

He blinked slowly, then turned around and headed back to the kitchen. I followed like a lost puppy and wished someone would put me to sleep. Dumb shit.

"I hope you like lasagna. My entire repertoire consists of lasagna, and mac and cheese."

"It smells great."

"Oh, it *is* great. I don't do a lot, but what I do, I do really well."

"Is that your cooking philosophy, or does it apply to life in general?"

"Applies to everything," he said, as he took a foot-square lasagna pan out of the oven. I thought it would feed me for a week. Or Myrtle for a day.

Turning, he hustled it past me to the counter. "There's another oven mitt there. Would you grab the garlic bread?"

*Garlic bread, too? Is he trying to seduce me or fatten me up for slaughter?*

"If there's dessert, you might get lucky tonight. And if it's chocolate, I'll blow you." I clapped a hand to my mouth to silence the evil whore who'd said all that, and as I did, I noticed my third drink was almost gone already.

"I will find chocolate for dessert if I have to tear this place apart," he said when he finally stopped laughing. "You're quite something with a couple of drinks in you."

"Yeah, so I've been told." I took the garlic bread to the counter, grabbed a bread knife and started slicing it while he piled giant hunks of gooey lasagna onto a pair of thick plates and carried them back to the table. I followed with the sliced, steaming bread. No salad.

*God, is this guy too good to be true, or what?*

*Down, girl. Vodka goggles, remember?*

*Whatev.*

So we ate, and I had another drink and couldn't stop thinking about banging him. When we were finished, he cleared up while I fed Myrtle—again. No wonder the poor thing was such a tank, but she looked so pathetic that how could I resist? I offered to help and he said no, so I sank onto the big teddy bear sofa near the fire, and he came back in with freshly brewed coffee, two cups of premade chocolate pudding just like the ones like my mother used to put in my school lunch box, and a shit-eating grin on his face.

I grinned back and when he sat beside me, I sipped, watched the fire and ate my pudding.

And then I said, "You know, I've only been a sighted adult for a few months now."

"And how are you liking it so far?" He was licking his spoon.

*That's it. God must want me to screw him.*

"Loving it," I said. "As independent as I thought I was before, it didn't compare. I can drive. I can redecorate my house in the brightest colors I can find. I can... well, hell, I can *see*."

"Must be like a whole new world for you."

"It is. And I want to explore every corner of it. I want to check out everything before I commit to anything. Even a little bit. You know?"

"I guess."

I nodded, even though he was looking at me like he was starting to wonder where I was going. "Good. So you'll understand when I tell you that this is just this. Nothing more."

His dark brows bent until they touched. "This... what?"

I took a breath, stood up and figured I might as well go for broke. It wasn't like he would refuse me. He'd been sending signals all night. So I bit my lip and dropped my robe. Just that simple. "This."

"Hot damn, I was hoping you'd say that." He stood up slowly. Didn't touch, except with his eyes, which were scanning me from head to toe and back again. "And I'm liking what I see."

"Which part?"

"All of it." He smiled, one side of his mouth crooking up higher than the other, and then he pulled me hard against him and kissed my face off.

Oh, yeah, this had been a very, *very* good idea.

# 19

I woke up about 1:00 a.m., because he was a blanket hog and I was shivering. We were curled up back to back, with only our butts touching. The sex had been amazing, and frequent, and pretty damned creative to boot. I was still tingling from it.

I rolled onto my back, stared at the ceiling and wondered if I was going to regret this in the morning.

*I don't regret it yet. Good sign, right?*

*That's probably just because the afterglow thing is still in effect, dumb ass.*

*Three hours later? Does afterglow last that long?*

*It was good sex.*

*Yeah, it was really good sex.*

At least myself and I could agree on that much. I peeled back the covers and eased out of the bed as carefully as possible, because, A, I wanted to avoid the awkward moment when we both woke up in the morning and had to say something, B, I didn't want to wake Myrt, who we'd hefted onto the bed after our playtime was done, and C, I fully intended to spend the night in Eric's room.

I don't know why. Maybe to prove to myself that I could, or maybe I was hoping to figure something out while I was in there. Who can tell?

I got there by way of the bathroom, because I had to pee, and I almost scared myself when I passed the mirror. Going to sleep with wet hair is never a great idea.

Then I was back in Eric Brown's childhood bedroom. I doubted I would ever get to sleep, but I was damned well going to give it my best shot.

I lay there for a while. I tossed and I turned. I cussed under my breath and thumped my pillow. I figured I'd been lying there for an hour or so when I finally conceded defeat and sat up.

The bed rocked a little with my motion, and I heard the gentle slapping of oars in water. What the hell? It was still dark, but when I looked around I knew I wasn't indoors. There was cool night air on my face and mist rising all around me.

*Ahh another dream, then. Okay, let's see where this one goes.*

The oars, it turned out, were in my hands as I rowed a small boat across the water. It was nighttime, and the mist made it hard to see how far away the shore might be, but I could see a few stars winking high above. And as I settled more deeply and comfortably into the dream, I could smell the air, the wet fishy scents close to the boat and the pines farther away. The dampness of that mist was like the air kissing my skin.

I was rowing, and I was crying. But as before, I wasn't me. I was riding along inside another body, looking at the world through another set of eyes. A killer's eyes.

*Hell, this is Eric. I'm in Eric's head. What is this? A memory?*

I tried to focus, to really look at my surroundings, at my body. I could see my legs, big, male legs clad in jeans and badly stained work boots. Wait, there were other feet in the bottom of the boat. Someone else was there.

*Don't look don't look don't look.*

I forced myself to look further, up the long, skinny legs, also dressed in jeans, and then higher, to the button-down shirt that was buttoned only partway. To the white T-shirt beneath it, red stains making my heart beat faster. Higher, to the pale skin of the neck, past a mark on one side of it, to the face, the head, but I couldn't keep my focus there. One glance, that was all. Hamburger. He looked like hamburger. I jerked my vision lower again, and this time, I paid attention to the mark on his neck. It was a badly done tattoo. A tiger, upright and climbing the neck like it was a tree.

*It's Tommy.*

The person whose body I was inside stopped rowing and brushed tears from his eyes/my eyes with a big hand. He was thinking, *This is the last time. This is the last time. I can beat it, I know I can.*

He leaned over and grabbed a length of rope I hadn't noticed before. He knotted the rope to one of my brother's wrists, then looped it around both of them and tied them together.

*I can't watch this. Wake up now. Come on, wake up.*

I closed my dream eyes, then opened them again, hoping I would wake up in reality, but no. I was still in the boat, and another length of rope was being knotted around my brother's ankles. Then the killer turned and picked up a pair of cinder blocks, connecting the free end of each rope to one of them.

Sobbing loudly now, the killer picked Tommy up and lowered him into the water, just as gently if he were handling a beloved child. As Tommy began to sink, the killer tossed the two cinder blocks over the side, as well, and then he sat and watched the body descend into the weeds and vanish from sight.

When it was gone, he grabbed the oars again and started rowing away. The mist was clearing a little. I could see the shape of the shoreline in the distance. The sun was starting to rise and the sky was growing lighter, making a silhouette of the trees.

I tried to squint things into better focus, and the scene turned into a window with the same trees and the same sky beyond it. I was sitting up in bed, wide-awake now, and looking through Eric's bedroom window at the paling sky outside.

I pressed my hands to my eyes. Dammit, I'd just seen Mason's murderous bastard of a brother dump my own brother's body.

*Well, that was what you wanted, wasn't it? That was why you slept in here, to see if you'd dream up more information about what happened to Tommy. Right?*

Right. So now I knew. Tommy was at the bottom of a fucking lake.

*A fucking lake.*

I looked at the window again. There were, I realized, probably a couple of hundred lakes in the Adirondack Preserve.

*But how many of them did Eric Brown have a personal connection with?*

I got up and got dressed, tamed my hair down and ponytailed it, then padded quietly downstairs, because I didn't want to wake Mason. No, I wasn't just being polite. I was still avoiding the awkward, post-sex discussion we were going to stumble through eventually. I made coffee, filled a big mug of it to take with me and then pulled on my jacket and the cute brown knit hat and scarf Amy had bought me last winter.

Coffee in hand, I went to the French doors and out onto the big redwood deck for a better look at the lake. Leaning against the rail, cupping the warm mug in my cold hands and sipping, I stared across the sloping expanse of back lawn to the water, some fifty yards distant. It was foggy, dammit. Mist rising from the water just like in the damned dream. It would burn off once the sun got up a bit higher, I thought, but for now I couldn't see a hell of a lot. Still, there was a set of redwood steps leading down to ground level, two short flights with a landing in between. Sighing, I decided to take them. At the bottom, I saw a pair of red kayaks leaning against the back of the house, under the deck. I walked through the wet grass, peering through the fog at the lake the entire way.

Birds were singing like maniacs. It was even louder than what I'd heard last night, because apparently most birds were morning people. Unlike me. You know, except for when I spend the night in a serial killer's bed, or in a serial killer's head, or both.

There was a wooden dock extending into the water, with a couple of little boats bobbing serenely, tied up on either side. One was a canoe. Gleaming hardwood, shining and glossy, with a stripe in pine green and the

words *Old Town,* which I figured was the brand name.
That was on the left. On the right was a flat-bottomed
metal rowboat that didn't even come to a point in the
front. It was boxy. The bow tapered a little, but then
squared off, and the stern was identical. It had two built-
in bench seats, and oars in the oarlocks.

I stood there staring at that boat and wondering.
Could it be the same one I saw in the dream? I stepped
into the thing and then crouched to grab the sides when
it rocked way more than I'd expected. I damn near
tipped it over, but no, it steadied. I sat myself down on
the bench seat, my eyes riveted to the floor at the stern.
And then, leaning forward, I put my hands there, right
where Tommy would have been lying if this was the
same boat.

I stared hard, trying to recall the image of my dead
brother and the boat from the dream, so I could compare. I strained to see any trace of blood, but there was
nothing. Nothing obvious, anyway. And all the while,
I pressed my hands to the cold metal.

*Were you here, Tommy?*

Blinking away hot tears, I stared out at the water.
The mist was starting to dissipate a little, and I could
see the shape of the lake better now, along with the
trees lining the shore. It looked a lot like the lake from
the dream, but then, so did most of the other lakes up
here, I imagined.

*Are you out there, big brother? Are you out there in
that dark water somewhere?*

"Going for an early-morning boat ride?"

I jumped so damned hard I almost capsized, sucking

in a breath that could have busted a lung, and twisted my head around like a freaking hoot owl.

"What the fuck are you doing here!" It wasn't a question.

David was standing on the dock, handsome as all hell in his bomber jacket with his *GQ*-model blond hair just perfect, despite the morning breeze. He had his hands in his pockets but offered me one when I started to climb out of the little boat.

I didn't take it. I was good and pissed. And yeah, maybe that was partly because I'd just realized that my brother might be anchored to a pair of cinder blocks not far from me, but mostly it was deserved.

"I decided to drive up for the weekend. I told you I like to camp up here sometimes, didn't I?"

I was on the dock now, facing him and not trying one bit to hide my temper. "You came up here because I came up here with Mason and you're jealous. The question is, how the hell did you know that?"

"No, you've got it all wrong," he said. "I *told* you, I camp up here sometimes," he repeated. But his tone had turned grim.

"And *I* told *you* I didn't want any strings. We had a few good times together, but now it's done. I think there's someone out there who's a much better match for you than I could ever be."

"Oh, come on, Rachel. You don't mean that. Any guy would be worried if his girlfriend was out in the middle of nowhere with some—"

"David, I'm not your girlfriend. We don't know each other well enough for that."

He lowered his head, but I got the feeling it was more

to hide his burgeoning temper than out of sadness because I was breaking up with him.

"Please," I told him. "Go home. Get a start on finding that right woman."

His gaze came level. He met my eyes, and I didn't like what was in his. It was dark. "You can't just end it like this."

"There was never anything to—" I bit my lip, because he was, at the very least, a stalker. And at most? God, could it be him?

"You're ending it because of him, aren't you?"

I softened my tone considerably, glancing past him toward the house. I thought I saw movement just beyond the glass doors. "David, I've only had my eyesight back for a couple of months," I said, using the rationale I'd been using to convince myself not to get involved with Mason. "I need time to be independent before—"

"I suppose this is independence. Coming up here with him."

"He's a cop, David. He's trying to help me find my brother." I tried to walk past him, but he stepped right up and blocked my way.

"Right, and you had to screw him to get that help?"

I was getting pissed now. "Get out of my way and let me pass."

"No. I'm not moving until we talk about this."

I shrugged. "Have it your way." I shoved him hard, both hands to the chest. He staggered backward a step and a half, then lost his balance and hit the ice-cold water with a splash that should have lowered the level of the lake.

By the time he came up spluttering, I was sprinting back across the lawn to the house. But I could hear him cussing me out in a way no one ever had. And the anger in his voice shook me in spite of myself, especially when I sensed he was out of the water, on the shore and coming after me.

Mason met me halfway, clasped my shoulders and put me behind him. I could see the gun tucked into his waistband and nestling in the small of his back.

David stopped where he was, glaring and dripping wet.

Mason faced him squarely. "Go on home, pal. We don't need any trouble."

"You've already got trouble, *pal,*" David replied. "When you take another man's woman on a romantic weekend, you've *always* got trouble."

Without turning, Mason said, "Go on to the house, Rachel."

"Fuck you both. I can fight my own battles." I stepped around Mason, pulling his handgun from the back of his jeans as I did. I didn't point it. Just held it. "Back off, David. Get out. And don't even *think about* coming back here, or calling me when I get home."

His jaw twitched, he was clenching his teeth so tightly. "This isn't the end of this."

"Oh, it *so* fucking is." I was shaking. The guy was clearly warped, his rage way out of proportion to our handful of dates.

He sighed so hard it was a growl, then started toward me. Suddenly I heard a car horn, followed by a child's voice calling, "Uncle Mason?"

I turned to see Joshua come racing around the house and over the lawn at breakneck speed. Behind him, on the deck already, stood Jeremy and two women, one old, one young. Angela and Marie, I presumed. They must have gotten on the road by four to have made it here so early.

"We'll settle this later, David," Mason said. "Go home now. My family's here."

David looked at Josh, who stumbled to a halt a few feet from us, clearly aware that something was up. David glared at him hard enough to break something but finally stomped away. He was out of sight in a minute, and I heard his tires spitting gravel in their wake when he roared away.

Mason looked at me, and I looked back at him. I wanted to remind him that David was a transplant recipient, but I could see he was already thinking the same thing. I wanted to tell him that I thought the lake might be his brother's dumping ground, and ask how he thought David had found us way up here in the middle of nowhere unless he'd followed us, along with about a dozen other things, but Josh was rushing in for a bear hug and time was up.

How the hell was I going to bring all this up with Eric's grieving mother, pregnant widow and fatherless sons here?

Marie took over the kitchen, while Josh ran from room to room shouting at the top of his lungs.

Okay, that wasn't really what the kid was doing. It was just what it felt like. Why the hell are kids so damned noisy?

Not Jeremy. He wasn't noisy. He was petulant, which was worse. He heaved loud, overblown sighs any time anyone so much as looked at him and sat morosely like a lump. Yes, I know that sounds petty, considering the kid had just lost his father a few months ago. And yes, I knew that and still wanted to smack him upside the head.

I played nice, pretending my life wasn't on the line, and that my brother wasn't, in all likelihood, feeding the fish in their pristine fucking lake. I brewed another pot of coffee and filled cups for the four of us.

"What do you take, Marie? Cream and sugar?"

"Black, please." She took the sizzling bacon pan off the burner to join me at the nearby counter, I handed her a coffee, and fixed my own. "How about Angela?"

She looked blank. "Um—"

"Cream and sugar," Angela said, stepping into the kitchen. "Same as I've taken it for as long as you've been in the family, dear."

*Oooh, some tension there.*

"And one for Jeremy, if there's enough. Black," Angela said.

*To prove he's a manly man, I'll bet.*

Angela took her mug from me, and I carried mine and Jeremy's into the living room, since Marie didn't seem to want my help with the overblown breakfast she was making. I figured she needed to throw herself into something. Anything, I imagined, would be a welcome distraction from life as a widowed mother of two. Soon to be three.

"Hey, Jeremy," I said, handing him the mug. I sat on the sofa beside him. "So why are you acting like such an asshole today?"

Angela gasped and damn near dropped her cup.

Joshua laughed his ass off. Jeremy glared at me for a second, then shrugged. "Because I don't want to be here any more than you probably want me here," he said.

His grandmother gaped at him. "That was rude, Jeremy." Then she looked at me. "And while I hate to criticize at our first meeting, Ms. de Luca, so was what you said."

I met her eyes. "It was honest. You're not going to get anywhere tiptoeing around and pretending it's okay for him to act like a jerk. And call me Rachel."

"He's just in a mood."

"We all have our moods. We don't all put them on public display and use them to beat up on our relatives." I shrugged. "So if you want to mope, go mope in private."

"I just want to go home."

"You will, sooner or later."

"This stinks on ice."

"I couldn't agree more."

Jeremy got up, coffee mug in hand, and headed for the stairway to the basement where his room was.

I was suddenly suspicious of how willingly he'd obeyed me. "Where are you going, Jeremy?"

"To my room. Where does it look like I'm going?"

"To sneak out the basement door and try to get home on your own."

He turned to stare at me, eyes wide as saucers, so I knew I was right.

"How about this? Try to act human and I'll let you drive me into the nearest town this afternoon. We desperately need junk food in this place." He was sixteen and male, right? So driving was bound to be his passion.

"Your T-Bird is up here?"

"Uh, no, and even if it was, I wouldn't let you drive it. Are you kidding me? I love that car."

"What, then?"

"Mason's rented Jeep."

He looked at me curiously. "And what do I have to do for this?"

"Be nice, stop moping, have a conversation. Act like your uncle for a while. Think you can do that?"

He heaved a sigh. "All right."

"Good. No more of those heavy sighs, and absolutely no eye rolling."

"Anything else?"

"I'll let you know." I could see Marie moving back and forth, putting vats of food onto the kitchen table, so I presumed breakfast was served. I tipped my head toward the kitchen, and Jeremy shuffled out there and took a chair. *I* sighed, then rolled my eyes to boot, but I followed him.

Behind me, Angela whispered to Mason, "*She's* a famous self-help author?"

"Yep. And she's *good,* isn't she?"

I smiled a little, warmed a little when I heard that, then slapped myself down again. "Don't listen to him, Angela. He wouldn't know, having never read a word I've written."

"Actually, I've read the last three books," he said.

I looked at him with my jaw dropping. "You have not."

"I have. Rosie's wife, Marlayna, loaned them to me. Good stuff." He walked past me, leaned close and whispered, "You should practice following your own advice."

*Well, I'll be dipped.*

* * *

The morning dragged, and Mason could see that Rachel was itching to get him alone, either to talk about David's behavior and bounce him around as a suspect, or to talk about the wild and amazing sex they'd had the night before.

He didn't want to talk about that and hoped she didn't either. It was sex. It was incredible sex. But it didn't have to mean anything, she'd said so herself. And he hoped she was still on board with that, because if she wasn't it could really make a mess of the work they had to do.

Rachel was gifted. There was no question she could tell when someone was lying, and she seemed to read their emotions as if she could look inside their skulls and interpret their brain waves. That had already been a huge help with this case.

Besides, he liked her. So he hoped to God the sex last night hadn't screwed that up. And he hoped to put off the morning-after conversation for another day or two. Or forever.

## 20

I couldn't wait for Mason. For all I knew, David the nut case might be out beating someone's brains in with his handy hammer right this minute. I had to know if it was him. And I was itching to get out on the lake, as if the answer was out there. As if *my brother* was out there.

And maybe he was.

I didn't know shit about boats, but I figured I ought to be able to handle a rowboat, and I was right. It was fairly simple. Sit in the seat and row. The oars were attached to the sides with oversize metal pins that dropped into oversize metal holes, so it was impossible to make much of a wrong move. I pushed my end of them forward, lowered the flat ends into the water and pulled back. Lift up, push forward, lower and pull back. Nice easy rhythm, and a pretty good workout, I figured. As I started out from the shore, the oars came up bearing tangled, dripping seaweed, but once I got out into the deeper water that stopped happening. I looked back toward the house, but I didn't think anyone had noticed I was missing. And that was just as well. I didn't want to have to explain what I was doing out here.

*And just what the hell am I doing?*

Rowing. And that was enough.

I had a notion to make my way around the perimeter of the lake, far enough out from shore to avoid the weeds, but near enough in to pay attention to the look of the shoreline, the shapes of the trees. The ones from my dream were burned into my brain, and I thought I could spot them again pretty easily.

Only I couldn't. Everything looked alike, and it wasn't long before I started to wonder if it was even this lake that I'd seen in my dream. And then I started to wonder if I would even be able to find my way back to the lake house.

*Just follow the shoreline, dumb ass. You'll see the house when you get to it. And the dock and the little wooden canoe will still be there. Easy.*

Right. Easy.

Still, after an hour, I decided this was a stupid idea. The trees all looked the same, and I wasn't going to be able to search the entire lake, which was apparently way bigger than my imaginary estimate, all by myself. And what would I see if I did? It wasn't like the bodies would be on the surface. There had been cinder blocks in the dream.

I pulled in the oars and sat floating for a minute, because my arms needed a rest. It was nice out here, I thought. Birds singing, and here and there some waterfowl swimming along. I saw ducks. I saw loons. I saw what I'm pretty sure was a blue heron, standing in the cattail forest of the shallows like a ghost. They hadn't migrated south yet, I guessed. But it wouldn't be long. Today was nice, nicer by the minute with the sun beam-

ing down full force now. I took off my coat as the temp
pushed up toward sixty. With the exertion of the rowing, I was plenty warm without it.

The boat drifted of its own accord, and I was content
for a moment to lean back and let it. It seemed hard to
believe, lying there, staring up at the bright blue sky,
that this lake was hiding any dark secrets.

I sighed, closed my eyes. This was nice. I was glad
I'd come out here, despite the fact that it hadn't accom-
plished anything. I'd needed to relax, to work off some
stress and unwind, alone. After all, my brain had been
like a hurricane lately. I tried to push everything aside.
The murders. My brother. The dreams and visions. But
the one thing that refused to be pushed aside was what
had happened last night with Mason. I couldn't stop
thinking about that. And more and more, what I was
thinking was that it was going to be damn hard not to
go back for more.

Something splashed, and I sat up fast, spotting a tail
that vanished beneath the surface of the water and then
the ripples that emanated from the spot where it had
been. A fish. A big one, I thought. And I wondered
for the first time if it would be fun to go fishing, or if
I would hate it.

Looking at the water, I glimpsed a flash as the fish—
or maybe some other fish, how would I know?—swam
just below the surface. The water was clear out here, I
realized. You had to sort of refocus your vision to look
past the reflection of the puffy clouds, to see the crea-
tures underneath. And this one fish, or however many
there were, kept swimming past, vanishing deeper, sur-
facing again. It jumped as I watched like an excited kid.

Shiny, with speckles and rainbow colors flashing before he splashed down again. And I realized there was a little swarm of bugs just above the surface right there. They looked like a tiny puff of smoke but were in fact bugs, and the fish was happy to eat them.

I leaned over the side a little, watching for the fish, smiling in spite of myself when he swam past again. Damn, was I going soft or what? Getting all Zen and basking in nature like this. It was like what I advised my readers to do in times of stress, but I'd never taken my own advice to heart. I'd been mostly rehashing what other modern-day gurus taught, just putting my own sassy spin on it.

I saw another fish, this one down a little deeper. Oddly, it wasn't moving.

Did fish sleep? It was just sort of floating down there in the weeds. Maybe it was dead. Curious, I took one of the oars out of its oarlock and thrust it down to poke at the lethargic creature, and sure enough it came loose from the tangled weeds and bobbed up to the surface.

*Huh, that's not a fish....*

It was a hand and part of an arm.

I jerked backward so fast the boat rocked and I went backward over the side. The shock of the ice-cold water made every muscle in my body tighten and try to pull free from my bones. I couldn't even move for an endless moment.

Then I forced my eyes open and stopped thrashing. I was sinking, and I told myself I needed to swim, that cold or not I needed to—

*Oh, my God.*

I was in a weed jungle, and I was surrounded by bodies. They were floating at various heights, ropes anchoring them in place, some upright, some lying facedown like skydivers, some so rotten you couldn't tell what they were, some with parts missing, all of them with hamburger heads.

My heart jolted and took off at a full gallop, and my arms and legs did likewise, while my lungs screamed for air. I surged upward, wondering how the surface could be so far away, and as I did, I saw a cinder block go floating past me, heading to the bottom, towing a rope behind it…a rope that was towing a *body* behind it. One foot was bare, one wore a penny loafer. Jeans, a shirt floating up like a parachute to show me the pale skin of the belly, the chest. I could count his ribs. His head was hidden by the shirt, floating up as he descended, and his long arms stretched above him like an extra in a spaghetti western when the bad guy yells, "Reach for the sky!"

*Wait, go back. Descending? He's descending?*

*He's descending!*

I was breaking the surface and realizing the awful truth at the same time.

*This body, this skinny male body, had just been dumped.*

I wiped the water out of my eyes and looked around me, saw the lake, the distant shore, the sky—

Hands came around my neck from behind, and I was pulled out of the water. The hard side of a boat scraped my back as I kicked and clawed and swore. I landed faceup in the bottom, and then something clocked me in the head and it was lights out.

* * *

"Has anyone seen Rachel?"

Mason had been busy trying to keep Josh from dying of boredom and his own mother from picking fights with Marie, not to mention trying to keep one eye on Jeremy so he didn't do something stupid, like take off. He'd lost track of Rachel after she said she was going to take a nap in her room and was only now realizing it had been a couple of hours.

"I thought she was in her room," Angela said, sending a frown back at him.

"I just checked, she's not in there," he said.

Mason sent the same question to the boys with his eyes. Josh shook his head no, then said, "I'll go check downstairs!" and was thundering away before he finished speaking.

Jeremy looked worried. "I saw her down by the dock earlier. Didn't want to bother her."

"When?"

"When Mom made those sandwiches. What time was that, Mom?"

"Noonish." Marie looked concerned.

Mason didn't say anything else, just crossed to the patio doors, and went out and down the back steps. He crossed the grass in long strides that came faster as his gut wound tighter. Something was wrong. Every cop instinct he had was telling him so.

*The rowboat's gone.*

He saw it before he got to the dock, the slightly green-tinted water with sunlight flashing from every minuscule crest where the boxy fishing boat should have been.

*Why would she take the boat out?* He knew that she'd wanted to talk to him—had been trying to get him alone all day—but it had been impossible with the family all over him.

*Bullshit. You didn't want to get her alone because you were afraid she wanted to talk about the sex last night, not to mention you want to do it again so bad you can taste it.*

"I'm gonna take the canoe and go out after her."

"Do you really think that's necessary?" Marie tipped her blond curls sideways.

"I doubt she's ever even been in a boat, Marie. And you know I have reason to believe she's in danger. That's why I brought her up here. And why I wanted the rest of you up here with us. I was afraid it wasn't safe at home, but now I'm not so sure it's safe *here,* either."

Jeremy came out the back door with Mason's fleece-lined denim jacket over his arm, jogged down the steps to the ground and sprinted the remaining distance. He was wearing a parka and a knit hat, and he shoved Mason's jacket at him.

"Thanks, kid."

"I'm coming with you. If she's in trouble I—"

"I need you here, Jer. I need somebody to watch the family. Keep them safe. Get 'em inside, lock the place up and stay put until I find out what the hell is going on here. Anyone shows up here, and I mean *anyone,* you call nine-one-one. I mean it."

Jeremy backed up a step, and Mason knew it was pure fear that pushed him. "What's going on?"

"I don't know yet. Just do what I said, okay? I'm

counting on you. I'll be back as soon as I can. Go on now. Go."

Jeremy nodded, backing off the dock, wide-eyed, and finally turned to his mother, saying, "You heard him. Let's get inside."

Mason sighed in relief, zipped up his jacket and eased into the canoe. He'd gone a half mile before he looked down and saw the knit hat sticking out of one coat pocket, the gloves sticking out of another. "Nice, Jeremy. Maybe you *are* growing up after all." He laid the paddle down long enough to pull on the hat. Then he was pushing hard, quickly stroking the paddle through the calm, deep water, then switching to the other side, then back again. Falling into the mindless rhythm, he tried not to let his thoughts wander too far afield.

*She's fine. She got bored and decided to go for a row. That's all. There's nothing bad going on here. David isn't the killer. He came here because he's a jealous loon, not to take her out to—*

*Stop it. Just stop it already.*

"Ah, shit." The rowboat was up ahead, and there was no one in it. One of the oars was floating up near the stern, knocking gently against the metal, over and over.

He paddled up beside her, looked inside. The life jacket was there, lying on the floor, dammit, along with the fishing box and rod that were left aboard from April to Halloween every year.

Then he saw something else in the water, something floating, white and bloated, with a rope writhing snake-like by its side. What was it?

"Shit!" It was a hand.

*Not hers, not hers, not hers.*

*Of course it's not hers. Look at it. It's been here awhile.*

*The rope. It had been tied down.*

*Shit, is this where he dumped them?*

*Did he dump her, too?*

"Rachel!" He tore off the coat and hat, and dived into liquid ice. Fighting past the paralyzing cold, he stroked downward and found them. The garden of bodies, in various stages of decomposition. But not her. He didn't see *her*.

And then he had to surface, gasping, stiff with cold almost to the point where his muscles would no longer respond to his commands. He dragged himself back into the canoe, no easy task. He'd done it a hundred times, of course. As kids he and Eric would row out here together to swim and raise hell.

*And this is what it meant to him?* This?

But he'd never gone swimming in water this cold.

He was lucky. The sun was at its warmest, and it had been in the upper fifties when he'd left. He wouldn't freeze to death. Not right away, anyway.

He peeled off his wet shirt and put on his dry jacket, zipping it all the way to his chin with shaking fingers. He wrung out his hair and pulled on the hat, put on the gloves and picked up the paddle.

Something else caught his eye out in the water, too far away to see. He paddled nearer. A boat cushion.

*Not one of ours.*

*There was another boat out here!*

Okay, okay, that meant she might still be alive. He pulled the boat cushion aboard, then paddled directly toward the shore, because that was what made sense to do. If you'd snatched a fighting, feisty woman like Rachel off her boat and onto yours, that was what you would want to do. Get off the water as fast as possible, before she drowned you both.

Mason pulled out his cell phone, praying there would be a whisper of a signal. There was service at the lake house, but out on the water it was iffy. He needed to report this. Bodies in the lake. Rachel missing. But not a single bar showed. He pulled up the text message screen and didn't have to consider who to contact. Jeremy's phone was never turned off and never far from his hand. And sometimes texting worked even if there were no bars showing. He typed a quick message. Call 911. Bodies in lake. Rach missing, prob abducted. Suspect David Gray.

His finger hovered over the send button. He hated to send such a dramatic text to his nephew. But he had no choice. Rachel's life was on the line, and Jeremy was his best bet at making contact. He hit the button and watched a narrow blue line creep across the screen as the message started to go.

"Come on, come on."

The blue line stopped just before it reached the end, and it didn't start up again.

"Dammit!" He jammed the phone back into his pocket, furious at himself for wasting precious seconds, then grabbed the paddle and headed toward the forested shore again. Twenty feet out he turned the canoe and followed the shoreline in the shallows, aiming for silence but pushing for speed as his eyes scanned the woods in search of anything—any sign of her or the other boat.

After what seemed like an hour but he knew had

been more like ten minutes, he glimpsed smoke and the shape of a cabin in the woods.

As he drew closer, he saw a boat. Someone had dragged it up onto shore and left it between two clumps of brush, deliberately trying to camouflage its presence.

*Has to be Gray. He said he was camping up here.*

Mason bent low to avoid creating a big silhouette and catching anyone's eye, and let the canoe drift past the boat, then he sat up again and stroked to shore.

*Why the hell does my head hurt so much?*

I squeezed my eyes shut tighter against the throbbing pain and automatically went to press my hand to the spot where it hurt, but my hand wouldn't move. My *arm* wouldn't move.

What the hell?

I opened my eyes. I was in a room. A house. A log cabin. On the floor in a corner with my hands tied behind my back and what I guessed was a strip of duct tape over my mouth and wrapped around the back of my head. And there was a man pacing back and forth in front of me.

About that time the memories came back to my addled and probably concussed brain. The ice-cold water, the bodies, including the newly dumped one, and the sudden realization just as I came up for air that the killer had to be there waiting.

Then being yanked onto the boat, dropped onto my back and bashed in the head with something.

*Oar,* my inner genius guessed.

He turned my way, and I quickly closed my eyes again, all the while working on the duct tape with my tongue, pushing it away from my lips, poking behind it, and panicking about what would happen if I developed a stuffy nose.

"She's a woman," he said to no one. He shook his fist. "She's not what you want."

"She knows. She has to die." It was a deeper voice, a meaner one, and I opened my eyelids the merest slit, trying to see who the speaker was, but he was turned away and I couldn't.

"I don't want to," said the almost familiar voice. It wasn't clicking into place, because I'd expected it to be David's. And it wasn't.

"I don't give two shits what you want," said the other voice, the completely different one. Except there was only one man and that voice was coming from the same set of lips.

Whoever he was, he was batshit crazy.

"Kill her now, before she wakes—unless you don't have what it takes. In that case, just let me...for heaven's sakes." He laughed. It was low and dark, very brief. Clearly he found his rhyme scheme clever.

*Rhyming! Oh, God, it's him. He's here, somehow!* "I don't. I don't have what it takes. Not a woman. Not her."

Wait, that voice...I almost had it now.

"Fine. Stop fighting me, then, and let me do my job."

"This isn't what I wanted. I'm leaving, I'm done." He reached for the door, just as someone kicked it open.

*Mason!*

He sprang into the room, gun drawn, as the lunatic fell backward onto the floor, but the creep just rolled and scrambled over to me, looking right into my face in the split second before he pulled me in front of him and put a knife to my throat.

*Dr. Vosberg?*

Mason stood there, pointing his gun at the guy. It was hard to see him, silhouetted against the light spilling through the wide-open door behind him. Was I the only one to notice that the gun, like Mason himself, had water dripping from it? Would it even fire?

"Dr. Vosberg?" he said. "What the hell?"

"It's not me! It's not me! It's the damn heart I got. It's evil, it's taking me over!"

Mason's eyes shifted to mine, and I shrugged.

"You had a heart transplant?" Mason asked.

"Was on the waiting list for a year." His hand was shaking. "That's when I did the research, wrote the book. But it was only two months ago, a little over, when I got the heart."

"Okay. Okay." Mason was keeping his tone calm, soothing. "Just let her go and we'll talk about it. This isn't what you want to do."

I felt the doc stiffen behind me. And then the shaking stopped and his grip on me became brutal, the blade pressing close, maybe even cutting a little. His voice changed again, deeper, crueler, and he said, "Hello, little brother."

Mason blinked. Clearly the greeting shook him. "You're not my brother," he said.

"Yes, I am. The only part of him that's still alive, anyway. He called me the rat. But I'm no rat. I'm a man."

"You're not a man. You're a fucking sickness." Mason advanced a single step.

That resulted in the knife blade slicing into my skin.

Maybe it was only a little, but it felt like a lot, and I whimpered from behind my tape as I felt warm blood trickling down my neck.

"Okay, okay. Easy." Mason held up his hands, one of them still holding the gun.

"Drop it, or I'll cut her jugular and you can watch her bleed out on the floor."

"Dr. Vosberg—Raymond, listen to me."

"The doctor is out right now. Would you like to make an appointment?" He laughed again, and the knife jiggled against my neck, cutting deeper every time. Then he stopped laughing and practically growled, "Mason better drop the gun, or brother's knife will have some fun." His tone was low and ice-cold.

Mason dropped the gun.

"Kick it this way."

He used one foot to push the gun carefully our way. I tugged at whatever bound my hands behind me, but it was useless. Shit.

The Eric-possessed shrink reached out with his own foot to drag the gun closer, and then he let go of me with one hand so he could pick it up. The knife was still at my throat, but when he bent and twisted, it moved away a little.

Enough.

I jerked backward hard, bashing my head into his, then threw my entire weight sideways, away from the knife. I landed on top of the gun, and by the time I did, Mason was on the guy. They were a giant tangle, and then I heard a grunt as Mason staggered backward, one hand on his belly.

Oh, God, blood was oozing from around it.

I jumped to my feet and plowed into the doc head-first, driving him backward until he bashed into the wall.

He dropped the knife but grabbed me by the throat a second later and started squeezing. That just about decided it. I couldn't breathe at all, and he was squeezing still tighter. Black spots started blocking out my vision.

Then I heard an explosion, and the hands around my neck eased. The eyes staring into mine widened, and Dr. Vosberg slowly sank to the floor.

I turned to look behind me.

Jeremy was standing in the middle of the room. The door was still open behind him, the gun still smoking in his hands.

And Mason was still on the floor bleeding.

I ran to Jeremy, turned my back to him. "Untie me." When he didn't move immediately I shouted, "Fucking untie me, Jeremy!"

He did. Turned out my bonds were tape, not rope, and he picked up the killer's knife and cut through them.

I removed the tape and dropped to my knees beside Mason. "Jeremy, we need help. Is anyone else coming? Are you alone?" I pressed my hands to the wound in Mason's belly, trying to slow the damned blood down. "Fuck, Mason, you're bleeding like a stuck hog."

"Sorry, I'll try to quit that."

I shot him a look. The first time I'd looked at his face since he'd busted in here. It was twisted up into a tight grimace. But his eyes stayed fixed on mine. The little wrinkles at the corners made my heart hurt.

"Jeremy," I said again, not looking away. "Come on. Your uncle's bleeding out here. Snap out of it!"

He finally moved. I heard him come closer, felt him set the gun down. "The police are coming. I didn't want to wait. I brought the kayak."

"It's a good thing you did," I told him.

"Check on Vosberg," Mason said. "Make sure he's dead."

I took Jeremy's hands, pressed them to the wound. "Keep pressure on it." Then I crawled over to the good doctor, who was only a few feet away. Still kneeling, I leaned over him. He'd fallen on his back, but he wasn't dead. "Jeremy?"

"Yeah?"

"You still got that gun?"

"It's right here."

"If this asshole tries anything, shoot him again."

Vosberg's lips pulled into a smile, a sick one. His eyes opened, wider than I would have thought they were able to. "No need for that. I'm done."

Dr. V stared at me. Only it wasn't Dr. V, I was sure of it. There was a stranger looking out at me through his eyes. He coughed. I angled my gaze to his chest, where bubbling red foam was spreading, then back to his face again. "I knew you were going to catch on," he said. "It was only a matter of time. Framing you didn't work, thanks to my little bro—"

"Shut up!" I glanced behind me at Jeremy. He didn't need to hear what the bastard was going to say.

"You might think I'm dead and gone," the monster speaking through Dr. Vosberg went on. "But part of me lives on and on." His smile broadened. "*Parts* of me, that is."

The light went out then. I saw it. It just left. His eyes

went from a living gaze to a pair of lifeless marbles. His jaw went slack. The bloody foam stopped bubbling. Just like that.

The cops came busting in, and that was it.

The nightmare was over. At least, I hoped it was.

# *Epilogue*

My brother's body was recovered, along with the other victims of the Wraith. The crimes were placed at the feet of Dr. Raymond Vosberg, a man whose wild ideas had been published, making it easy to believe he was completely insane. Terry Cobb, a patient of Vosberg's, had been written off as a copycat, maybe even a protégé, who'd killed once and then realized he couldn't live with being a murderer. David, it turned out, was just an overly possessive, jealous jerk, but otherwise harmless.

We'd buried Tommy that afternoon in a beautiful spot overlooking the reservoir, and I liked to think he'd found some kind of peace. The funeral was over, and everyone had gone back to my place for comfort food. Everyone but me. I was still standing near the grave, with the shiny casket all flower-strewn on its stand above a thinly disguised hole in the ground. Myrtle was sleeping on my feet. She was wearing her pink plush jacket, and I was huddling into my long wool coat. The leaves were mostly gone, trees bare, and the breeze was brisk.

I felt him before I saw him. Mason. He walked up to stand beside me, his hands in his coat pockets.

"I thought you'd left," I said.

"You thought wrong." He slid an arm around my shoulders. Friendly, supportive. Also warm and strong. "You okay?" he asked.

"Yeah. Yeah, actually, I am. How about you?"

"A little sore still." He put a hand on his belly, where he'd been stabbed, as he said it. "But it's healing fast."

"Good." I drew a breath, sighed it out again. "You believe there's an afterlife, Mason?"

"Hard not to, after what we witnessed, isn't it?"

"Yeah. Yeah it is." I blinked, and looked up at him. "I'd like to think Tommy's found some peace."

"It feels peaceful here. Maybe that's a sign that you're right."

"I hope so." I turned around, and he did, too, and we started walking slowly toward our cars, the only two left in the cemetery. "What did you decide to tell the family?" I asked. When I'd visited him in the hospital, he'd still been wrestling with that question.

"Nothing. I decided to tell them nothing. Marie's weeks away from giving birth. Jeremy and Josh are too young to handle it, and my mother would just refuse to accept it, anyway."

I nodded. "I think that's the right call."

"I hope so. Jeremy, though… He's still pretty haunted by what happened."

"Well, he killed a man. At sixteen. Is he seeing someone?"

"Yeah. And he's started reading your books, too."

I looked up fast. "No shit?"

"He likes you, Rache."

"I like him, too."

There was a long, tense silence when we reached

the cars. We stood there by his black behemoth and my bumblebee, parked side by side in the little lot. "So…" I said.

"Yeah."

"Look why don't we—"

"I don't think we have to—"

We both spoke at once, then stopped and laughed awkwardly. He gestured at me, a ladies' first sort of thing. So I had to go first.

"I think if we were to start…seeing each other…it might go somewhere I'm not ready to be just yet," I said.

"I think I agree with you on that."

We were standing close, face-to-face, but I was looking down at my dog to avoid his eyes. "I just need a little time. To process everything that's happened. To figure out who I am as a sighted adult without a serial killer in her head. At least, so far. You know?"

"I hear you. I've got lot of people depending on me, now. The boys, especially. And shit of my own to work through, too."

No lie. His brother had been a serial killer, and he was carrying that heavy secret squarely on his shoulders. He would be lucky if he didn't need to spend a few years in therapy himself.

"So for now…friends?" I asked. When he didn't answer, I lifted my head.

"For now." He held my eyes, and then he slid his arms around me and slowly pulled me to him, then lowered his head. I wound my arms around his neck, and we kissed. It was long, deep, luscious, and it made my heart hurt.

When he lifted his mouth away from mine, he said, "Starting now."

"Starting in a minute." I laid my head on his chest, and we just stood there, holding each other, while the wind blew over the naked trees and the tombstones, and over the two of us.

\* \* \* \* \*

*Turn the page for*
*an excerpt from*
*WAKE TO DARKNESS,*
New York Times *bestselling author*
*Maggie Shayne's*
*next novel featuring*
*Rachel de Luca and Mason Brown,*
*coming from Harlequin MIRA*
*in December 2013.*

*Wake to Darkness*
Maggie Shayne

Mason had never seen the side of Rachel he saw on that stage. He had read her books—the last three, anyway—and they were pretty much all the same: all about positive thinking and creative visualization and everything happening for a reason. He would probably have read more, because the message was so uplifting and empowering, if he hadn't known that she didn't believe it herself. Not a word of it.

It was the one thing he'd never liked about Rachel. God knew he liked everything else about her a little *too* much. But that she was selling this spiel to the masses when she didn't believe in it herself felt a little too cold, too calculating.

But just now he'd seen a hint of something else. She might *say* she didn't believe the stuff she wrote about. She might even *think* she didn't believe it. But she *wanted to.* She had practically glowed on that soundstage when she was spouting her message. He was beginning to think it might not be an act at all.

Or maybe that was just wishful thinking on his part.

She'd kept the mask in place as she'd said her good-byes to her hostess, and the entire time she'd signed autographs for the group who'd gathered outside on the sidewalk, even though it was cold and starting to snow. Then the crowd fell away as he led her off to find a place for lunch.

"It's a great time of year to be in the city," he said.

She nodded. The Rockefeller Center Christmas tree was all lit up, and every store window decked to the nines. "I wish I could stay, but I've gotta get home to the kids."

"Kids? Don't tell me you got another dog."

"No, Myrtle's plenty. My niece Misty is dog-sitting, though."

"At your place?"

She nodded.

"You're a brave woman, leaving a sixteen-year-old alone in your home overnight."

"Amy's staying over, too."

He grinned. "I don't think your assistant is going to be much help, unless it's to buy the booze for the inevitable party."

"Don't judge a book by its cover," she quipped.

He laughed and meant it. It had been a while since that had happened. "Why is only one twin dog-sitting? Is your other niece a cat person?"

"My sister and Jim took Christy with them for a two-week Christmas vacation in Aspen."

"And Misty didn't go?"

"Misty had the flu. Or at least she convinced my gullible sister that's what it was. Frankly, I think it was more a case of not wanting to leave her latest boyfriend behind. The priorities of love-struck teens never fail to make me gag." She mimed the finger-in-the-throat thing.

"I've missed the hell outta you," he said, smiling at her gross gesture as if she was a supermodel posing in front of a wind machine. "And your little dog, too."

"She's missed you, too."

But she didn't say *she* had.

She'd stopped walking, and it took him a beat to realize she was indicating that they should eat at the deli whose wreath-and-bell-bedecked door they were currently blocking. He opened it, and she preceded him in. They moved through the line to the counter, ordered, and then she picked out the quietest table in the crowded, noisy place.

She was sparkling. Her eyes, her smile, told him she was as glad to see him again as he was to see her, whether she was willing to say it out loud or not.

"So how are the nephews? I'll bet this is a hard time for them."

"It's rough. Their first Christmas without their dad. It's hard on all of us."

She nodded slowly. "It's my first holiday without my brother, too. I think that's probably why Sandra wanted to get away. It's too hard."

"Sometimes I wonder if it would be easier if they knew the truth about Eric." He looked at her as he spoke. It was one of about a million things he'd been dying to talk to her about.

"No, Mason," she whispered. "No one would be better off knowing their father, husband or son was a serial killer. No one. Trust me on this."

He nodded slowly. "It's been eating at me. Keeping that secret."

"You did the right thing."

God, he'd needed to hear her say that again. He didn't know why, didn't need to know why. It was a relief, that was all.

"They must have that new baby sister by now, though, right? Marie was out to *here* last time I—"

"Stillborn," he said softly.

"Oh, my God. I'm so sorry, Mason. I didn't know. You should've called."

"What good would that have done?"

She blinked what he thought were real tears from her eyes. "Poor Marie. First her husband and then her baby. I'd ask how she's doing, but…"

"Yeah, she's having a hard time of it. Keeps saying she's being punished."

"For what, for heaven's sake?"

"She's grieving. We can't expect her to make sense."

"And the boys?"

"Josh is good. He's eleven, you know? It's Christmas. They bounce back at that age. They spend a lot of weekends at my place. I pick them up after school and take 'em to the gym to shoot hoops every Wednesday."

"But Jeremy, not so much?" she asked, homing in on what he'd left out. She was good at that. Good at reading between the lines, good at sensing the things people didn't say. He'd never seen anything like the way she could tell when someone was lying or read the emotions behind their words.

"He's seventeen." He said it as if that said it all, then reminded himself that Rachel had nieces, not nephews, and it might not be quite the same. "He's not bouncing back like Josh. He's brooding. Quiet. Withdrawn. Didn't even go out for basketball this year. Would've been his first year playing varsity, too."

"Sounds like he's depressed."

"Marie thinks he's been drinking. Said she smelled it on his breath when he came in late one night."

"Shit. I'm so sorry, Mason."

He shrugged. "It is what it is. They'll come back around—it just takes time."

Then he lifted his head and tried to bring his mood up a notch. "I'm sorry. I didn't mean to dump all that on you. I should be focusing on the positive, right? That's what your books say."

"It's hard when there's so little positive to find," she said. Then she stabbed him with those insightful eyes of hers. "What about you? How are you doing, Mason?"

He lowered his head again. "I don't know, Rache. I feel like I'm in some kind of limbo. Waiting for something really big and really bad." He met her eyes again. "Like it's not finished yet." He knew that she knew what he was talking about.

"It's got to be finished," she said, but she said it really softly. As if she was afraid to press their luck by saying it out loud.

The waitress brought lunch, and as soon as she left he got to the point of their meeting. "So, about this case. The one I contacted you about."

"Missing person," she said.

"Yeah. But the name was familiar, and I realized it was one of Eric's organ recipients."

She went still, but only for an instant. Then she shrugged and said, "Coincidence."

"There's no such thing as coincidence. You wrote that yourself."

"Every self-help author spews that line. No one even knows who came up with it first. It's universal. Doesn't make it true."

"I kind of think it does." He paused, then said, "I figured I should at least ask if you'd had any dreams. Like before."

"Before, when I was riding along inside the head of a killer, you mean?"

"Inside the head of another person who got one of my brother's organs. If you can see them when they're *committing* crimes, maybe you can see them when they're the victims, too."

She took her time before answering. "It was so traumatic that I think my mind kind of...took over."

"In what way?"

"Every time I start to dream, I wake up. I have the same startle response you have when you dream you're falling."

"So is it any time you dream, or only when it's one of those...psychic-connection dreams?"

"How the hell would I know? The dreams never play out."

"*No* dreams ever play out?"

She averted her eyes and her cheeks turned red. "Well, sure. Some do."

Was it crazy for him to hope that blush was because those dreams were about him? And that they were sexy as hell? Like the ones he'd been having about her ever since he'd seen her last?

"But I *can* say for sure that I haven't had *any* dreams about *any* harm being done to *any* people. Besides, you said this was a missing person, not a murder victim, right?"

"Right. But to the family, this isn't someone who would just up and vanish. Housewife. Soccer mom. PTA, all that. You know?" He got an idea and ran with it before his brain told him not to. "It would be like if your sister suddenly just up and vanished. You wouldn't think Sandra did it voluntarily, right?"

"No, I wouldn't. Not like when my transient addict brother up and vanished, and I assumed he'd just turn up after a while, like he always did. Until he didn't."

"I'm sorry. That was a bad— I'm sorry, Rachel." He covered her hand with his.

She nodded, then twisted her arm to look at her watch. "I have to go."

"How are you getting back?" he asked.

"Alone, Mason. I'm getting back alone." She left half a sandwich on her plate. "Thanks for lunch. I hope things get better for your family soon."

He nodded. "Thanks. Merry Christmas, Rache."

"Merry Christmas, Mason."

And then she was gone.

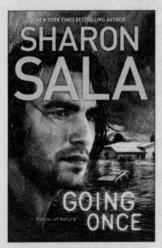

**USA TODAY** bestselling author

# Antoinette van Heugten

**Max Parkman—autistic and whip-smart, emotionally fragile and aggressive—is perfect in his mother's eyes. Until he's accused of murder.**

THE *USA TODAY* BESTSELLING NOVEL

Antoinette van Heugten

saving max

Attorney Danielle Parkman can't deny her son's behavior has been getting worse—drugs and violent outbursts have become a frightening routine. But the diagnosis that Max is deeply disturbed—and dangerous—is too devastating to accept.

Until she finds Max, weapon in hand, at the bedside of a fellow patient who has been brutally stabbed to death.

Trapped in a maelstrom of doubt and fear, Danielle's mothering instincts snap sharply into focus. The justice system is bearing down on them, so she must use her years of legal experience to find out the truth, no matter what that might be....

### Available wherever books are sold.

**Be sure to connect with us at:**

Harlequin.com/Newsletters

Facebook.com/HarlequinBooks

Twitter.com/HarlequinBooks

HARLEQUIN® MIRA®
www.Harlequin.com

MAVH1469

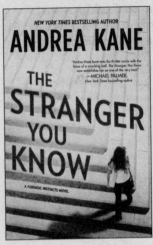

# REQUEST YOUR FREE BOOKS!

## 2 FREE NOVELS
## FROM THE SUSPENSE COLLECTION
## PLUS 2 FREE GIFTS!

**YES!** Please send me 2 FREE novels from the Suspense Collection and my 2 FREE gifts (gifts are worth about $10). After receiving them, if I don't wish to receive any more books, I can return the shipping statement marked "cancel." If I don't cancel, I will receive 4 brand-new novels every month and be billed just $6.24 per book in the U.S. or $6.74 per book in Canada. That's a savings of at least 22% off the cover price. It's quite a bargain! Shipping and handling is just 50¢ per book in the U.S. and 75¢ per book in Canada.* I understand that accepting the 2 free books and gifts places me under no obligation to buy anything. I can always return a shipment and cancel at any time. Even if I never buy another book, the two free books and gifts are mine to keep forever.

191/391 MDN F4XN

| | |
|---|---|
| Name | (PLEASE PRINT) |
| Address | Apt. # |
| City | State/Prov. | Zip/Postal Code |

Signature (if under 18, a parent or guardian must sign)

### Mail to the Harlequin® Reader Service:
**IN U.S.A.:** P.O. Box 1867, Buffalo, NY 14240-1867
**IN CANADA:** P.O. Box 609, Fort Erie, Ontario L2A 5X3

**Want to try two free books from another line?**
**Call 1-800-873-8635 or visit www.ReaderService.com.**

* Terms and prices subject to change without notice. Prices do not include applicable taxes. Sales tax applicable in N.Y. Canadian residents will be charged applicable taxes. Offer not valid in Quebec. This offer is limited to one order per household. Not valid for current subscribers to the Suspense Collection or the Romance/Suspense Collection. All orders subject to credit approval. Credit or debit balances in a customer's account(s) may be offset by any other outstanding balance owed by or to the customer. Please allow 4 to 6 weeks for delivery. Offer available while quantities last.

**Your Privacy**—The Harlequin® Reader Service is committed to protecting your privacy. Our Privacy Policy is available online at www.ReaderService.com or upon request from the Harlequin Reader Service.

We make a portion of our mailing list available to reputable third parties that offer products we believe may interest you. If you prefer that we not exchange your name with third parties, or if you wish to clarify or modify your communication preferences, please visit us at www.ReaderService.com/consumerschoice or write to us at Harlequin Reader Service Preference Service, P.O. Box 9062, Buffalo, NY 14269. Include your complete name and address.

SUS13R

# MAGGIE SHAYNE

| | | | | |
|---|---|---|---|---|
| 32980 | TWILIGHT PROPHECY | ___ $7.99 U.S. | ___ $9.99 CAN. |
| 32875 | BLUE TWILIGHT | ___ $7.99 U.S. | ___ $9.99 CAN. |
| 32871 | TWILIGHT HUNGER | ___ $7.99 U.S. | ___ $9.99 CAN. |
| 32808 | KISS ME, KILL ME | ___ $7.99 U.S. | ___ $9.99 CAN. |
| 32804 | KILL ME AGAIN | ___ $7.99 U.S. | ___ $9.99 CAN. |
| 32793 | KILLING ME SOFTLY | ___ $7.99 U.S. | ___ $9.99 CAN. |
| 32618 | BLOODLINE | ___ $7.99 U.S. | ___ $8.99 CAN. |
| 32498 | ANGEL'S PAIN | ___ $7.99 U.S. | ___ $7.99 CAN. |
| 32497 | DEMON'S KISS | ___ $7.99 U.S. | ___ $9.50 CAN. |
| 32244 | COLDER THAN ICE | ___ $5.99 U.S. | ___ $6.99 CAN. |
| 32243 | THICKER THAN WATER | ___ $5.99 U.S. | ___ $6.99 CAN. |
| 31421 | BLOOD OF THE SORCERESS | ___ $7.99 U.S. | ___ $9.99 CAN. |
| 31333 | MARK OF THE WITCH | ___ $7.99 U.S. | ___ $9.99 CAN. |
| 31267 | TWILIGHT FULFILLED | ___ $7.99 U.S. | ___ $9.99 CAN. |
| 29060 | PRINCE OF TWILIGHT | ___ $7.99 U.S. | ___ $9.99 CAN. |

*(limited quantities available)*

| | |
|---|---|
| TOTAL AMOUNT | $ _____ |
| POSTAGE & HANDLING | $ _____ |
| ($1.00 for 1 book, 50¢ for each additional) | |
| APPLICABLE TAXES* | $ _____ |
| TOTAL PAYABLE | $ _____ |

*(check or money order—please do not send cash)*

To order, complete this form and send it, along with a check or money order for the total above, payable to Harlequin MIRA, to: **In the U.S.:** 3010 Walden Avenue, P.O. Box 9077, Buffalo, NY 14269-9077; **In Canada:** P.O. Box 636, Fort Erie, Ontario, L2A 5X3.

Name: _____

Address: _____ City: _____

State/Prov.: _____ Zip/Postal Code: _____

Account Number (if applicable): _____

075 CSAS

*New York residents remit applicable sales taxes.
*Canadian residents remit applicable GST and provincial taxes.

**HARLEQUIN®** MIRA®
www.Harlequin.com

MMS1013BL